Praise for *London, Can You Wait?*

GOLD MEDAL FOR ROMANCE
2018 Independent Publisher Book Awards

Featured by *NBC's TodayShow.com, USA TODAY,*
Redbook.com, Buzzfeed, PopSugar, Hypable,
Brit+Co, Your Tango, and *Coastal Living*

"…Middleton has mastered chick lit…The narration is well-crafted, full of seemingly innocuous tidbits that later become significant, raunchy banter between friends, and the kind of sweet nothings that hopeless romantics die for…A winner for romance and chick lit fans as well as Anglophiles and geeks."

—Kirkus Reviews

"*London, Can You Wait?* is just as delightful as *London Belongs to Me*. It's a fantastic and truly wonderful page-turning read. TOP PICK! 4.5/5."

—RT Book Reviews

"Perfect for fans of *Bridget Jones's Diary.*"

—NBC's TodayShow.com

"Jacquelyn Middleton's *London, Can You Wait?*, the sequel to *London Belongs to Me*, will both break your heart and make it swell. Sometimes in rapid succession, sometimes at the same time. And you 1000% should pick it up and read it!"

—Hypable

"A passionate, witty page-turner. Middleton has written a delightful and worldly novel with interesting characters and romantic twists and turns!"

—Renée Carlino, USA Today bestselling author of
Wish You Were Here

D1096400

Praise for *London Belongs to Me*

Featured by the *Huffington Post, Elle.com, USA TODAY, Cosmopolitan.com, Buzzfeed, MSN, PopSugar, Redbook.*com, *Reader's Digest Canada, Today's Parent, Yahoo! Beauty, Parade, Brit+Co,* and *Culturalist*

"Middleton's novel is a love letter to London ... even the most skeptical or cynical readers will surrender to the many delights of this compelling narrative. Prepare to be seduced by engaging characters, irresistible in their own quirky way, and transported by keen descriptions of the sights, sounds, and tastes of London."
—*Kirkus Reviews*

"Middleton's novel is everything a chick-lit story should be. The heroine is so well-developed—with her quirks, nuances, and relatability ... and Middleton's writing style helps the story flow beautifully and freely ... This novel comes with our highest recommendations because it truly makes for a perfect read by the fireplace on a cold winter day. Top pick! 4.5/5 stars."
—*RT Book Reviews*

"The lovers of Bridget [Jones's] single girl, younger days in London are going to adore *London Belongs to Me*, the coming-of-age story of a girl (who could be Bridget's younger American cousin!) coming to London to find love and adventure."
—*Redbook*

"Wow, folks, this new London-based novel will send your heart swooning. A stunning portrait of modern London life, with unput-downable prose, this [debut novel] belongs on every Anglophile's bookshelf!"
—*PopSugar*

Until the last star fades

Jacquelyn Middleton is an award-winning author and freelance writer. She previously worked in television broadcasting and now lives in Toronto with her husband and Schipperke. She's addicted to Bookstagram, loves London, and adores theatre a little too much.

Until the Last Star Fades is her third novel.

Follow Jacquelyn:
Instagram @JaxMiddleton_Author
Twitter @JaxMiddleton
Facebook @JacquelynMiddletonAuthor,
or visit her webpage at www.JacquelynMiddleton.com

Also by Jacquelyn Middleton

London Belongs to Me
London, Can You Wait?

Until the last star fades

A NOVEL

JACQUELYN MIDDLETON

KIRKWALL
BOOKS

KIRKWALL BOOKS

USA – CANADA - UK

Until the Last Star Fades

ISBN: 978-0-9952117-8-0
Copyright © 2018 Jacquelyn Middleton
First Paperback Edition, November 2018

Until the Last Star Fades
is a love story about...

a girl and a guy,
a daughter and her mother.

This book is dedicated to my favorite mums,
all strong women I love and admire:

Sally, my dear friend
who lovingly looks after my Zoey when I can't,

Val, my mother-in-law
who loves me like one of her own,

and

Mum, you're in these pages, you're in my heart,
thank you for the 'signs' to keep going...
I miss you & love you, always

xoxo

DEAR READERS,

Until the Last Star Fades blurs the line between a slow-burn, friends-to-lovers romance and women's fiction. Riley and Ben's story is a standalone that takes place in the same 'world' as my two previous books.

Enjoy!

P.S. I've included a glossary at the back of the book to explain a few terms that might not be familiar to all readers.

Love music? You can find the *Until the Last Star Fades* playlists on my website at www.JacquelynMiddleton.com listed under 'Extras'!

ONE

"Remember that everyone you meet is afraid of something,
loves something, and has lost something."
– Paul Tournier

New York City, March 17, 2018

Riley couldn't do it. An elbow to the kidneys, a strategically delivered shove—even a well-timed foot placed in an unsuspecting
path—all viable options, according to her best friend Piper.

"Rye, just do it already!" The fast-talking voice barked through
her secondhand phone. "Force your way to the front. If you don't
leave soon, you're going to miss St. Paddy's Day completely!"

"Yeah, and if I follow your advice I'll be spending it with the
NYPD—in a jail cell." Riley scrunched up her nose, peering at the
sizzling red LED display listing flights awaiting luggage. Raised
voices bounced off the walls as passengers from Los Angeles, Toronto, and Minneapolis—her connecting flight from Grand Forks,
which had landed a ridiculous ninety minutes earlier—pushed closer to the baggage carousel, hoping to spy their delayed suitcases,
grab what was theirs, and exchange the stuffy fluorescent-lit hell-
hole for the last gasp of the day's dwindling brightness. A snow-
storm in the Midwest had unleashed post-spring break chaos at air-
ports across the country, and LaGuardia's terminal D hadn't escaped unscathed. Sweaty, hangry travelers gave each other stink eye
as an avalanche of suitcases burst through the rubber partition, piling up and creating a moving mountain of plastic, nylon, and tiny
wheels, many rattling and spinning defiantly.

A heavy sigh left Riley's lips, her stomach as off-kilter as the
precarious cliff of cases. "Pip, I could do without an assault charge,

1

thank you very much." Jockeying for a position along the path of the U-shaped belt, the New York University senior dragged her hand through her wavy ponytail. "I'm not the elbowing type."

"Yeah, about *that*." Piper snapped her gum.

I walked right into that one. Riley winced. "I couldn't go through with it."

"Rye, you completely ignored what we talked about before you left. It's like those conversations didn't even happen."

"I *know*, but..." Clenching her jaw, she adjusted the Strand bookstore tote on her arm and stretched up on the toes of her boots, fighting for a glimpse of the luggage parade over the shoulders of two ridiculously tall suits. *What are you dudes, part giraffe?*

"You're delaying the inevitable," said Piper. "Why *did* you go to North Dakota, huh? 'Cause it sure as hell wasn't to freeze your butt off watching hockey for five days straight. You could've done that here..."

As Piper rattled on, a chubby bald man who looked like a giant toddler wrestled with a large hard-side roller bag sailing by on the belt.

"...but hey, at least I didn't have to go with you. I'm still shaking off the cold I caught watching NYU play. I'm lucky that frozen bench didn't give me terminal hemorrhoids, the frostbite was bad enough—"

"Terminal hemorrhoids? Jeez, Pip, that's a new one!" A chuckle burst through Riley's lips. "And you didn't catch frostbite! You ditched me for a warm bar after twenty minutes!" Yawning through a smile, Riley spied a midsized pink case wedged underneath a heavy duffle bag. "Oh! Wait a sec." She fought with the still-moving baggage, tugging her wheelie case from the mound. The bag's swinging momentum almost t-boned one of the giraffes mid-conversation.

Thank God! A huge breath released from Riley's chest. She extended the case's handle, returning her phone to her ear as she squeezed through the frowning crowd, her suitcase rolling happily behind her. "Got my case. Look, meet me at my place in an hour

2

and a half, okay?" A large family blocked her path to the exit. "I'll tell you"—she glanced back at her belongings, her eyes focusing on the ID tag flapping from the side handle—"everyth..." Her stomach plunged into free fall. "*FUCK!*"

The mother covered her little boy's ears, her eyes shooting daggers at Riley.

"*Aaand* now I'm deaf, too," Piper whined. "Thanks, Rye."

"Shit!" She lifted the case, her pulse charging, her eyes chasing the swirly girly handwriting on the luggage tag that wasn't hers: *B...something*—the last name impossible to decipher. There was no phone number, no address, just *B. Something* in the most frustratingly illegible cursive Riley had ever seen. Her heart tripped into an unhappy dance. "Pip, I gotta go."

"Wha—"

The twenty-two-year-old's eyes darted to the unmanned airport help desk...to the cases wheeled away by weary travelers...to the exit and a bright pink blur scooting through the parting glass doors. "Someone stole my case." Hitting disconnect, Riley cut Piper off.

"Sorry! Excuse me!" She dashed around the family and a pack of slow-walking, fast-talking French tourists, their elegant parley cut short by the terminal's doors whisking shut behind her. She inhaled sharply, the frosty air invigorating her senses as a chorus of honking taxis and the stench of bus fumes welcomed her home. *Whoever you are, don't get on the shuttle! Don't disappear!* Her eyes scurried across the slushy pavement crowded with boots and every shape, color, and size of luggage. *Dammit. That was the whole point of choosing such a loud color...*

YES! There it is! Identical to the one trailing behind her, it was fugly—bubblegum pink and covered with a rash of white polka dots. But, despite its obnoxious appearance, this case suited her strapped student budget just fine and it was right there, resting beside the salt-stained UGGs of a twenty-something brunette leaning on a row of luggage carts, checking her phone. Riley's brows eased their ascent as she wriggled past a kissing couple and a guy wearing a green Boston Bruins cap. *Oh, thank God.*

3

A stroller cut her off. *Woah!* Giving the harried father a wide berth, she turned back to her missing case as the arm of a thin jacket unsuitable for a New York winter swooped in and claimed its extended handle. Salty boot girl didn't react—at all.

Green cap guy? What the—? "Hey!" Lunging for the thief's arm, Riley tripped over her own boots and barely saved herself from kissing the pavement.

"Fuck!" The guy stopped and lifted the peak of his cap, revealing a mop of misbehaving dark hair falling into his blue eyes—eyes that might've made her catch her breath if they hadn't been so puffy and bloodshot. He was about Riley's age but appeared pale and drained under his five o'clock shadow, like he was on the losing end of a twenty-four-hour bender. The closer Riley got, the more a waft of whiskey and sweat punished her nostrils, proving her first impression right. The guy scratched at the purple hood poking out from the neck of his jacket, his full lips parting into a charming smile. "You all right, love?" His English accent hung in the air.

"I think you guys have my case." Riley's glare darted from the Brit to the woman. "Which one of you is *B. Something-or-other?*" She gestured to the identical luggage behind her. "I can't read the last name."

With a sneer, the brunette side-eyed Riley and the guy then walked away, making a call on her phone.

"Hey! Wait!" Riley waved her arms, but the woman didn't stop. "I'm talking to you—"

"Actually, it's me you want." His six-foot frame lurched toward her, his grin unwavering underneath cheekbones male models would kill for. "Let me sort this." His right hand, swaddled in a bloodstained bandage, yanked the tag on the case in his possession, snapping its buckle and sending the owner's information fluttering to the damp pavement. "Sh-Sh-Shit." He chuckled and bent over, his earbuds tumbling from his ears and snapping to a halt above the winter muck like two miniature bungee jumpers.

They both fumbled for the card, but he reached it first. He slowly stood up, adjusting his backpack with a jerk and invading her personal space. He squinted underneath the brim of his cap at the neat penmanship on her tag like he was deciphering a secret code spelled out in hieroglyphics.

"See?" Riley pointed. "It says R. Hope—right there. My email, RHope@...the tag on the case I have says B. Something." She leaned away, her eyes telling him to give in and back off.

He sniffed. "RHope...yeah, that's definitely not me." His watery eyes blinked lazily at her. "Soz, Ms. R. Hope. I fucked up." He laughed, sending boozy, steamy breath into the frosty air. "I can't believe you've got the same shite taste in luggage as my mum—"

"Lucky me." Riley didn't care about his mother or her taste in suitcases or that this hot mess with an accent was adorable. She just wanted to hop on the first shuttle bus and get the hell out of there. She pulled her case away from him and wheeled his mother's pink monstrosity forward, their transaction complete. "Well, thanks." The words flew from her lips without a breath between them. "Happy St. Patrick's."

Turning away, she left the hungover dude holding her broken tag. She could catch the Q70 shuttle bus boarding at the far curb and be riding the R train down to the 8th Avenue-NYU stop in the East Village in ten minutes. Racing through the dirty slush, she reached into her tote and pulled out her Pay-Per-Ride MetroCard.

"R. Hope! Wait! I have your..."

Riley kept walking and threw a pinched glance over her shoulder. The cute guy was sliding along the sidewalk, holding her luggage tag. She stopped at the fare machine and locked eyes with the bus driver, pleading with him to wait.

"Sorry." The Brit handed it to her.

"Thanks." Pursing her lips, Riley stuffed it in a pocket and threaded her MetroCard into the machine.

"This is my first time here. I'm a bit lost, actually." Rounding his shoulders, he stuffed his hands in his pockets. "Do I need one of those yellow cardy things for the bus?"

I can't chit-chat—the bus is gonna leave! Snatching her MetroCard from the slot, she collected her ticket and turned to him. "A

MetroCard, yeah, or if you've got coins"—she waved at the smaller machine to her right—"you can pay there."

Shivering non-stop, a shaky hand braved the elements to scratch his stubble. "Coins...I can't add at the best of times, but feeling as rough as I do now? Ugh." He swallowed, his nose a chilled pink. "You wouldn't happen to have the right change, would you—please?"

PFFFFSSSSSSSSSSSSSST!

Riley looked up, catching the bus's doors closing. *For fuck's sake.* She waved furiously. "NO, WAIT!" A warm puff of breath left her lips. "I'm COMING!"

The guy rushed past her, each coltish stomp plunging his worn sneakers into the gray slush. "Hey, mate"—he slipped, his shoulder smacking into the bus's front door—"don't take off on us!"

The driver rolled his eyes. *PFFFFSSSSSSTTTT!* The doors opened with a protracted hiss, like they were sarcastically passing judgment.

"Thanks! Don't let him drive away." Riley's fingers jabbed at the machine, repeating the payment process with her MetroCard. She locked stares with the driver. "I'm paying—for him."

The Brit gleefully bounded back to her side. "Oh, cheers, darlin'! You're the best."

Riley nodded as he loaded both suitcases onto the bus.

TWO

"Only aisle seats left." Brit boy pointed at two blue plastic seats at the back and picked up Riley's case, lifting it onto the luggage rack. He reclaimed his own and stowed it safely beside hers.

"I like the aisle," said Riley, gripping the yellow poles lining the path to the vacant seats. She hesitated, bracing herself as the bus veered around a corner.

"Me too. I'm all about the quick exit, you know?"

Riley unzipped her parka and sat down. *Jeez, it's warm in here.* She typed a quick text to her mom, Maggie, and hit send.

On bus. Meeting Pip at home. x

The guy slouched out of his backpack and dropped onto the hard seat across from her. His shoes and the calves of his baggy jeans were soaked from his sprint to the bus, but he didn't seem to care. "So, you live here, eh?"

"Yeah."

"How long?"

"I was born here—Staten Island. It's a New York borough, south of Manhattan." She smiled, relieved to be on the bus and headed home.

"Where are you coming back from?"

Is he gonna chat the whole way there? "Spring break."

"Oh, I've heard about spring break. Love the sound of it." He sniffed and started to unbutton his jacket. "Beaches, booze, shagging—my kind of holiday."

"Try blizzards, hot chocolate, and skating." Her brows furrowed as his light jacket opened to unveil an oversized purple hoodie and hints of a plaid flannel shirt, some sort of red zippy track jacket, and a t-shirt. One, two, three, four—five layers. *Is he wearing everything he owns? He's like Joey from that old* Friends *episode.* She pulled a clean tissue from her bag and handed it to him.

7

"Ah, cheers!" He grinned behind the Kleenex.

"I was in North Dakota visiting my boyfriend."

"Oh! North Dakota, eh? The beautiful rugged Midwest?"

"Oh, you've been?"

"No, but when I was little I loved atlases, dreaming of far-flung adventures." He stuffed the tissue in a pocket and swiveled to face her head on, leaning into the aisle. "Long-distance relationship? That's hot."

Riley shimmied out of her parka, revealing a sweater and a pair of distressed secondhand jeans. She stood up, folding her coat into a small bundle as the luminous headlights from passing cars invaded the bus and swept over her. "You wouldn't say that if you were in one."

The guy dipped his head and his eyes discreetly checked her out underneath the brim of his cap. He cleared his throat and sat up. "What's he doing so far away?"

She stuffed her coat on the seat, sitting on top of it. Her body swayed with the movement of the bus. "He's a senior at the University of North Dakota, studying entrepreneurship."

"Oh, so he's from there?"

"No, Staten Island, same as me. He's on a scholarship. The Minnesota Wild drafted him three years ago."

"Minnesota what?"

"Wild." She stuck her hand in her tote, feeling around for her library book.

He widened his eyes. "He was drafted…I don't get it—by who…Wild?"

"They're an NHL team."

He shrugged and shook his head.

"The National Hockey League? Pro hockey—*ice* hockey?" She pointed at his hat. "You're wearing a Boston Bruins cap…"

"Am I?" He chuckled. "I don't know. I just liked the B on it!"

Riley giggled and pulled a well-thumbed novel from her tote. "Well, he'll join the Wild next fall."

"Holy hell, you're a WAG?!" He laughed, smacking the metal

handle on the seat back in front of him. The woman sitting there didn't notice—her headphones were cranked, leaking Fleetwood Mac's "Go Your Own Way".

"Shh!" Riley glared and retreated into her seat. Her admonishment pulled him farther into the aisle.

"What?" he whispered back.

"I HATE that term!"

"Well, you're dating the wrong guy, then." He nudged his cap above his eyebrows, giving Riley a better view of his eyes, which were waking up with a sparkly playfulness. "'Wives and girlfriends' of athletes—"

"If the tables were turned and *I* was the athlete, he wouldn't get labeled with such a dismissive nickname."

"Do girls even play ice hockey?"

"Yes!" With a sneer, Riley nodded her head. "I do! Well, I did…"

"You're fun to tease!" He laughed. "Why'd you stop playing?"

"Why'd *you* get drunk and board an airplane?"

"Ahhh! I was celebrating."

"What were you celebrating?"

He smirked and narrowed his eyes, not answering her question. "A hockey-playing WAG. I would've guessed sociology student…maybe languages? Never a WAG."

"So…you're saying I'm not hot enough to be a WAG—"

"Hey, don't get your knickers in a twist. I'm sure you are…underneath that scarf and…" He scratched the dark stubble on his chin. "Jumper."

"Jumper?"

His bandaged hand waved in her general direction. "Your sweater."

"The English have strange names for things."

"I'm Scottish, actually."

Riley shook her head. "My best friend's dad is Scottish—you sound nothing like him."

"I was born there"—he shifted in his seat—"but grew up in

9

England." He tapped his finger against his generous lips. "Nah, thinking about it—you're too classy to be a WAG."

"Obsessed much? Are you a wannabe soccer—oh, sorry, *football* player?" Riley's thumb flipped the corner of her book. "Do you play?"

He raised an eyebrow. "Would it turn you on if I did?"

"Yeah, right!" She chuckled sarcastically.

"Back home, WAGs are all flash, no substance. You know: cosmetic surgery, high heels, designer frocks—totty with a taste for living large."

"Nice." Riley curled her lip. "Good to know stereotypes are alive and thriving over the pond. Heaven forbid women be celebrated for their brains instead of their breasts."

"Hey, don't shoot the messenger. I'm just saying how it is. I'm not saying it's right…"

"Well, good."

She opened her library book, drawing their exchange to an abrupt close. They sat quietly for several minutes, their silence invaded by more Fleetwood Mac, cars honking outside the fogged windows, and a restless baby sobbing a few seats ahead. Riley's phone buzzed on her lap with a text from her mom.

All good here. Say hi to Piper. Love you. x

Looking up from her phone, she saw cute Brit guy's attention had drifted to the snow globe world passing by outside, and his fingers were toying with something on his right wrist above the bloody bandage. Wide-eyed, he seemed a bit lost. "What happened to your hand?" Riley searched through her tote, unearthing her reusable water bottle. Two crumpled candy wrappers floated to the floor.

He leaned over and rescued them. "These must be good—"

"They're peanut butter cups." Her hand reached impatiently.

"Mmm!" Beyond her grasp, he examined the empty brown paper cups and orange wrappers. "Two packs and not a crumb left? Someone's greedy—"

Riley snatched them from him, hiding the evidence in her bag. *Greedy? You should talk, drunk boy!* Her glare made him turn away, his smile vanishing. She sipped her water and got lost in her Instagram feed.

Neither spoke for a few minutes. The guy reached into his jacket, fumbling with the zipper on the hoodie underneath. Riley scrolled through photos, her annoyance melting away, replaced by embarrassment for being a grump. It wasn't this guy's fault she was stressed, drained, and feeling bluer than her Levi's. She glanced across the aisle, catching his eye as he sat back in his seat. His muted grin grew as she asked, "So, where are you coming from?"

"I'm an actor. I flew in from LA—you know, pilot season?"

"LA?" Riley's face lit up with genuine interest. California, its palm trees and sea breezes, swimming in the ocean whenever she desired—her dream life. "Did you like it?"

"Yeah, I didn't want to leave."

"Don't blame you. I love California."

"Really? I read for a great part in a Netflix series, and I made quite the impression! They think it's going to be massive—merchandising, comic con tie-ins, maybe a film, eventually."

"Wow, sounds promising. No wonder you were celebrating." Riley's eyes dropped to her phone, catching Piper's latest Instagram story.

"So, what about you? Women's studies? Philosophy?" He ducked his head, trying to read the title of the book in her lap. "Future librarian? I love books, me."

"NYU, Tisch School of the Arts. I graduate in May."

"NYU, eh? Sounds impressive. Hey, maybe we'll perform together one day."

"I doubt it."

"Well, at least tell me your name so when you're famous, I can tell everyone 'I used to know her.'"

She looked up. "Oh, I'm not an actress. I'm a film and television major. I want to work *behind* the scenes…in casting or as a director."

"That makes sense."

"Why?"

"You're bossy."

A forced laugh left her lips. "Jeez, thanks a lot!"

"Hey, bossy is a compliment!" His adorable smile made an appearance again. "You're feisty, a go-getter. You like to be in charge. I think it's great. You should embrace it."

When you put it that way... Riley grinned. "Oh, you're a charmer!"

"I am!" He promptly offered his hand to her across the aisle. "Benjamin Fagan—Ben."

Riley squinted at the bloodstained bandage and accepted his hand carefully, barely touching it. "Riley Hope."

"Ah, sorry." He frowned, tucking his hand away. "Wanna hang tonight, Riley Hope?"

She returned to her phone. "I can't..."

"Why not? *Technically* you're still on holiday, right?"

"You look and smell like you're on a permanent holiday."

"Envious?"

"No." She laughed.

"Go on, admit it—you're envious. No classes on Monday, no essays to write, no rules, just...freedom to do what I love and have a blast doing it, you know?"

Sounds perfect... Riley flicked her thumb along her screen, scrolling at warp speed.

"Come on! Put the phone down, live a little. You seem down about...something, and it's Saturday night—St. Patrick's Day! Let me repay you for helping me. Let me cheer you up."

"I don't need cheering up."

"You don't? *Really?* For someone coming off holiday, you're really bummed. It's your eyes—something's bothering you."

Shit! Is it that obvious? Riley continued scrolling.

"Want to tell me? I'm a great listener. I won't tell anyone."

Like I'm going to tell someone I just met.

"Or we could get pissed and forget? C'mon, it'll be a laugh, once we get out of this...tin can on wheels." He pulled out the tissue she had given him, dabbing his nose. "This bus reeks of wet dog and piss—it's totes stuffing me up." Ben nudged her arm with his non-bandaged hand. "Hey, not only will I buy you a drink, I'll also buy you more of those peanut butter things."

Oh, I'm SO done with those peanut butter things.

"Earth to Riley?"

"Thanks, but I'm meeting my friend."

"Cool, bring her—or *him*—too. Look, I think you've got the wrong end of... I'm not auditioning girlfriends, I just want some fun, you know? A proper night out in the Big Apple, see what all the fuss is about. You up for it?"

Riley looked up from her phone. Ben tilted his head, beckoning. His wide smile consumed his face, his eyes almost disappearing into happy-go-lucky crescents. There was something about him that held a promise, a challenge, his adorable grin offering an unspoken invitation: *I'll bring fun and mischief—come hang out with me.*

But Riley didn't have time for fun, not anymore, and mischief was a luxury she couldn't afford. No, Ben's persuasive smile wouldn't work its magic on her. It would have to charm another partner in crime. Riley wasn't that girl.

The bus came to a sudden stop, lurching the two of them forward and breaking Ben's smile.

"This is it—the subway." Riley grinned, stuffing her belongings in her bag as she stood up and collected her parka, letting the woman seated beside her exit first. "Do you know where you're going?"

Ben stared out the steamy window into the darkness crowding the Roosevelt Avenue-Jackson Heights subway station. "Um, not sure—downtown somewhere, an Airbnb." The man beside him stood quickly, forcing Ben to vacate his seat for the aisle. His hand dipped into one of his many jackets' pockets, pulling out a crumpled piece of paper stained with God knows what. "Canal Street?"

"That's two stops past mine. C'mon."

Ben stood up and smiled, following Riley toward the luggage rack.

THREE

The R train shuddered and screeched, arriving at the Times Square-42nd Street station. Twenty-five minutes into their subterranean journey, Ben and Riley had barely shared more than ten words. Two overwhelmed tourists from Munich had glommed onto Riley, who surprised Ben with her rusty high school German. For the past eleven stops, the couple had sat beside her, asking questions with hand gestures, a little English, and a lot of German, seeking reassurance that New York was safe. Riley answered carefully and calmly, but the tourists didn't seem satisfied, volleying question after question back at her.

Swaying with the train's vibrations, Ben kept a tight grip on their twin suitcases, preventing a rolling getaway. He couldn't pull his eyes away from the leggy student; specifically, he couldn't pull his eyes away from Riley's pale pink lips. His thoughts tunneled into a single focus. They were soft, slightly pouty—perfect. *They're just asking to be kissed.* A surging warmth started to harden underneath the zipper of his jeans. He glanced down at his crotch. *Now?! Seriously? Er...down boy! Don't be THAT guy!* He fidgeted on the hard orange seat next to her, crossing his legs.

Answering question #124, Riley licked her bottom lip and glanced back at him. *What if she notices! Worst timing ever.* He picked up his backpack from the floor and set it on his lap, hiding his embarrassment.

She turned again, her green eyes squinting quickly, which Ben took to mean, *I'd much rather be talking to you*, though maybe that was wishful thinking. Her willingness to help these strangers, her taking him under her wing at the airport made her even more attractive. She was kind, self-assured—so damn hot. *Shame she won't flirt with me. I blame the boyfriend. She's the loyal type, lucky bastard.* He hugged his backpack, his eyes darting down the subway car, desperately searching for something—anything—to short-circuit the throbbing ache in his boxer briefs. *C'mon, think of something else! There—that dirty bloke with the pineapple. Wait...a pineapple? Is he actually...talking to it?* Ben pulled down his cap, so the strange dude didn't catch him staring.

A few minutes later, the train arrived at the next station, and Ben's discomfort had eased.

"Und diese Haltestelle ist der 34th Street-Herald Square—Macy's department store." Playing impromptu tour guide, Riley pointed out the window, and the tourists leapt to their feet, rushing through the closing metal doors with barely a "danke" leaving their tongues.

"Is this their stop?" Ben moved his backpack off his lap onto the empty seat beside him.

"Err, no..." Riley scratched her head. "They had ten to go. They were headed to Whitehall Street—the Statue of Liberty."

Ben chuckled as the momentum of the train pushed him sideways into Riley's right shoulder. He didn't pull away and she didn't either. *Result: physical contact—my own miracle on 34th Street.* "I'm sure they'll find their way. How many more stops for us?"

"I have four, you have six."

Ben's stomach tightened. It was now or never. "You know, Riley, I'd probably still be standing outside the airport wondering what to do if you hadn't helped me out."

"You would've figured it out eventually."

"I know you have somewhere to be, but...please come for a drink—just one? Just so I can say thank you."

"Benjamin—"

"Riley." He smirked.

15

"Ben, I'm already late. My friend's probably waiting outside my apartment right now, cursing me for catching hypothermia..."

"*This is 28ᵗʰ Street.*" The automatic announcement crackled through the train's speakers as it slowed to a creaky stop.

"Your friend can come, too. We can talk about California, you can tell me about New York, making TV programs...*ice hockey...*"

"I appreciate the offer, but I really have stuff to do, sorry."

"So, you're gonna leave me to fend for myself?"

Riley rolled her case closer to her boots. "You'll be fine. Americans love British accents. Go into any bar and you'll have lots of female company. You don't want me cramping your style."

"I do! You're my only friend in New York."

"We've only just met!" She laughed. "You'll make new ones."

Ben's stomach sank. They sat quietly for a few minutes.

"*This is 23ʳᵈ Street.*" The doors opened, allowing the train and platform to exchange passengers.

He shifted his backpack on top of his case so an old woman could sit down. "You know, it's okay. I'll find my way in the big city. I'm sure I'll pick up friends before long."

Riley bit her cheek and checked her texts.

She looks like she just kicked a puppy. Ben's gaze darted out the window at the mosaic tiles on the station wall. "What's with all those floating hats?"

Riley looked up. "Apparently, they're hats worn by famous people who passed through this area: Oscar Wilde, Eleanor Roosevelt—the actor, Ben Fagan..." She grinned, returning to her phone as the train began to move.

Ben smiled as he adjusted his Boston Bruins cap. "Maybe one day, eh?"

"Oh, shit."

"What?"

"Piper wants me to pick up"—her finger slid up the screen—

"Cookie Butter…and Cheddar Rocket Crackers from Trader Joe's. With what? Magic beans?"

"Where's that, then?"

"14th Street."

Ben's eyes shot to the subway map near the doors. "Oh—next stop?"

"Yeah, sorry Ben."

So, I guess that drink really is out of the question…along with any hope for a snog ever, I reckon. Bollocks. The twinkle left his eyes.

With a tight half-smile, she quickly looped her scarf around her neck and zipped up her parka. "Make sure you get off at Canal Street. It's three stops after 14th Street, got it?"

"Yeah…" Pulling out his phone, he deflated in his seat.

Riley packed away her phone and tugged on yellow mittens with TAXI stitched down the hands. Eyes darting to Ben, she pressed her lips together. "Ben, you'll be fi…" A heavy exhale left her lips. "Look, I know New York can be overwhelming, so I'll give you my number—for emergencies *only*, 'kay?"

Result! "Really? That's brilliant! Cheers, Riley!"

She rattled it off and Ben typed it into his phone, a smile lighting up his face. "When I'm back on street level, I'll text you so you'll have mine."

"Sure." She nodded, standing up to corral her suitcase. "On Canal, I think you need to head toward Mercer Street. If you pass McDonald's, you're going the wrong way. You want to head toward Dunkin' Donuts."

"So, burgers—bad. Donuts—good. Got it."

"It's been nice meeting you, Benjamin. Welcome to New York." She joined the cluster of people waiting by the doors.

"It's been awesome meeting you, Riley. Welcome home."

With a quick wave, she was gone.

FOUR

Crossing Third Avenue to St. Mark's Place, Riley checked her phone one more time. New texts had arrived since her last peek ten minutes earlier.

Her boyfriend, Josh King: *Babe, missing you!* with a photo of two pugs dressed as leprechauns.

Piper: *Are you close? This weather's aggravating my asthma. Hurry!*

Josh again: *Everyone's buying me drinks! #MVPperks*

But still nothing from cute Ben. Riley hoped he wasn't lost somewhere, wandering solo through the slush and noisy packs of shamrock-wearing partiers, his mother's pink case in tow. New York City could feel so lonely when you were on your own. Maybe he was downing pints in a Soho bar and fighting off women who loved his accent; she hoped it was the latter.

Hood up and head down, Riley weaved through the boisterous Saturday night crowd, their phones glowing bright in the night and their heightened sense of anticipation electrifying the air with a primal, youthful energy. Their laughter, imbued with a carefree spiritedness, triggered Riley's FOMO. An ache squeezed her chest. The excitement of a fun evening out, of no worries weighing you down—what's that like? I wish I could remember.

She hid her frown, replacing it with a more weekend-appropriate grin. Smiley Riley, her classmates called her thanks to her sunny, upbeat personality and her fun social media feeds, which told a happy tale of walking shelter dogs, her job at Sephora and internship at BBC Studios, and life in New York City. She had achieved excellent grades in college, had three ride-or-die friend-

18

ships in Piper, Casey, and Erika, and a mom who made Lorelai Gilmore look like a parenting slacker.

But Riley's put-together persona and outer cheeriness had become a well-rehearsed act, honed to near perfection. Underneath the happy-go-lucky façade, the real Riley was hurting and treading water, struggling to stay afloat amid tumultuous waves of sadness and despair.

Riley's feelings weren't new. Her mom, Maggie, first noticed something wasn't right during Riley's junior year of high school. Hanging out with Erika and their friends, her fun-loving daughter was happy and energetic, but when they weren't around, Riley seemed adrift, slipping into a downward spiral of hopelessness. She lost interest in things she loved like reading, playing board games, and researching family trees with her mom, her indifference leading to hours spent alone behind her bedroom door. Every time Maggie asked what was bothering her, Riley denied anything was wrong, but she eventually agreed to see a psychologist if her mother would stop nagging. The diagnosis was a surprise: smiling depression. "That's a thing?" Riley had asked the therapist. The strange dichotomy fit her perfectly, though: smiling on the outside, hiding her dark feelings inside. That was the thing—Riley never looked depressed. Always neatly dressed, always encouraging and thoughtful toward others; none of her friends had a clue.

After a dozen therapy sessions, Riley said she felt better and stopped going. Favorite activities resumed with her mom and she spent less time alone, but she still experienced crushing bouts of feeling lost, sad, and lonely. Riley vowed to control her emotions without therapy or involving Maggie—she refused to become a burden for her mom—so she pledged to be shiny and smiley even if she was hurting and battling a nagging emptiness inside. Her illness would remain invisible. No one likes a Debbie Downer. Keep it together, girl.

Faking it, Riley believed she had fooled everyone and wanted to keep it that way. Her mask never slipped, but today on the bus, had Ben—somehow—seen through her façade? *'You're really bummed. Something's bothering you. Let me cheer you up.'*

Her eyes left her phone, landing on her four-storey building and its zigzagging fire escapes a few doors away. Located above the blindingly bright yellow awning of Funky Town, an East Village shop with an extensive selection of heavy metal t-shirts, her apartment—lovingly labeled 'the shoebox' by Piper—offered a cramped yet convenient home on the fringes of NYU's campus. It also placed Riley in the midst of what had arguably been New York City's hippest street, once upon a time. Today, its quirky glory was faded and grimy, its rebellious counter-culture vibe relegated to its remaining hold-outs—vintage clothing stores, piercing places, and bong shops—but there was no debating the street's illustrious pedigree. In its heyday, hippies, punks, and famous trail blazers like artist Andy Warhol and singer Debbie Harry had guaranteed St. Mark's place in pop culture history.

In the midst of the karaoke bars and tattoo parlors, Riley spotted Piper Paisley scrolling through her phone, its screen lending a harsh glow to her pretty face. Wrapped in her pink faux-fur coat and wearing a sparkly silver mini-dress and oversized plastic sunglasses—at 8:15 p.m.—Piper looked like 1960s New York it girl, Edie Sedgwick. Her bleached blonde pixie cut and pointy-toed three-inch heels left no doubt that she was channeling Andy Warhol's famed muse from head to toe, but on her own terms. She accessorized her outfit with a devil-may-care joie de vivre few college seniors could pull off. Eyes closed, lost in her favorite Japanese pop—Pizzicato Five—trilling through her headphones, Piper was oblivious to the merrymakers spilling out of an Irish pub, lobbing offers of drinks from across the street.

"Piper." Riley's mitten nudged her friend's fluffy shoulder.

Piper bucked to attention. "What the f—?" Her glossy sneer stretched into a crooked smile. "Yay! Finally!" She yanked away her music and sunglasses, revealing heavily kohl-lined eyes, another Edie signature.

"It's your fault. You sent me on a wild goose chase for ginger-bread spread and cheesy crackers."

"Did you get them?"

"Sold out."

Piper sighed.

"How's your asthma—" Riley's phone broke out into Sia's "Chandelier". Her eyes dipped down to the lit screen. *Josh.*

"Yo, Pink Lady!" Across the street, a tall guy wearing an over-sized felt St. Patrick's Day hat flicked his cigarette to the curb and hollered over the passing cars. "Looking at you, I feel like the Re-public of Ireland—you know why?"

"God, where's this going?" Snapping her gum, Piper jutted out a sparkly hip.

Riley searched her tote for her puffin keychain. "No clue."

The guy pointed at his khakis. "Looking at you, my dick is Dublin!" His friends howled with dirty laughter.

Riley grimaced. "Nice to see your future husband decided to join us, Pip."

"Ugh." Piper groaned, following Riley to her building's brown metal door. "How do I attract these losers?"

"Another bad date last night?" Riley unlocked the door and held it open.

"Yup." Picking up Riley's case, Piper carried it inside. "He in-vited me back to watch a movie. It was—cringe—his own sex tape with two girls."

"Eww!" Riley checked her mailbox. "So not sexy!"

"Seriously!" Piper set Riley's suitcase by her feet and stuck a hand in her MoMA tote, pulling out an asthma inhaler. "I hit it off with guys on apps, we chat for freakin' forever, but then if—IF—we go on a date, they turn out to be shower dodgers, impotent, or fans of dick pics." She strangled the inhaler, shaking it violently.

"Maybe try a different app?"

"Maybe, but I'll have to add a 'no threesomes' note to my profile. Why do guys think if you're bi, you're desperate for a three-way?" Piper stuck the mouthpiece between her lips and plunged the canister, releasing a puff of medication.

"Blame porn," said Riley, her fingers sifting through a stack of mail and fast food flyers.

"I've never had this problem with women." Stashing her inhaler in her tote, Piper swiped a flyer from Riley's hands. "Oh, yum! Let's go grab falafel before bar hopping!"

I can't afford that. Riley swallowed heavily and stared at two business-size envelopes, a red 'PAST DUE' screaming for attention. *I'm drowning.* The mail in her hands didn't go unnoticed by Piper.

"You know what…" She dropped the flyer into the vestibule's trash can and shifted her weight onto her right foot. "These shoes? Blister fucking central! Can we stay in?"

Piper was lying, but Riley loved her for it. "I can make us nachos?"

"And I have tequila." Piper patted her tote. "Who needs green beer and drunk fuckboys?"

They climbed several flights of stairs to the third floor, the smell of weed and stale pizza embedded in the wallpaper. Once inside, Riley flipped the light switch and abandoned her Strand tote and pink case by the door. There was nowhere else they could go. Her home wasn't a really an apartment. It was more like a claustrophobic dorm room—a ninety-square-foot sliver with a communal bathroom down the hall and no kitchen—but at a fraction of dorm room prices. At least the large, curtain-covered window facing the street gave the promise of breathing space beyond the four walls.

Riley hung her parka on the back of the door and removed her boots. She whipped off her sweater, the only way to avoid sweating to death at the hands of the room's overzealous heater. Pulling down the creeping hem of her tank top, she turned on the faucet of the tiny sink wedged in the corner, the water pipes moaning as she washed the subway off her hands. "Toaster oven nachos coming up!" She tugged open her mini fridge, home to a carton of milk, a chunk of slightly moldy cheese, a jar of salsa, lemonade, and little else. *That'll do.* Stretching up on tiptoes, she rooted through cereal boxes, glassware, and dishes hogging two wall-mounted shelves. Her sock-covered heels returned to the hardwood floor, which creaked its displeasure. "No tortilla chips, but"—she held a bag and a box—"I have plain potato chips and Corn Chex cereal—that works, right?"

Piper kicked off her shoes. "After eating Chef Boyardee ABCs the past four days, potato chip nachos are haute cuisine." She wrestled the tequila from her bag, proudly setting it on the counter hovering over the fridge. Making herself at home, Piper grabbed two glasses and twisted off the bottle's lid, pouring equal measures. A splash of lemonade and her bartending job was done. "Cheers, lady." Glass aloft, she backed up, bumping into the ladder that led to Riley's bed—a twin mattress suspended overhead. Elevating the bed gifted Riley enough space to have a compact loveseat underneath, and across from it, a narrow chest of drawers topped with her PEZ dispenser collection. A clothing rail leaned against the remainder of the wall, plastered with photos of friends and family.

"Cheers, Pip." Riley swallowed a large mouthful and winced, removing a plate and some foil from her shelves. She didn't expect Piper to help with the cooking; her place was too cramped to even go there. "Hey, did you order your cap and gown yet?"

"Yup. Can't wait to rock that tassel." Piper sucked in her stomach and inched through the tight path between Riley's hanging clothes and the poles holding up her bed. She set her drink on a plastic milk crate—an improvised coffee table—and swept the blue curtain aside, grunting as she heaved open the window. "Did you?"

"I will after payday."

Piper spun around, snatching the TV remote. Pointing it at the small television clinging to the wall, she pulled up Netflix, the password to which she'd shared willingly with Riley and their friend Casey. "See this? Season two of *Lairds and Liars* has been added. My little Scottish heart is dying for another highland fling!"

"Been there, done that!" Riley laughed, arranging chips and cereal on the foil-lined plate. "Mom and I binge-watched. Hope they add season three soon."

Piper shrugged off her coat and reached under her dress, pulling down her black tights. "Your super sucks. It's still a sauna in here, gross!"

"He won't fix anything until I pay the rest of last month's rent. I might get a second job. I was looking at tutoring or babysitting—"

"With what time? You have to sleep, you know!" Piper yanked the tights from her sweaty feet, her eyes flitting to the TV. "Ahh, Mark Keegan—ooh, I would!" Captivated by the raven-haired Irish actor portraying an 18th-century Scot, she sank into the loveseat, digging her toes into the shaggy throw rug.

"Who wouldn't?" Riley peeked at the TV, catching her favorite actor. "Even Casey would. His man-crush is out of control." Despite Casey's admiration for Mark Keegan, he was wholeheartedly a heterosexual male—albeit one who hadn't dated or had sex in over two years.

"Well, he's got to have some fun," said Piper. "Imagine swearing off booze, sex, and girls? The freak. I know he probably got a hard-on when he heard his documentary was accepted to the Tribeca Film Festival, but come on! Live a little, dude."

Casey Hernandez was the Hermione to Riley and Piper's Harry and Ron, the third member of their Tisch trinity. A dog lover, a coffee fanatic, and an expert at winning stuffed toys from claw machines, Casey had dreams of becoming a documentary filmmaker. He and Riley had one awkward date during freshman year but realized they didn't want to mess up their friendship. Months later, Riley started dating Josh, and Casey began a short-lived relationship with a communications major who broke his heart when she was caught in the restroom of his favorite pub, straddling the bartender. He gave up booze and dating that night, vowing to pour all his passion into his film and television degree, and his volunteer work at an East Village no-kill animal rescue. Skipping St. Patrick's celebrations, he was busy editing his latest documentary.

Piper stared at the TV. "Have you seen photos of Mark's girlfriend?"

"Yeah, she's pretty—and American." Riley chopped off the cheddar's moldy corners.

"Lucky bitch." Piper nodded.

Sia burst out into song from Riley's phone again. She glanced at the screen glowing beside the cutting board and ignored it, lifting the cheese grater off its hook. "We'll work on your dating profile tonight."

"No, we're discussing North Dakota."

"Piper—"

"That's Josh, right? Calling again? He's so predictable, so annoying."

"He feels bad," said Riley. "I barely saw him. All he did was eat, sleep, hockey—repeat."

"Like I said, predictable…and annoying. At least you got something out of it—God, I miss sex."

"We only did it twice."

"But he made sure you came, right?" asked Piper.

"Pip…!"

"So, that's a no, then—"

"He had early morning practices."

"Like that's an excuse for ignoring your needs. Did you go with him?"

Riley shook her head. "His coach has a girlfriend ban before a big tournament. He thinks the players won't sleep, so I couldn't show up." She tortured the block of cheese, pressing it hard against the grater's metal spikes. "It's my fault. I should've visited another time."

"Wait, wait—everything you're saying is total crap AND grounds for dumping." Piper set down her drink and counted on her fingers. "Selfishness between the sheets, hiding you away from the world, putting a stupid sport ahead of you? That's three strikes— you're OUT!"

"Wrong sport, Pip."

"Oh, whatever!" Her voice spiked. "You ignored what we discussed, so what was the point of going to North Dakota? To be ignored? Better get used to it, Rye. PuckHead loves his hockey stick more than he loves you—fact."

"Please, dramatic much?" Riley laughed, sprinkling cheese on the potato chips. Piper always went way over the top with digs at Josh. "He needs to focus on playing well so the Wild's scouts—"

"Rye, stop it."

"What?"

"Stop making excuses, convincing yourself you're happy with him. You did the same thing at Christmas."

"No, I didn't."

"Hello? Last fall? After every FaceTime call? You'd complain—'*Josh doesn't listen, Josh changes the subject when I mention LA*'—Every. Single. Time. Then he came home for Christmas, and I don't know what magic he worked on you, but you babbled on about how amazing he was, walking shelter dogs with you, going skating—"

"Things were good at Christmas. He was like old Josh—"

"Yeah, but most of the time he's *new* Josh: self-absorbed, pushy, and increasingly arrogant. You finally clued in after winter break. All the doubts—"

"Piper—"

"You said nothing had changed—*Josh* hadn't changed. God, the earache you gave me! I was so relieved when you said you'd dump him on spring break."

"I never said I'd *dump* him." Riley yanked a spoon from a glass stuffed with cutlery.

"Not in so many words—"

"No, what I said was, I might suggest we *take* a break."

"Whatever. The reason's the same: you're not happy with him."

"Not all the time, no, but I think that's normal." Riley cracked open the salsa and swirled the spoon around the half-empty jar.

"Oh, come on!" Piper rolled her eyes. "Any guy who puts his career plans before my best friend can go fuck *himself*—not you!"

"Piper, three years together is a long time. You just don't throw a relationship away when things get rough. You work through it." Riley slopped salsa over the cheese and chips.

"Just because my longest relationship only lasted two months doesn't mean I don't understand."

"Yeah, but you don't." Riley huffed, a tightness squeezing her jaw.

"But I understand *you*." Piper lifted the remote, muting Mark. "I know you've been feeling down lately. I know you're scared, and I would be too if I were you, but you're not alone. You've got me and Casey. We're your family. I know we're dysfunctional as fuck, but we love you, 'kay? You don't need that selfish idiot."

Piper, you don't know the half of it...

27

"No matter how he spins it—"

"Josh proposed." Her words hung in the air, freezing the room into silence.

FIVE

Her spoon clanked loudly on the counter. *Fuck. I didn't want to tell her like that.*

"What?!" Piper snapped her gum and dropped the remote. "Did you say yes?"

Riley opened her mouth, about to say something, but settled into a silent pout. She scattered more cheese and then stopped, her eyes fixed on the plate. "I *was* going to suggest we take a break. With everything going on, I thought we could both use some space, focus on school and stuff without the constant obligation of checking in with each other every day. Then after graduation, we could see if we wanted the same things—see if we wanted to stay together." She spun the plate around, her finger trailing along its edge. "On Thursday, we were alone—finally—and I think he sensed something was up. He took me out for a surprise meal. Fucking great, right? I'd have to do it in a public place. Not ideal, but I was running out of chances since he'd be playing hockey again the next day...but before I could say anything, he asked me. I couldn't believe it! He got down on one knee with two packages of Reese's—"

"That's lame."

"He had a toy ring underneath the candy. He said he loved me so much he couldn't wait any longer to make things official. He doesn't want to spend another winter without me and..." Her eyes drifted across the wall, settling on her *Lairds and Liars* calendar.

"And what?"

"He said..." As Riley shifted her weight from foot to foot, the floorboards creaked underneath her socks. "He said when he signs with the Wild this spring, he'll take care of everything...bills and all that..."

"He what?" Piper squinted at the mail on top of Riley's suitcase. "Oh, so now he's bribing you? Fucker—"

"He's not bribing me. It's what committed couples do, Pip. They support each other emotionally, physically—financially. He says he doesn't want me to worry—"

"Worry? Jeez, it's a bit too late for that. My God! Be still my cold heart. Josh is *such* a romantic." Piper curled her lip. "The manipulative dick, I'd like to cut—"

"His balls off—yeah, you've told me a million times."

The veins in Piper's neck bulged. "He's totally playing with your emotions!"

Riley opened the toaster oven and slid the nachos inside. "No, if anything, he's being...practical. He knows we've grown apart because of the distance, and he knows how desperate I—" Her words stopped abruptly as tears began to sting her eyes.

"Aww, don't sweetie." Hopping to her feet, Piper swerved around the ladder and wrapped herself around her best friend. "I didn't mean to make you cry. It's just..." She paused, choosing her words carefully. "Josh complicating matters isn't helping."

"Don't you think I know that?" Wiping her nose, Riley withdrew from the hug and retreated to the fridge. Leaning down, her tired, watery eyes searched its bare interior. "My worst nightmare's coming true and there's nothing I can do to stop it, but Josh's money might make a difference."

"Why don't you ask Erika instead?"

Riley selected a crusty bottle of ranch dressing and closed the door. "I know we joke about her being loaded, but it's Scott's money, not hers—and besides, they're saving for their wedding." She opened the lid and sniffed the contents.

"Yeah, which will cost the same as two years' tuition and be splashed over Page Six—the hockey star and his ballerina princess."

"She hasn't danced for years, Pip. You wear more tutus than she does."

"I'm just saying you could ask. She's got money to burn."

Riley left the bottle on the counter. "No way. Talk about putting her in a really awkward position. I can't do that to her. And Josh offered—"

"Yeah, putting YOU in a really awkward position. Funny how he never made that kind of financial offer before—"

"He didn't have money before!" Riley pulled open the toaster oven, peering at the bubbling pool of cheese. "He won't actually get it until he signs with the Wild after graduation."

"He was drafted three years ago, right?" Piper hovered, chasing breaths as her voice grew louder. "He's known about this signing bonus he'll be getting for THREE YEARS!"

"Piper, enough! You'll have an asthma attack." Riley scowled over her shoulder, slamming the toaster oven shut. "Go sit down, you're in the way—"

"Why didn't he offer to help eighteen months ago, huh? When everything kicked off? He's such a fucking dick! He watched you cry over FaceTime, applying for loans, struggling to keep up with school…he only offered when he realized he might lose you."

Riley threw her a dirty look. "No, he offered because he loves me."

"That's not love, that's manipulation—and when was the last time *you* said you love him and meant it?"

"I *do* love him."

Piper huffed loudly. "He's holding your heart hostage at the worst possible time and you're falling for it!" Her eyes swept Riley's fingers for the toy ring, but the only jewelry was the small moonstone ring of her mom's that always graced her right hand. "You didn't say yes, did you?!"

THWUMP, THWUMP, THWUMP!

Riley jumped, her wide eyes glaring at the wall. "Great, my neighbor. She'll call the super—fucking awesome." She scowled. "Just...stop yelling! And stop calling Josh a dick. I hate it. I wish you guys would get along—"

"Rye, tell me." Piper lowered her voice. "Did you say yes?"

She fiddled with her glass. "I'm thinking it over."

"Riley, no, there's got to be another way. We'll figure it out...together." Piper rubbed her friend's arm. "If you say yes, you'll move to Minnesota and end up hitched to a guy you don't love, raising his brats, and all your dreams of California and a TV career will be gone. Promise me you'll follow your dream, not some boyfriend? Please don't throw away your happiness."

"I'm not. I'm trying to do what's best—for everyone." Riley handed her the tequila and lemonade bottles. "And that includes you. Now, let's drink, eat nachos, and rewrite your dating profile, okay?"

Biting her tongue, Piper tilted the bottles and poured and poured, filing Riley's glass until lemonade and tequila tickled its rim.

Six

Impatient taxis and drunken shouts rose from the street as Riley watched Piper turn the corner, disappearing into the darkness. Her best friend's room in NYU's Alumni Hall was the next street over, and she'd be safely home within minutes. With Piper gone, Riley could finally exhale.

She picked up her iPad (a hand-me-down from Erika), and flopped on the loveseat, propping up her phone on the cushions so she wouldn't miss Piper's 'I'm home' text. With a finger flick, she popped the button on her jeans. *Grrrrrrrowlllllll!* Her stomach wasn't happy—too much cheese or too much angst? The argument with Piper had left her unsettled during *Lairds and Liars*, dizzy with tequila-soaked questions about the past week, the future, and what made her happy. *Josh's mind might be cluttered with dreams of hockey pucks and trophies, and he's more hyped about me being a WAG than a TV director in California, but that doesn't make him a bad person...does it? He loves me.* Her thoughts tangled into a dull headache. Piper meant well, but Riley's relationship with Josh was complicated. More was at stake than a broken heart.

She fanned her flushed face and tapped her tablet, unleashing the high-pitched FaceTime ring. It cut out, replaced by thumping bass and *"YEAH...YEAH..."*—Usher's assured vocals blasting through the speaker. Josh's scruffy moustache and beard, grown for good luck during the tournament, appeared first and then the picture swept up his face, capturing his slightly crooked nose and hazel eyes, muddy and half-lidded.

"Hey, baby gurrrrl!" His voice fought with what sounded like the entire population of Grand Forks, North Dakota, crammed into

33

whatever drinking establishment he was in. His phone lurched, sailing over a table crammed with empty glasses and surrounded by boisterous males downing inky-colored shots. The guys were familiar: Josh's North Dakota Fighting Hawks teammates, all oozing ego and entitlement—not to mention booze—through their sweaty pores. "Guys, GUYS!" Josh demanded off camera. "Say hello to the future Mrs. King!"

Red faces flooded the screen, their slurring voices competing with each other.

"Kingy shoots, he scores!"

"Fuck the trophy, man—she's the real prize!"

Josh started his own chant. "She said yes! SHE SAID YES!"

"Hey! Hi guys." Riley waved politely, blushing.

The drunken chorus grew louder, hammering her phone. "WE'RE NUMBER ONE! NUMBER ONE, BABY! NUMBERRRR ONNNNNE!" The chants sloppily swerved into a shouty out-of-tune rendition of the college's fight song, the lyrics an incoherent mess.

"JOSH!" Riley raised her voice, waging a losing battle for her fiancé's attention. "Sorry I missed your calls." She winced as the screen bobbed from face to face. "I was with Pip—"

"Argh, Hyper Piper!" Josh sneered. "Did you tell her the good news?" His lips curled into a smile. "My baby said YES!"

Riley's phone lit up on the loveseat—Piper texting she was home. "Um…no. Wasn't a good time."

"Is it ever with her? *Anyway*…Rye, my goal! It was EP-IC! Their defenceman was clinging to me, pulling me backward, but I dragged him and the puck over the blue line, across the slot, then my wrist shot—"

"*MVP*! *MVP*!" Teammates pumping the air with bottles invaded the screen, their deafening chants sending Riley's fingers scrambling to lower the tablet's volume. They jumped around, slopping beer on each other without regret or concern. *"MVP! MVP!"* They tried to hoist Josh up on their shoulders, but he wrestled them off with laughter and a round of aggressive high fives.

"YASSS!" With each smack, the vibrations jarred Josh's phone, distorting the picture. "I am! I am the FUCKING MVP, right, *fiancée*?!"

Riley nodded with a tight smile. She was happy for Josh, for all of them. Their season had been a rollercoaster ride of nail-biting wins and devastating losses. Going into the tournament as under-dogs, their guts and grit captured the title, and her guy—the science nerd from school who was bullied as a preteen for competing in figure skating—was now a sculpted, six-foot-two hockey god who could outskate all competition and had scored the game-winning goal two games in a row. Celebrated in chants, plied with booze all night, and destined for the NHL in six short months, Josh was prov-ing wrong all those bullies who called him weak, weird, or a waste of space. What had made him a target as a kid was now his gift. He was the MVP—and her fiancé.

Fiancé. Most f-words I have no trouble saying, but this one...?

High fives morphed into 'I love you, man' hugs, bro back slaps, and Josh's phone zooming into some guy's plaid shirt.

Riley exhaled heavily. Anything she said now wouldn't be heard. *I should let him go...*

His red face flew back on screen. "Aww, babe, wish you were here." He pushed off another teammate invading their conversation. "Make sure you tell your mom about our engagement, okay? Tell her."

"I will, when I see her." She grinned. "You should go, have fun. I'm glad I got to see you..."

"Rye?"

"Yeah?"

"Wait." He covered his phone, only a flicker of light making it through the gap between his fingers. The booming bass and locker room chants faded, replaced by the brief squeal of a hinge. "Woah, c-c-old!" Josh gasped and his phone shook, revealing a flash of dirty Nikes crunching snow underfoot. "It looks like Christmas…see?" His phone tilted, sweeping across the woodland bordering the bar's property. Snow-kissed evergreen trees stood still, pointing toward a jet-black sky pierced with tiny dots of tinsel, faraway stars twinkling hello. No wind, no voices, just the passing splash of tires through slush on the road and the muted *thump thump thump* of bass from the bar keeping them company.

Returning to the screen, Josh chuckled, muting another hiccup. "The chill…it's sobered me up a bit." He inhaled deeply, blowing out a cloud of breath. "So, fiancée…" A sly smile raised his cheeks. "I couldn't be happier. It's what everyone wants—you and me engaged!"

Not Piper. Piper thinks I should dump you—now.

"My parents, Erika, your mom—yeah, think about how happy Maggie will be."

Erika wants another WAG-y partner in crime, and Mom? How will Mom feel?

Josh stared, his eyes dropping to her thin tank top. "Hello…Riley? Are you thinking about our wedding night? I am! *Riley?*"

She blinked, rejoining the conversation. "Yeah."

"Aw, babe, you and me in the same city, our own apartment with actual rooms—not like that shitty dump you're in now. We'll have a huge bedroom with a king-size bed, an en suite bath, maybe even get a place with a pool so you can swim whenever. I'll take care of you—of us. I've got this."

"Josh—"

"I know. Maggie raised an independent girl and you hate letting a guy take care of you, but that's what a husband does." A laugh burst from his lips. "I'm so gonna let you pick out a massive ring with my signing bonus."

"You can't blow your bonus on me, Josh."

"Can't I spoil my fiancée? Make sure everyone knows you're mine? The Wild veterans, man, they're gonna be so impressed—and envious. I may be a rookie on the ice, but off it—with you—I'm anything but! I'm dying to show you off. You'll be the hottest girl at the rink."

You want me to play a role that's not real—that's not me. "Those girls will think I'm a freak. I'm not into shopping or babies. I hate manicures. I have more in common with your future team-mates than their girlfriends—I actually know what a failed offside challenge is."

"Erika and Leia don't think you're a freak."

"Leia does," Riley shot back. Erika's bestie wasn't her biggest fan.

"Leia shouldn't talk. She's named after a *Star Wars* character."

"She hates *Star Wars.*"

"Yeah, and that's why *she's* a freak. Look, when we move to Minnesota, you'll meet girls nicer than her and Erika with none of that snotty New York 'tude. Sometimes I think that city's a bad in-fluence..."

Riley pulled the elastic from her hair, letting it fall long and wavy to her shoulders.

"Babe," Josh groaned, his words slowing down. "Your hair...so soft, so fucking sexy. I wish I could get lost in it, spread out on the pillow beneath me..."

She gave him a wistful smile.

"I'd kiss your neck, suck your boobs...while your hands—" He gasped. "Your hands would play with my hard cock." He licked his lips. "Baby, remember how good it feels? How wet it makes you? I can't have you forgetting your MVP, your most valuable..." Josh stared half-lidded into his phone.

Player...

"Penis." Josh breathed heavily. "MVP, get it?"

Typical guy. "Yeah, I get it."

"Ahh, babe." Josh let out a shuddering breath, his eyes needy. "I'm dying here. You should've stayed another night. I should've made you stay." He fell into a whisper. "Rye, if I went into my truck, would you..."

She slouched into the cushions. "Josh—"

"Babe, c'mon." He shivered. "I won't take long."

You never do. She exhaled, not budging. "It's getting late..."

"Oh...right." He nodded, shoulders slumping. "Rye, I love you."

"*I...*" Riley's stomach pinched. "I love you, too." The mumbled words slipped through her tight lips without being fully formed, a reflex, a force of habit—a lie, now impossible to pull back. "Night."

"Night, babe." He waved and the screen went black. 1:06 a.m. popped up in his place, but sleep would have to wait.

Riley stepped over to the sink, squeezed a green blob of dish detergent into the small basin, and turned on the faucet. The FaceTime conversation replaying in her head, she mindlessly swirled a dish cloth through the water, encouraging bubbles to grow and overtake the dirty stack of plates and utensils. Waiting for the soapy cloud to consume her hands, tears began to sting her eyes. She looked up past the NYU pool schedule tacked to the wall to the *Lairds and Liars* calendar hanging above the faucet and the appointment circled in blue marker on Monday's square—11:15 a.m., Brooklyn Health Center.

SEVEN

Ben jolted awake, his eyes assaulted with a flash of red—a high ceiling coated with an obnoxious slick of scarlet paint. The scent of coffee teased, and childlike voices squealed from afar, chased by a tinny laugh track. *Can't be real kids. TV...cartoons?* He rolled to his right and the edge of the lumpy sofa, the coarse but colorful knitted blanket on his bare chest falling toward the floor. Grabbing hold and covering himself, his fingers poked through the blanket's holes, his blurry eyes focusing, sliding along a black wall to meet two round, tanned—*butt cheeks?! What the FUCK?* Shifting up on his elbows, his bare heels digging into the sofa, Ben backed into the armrest, creating as much distance as he could between himself and Mr. Rock-Hard Buns crouched in a low squat.

"Hey!" The naked squatter looked over his shoulder. "Sorry, did I wake you? I'm Hunter." He began to swing around, a musky scent accompanying his arrival.

Oh, good God, don't! Ben squinted, but it was too late. Mr. Rock-Hard Buns, AKA Hunter, was full-on full frontal, his nine flaccid inches swinging with pride. Ben gulped, his eyes widening. *He's hung like a fucking donkey!* He quickly looked away, his eyes scrambling for somewhere safe to land.

"Gotta get my squats done before jogging to the gym." Hunter held his head high and scratched his head through his close-cropped brown hair. "They warm everything up, ya know?"

No, I don't know, actually. A stack of men's fitness magazines on the hardwood floor held Ben's stare. He cleared his throat and played with the dark hair on his forearm, unsure where to look next. Hunter leapt into jumping jacks. "Glad you got the keys off my neighbor, let yourself in. I meant to be here when you arrived, but work called. Did you sleep okay? Sorry it's not big."

Ben looked up—a big mistake—and got an eyeful of bouncing penis. "Oh, it's big—"

"What?' Hunter stopped jumping and scratched his rapidly rising and falling pecs, which were pumped up, hairless, and sculpted to male model perfection.

"Uh, I mean it's big *enough*—the sofa, it's great, thanks." Ben gave an awkward double thumbs-up and bowed his head, keeping his sightlines PG.

"I know it's not ideal." Hunter exhaled heavily, surveying his home. "Most Airbnb guests only stay for a night then go elsewhere."

Yeah, I wonder why, mate. Ben smiled politely and ran a hand through his messy hair, trying to tame the pieces pointed toward the red ceiling.

"Sorry about…" Hunter casually swept his hand down his naked body. "I usually warm up in my bedroom, but I'm storing stuff in my there for my new business venture. I like to stretch and warm up naked. It lets me see how my body reacts—it's become a habit."

"It's okay, really. It's nothing I haven't seen before."

"Exactly, dude! Hey, if you don't mind the sofa, you're welcome to stay as long as you'd like. Your email said something about a couple weeks?"

"Hopefully, yeah, but I need to find a job, otherwise…" Stomach growling, Ben brushed his hair from his eyes. "I can't afford to stay on anyone's sofa. Time's a-ticking." He squinted toward the half-tilted window blinds and the gray day peeking in. "Speaking of, what time is it?"

Hunter squatted, picking up his phone from the floor. "Quarter to nine, the Sunday after St. Patrick's Day—first one I've greeted without a hangover, I think…"

"Yeah, me too." Ben nodded. "Hey, do you have a laptop or a tablet I could use? To search for jobs?"

"Want something under the table?" Hunter scrolled through his phone.

"Maybe." Ben's eyebrows furrowed. "Why do you ask?"

"Your accent—Australian?"

"British."

Hunter nodded. "My buddy's Spanish, here illegally. I've become an expert at finding cash-in-hand work. I might be able to help you land something…" He stared at Ben's bandaged hand. "I was going to suggest joining his flat-pack furniture assembly biz, but—"

"I can do that." Ben sat up, eyes keen and bright. "My hand—it's just a cut. I'll do anything."

Anything, huh?" Hunter chuckled, giving Ben a once-over. "Okay. I'll make some calls."

EIGHT

Lining up boxes of perfume just so, a yawn escaped Riley's pout. Her hand quickly ran interference, covering her mouth as her puffy eyelids flickered and fought to stay open under the headache-inducing fluorescent lights. It was no use—this yawn would not be muffled. *Wake up! Look alive.*

A co-worker snickered. "Rough St. Paddy's, Riley? Grab my extra espresso in the break room—you need it more than I do."

"Aw, thanks…" Riley yawned again, straightening her black Sephora tunic over her hips. "You're a lifesaver." Her eyes swept the shop floor, searching for her manager, who had already told her off once for looking pale and exhausted that morning. A quick get-away was imperative. She had to be peppy and back in place for the arrival of Sunday's first customers. Boss nowhere to be found, Riley made a dash, leaving her post in 'fragrance world' for a much-needed rendezvous with the two Cs—concealer and coffee.

A burst of chilly air sailed up the back of her black tights. *Shit, 11 a.m.—showtime.* She circled back to her department, smiling at the rosy faces emerging from wool scarves and fur-trimmed hoods. The shop in Soho was open for business whether Riley was ready or not. Her eyes strayed to the people passing by outside on Broadway, the morning foot traffic heavy despite yesterday's snow and the boozy St. Patrick's Day vibe that still hung over the city. An old habit roused itself—making up stories for people sailing past on the sidewalk: well-groomed women heading toward Balthazar for avocado toast, teenagers in unzipped parkas exercising their parents' plastic in Uniqlo, the lanky dark-haired guy hidden underneath a green ball cap shuffling to—*wait! Ben? It's Ben!* A strange sense of

42

giddiness lightened her mood. The place where he was staying was a few blocks away so it made sense to see him around. Riley smiled, happy he was okay. He looked snug in a quilted coat ideal for a New York winter. *Thank God he ditched that light jacket!* Snow began to dance in the blustery air as he slowed his pace and adjusted his hat, lifting the peak and turning his head. She raised her hand in a half-wave and his eyes met hers, delivering a blank stare—under a New York Jets cap. This guy's hand wasn't bandaged. His lips were thin and unkind, displaying zero joy or interest, his cheekbones unremarkable, and his eyes...steely and impatient. Even if she never saw Ben again, she wouldn't forget his sparkly blue eyes, carefree and inviting—fun. Ben was like a friendly puppy, all gangly and unable to sit still...unlike this guy. With a double take, he frowned, stared at his phone, and stiffly strode away, out of sight, out of mind, instantly forgettable—unlike Ben.

Riley's smile dissolved as quickly as it had appeared. *Why hasn't he texted to say hi?* She stood up straight, the freezing air pushing past the open doors, waking her up. *Riley, you told him your number was for 'emergencies only'. That's WHY, stupid. Hopefully he's all right. New York alone is...well, I hope he's okay—*

"Riley!" Frustration tinged the woman's tone. "A client's waiting."

Ugh, the boss. She snapped to attention. With an apologetic smile, Riley slipped her fingers down her sleek ponytail and smoothed her tunic. She turned around, meeting two familiar faces.

"Gotcha!" Underneath the hood of her shearling coat, her oldest friend, Erika Kobayashi, stood tall and posture-perfect, a grin raising the corners of her burgundy lips. "Like my angry boss voice? I'm practicing for when I get that promotion. It's good, isn't it?"

Riley nodded with a sleepy smile. "Almost too good. You'll have 'em quaking in their boots and eating out of the palm of your hand."

"Aw, you really think so?"

"Yep. The Four Seasons would be crazy not to give you that promotion. Plus, you always get what you want."

"That's true." Leia McClelland, Erika's best friend and fellow New York Islander WAG, stuck her hands in the pockets of her wool coat and tapped her foot. Willowy and ethereal with a thick mane of long red hair, Leia was bewitching yet unassuming. Wherever she went, she drew envious stares, and today was no different, her makeup-free complexion still lightly sun-kissed from her Caribbean vacation with Erika six weeks earlier during the NHL's all-star break.

"So, what are you doing here?" Riley looked around her friends, ensuring her boss wasn't hovering. "Erika, weren't you and Scott booked for a spa day?"

"You never get out anymore. I had to ambush you." The twenty-four-year-old carefully lowered her hood, revealing her sleek black tresses immaculately coiffed into a bun. Not a hair, not an eyelash, not a sweep of blush was out of place—but that was Erika, always ready for her close-up. The Japanese-American stunner and former teen ballerina was perpetually dressed to impress for any high-profile occasion that might roll her way, be it a star-studded Midtown fundraiser, or an impromptu casting session for the *Real Housewives of New York*—her favorite TV series. Riley was always amazed by her high school friend's elegance and had no clue how she kept it up, rain or shine, weekday or weekend. "Scott blocked a shot last night, puck hit his arm."

"Ouch! In the gap?"

"Yeah, between the glove and elbow pad. It ballooned and turned purple. The doctor's examining it again, so I'm here, ready to take advantage of your staff discount."

Riley slouched into a whisper. "Not today, okay? You know I

would if I could."

"Well, save me some of your gratis products, then."

"I gave you a bag full last month, greedy guts, and it's not like you can't afford them—"

"You can take the girl out of Staten Island, babe. Besides, everyone loves free stuff!"

"Yeah, you more than most, Eri." Leia yawned, her blue eyes hopping to Riley, who was fiddling with her ponytail. "I'll be over in hair products." The twenty-five-year-old's boots scuffed aimlessly toward the rear of the shop.

"Was that a dig?" Riley examined the ends of her hair.

"No! Your hair looks super cute today! But—"

"What?"

"Your eyes look puffy— you *did* go out last night!"

"No! I was up late with Pip and her tequila." Riley looked over her shoulder, praying her boss wouldn't swoop in and catch her socializing. Thankfully, her engagement news would have to wait. She exhaled quietly, relieved that Erika—who was eating, breathing, and sleeping weddings—could be kept in the dark a little longer. One whisper of Josh having proposed and Erika's delighted squeals would be heard all the way back to Staten Island and their old neighborhood. Riley's boss would probably celebrate, too—by firing her.

"Aw! I get it. I used to drink when I missed Scott. It sucks being apart." Erika sighed and rifled through a row of perfume boxes. "Want to do lunch? Tell me about spring break? I don't have to pick up Stanley from daycare until three." Stanley Pup was Erika and Scott's Boston Terrier, named after the Stanley Cup, the NHL's top prize. Riley adored him. In many ways, she preferred dogs to people—they were loyal, reliable, uncomplicated.

"Can't—I'm broke." She straightened the scents Erika had messed up. "And I'm here 'til closing, doing a double."

"Is that smart?" Erika's eyebrows lifted. "You look like you're running on fumes, and isn't tomorrow—"

"Did you see these?" Riley snatched a frosted bottle from a shelf, trading the rest of her friend's sentence for a decadent eau de toilette spray. She waved it under Erika's nose. *Look! Shiny things!* If it was new, heaven-scented, and eye-catching, Erika would latch on and forget what they had been talking about. "Just arrived. Limited edition."

Erika's eyebrows launched toward the ceiling, buoyed with competitive zeal. "Ooh! Leia doesn't have that one!" Her pale manicure flew down the buttons of her coat, unveiling a designer dress yet to hit stores. "So! Get this—my bachelorette is almost planned!"

Riley cradled Erika's perfume and started down the aisle. "Which one?" Leia was organizing all of Erika's pre-wedding parties and gift grabs.

"Which one! The *first* one." Erika's intense concentration climbed the shelves. "Leia thinks she found the perfect club."

"Male strippers? Seriously, that's still the plan?"

With a nod, Erika's chandelier earrings tinkled cheerily.

Riley scrunched her nose. "That's such a cliché."

"Babe, I *want* cliché. Every aspect of my life is ordered, professional, top notch. I want sweaty pelvises grinding in my face. I want handstands in banana hammocks! I want penis-shaped cake! Don't be a killjoy—let me have my smutty fantasy." Erika giggled, dumping several boxes of perfume into Riley's arms. "Leia's taking this research seriously. She has one more club next Friday and then she'll make her decision. The timing couldn't be better."

"Why?"

"The Islanders' western road trip? Tyler won't be around to distract her and with Scott gone, I can get the 411 about the dancers! But only if his arm is better and he travels with the team. He's dying to get revenge on the LA Ducks."

"You mean LA Kings." Riley smiled politely at a passing customer.

"Ducks, Kings—all I care about is the guys being gone for six days, and Leia and I are taking full advantage. You should, too! We'll have a girls weekend! Cocktails, manis, pedis—my treat. Oh! And we can check out her apartment reno and try on her new upcycling designs. There's a dress screaming my name!"

More things I can't afford. "Does Leia know you're inviting me?"

Erika crossed her arms like a teacher disciplining a student. "Rye, I need my maids of honor to get along."

I shouldn't have let Erika guilt me into this. Being a bridesmaid is sucking the life out of me—and my bank account. I can barely afford groceries let alone my dress...

"Scowls will ruin my wedding photos—"

"Talk to Leia, then." Riley checked her whereabouts. Leia was at the back of the store slouched beside a black and white striped pillar, checking her phone. "She gives me the cold shoulder and *I'm* the one getting the lecture? It's been four months and I'm still waiting for a thank you. I spent three weeks filming and editing that reel for her boss's Fashion Week charity. I guess it created itself, right?"

"I know, I know. It's just..."

"Easier to tell *me* to play nice? Eri, I know you want to stay in her good graces—"

"I can't miss the Met Gala!"

"You act like it's life or death."

"It is—" Erika caught herself. "Well...socially." She added two more boxes to the haul in Riley's arms.

She stared at the lavish stash teetering in her arms. One careless nudge and her paycheck would be splattered across the floor. "Uh, want a basket?"

Pausing at a mirror, Erika flashed a gleaming smile, a perk of

Scott's endorsement deal with a teeth-whitening brand. "I'm one degree of separation from landing on the most coveted guest list. The Met Gala is THE big get, and with Leia working part-time at the Costume Institute—"

Riley rolled her eyes. "Kissing her butt so you can go to a celeb-filled party..."

"It might sound silly to you, but it's everything to me."

"I'd apologize to Leia if I'd done something wrong, but..." Riley curled her lip. "She acts like I slept with Tyler. Yuck—as if!"

"Honestly, who *hasn't* slept with Tyler? Have you heard the latest?" Erika pulled Riley into a Leia-free corner. "You know that Fashion Week model, the one with the twin sister who dates that douche from *SNL*? Apparently, she's the latest."

"Ugh, I don't get the attraction." Riley frowned. "He's so cocky—like he's God's gift, boasting about his blue line prowess at your Christmas party. Remember when I rattled off his embarrassing plus-minus stats? That shut him up."

"Yeah, he looked like a puck hit him in the groin," Erika snickered.

"The Pittsburgh scandal would've done it for me. I can't stand cheaters—I can't stand *him*."

"And that's the problem." Erika exhaled heavily. "That's why Leia is frosty. She knows you don't like him—"

"That's the reason?!" Riley flinched at her loud retort and settled into a whisper. "But I'm on *her* side! All I said was that she deserved better."

"I know, but nobody's allowed to diss Tyler, except her..."

"She's being naïve: once a cheater, always a cheater. Why won't she leave him? He slept with his teammate's wife, for fuck's sake!"

"Love makes you do crazy things, Rye. All she wants is Tyler and his babies, and if she has to break her vows to make him jealous, so be it. Personally, I think someone's going to get hurt. I told her as much and she freaked out at me, said I wasn't supportive and froze me out for a week. You being weird could set her off again…"

As much as Riley liked Erika, she didn't like the melodrama that accompanied her pro hockey clique. Rumors of affairs, fickle friendships, the competition to have the best clothes, the biggest homes, and the most jaw-dropping parties was never ending and exhausting. Rich people's problems—so foreign, so not her. The more she was exposed to it, the more Riley hated it, but with tomorrow looming, her fight was needed elsewhere…and Erika had kindly covered every night out since fall, so she owed her—literally. *Hold your nose and just agree to it.*

"I can't have you relegated to the penalty box." Riley gently kicked a shopping basket toward Erika, careful not to shift her perfume pyramid. "Fine, I'll be extra nice to Leia—and Tyler—for you."

"Babe, you're the best!" Erika claimed her items, placing each one lovingly in the basket. "But speaking of *the worst*…guess what Mom called about this morning?" She didn't allow Riley to answer. "Her dress. She hates it! I said, 'Mom, it's Gucci—deal with it!' Then, she said a chocolate fountain mimicking the Stanley Cup was tacky…"

Riley zoned out. Mother-daughter arguments, weddings, hockey husbands…every bit of it soured her empty stomach.

NINE

Riley was battling a serious case of the Mondays.

Her 'Directing the Camera' workshop ran late, leaving her scrambling for the appointment in Brooklyn. She cursed the B train from Broadway-Lafayette for being so slow, the worn treads on her boots for hindering her progress on the slippery sidewalks, and God—if there was one—for being cruel and unfair.

Stomach growling, she weaved around people rushing past, their fluffy conversations and laughter in wild contrast to the fear squeezing her heart. *These people—they don't know how lucky they are. Everyone's lives just go on while mine is tearing apart at the seams...*

Large storefront windows topped with blue awnings signalled she'd arrived. *Breathe, Riley.* She pulled open the door and hurried inside the modern space, passing by crisp, white lab coats and slow-moving people—*patients, family members*? Her wet boots squeaked to a halt on the shiny floors in front of a simple yet stylish white desk, topped with a flourish of silk flowers.

"I'm sorry, I'm late—"

"It's okay, Riley. Take a seat." The woman gestured to the area behind a large white wall punctuated with cut-out square shapes, each one home to a colorful vase or piece of blown glass. "Your mom's here."

"Thank you." Riley nodded and stepped around the wall.

Rooting around in her purse, Maggie Hope sat alone in the waiting room on a sky-blue couch. A lush indoor garden of non-fragrant flowers defied the gray coldness lingering outdoors. Riley's heart surged into her throat. It had been a week since she'd seen her mom, but it felt like an eternity. So much had happened during the past seven days, and the first person she always turned to with good or bad news was only a few steps away. Sometimes you just need your mom.

Riley rushed over, unzipping her parka. "Sorry, Mom! Class ran long." She plunked down on the cushions, dropped her tote and backpack, and wrapped her arms around her favorite person in the world. Maggie, still cozy in her winter coat, smelled of vanilla and coffee, of comfort and happy memories. Riley sank in and exhaled a halting breath, hesitant to pull away and let go, hesitant to face what was coming.

"Remind me again—why are you going to that fancy college if that's your best excuse? I thought you were more creative than that." Chin resting on Riley's shoulder, Maggie laughed, trying to dampen her daughter's worry. "Mind you, my excuse isn't any better—construction on Staten Island. I got here two minutes ago." Maggie leaned back, her expressive brown eyes full of warmth. "Sweetheart, it's going to be fine." She squeezed Riley's cold hand. "We'll get through this together like always. I love you."

"I love you, too, Mom."

Maggie smiled and ducked out from her coat's hood. Not a wisp of an eyebrow or lock of silky brown hair graced her head.

A nurse stepped around the wall. "Maggie, we're ready for you now. "

TEN

Maggie flinched in the infusion chair as the cold rush of saline coursed through her vein and up her arm. She smiled sheepishly. "You'd think I'd be used to this."

"Wimp," Riley joked. She had to make light of the situation. If she didn't laugh...

"Your mom's one tough cookie," said Dominique, Maggie's usual nurse, an older woman with a melodic Jamaican accent and a tidy bun the color of spun silver thread. She flipped a page of Maggie's medical history on her clipboard, reading the need-to-know info aloud so a young nurse wearing pink scrubs and oversized glasses could learn and follow along. "Maggie was originally diagnosed with cervical cancer in 2012, then Stage 2A ovarian cancer four years later. Following surgery and treatment, both went into remission, but a third diagnosis was made last November, a recurrence of ovarian cancer—Stage 3C."

"The chemo's been tougher this time." Riley settled in a chair beside her mom. "The fatigue and joint pain have been a lot worse."

"But all this discomfort means the cancer cells are being destroyed." Maggie yawned. "All for a good cause, right? I'll be better before you know it, despite the hand numbness, chemo brain, and my itchy butt."

"Especially the itchy butt." Riley laughed.

"Did you celebrate your birthday?" Dominique turned to the young nurse. "Maggie's birthday was a week ago, the eleventh."

"At home with my girl." Maggie winked at her daughter. "But we didn't let cancer cramp our style. We traded our sweats for dresses, put on glittery makeup, did our hair—well, I say that, but I just tossed on a wig."

"Good for you," said Dominique, patting Maggie's arm.

"That wig lasted all of five minutes," said Riley.

"Too hot." Maggie crinkled her nose. "And besides, bald is beautiful."

"You're lucky you have a nicely shaped head." Riley looked over her shoulder at Dominique, who was jotting down notes. "I made pizza, salad, and cupcakes, but some birthday traditions had to be axed—raw cookie dough was on the no-go list."

"Cancer's such a killjoy." Maggie laughed, holding her daughter's hand. "But we were together—that's all that counts."

"So true." Dominique smiled, unveiling her beautiful gap-toothed grin. "You've got a terrific attitude. Cancer picked the wrong woman."

"Yep, third go-round, but my third and final time beating its butt."

"Third time lucky," said Riley.

"Third time lucky, you know it!" Maggie squeezed her daughter's hand and let go.

Dominique checked the saline bag, ensuring the clear liquid was dispensing at the correct rate. "Your chemo cocktail should arrive in about twenty minutes, so sit back, relax, and we'll get this party started soon, okay?"

"I'll be here." Maggie nodded, watching the nurses leave the treatment room. She reclined in the chair, turning to her daughter. "So, c'mon, spill. How's Josh?"

"Good…" Riley's phone vibrated in her lap, a text brightening the screen.

"Everything okay?"

"It's Erika." Riley's eyes followed the rambling message.

Fuck! Erika never swore. *Today sucks! Scott's on injury reserve list = no road trip for him. Leia canceled our girls weekend = no*

Sat fun for us. Stanley peed on my new trousers, the dry cleaner's closed and...

"Nothing important." Riley left her phone on the rolling table and picked up a grape popsicle. "Josh was really busy. We didn't spend a full day together until Thursday, so I read, went swimming. Friday was the semi-final. He scored the winner and my God, I screamed so much, I could barely talk, and then Saturday morning he was at the rink before I left for the airport."

"MVP, huh? Josh did good."

"He did really good." Riley tore away the popsicle's wrapper and handed the treat to her mother. Maggie usually developed debilitating sores in her mouth during treatments and the soothing ice helped keep them at bay.

"You know, honey, you didn't have to rush back. You could've stayed for the final—"

"I wanted to be here. A week was too long to be away." *I'd drop everything for you, Mom.*

"I know, but you're either at school, interning, working, or with me. You need to see your friends, Riley, go to parties, be a college kid. You're only young once—trust me."

Here she goes again with the 'You should have the true NYU experience!' Riley had wanted to commute from home, but Maggie insisted she live near campus. "You make me sound like a bore. I still swim."

"You better! It's the only me time you have." Maggie held the popsicle in her mouth for a few seconds. "I'd be fine here on my own. One of the volunteers would've driven me home. You and Josh have so little time together."

"Yeah, well, that's going to change..." She took a deep breath. "He proposed."

Maggie almost choked on her popsicle. "He *what?*"

"He proposed Thursday night—"

"Riley—" Their words stepped on top of each other.

"Sorry I didn't say anything before. I wanted to tell you in person."

"And here I thought our traditional post-chemo donut was today's highlight. So…" Maggie's smiled cautiously as she clasped her daughter's hand. "What did you say?"

"I said yes." Riley looked at her hand wrapped in Maggie's, her mother's soft warmth comforting. "He proposed with a toy ring hidden in a package of Reese's."

"Oooh, smart—you can't say no to peanut butter…"

"We were at Red Pepper, finishing our tacos, and he went outside to grab his phone from his truck. Next thing I know, my name's being called and he's down on one knee. The restaurant went completely silent. They even turned down the music so everyone could watch."

"Well, he is a big deal in Grand Forks, right?" Maggie squeezed Riley's hand.

"Yeah, fans stop him all the time, but thankfully no one did mid-proposal. He was so nervous."

"Couldn't have been easy with an audience."

It wasn't. Riley nodded. "He was holding the peanut butter cup packages and said, 'Some might say I'm 'nuts' getting engaged at twenty-two, but I can't think of a 'butter' way to say I love you. Will you marry me?'"

"Oh, Josh." Maggie scrunched her eyes.

Laughing, Riley let go of her mom's hand. "I know! It's cheesy as hell, but it was like he reverted back to junior high Josh. Remember how small and geeky he was? Zero confidence, jokes so bad they made you groan, the only boy at school into competitive figure skating…"

"He certainly got picked on, but you were always there for him. I can't count the number of times you were late for dinner, practicing wrist shots on his backyard rink."

"Yeah, when we weren't making volcanos for the science fair!" Riley smiled. "But now look at him: an NHL second-round draft pick! I bet some of his school bullies will ask for his autograph one day without realizing he was the scrawny figure skater they used to beat up."

"It's strange how life turns out, isn't it?" Maggie returned the popsicle to her mouth.

"Yeah." Riley nodded. "Josh says he wants to build a solid foundation for our future together. He wants to take care of me, which is lovely…" She sighed heavily, her eyes drifting to the floor.

"Sweetheart, what is it?" Maggie tried to read her daughter's face.

"Part of me…I don't know. I was thinking about Dad…"

"Oh, Riley—Josh is nothing like your dad."

"But I can't forget how he—"

"You don't have to forget, but just remember, not every man takes off when times get tough."

Yeah, some propose instead. With a nod, Riley's forehead wrinkled in thought. "It's the next step, right?"

"If you're happy, sweetie. If you love him and want to spend your life with him…then hell yeah." Maggie leaned forward, searching Riley's eyes. "But if you're not sure, it's okay to say no. You're only twenty-two—there's no rush. I remember you seemed to be having doubts a few months ago, so don't feel pressured to say yes if you're not ready or it doesn't feel right."

"I know." Riley swallowed heavily. *There are so many reasons why I should've said no and one big reason why I had to say yes.*

"If you're worried saying yes to Josh means saying no to your career…"

Yeah, that's one for the no column, sure. She nodded.

"Riley, you don't have to choose between a job and Josh. There are TV stations in Saint Paul."

"But I won't be able to work toward directing or casting programs there. I don't want just any TV job, Mom. I've spent four years at Tisch with the goal of getting an entry-level job in production. That's been the plan since sophomore year, me and Piper going to LA together."

"Well, that's still an option. You could go with Piper this fall, test the waters and see if you get hired, and maybe Josh can ask for a trade to the LA Kings in a year or two so you can be together. Sometimes we have to wait a little bit for what we want most." Maggie chewed the last piece of popsicle. "Do you remember your dad's thirtieth birthday?"

"Maybe." Riley squinted, not sure what was coming.

"You were three years old, my little shadow, sitting on a chair watching me make his cake—"

"Red velvet with fluffy white frosting?"

Maggie nodded. "That's right! I explained the cake was for your dad's birthday and we couldn't eat it until he blew out his candles, but I said you could have a spoon of frosting when I was done icing the cake."

"Ooh, my fave part of baking."

"Your eyes grew three times their size when I gave you that spoon. You sat there licking away, frosting all over your face, happy as a clam. I turned my back for one minute, and you stood up on the chair and plunged *face-first* into that cake!"

"I was such a little pig!"

"You were adorable! But when I lifted you away, you cried. You saw cake and thought, *Mine*. I tried to explain that you can't always have what you want *when* you want it." Maggie discarded the popsicle stick on the table. "Maybe this is the same lesson…"

Riley nodded. *I wish I could be patient…but more than that, I wish I didn't feel trapped. I wish I could help pay Mom's bills and get her the best treatment on my own, so I didn't have to say yes to Josh.*

"What did Piper and Erika say?"

Riley stood up. "I haven't told them." She picked up a jug of water from the table. "I wanted time to enjoy our news before everyone offers opinions on dates, dresses…" Her chest felt tight, her voice flat…lying to her mom—the worst. She poured some water into a paper cup and added an angled straw, which bobbed and pointed back at her like an accusing finger. *I can't tell her what Piper said…the doubts. Mom would start questioning, even more than she is now. She can't find out the truth. She'll make me call it off.*

"Smart move. Everyone's got an opinion."

Riley handed her mom the cup. "I wanted to tell you first."

Maggie softly smiled and took a sip. "So, where's this ring, then?"

Riley winced. "The candy wrappers fell out of my tote on the bus…"

"You kept the wrappers? That's my girl. Sickly sentimental…or maybe scary hoarder?"

"Mom! The ring wasn't in the wrappers or my bag when I got home…I lost it."

"Aww. But I doubt Josh expected you to wear it."

"You'd be surprised. Wanna bet he'll ask about it? He's so excited, he'd tattoo 'fiancée' on my forehead if he could." Riley chuckled nervously.

"Did you discuss a date?"

"Only that it won't be this year."

Maggie smiled and held Riley's hand, both refusing to verbalize what they were thinking.

"Mom, if you need chemo this fall, I'll delay the move—"

"Ah, that's a big if, sweetheart. Don't worry, everything will work out fine, you'll see."

I hope so. I'd do anything for you, Mom. Anything.

Dominique returned carrying several bags of clear fluids. "Okay, Maggie, got your usual. Anti-nausea and anxiety meds first, then the chemo drugs." She hung the bags on the IV stand.

"I'll get more popsicles." Riley inhaled deeply and headed to the kitchenette.

"Whoops!" Riley's boots kicked something across the tiled entranceway of Maggie's Staten Island apartment. She peered over the groceries in her arms and leaned her shoulder into the door, keeping it open for her mom. Several pieces of mail, now scarred with dirty tread marks from Riley's winter footwear, fanned out on the floor. 'FINAL NOTICE' in red block letters screeched across one business-size envelope; another sneered 'OVERDUE'. A few more envelopes made up the scattered mess, but they were face down and Riley couldn't tell who they were from without stooping down. "Mom, I worked a double shift yesterday. I can—"

"No, you have rent to pay. I'm just a little late in my payments, no need to worry." Maggie stepped out of her boots, hung up her coat, and walked into her pokey kitchen.

Riley followed, leaving the single bag of groceries on the counter.

"I *know* you're living on cereal and apples." Reaching into the bag, a quick laugh left Maggie's lips. "I'll whip together a green salad, chicken fingers, those smiley face potato things you love, and you can tell me more about North Dakota. Those winds are picking up outside—I don't want you catching the ferry too late."

Riley returned to the entranceway and kneeled down, picking up an envelope—an insurance letter, probably demanding a deductible before they'd cover the cost of treatment. She picked up another—a heating bill. Even with her coat on, the chill of Maggie's apartment made Riley shiver. "But Mom—"

"No! Riley…please. I want to celebrate your good news with a home-cooked meal before the nausea kicks in. Just let me be your *mom* tonight, okay?"

"Okay." Riley stood up, ready to help any way she could.

ELEVEN

A week and a half later

Late for class due to Casey's insanely complex Starbucks order, Riley tilted hood-first into a bone-chilling gale, careful not to wipe out on icy Astor Place. "I don't think you should worry, Case. People will show! Tribeca is always sold out and your documentary's fantastic. I cried twice!"

"Yeah, but you've volunteered at a dog shelter for years—you *get* it." The snowy gust roared with evil intent, swooping down between the buildings, sending discarded coffee cups airborne and forcing Casey's gloved hand on a rescue mission, saving his flat cap—a gift Piper brought back from London the previous year— before it blew away. "But some festival goers might be all, 'No-kill animal shelters are SO five years ago.' Documentary lovers can be jaded. I should know—I am one!"

"But Tribeca wouldn't have accepted it if it wasn't good or important." Riley sniffed behind her scarf. "It gave me goose bumps. You can tell you put your heart into it."

"And many tears and sleepless nights." Casey sighed. "If it raises awareness and saves even one dog, I'll be happy."

"I bet it'll save tons of dogs."

Casey smiled and leaned into the wind, employing a death grip on his venti quad, no whip, coconut milk, extra hot mocha with caramel drizzle, extra vanilla syrup, and dark chocolate curls. He regularly skipped meals to feed his caffeine addiction. "Hope so. God, it's going to be a long month."

Don't let him dwell. Cheer him up. Riley's eyes settled on his wool coat. "Case, you're looking very Harry Styl-ish today. That coat looks like the one he wears in the "Sign of the Times" video." Her warm breath was snatched away by another blustery attack.

"You think? It's secondhand, but that's what I was going for. Cheers, mate!" Casey religiously followed Harry Styles online, copied his sartorial choices (the best he could with his student budget), and wore his brown hair exactly like him. Currently, it was short back and sides, and long and swept back at the front. "His clothes are pukka."

"Case! I'd roll my eyes, but I think they're frozen. You're doing it *again*."

"What?"

"Using British slang. It's insulting to real British people." *Like Ben, I'd bet...wherever he is.*

"Who? Piper?" The wind whipped up again, and Casey braced himself against Riley. They barged across the Astor Place-Broadway intersection, the traffic signal already flashing its red 'stop' hand. "She finds it endearing."

"So endearing, she calls you Brit Twit—to your face. How would you like it if Piper pretended she was Mexican?"

"Wouldn't bother me at all. Live and let live. I may have been born in the Bronx, but my soul belongs to Britain—and anyway, Mom thinks her granddad's ancestors came from England, so I have *some* claim."

Riley's phone began to sing. She yanked off a mitten, a smile rising from her bundled scarf. "Hey, Mom! Were you in the shower when I called?" The snarling wind bit into her bare skin, sending searing throbs through her hand and twisting her grin into a clenched wince. "Whatever you do, don't go out. My face feels like it's about to shatter and fall off."

"I just got in." Contentment hugged Maggie's voice.

Mom never goes out early unless... A twinge jabbed Riley's stomach. *Not again.* "Were you at the hospital? Why didn't you call me? You shouldn't be on public transit!"

Casey leaned in. "Hospital?"

Riley offered a shivery frown.

"I didn't call because you have early class this morning. Speaking of which, shouldn't you be there *now*—?"

She stepped on her mother's question. "Are you okay?!"

"I'm *fine*. I felt a little short of breath after dinner, so I went to the ER."

"What? You were there overnight? If you went willingly, it had to be more than 'a little'. I had to drag you in January."

"Riley, stop worrying. Last night was like January. The symptoms were the same, the diagnosis was the same, and the treatment, same—a blood transfusion."

"A blood transfusion isn't like slapping on a Band-Aid, Mom."

Casey popped above his scarf. "Transfusion? Again?" he mouthed.

"I feel much better." A giddiness lifted her words. "Maybe I'm half-vampire—I do love *Twilight!*"

"Not funny!" Riley sniffed, her eyes and nose watering from the chill. "If you can't breathe every time your red blood cell count drops after chemo, they'll postpone your treatments again."

"They'll only postpone if my numbers don't improve. As of 6:30 this morning, my count was climbing and I was breathing normally."

"Yeah, after sitting there for hours—on your own."

"I was fine, sweetheart! I had my book and chatted with a little girl who kept popping through the curtain. Her grandma apologized, but I didn't mind. She was so cute, dragging around a stuffed dog by the ear, asking if she could be a blood donut."

"A what?" Riley squinted, trying to hear her mom over the howling wind and an open-top tour bus—devoid of passengers—

chugging south on Broadway.

"She was calling a blood donor a 'blood donut'. She reminded me of you at that age—inquisitive, wanting to help, dragging Puffin everywhere. You loved that stuffed toy so much—still do!" A smile lifted her words. "Anyway, I feel much better now, so I'm going to enjoy my toast, binge-watch something happy, and cocoon under my blanket."

"I wish you would've called me. I could've kept you company." Riley blinked away the snowflakes collecting in her eyelashes and glanced around the fake fur on her hood.

Casey nodded.

"Riley, it would've been pointless to drag you out of bed. If it had been serious, I would've called you, promise—and before you ask, I didn't take the bus. A neighbor drove me and a hospital volunteer brought me home. See? Nothing to worry about."

"Still..." Riley sighed as they crossed Waverly Place, school only steps away.

"Sweetie, I'm fine. I'm home, and Netflix is calling."

Above the entrance to Tisch, the purple NYU banner snapped and flailed, threatening to break free. Casey tugged the door open and gestured for Riley to enter first. "If anything changes, text me. I'm working later, but you can still call."

"Will do. Now, I'm hanging up and you're going to class. Bye!"

Riley tossed her hood off in frustration.

"Your mom's always been super sweet to me. I hate that she's going through this again." Casey showed his NYU card to the security guard. "Is she doing okay?"

Riley dug out her ID and flashed it. "I guess, but I don't think she's telling me everything."

"Being vague about bad stuff is in the parenting manual."

"Don't they realize that makes us worry *more*, not less? The unknown is scarier than reality. I'm not twelve—I can handle what's really going on."

Casey lowered his voice. "Remember when I told you my dad got laid off, a few years back?"

Riley nodded.

"I only found out because I caught him leaving a pawn shop—he'd sold an old watch, family bits and bobs. I remember his face. He looked shocked and angry, but I think more than anything he was ashamed. He said, 'Casey, I don't want your sisters worrying about any of this, so let's keep it to ourselves.' Maybe your mom's the same?" He pressed the elevator button, still wearing his gloves. His obsession with Harry Styles was matched only by his obsession for dodging germs. "If she called all the time and told you about every bad day, you'd never make it through college, and you'd never see your friends or go out. She's protecting you, Rye—"

"Yeah, but it's hard to have a 'normal life' when I'm worrying she's not being straight with me. Catch-22, right?"

"I know, but it's what she wants." He squeezed her arm. "You have to respect that."

"Do I?" Riley sighed and followed Casey into the elevator.

TWELVE

One week later

Swaying in time to The Weeknd's "Earned It" to be polite, Riley stifled a yawn and gave Erika a thumbs-up, watching her float onto the stage, cheeks aglow above a megawatt smile that screamed, *Fun like this should be illegal!* The bride-to-be was in total banana hammock heaven, and it didn't hurt that the male dancer leading her by the hand through the foggy haze was a dead ringer for Erika's favorite actor, Zac Efron. Dressed in a sexy, casual combo of a muscle-hugging tank and beat-up Levi's, his attire made a nice change from all the spandex short-shorts, trench coats, and cheesy fireman costumes (complete with big hoses) that had strutted across the blue-lit stage of the East Village club over the previous hour.

"You're next, Rye!" Erika shouted with a wink, her enthusiasm for Riley's just-delivered engagement news bordering on obsessive. She had already named herself Riley's chief bridesmaid and forced her to endure two nearly naked lap dances. Male dancers weren't Riley's thing, but witnessing Erika's overwhelming glee made her laugh, and the ear-pounding music meant she didn't have to make small talk with Leia—a win-win.

Riley's eyes flitted to the table behind them and the uncut penis cake that pointed at Leia's butt. With a snicker, she adjusted her pink satin sash with 'Hot Bridesmaid' embellished in silver glitter and joined the crowd, clapping to the beat as it swerved into the whistling intro of Maroon 5's "Moves Like Jagger". Five more dancers wearing Ray-Bans appeared through the smoke, echoing the Efron lookalike's uniform. They stalked the stage under the pulsing strobe lights, each slipping a hand under their tank tops, their faces feigning wonderment over their yet-to-be-revealed physiques. The scent of cologne and sweat hung in the air, a testosterone-charged calling card inviting the shrieking audience to pant and claw their way closer.

The six dancers circled around Erika's chair on stage, their bodies rolling seductively to the bass. Squealing with a naughty twinkle in her eyes, she bounced up and down, barely able to keep her hands to herself. Her white 'Sexy Bride' sash slipped off a shoulder, and the Zac lookalike grabbed hold and used it like a lasso to pull her closer. Erika opened her knees slightly and the dancer went to work, grinding his hips and lifting the hem of his tank higher, higher, up over his head. He clutched her eager hands, sliding them down his hard pecs and jaw-dropping eight-pack to his impressive abdominal V-lines. Erika screamed in hilarity.

"Go lower—LOWER ERIKA!" Leia shouted.

Riley smiled. *Okay, I admit it...this is hilarious!* Erika, the immaculate hospitality coordinator at the ritzy Four Seasons Hotel, was shaking off the posh persona she wore Monday through Friday and owning her sexual fantasies without apology. For once, she wasn't bothered about her image, who was watching, or what Scott would think, and was full-on enjoying herself.

Finishing her water, Riley set down her glass and caught the now shirtless men flexing their abs and rolling their denim-clad hips, whipping the women into a feral frenzy. With a well-timed pelvic thrust, they tossed their sunglasses into the audience, eliciting lustful howls and a surge of grabby hands lunging toward the airborne accessories. Most were out of luck as Riley, Leia, and two of Erika's work friends captured four of the six shades.

Licking her lips, Riley put on the glasses. "I hope these things are 3-D!"

Leia burst into laughter, the two women united in a common

goal—kissing goodbye to Erika's bachelorette status, one pelvic thrust at a time.

Head bobbing, Riley's eyes flitted from a handsy Erika getting carried away with Efron Junior to a dancer hanging back, seemingly playing catch-up. Out of sync with the music and choreography, his moves were *not* like Jagger—they were hesitant and off beat—and his chest and abs, while toned and sculpted, weren't as over-the-top stripperlicious as the other guys' muscles. Flicking his hair out of his eyes, he bumped into his fellow dancers and stumbled in the dark, almost falling off the back corner of the stage. *What's up with that guy?* She removed the cheap sunglasses, trying to see through the dry ice. *He's hot and his hair—my God, what an irresistible mess, but...is he drunk?*

He looked up and Riley's heart tripped.

BEN?!

BOLLOCKS! Is that RILEY?!

Freezing on the spot, Ben's stomach flipped. He gulped and spun clumsily behind Hunter, his arms wrapping around his bare chest. *She didn't see me, did she? Oh fuck!*

"Dude!" Hunter growled over his shoulder. "Get it together. Go dance with the bridesmaids."

"Uh, mate, I can't. I'm...erm..."

Hunter dance-moved behind and elbowed him in the back, forcing Ben forward. Caught off guard, he tripped over his own feet, face planting beside Erika's Jimmy Choos.

Great! Face down, center-fucking-stage. Nice one, you complete muppet.

Erika didn't notice. Eyes closed, her hands were dedicated to Zach's abs as he teased her neck with feathery, barely there kisses.

Ben pressed his forehead into the floor and held his breath, sweat gathering between his shoulder blades. *Jesus, I can't just lie here. FUCK. Improvise! Pretend this is part of the show.* Within seconds, he rose up on his forearms, humping the stage. He flipped over and stood up, briefly catching Riley's eyes before his gaze slipped to Leia, who arched an eyebrow and leaned into Riley's ear. Peering through his hair, Ben couldn't look away. *What's she saying?* A laugh flew from Leia's lips, but Riley didn't join in. She stared, eyes narrowing, jaw slack.

What the fuck did she say? With a sweep of his hand across his stubble and a roll of his hips, Ben was almost caught up to the other dancers, but his mouth sank into a frown. *I am such a loser. Kill me now.*

Hunter nudged Ben toward Riley. "Buddy, c'mon—work the crowd."

Ben obliged, each step off the stage pushing his heart higher and higher into his throat. He swallowed heavily, watching Hunter for guidance. His new roommate threw his arms triumphantly around Leia's waist, yanking her willingly against his jeans into a dirty dance that drew lustful screeches from the crowd. *Here goes nothing.* Avoiding Riley's eyes, Ben tentatively reached for her waist, his fingers sliding around her soft curves, the silkiness of her blue wrap dress conspiring to quicken his already rapid pulse. He fought the rush, inhaling slowly, closing his eyes as he released the breath with a shudder. *Sassy, sexy Riley*—but she leaned away, her wild stare tracing his bare chest. *Shit, is that pity? Disgust?* He glanced at Hunter, who was completely lost in Leia and their flirtatious bump and grind, and then caught the lascivious leers of several women mere inches away. *You can't hide. Everyone's watching. Get it over with—just do it.* A tortured half-grin floundered on Ben's face as he pulled Riley in, the kind, gorgeous girl he had hoped to bump into again. *Careful what you wish for...*

Ben swayed to the beat. Riley stiffly followed his lead, keeping a safe distance from his sweaty chest and the belt buckle protruding over his jeans. Her hands skirted his shoulders, barely touching him, like a shy preteen at a junior high dance. He briefly looked at her face, expecting disappointment but…a warmth rose in her green eyes and a soft smile grew across her cheeks. Her fingers traveled along his skin, her hands meeting behind his neck, pulling him closer. *Don't read anything into this. She's just being kind.*

They stayed locked together for the final minute of the song, each roll of his hips into hers, each sway as one unleashing shivers up his spine. Eyes closed, Riley didn't push him away or tell him to back off. *I bet she can feel my heart pounding like I can feel hers. Is she enjoying this? Or is she wishing it would end soon? Oh God, what I wouldn't give to kiss her…*

The rising catcalls and heavy bass flooded his ears, derailing his longing, forcing him back to reality with a heavy blink. *Fagan, stop! These feelings—you're wasting your time! She's taken. And anyway, commitment isn't your thing, mate.* He cleared his throat, his gaze drifting over her shoulder, avoiding the blur of female faces beyond.

Maroon 5's big hit began to mix into the next song, signalling that Ben's only performance was over. Riley opened her eyes and he loosened his hold, his hands falling from her waist as he stepped back. *Self-preservation…save some face.* Ben's shoulders lifted in a casual shrug. "Cheers."

Riley fumbled with her clutch, her lips opening to say something, but Ben fled into the shadows where excuses and explanations weren't necessary.

THIRTEEN

Ben's unexpected appearance and abrupt disappearance left Riley's complexion flushed, her heart racing, and her mind flooded with questions: *Why didn't he text me? Holy crap, he's hot! Has he been dancing long?* Riley giggled. *Actually, his 'moves' answered that question!*

Squeezing through the rowdy throng of women during the intermission, she crossed paths with a few shirtless dancers serving drinks, but Ben wasn't one of them. She craned her neck, looking over heads bobbing to the music and around arms waving colorful cocktails, but after a second loop of the club, there was still no sign of him. She gave up her search, slipping into the ladies' room. After a lipstick re-application and a fluff of her hair, "Pony" began to throb through the club's sound system. The midnight show—the dancers were on stage again.

Heading back, Riley's eyes shot over the sea of women in front of the stage, landing on the muscled hunk who had been dancing with Leia earlier, slick with body oil, thrusting away, his jaw-aching bulge barely contained in a tiny purple G-string. A woman to her right held up a sign with a huge purple emoji—the eggplant. *Of course.* Riley chuckled, veered to the left, and spotted a green baseball cap by the bar. *Ben?* She took a detour and a chance, weaving past several drunk women punching the air with large inflatable penises. Claiming a spot just shy of the guy's left elbow and his coat, which were piled up on the wooden bar like a barrier, she leaned in: Boston Bruins hat—check, dark hair flicking out underneath—check, cheekbones to die for—check. He turned his head and quickly turned away again. Vibrant blue eyes—fleeting, but check. He hung his head and slouched over three empty shot glasses. His left hand was entertaining itself in a bowl of bar nuts.

Is he okay? "Ben?"

He stared at the bar, plunging a finger of his now healed right hand into an empty glass, spinning it round and round. The bartender returned with two full shots of a clear liquid. Ben mouthed, "Thanks."

Vodka? Riley leaned in. The sleeve of his purple hoodie was torn, hinting at a tattoo of some sort lurking on the inside of his right forearm. She ducked slightly, trying to see under the peak of his cap. "Hey...again..."

He focused intently on the peanut bowl, not responding.

"I almost didn't recognize you up there without your hat. Is this research?"

"Research?" Avoiding her eyes, his chin retreated into his hoodie.

"Yeah, for a role. Going all Channing Tatum?"

He snorted, his posture stiffening as his hand abandoned the empty glass for a full shot. "Like anyone would want to cast me."

"What? Oh, jeez. The Netflix thing...you...?"

"Didn't get it." Ben tossed back the vodka and winced, promptly exchanging that glass for another.

"Oh, I'm sorry." Riley set her jacket down on top of his. "Did you find out today?"

He laughed joylessly, the full glass teasing his wet lips. "I found out mid-audition."

"Weeks ago?"

"Yep." He downed the shot and slammed the empty glass on the bar.

"But you were celebrating in LA. You said—"

He wiped his mouth with the back of his hand, still refusing to look at her. "Yeah, celebrating the end of my dream of being an actor. Why just celebrate our successes? I reckon we should celebrate our *failures*, too, send 'em on their way with a bottle of whiskey and a cheeky middle finger."

"So, why did you tell m—"

"I lied, all right? Because no bloke tells a pretty girl he's just met that he's a fucking failure."

Pretty? A slight smile raised her lips but quickly dissolved.

He shoved the empty glass away. "The audition was a disaster. They handed me a script I hadn't seen before, not the one my agent gave me to rehearse. I got nervous, couldn't even read the lines…"

"I'm sure it wasn't that bad. Maybe that role just wasn't right for you."

"No, I mean *literally*—I couldn't read the script. I'm dyslexic, okay?!"

"Dyslexic—really?"

"Yeah, really. I don't see things properly. Letters move around, words get jumbled up when I read, and it gets worse when I'm stressed out."

Her heart dipped. *Poor guy.* "You should've told them."

He shook his head. "They showed me the door in less than a minute. I was gutted, and furious. I smashed a mirror in the gents' toilets with my fist."

Riley glanced at his healed hand. "The bandage."

"Yeah. Smart, eh? Every time I saw it—a reminder of the truth." Ben made eye contact for the first time.

Riley felt an immediate wave of concern; he looked sad and defeated.

He gave her a tired smile, placing a finger to his lips like he was letting her in on a secret. "Want to know the truth, Ms. Hope?" Without waiting for a response, he leaned closer. "I'm just not good enough, and I'm done knocking my head against a brick wall. That's why I'm in New York—'cause I can't face going home…not yet. I can't be a fucking disappointment." He stuffed his fingers into one of the front pockets of his dark jeans, pulling out some folded cash. He opened the small stack, fanning the bills out on the bar. Riley counted one, two—two fifties, maybe three or four twenty-dollar bills, and a couple of crinkled ones.

"Ben—"

"Have a drink with me." He waved a fifty at the bartender. "Four more, please."

"Thanks, but I'm not drinking."

"Why?"

"I need to keep a clear head."

"Why?" He leaned on the bar, looking at her with a squint.

"Ben, more booze isn't going to help you."

He sat back, shaking his head again, his fingers digging through the bowl of peanuts. "You have no business telling me what to do! 'Specially not after giving me the wrong bloody number." He threw a hard glare her way, his hand flying from the bowl and scattering nuts across the bar. "Why didn't you just say, 'Ben, piss off you loser'? Bish bosh, message received loud and clear."

She narrowed her eyes. "I didn't give you the wrong number." She held out her hand. "Give me your phone."

Ben slapped an ancient smartphone with a cracked screen into her palm. He returned to the bowl, grabbing a fistful of peanuts and shoveling them into his mouth, chewing quickly and scowling at the rows of liquor bottles lined up behind the bar.

He's got the same old phone as me. No security code necessary, Riley skimmed through the few contacts he had, all listed by first names, no last names to go with them. She spotted 'Rilee', but the number was off by one digit. *He punched it in wrong.* "You tried to text me?"

He shrugged.

Riley didn't make a huge deal of it. "See the six at the end? It should be a four. I'll fix it and send a text to my phone so I have your number, too, okay?"

He turned his head slightly, barely looking at her. "Hope, go back to your friends and leave me alone. I'm gonna stay here and get pissed and blot out every little bit of my shite life."

She set his phone on the bar. "Ben—"

"I've got nothing: no career, no home, no—" He hiccupped, his eyes locked on the approaching bartender. "Let me have *something*...and right now, it's waiting for me in these wee glasses." The bartender lined up four full shots. "Cheers, mate." Ben raised one to his lips, the liquid gone in a gulp.

"I know losing out on the Netflix thing must be disappointing, but you know better than anyone that rejections are part of an actor's life, right? Sure, it hurts now, but it will fade and you'll get other auditions, other roles. You have to keep trying—"

"Oh, you think so, eh? Think it's that easy? Since drama school, I've only had a few acting jobs: some voiceover work, an advert or two, a play in a pub, and a small part in an indie film in LA, so all that crap about other auditions, other roles—tell it to someone who gives a shit."

Riley jerked her head back. "I get it, you're upset, but getting wasted isn't the answer, and what's your boss here going to say— seeing you drinking the bar dry?"

"My boss?" He laughed. "He'd say, 'Thanks for the wages back, loser.' Besides, I got sacked tonight."

"What—?"

"Yeah! I had two weeks to prove myself. Apparently, I didn't. How's that for shite? I can't even take my clothes off properly." He patted his cash on the bar. "And this is all I have to show for it." He downed another shot and chased it with a handful of nuts.

"So..."

Ben picked up the dish of peanuts and dumped the remainder

into his open mouth.

"Take a breath, Ben. It's like you were raised by wolves…"

He dragged another bowl across the bar. "I'm *starving*."

"Slow down."

"I have to take what I can get before the owner spies me and kicks me out. Can't a guy have some dinner?"

"Free peanuts are your dinner?"

"Yep, so if you don't mind, leave me to it. I'd rather dine alone." Downing another shot, he gave her a quick glance, but his sad blue eyes belied his liquor-soaked swagger. "I don't need *anyone*—never have."

He has no one here. That fear of being alone, of having no one pinched Riley's heart. She knew that fear well, that black cloud…looming, about to smother and suffocate, to blanket you with an unbearable ache that seeps into your bones. She blinked away the stinging suggestion of tears and picked up her coat then his. "C'mon."

"Riley, just go, okay?" He snatched a handful of his jacket.

"Fine, I will"—she shifted, pulling his coat out of his grasp—"but you're coming with me."

"No, I'm not!" He propped his elbows on the bar like a kid, mid-temper tantrum. "You can keep my coat. I don't need it. I don't need you…don't you get it?"

"Don't *you* get it? I'm just trying to be a friend. Jesus, you're being such a jerk!" Frowning, she dumped his coat back on the bar and turned away, stuffing one arm into her denim jacket, followed by the other.

Doing a double take, Ben peeked out from his cap, his eyes softening. He reached out, touching her back. "Riley! Shit…*I'm sorry*." His shoulders relaxed. "You're the last person I expected to see, and tonight hasn't been…well, you know—my finest hour." He winced. "And I'm a complete arse when I'm hungry."

Riley fidgeted with her clutch, snapping it open and closed, then faced him again. "Who isn't?" She breathed out slowly, her stomach snarling underneath her jacket. It had been twenty-four hours since her last meal. "I know a place with cheap 2-for-1 pizza slices…"

"I'm not a pizza fan."

"Okay, well, how 'bout a diner? You know, milkshakes, dinosaur-shaped chicken nuggets? Fries? You like fries, don't you?"

"Is my name Ben Fagan?" A slight smile curved his mouth.

"I don't know—is it?" Riley smirked and stood up straight, picking up his coat again. "Let's go."

"But…" He looked over his shoulder. Erika was waving Hunter's purple G-string in the air. "Won't your friends be pissed?"

She followed his stare. "Yeah, pissed drunk. They won't notice I'm gone. They've only got eyes for Vlad the Impaler—" *Argh, awk-ward!* Her cheeks flushed red as her eyes shot back to Ben, a cheeky grin creeping across his stubble. "Never mind, Tragic Mike. Let's get out of here."

FOURTEEN

Crossing the intersection of Norfolk and East Houston Streets, Riley decreased her speed, letting Ben's long, purposeful strides catch up. He had been walking a few steps behind, giving her privacy while she talked on her phone. "Sorry…"

"Everything okay? You barely said a word." Ben yanked open the door to a twenty-four-hour diner called Remedy, its name in sizzling red neon above silver double doors accented with round porthole windows. The restaurant was bustling with club kids, smitten couples, and coffee-addled college students. Following Riley, his eyes locked on tiers of cakes and gooey desserts teasing him from inside a glass case.

"Yeah." Riley fought a yawn and smiled at the harried hostess who waved them toward a vacant booth overlooking East Houston. "My boyfriend gets a bit hyper, can't sleep." Her phone lit up again—1:35 a.m. Saturday—a new text from Erika joining others she had sent during Riley's one-sided phone conversation with Josh.

Wear'd u go? U missed the beast part.

Drunk misspelled texts from Erika were a rare sight. Riley chuckled and sat down, laying her clutch beside her. *Beast— probably meant 'best'…although that purple thong guy was a beast, and as for his 'part'—*

"Why's he hyper?" Ben slid along his seat, promptly scooting out of his unbuttoned coat and unzipping his hoodie, a black and blue t-shirt for Sting's old eighties band The Police tucked into the front of his dark jeans.

"Sorry, just have to text Erika. She's wondering where I am." Mid-text, Riley did a double take as Ben removed his hat and pawed a hand through his thick dark hair. *My God, that hair—slightly wavy permanent bedhead, sexy as hell…If I were a guy with hair like that, I'd never hide it under a cap.* She finished her response to Erika, hitting send.

Friend emergency. Sorry! All OK. Chat tomorrow.

"So, your boyfriend…?"

"Josh, yeah. He was calling about the Frozen Four—the NCAA championship final. It's tomorr—ah, it's Saturday now, right?" She set her phone on the table. "It's *tonight*, and I'm going."

"*You're* going? You're flying to North Dakota—in a few hours?"

"No, it's in Saint Paul, Minnesota."

His eyes widened. "Mad!"

"Josh's team won the semi-final on Thursday, so tonight's the final. He's paying for me to go. It's definitely a flying visit. I'm back Sunday, so I won't miss classes or anything."

"Wow. You're his number one fan, then."

"Well, it's the biggest game of Josh's collegiate hockey career. Tons of media will be there, NHL scouts. It's a big deal—over 18,000 tickets have been sold."

Ben lifted his elbows off the table as the server swiped a damp cloth over its surface and set down two menus before toddling away to the kitchen. "All this for a *college* game?"

"Oh, college sports are massive here. Games are on TV, athletes get treated like celebrities—it's kinda crazy. Anyway…" Riley removed her jacket and steered the conversation away from the minefield that was her relationship with Josh. "How do you like New York so far?"

"It's bloody brilliant! Skyscrapers, yellow taxis—I feel like I've walked onto a movie set."

"Are you settled in at your Airbnb?"

The server delivered two glasses of water to their table. Ben

79

waited for her to leave before continuing. "Yeah, I'm staying at Hunter's place. He's the purple thong guy, the Aubergine?" He chuckled. "Fuck, sorry...British brain. He's the *Eggplant*."

The emoji sign from the club flashed through Riley's mind. "Oh! Right." *The beast part.* She giggled, lifting the bridesmaid sash over her head.

"I needed cash and Hunter hooked me up with the dancing gig. Being skint with zero connections, I didn't have much choice. Desperate times and all that, right?"

Riley picked at the glitter on the sash. "Right..."

"I thought it would be easy, but it was hard and I hated it!" Ben's attention followed a burger being whisked toward the next table. "Hunter said tips were amazing, but all I got were pity tips— one dollar here and there." He exhaled. "So, now I'm back where I started—unemployed and broke."

Riley checked out the menu. "Well, I couldn't believe it when I saw you onstage. You don't seem like the stripper type."

"There's a type?"

She laughed, hoping she could lighten his mood. Alone in New York without a job, without much money—she wouldn't wish that on anyone. She peeked over the oversized menu. "You know what I mean."

"So, what you're saying is..." He scowled, but the playfulness in his eyes suggested it was for effect. "I'm not *hot* enough to be a stripper."

"Oh, I don't know, I'm sure you're attractive enough under that hoodie, baseball cap, *jumper*..."

They both burst out laughing.

Ben stretched back in the booth, a smile growing. "They were desperate, someone quit..."

"You looked good up there..." Riley felt her cheeks heat up as Ben raised a cheeky eyebrow. "But no offense, Ben—those guys have muscles on top of muscles."

"No offense taken." He winced. "All those hours in the gym? I kept thinking of all the hours I'd miss in the pub."

The server returned. "Ready to order?"

Riley looked at Ben, waiting for him to peruse the menu.

"Go for it." He ran his hand through his hair, but it sprung back and flirted with his eyes again.

"Oh, okay. I'll have...hmmm, I'll have the California Wrap and...fries. I'm famous for eating my weight in potatoes, especially smiley ones..."

"What are smiley potatoes?" asked Ben.

"Oh, they're these frozen potato thingies in the shape of a smiley face. You pop them in the oven, make 'em all crispy. Mom made them when I was little." She hesitated, buying more time so Ben could read the menu. "Fries or onion rings...? Hmm, no, I'll just have the wrap. Oh, and something to drink..." She glanced up at Ben, but he was staring at her. "Actually, water's fine."

Ben slid the menu to the server without looking at it. "Do you have chicken nuggets, but shaped like dinosaurs?"

Riley chuckled.

The server narrowed her eyes. "Excuse me?"

He stifled a laugh. "Never mind. A burger and fries, thanks. Ooh, do you have milkshakes here?"

"Vanilla, chocolate—"

"Chocolate! Cheers." As the server turned, Ben winked at Riley. "I'm so going to have cake for dessert, too. Gotta put back all those calories I lost on stage tonight."

"Yeah, about that...were you freestyling up there? Your moves, Ben—my God."

"Oi, they weren't *that* bad! I'll have you know, I learned two routines."

"Two? Wow. So..." She toyed with the fork lying on her paper napkin. "What have we learned in the short time we've known each other? I'm a crappy WAG and you're a crappy stripper."

"Ahh, I'm also a crappy actor, so I'm one up on you. Sometimes you don't know until you try and fail miserably, right?"

Riley's face softened. "Ben, I'm sure you can act."

He scrunched his nose and scratched his stubble. "So, your friends at the club…WAGs?"

"Yeah. Did the huge rocks on their fingers give them away?"

"Kinda. They looked quite posh. You meet them through your boyfriend?"

"No. Erika, the future bride, was a year ahead of me in high school. We worked together on the yearbook and became good friends. Leia, the redhead—"

"Her name's *Leia*?"

"Yeah, like the *Star Wars* character. We don't get along."

"Oh." Ben's eyes lit up as his milkshake arrived.

"Nothing major happened, we just don't gel."

"Right. Well, it happens."

"I'm only friends with her because of Erika."

Ben tore the paper off his straw and plunged it into the bubbly chocolate froth crowning the tall glass of his shake. "So, three of you there tonight?"

"Some of Erika's work friends came, too. I don't really know them. When I hang with Eri, it's usually just us, sometimes Leia and the guys, too."

"All hockey players?"

"Yep."

Ben took a long sip of his shake, his eyes rolling back in exaggerated bliss then returning to Riley. "So, you said your boyfriend got drafted—what does that mean for you?"

Riley hugged her waist. "I'm moving to Minnesota—next hockey season, this fall."

"This fall? Why would you have to move?" His eyes fell to her arms wrapped around her stomach. "You weren't drinking earlier…jeez, he knocked you up?"

"No!"

"Well, why move? It's not like you're married or any—oh!" His gaze roamed to her hands, but they were still hidden behind her waist. "Shit, are you engaged?"

Eyes glazing over, Riley opened her mouth. "Y-Yeah," fell from her lips along with a soft exhale.

"Really?"

She answered with a business-like nod.

"Well, congratulations." His raised eyebrows contorted with confusion and concern. "You don't look very thrilled about—"

"I am thrilled!" Her face lit up with a defiant smile as she dragged her left hand through her hair.

Ben watched its progress through her locks and along her neck, where it paused to stroke her collarbone. "Where's your ring? Didn't he give you one? Is that why you're not all sparkles and rainbows?"

"I don't care about the ring."

"Isn't that what girls say when they receive a shite one?"

"No!"

He scoffed, playing with his straw. "What a naff proposal. No ring—"

"There *was* a ring! A toy one, something to have until he bought the real thing."

"But you're not wearing it." Ben leaned forward. "Blimey O'Riley, you don't wanna marry this bloke, do you?"

"I do!" Riley glared.

"No, you don't—not if you're keeping your engagement a secret, not wearing a ring…"

"It's not a *secret*!" The loudness of her sharp retort caught the attention of a couple waiting for takeout. Riley hunched over the table's edge, lowering her voice. "For your information, I lost the ring...on the bus, with YOU."

"How old are you?"

"What does that have to do—" She huffed. "Twenty-two."

Ben's eyes widened.

"What? Lots of people get married young."

"Yeah, if they're religious types, saving themselves until marriage. Oh, shit, sorry—are you like a Mormon or something?"

"I'm not saving myself. Jeez, Ben!" She scowled, watching two old men at the counter eating donuts. "It's none of your business, anyway."

"You're right, it's not, but if you're not keen—"

"I *am*. He's great—we're great."

The server appeared with her wrap and Ben's burger. "Do you need anything else? Mayo, hot sauce..."

"Malt vinegar, please?" Ben flashed a smile. The woman nodded and strolled away.

"Josh and I have been together three years." Riley leaned over her plate, her voice barely above a whisper. "I'm really proud of him and I can't wait for us to be together as a couple, okay?"

He smirked, flipping the bun off his burger. "If you say so."

"Ben, you don't know me. You have no clue what I want." She caught herself. Why was she getting so annoyed at him? He was just being curious, and perhaps concerned. She knew in her heart it wasn't his questions raising her blood pressure; it was the answers rolling off her tongue—the pretending, faking, lying, acting like all was well. *It's a miracle my nose hasn't grown five inches. Ben's right, about all of it.*

The server set a bottle of white vinegar on their table. Ben frowned but grabbed it anyway. "Okay, so tell me—what do *you* want, Riley? Because it sounds to me like you're following Josh's dream, not your own." He drowned his burger in a shower of vinegar, its smell prickling Riley's nose as he tipped the bottle farther.

Yuck, he's ruining his meal.

He set down the almost empty bottle and tucked the tablespoon sitting on his napkin into his hoodie pocket like it belonged to him. "Come on, be honest…"

Honest? What? She did a double take. "You—you just stole a spoon."

"I did."

"Why?"

"Needs must."

"What's that mean?" asked Riley.

"It means necessity compels. Hunter owns forks and knives—no spoons. Mad, eh? How do I put sugar in my tea without a bloody spoon? I hate stealing, but I need one so—"

"But you can't just *take* it."

"Oh, they won't miss it." He picked up his burger, but the soaked bun disintegrated into mush, spilling its contents on the plate. "Bugger!"

Riley chuckled. "That's karma for swiping the spoon."

He curled his lip, but a carefree glint shone in his eyes as he plucked the knife and fork from the table. "Fuck the spoon. I remember you saying you wanted to go to California, work your way into directing or casting…"

Riley was taken aback that he remembered. "Yeah. Someday…I'd like to work on sitcoms or dramas, happily ever after stories. I think there's enough sadness in the news and everyday life, so I want to make entertainment that's an escape, that helps people forget their worries for a while."

"Happily ever after like…" He stabbed a chunk of burger. "You and Josh—in Minnesota."

Riley scowled, stuffing a piece of chicken in her mouth. "Oh, forget it."

"C'mon, I'm just taking the piss. I'm sorry. It's great you want to use your creative talents in a compassionate way, to help people. It's admirable, really. Not a lot of people care like that. And I totally get the escape from reality thing."

"Yeah, I guess, being an actor." Riley's face softened. "Have you always known it was what you wanted to do?"

"No. When I was a kid, I wanted to be an astronomer. I loved stars and planets."

"Ah, that explains your tattoo."

"This one?" Ben stretched the neck of his t-shirt, revealing two hollow stars, one larger than the other, beneath the curve of his left collarbone.

"I spotted it earlier. It's cool."

"Thanks. Shame a passion for something can't make up for shit grades."

"Because of your dyslexia?"

"Maybe...probably." He raised his fork to his mouth, chewing a bite-sized piece of burger quickly. "God, I hated school." He spun his plate around so his fries were facing Riley. "Help yourself, 'kay?"

She nodded with a smile.

"The teachers said I had a learning disability, behavioral issues, and you know what kids are like. They called me a div."

"A div?"

"Stupid person, a moron."

"Aw, that's awful!"

"Yeah, well, I wasn't going to win any academic awards. I did okay in drama class, though, so I thought, why not? I aced my auditions for drama school, received bursaries to help pay for it, got my BA, and here I am."

"But how do you learn lines?" Riley peered into her wrap.

"What do you see when you read?"

"Depends. Sometimes letters get mixed up or they move…it's weird. If I'm relaxed or have time to partially recognize the words, I'm pretty good. It takes me a while, but I get there. I love books and reading, so I invest the time, but when I'm learning lines, I record myself reading aloud on my phone. Then I listen to it over and over, imaging a mini movie in my head, relating the actions to the words."

"That's a lot of work." Her eyes fell to his plate. "No wonder the Netflix audition threw you—no prep time."

"Cold read auditions are the death of me. It's like reading aloud in school all over again." He pulled the straw out of his shake. "I want to make something of myself, make my mum proud, but I've lost out on a dozen or more acting gigs on the trot, so I'm taking the hint." He tilted his head, contemplating the chocolate dripping back into the glass. "I'm gonna quit."

"Quit? How old are you?"

"Twenty-three."

"You've been out of drama school for…?" She picked up her phone and tapped at the screen.

He squinted at her flying fingers. "Almost three years."

"And you're quitting? Already? Imagine if J.K. Rowling gave up after her first rejection letters! You gotta keep chasing your dream, Ben. That's what they're there for—to keep you going." She turned her phone around. "Look, these actors are all dyslexic: Kiera Knightley, Tom Cruise, Orlando Bloom. If they can do it…"

"Wow, you're great." His eyes brightened. "Care to follow me around and give me a kick in the arse when I need it?"

Her fingers scrolled the screen. "And it says here dyslexia doesn't signify low intelligence. Ben, those kids at school were ignorant assholes. In a way, you'll be letting them win if you quit—"

"How can you say all this to me but let your own dream die?"

"I'm...I'm not letting it die." *Aren't I?* Riley looked down at the bridesmaid sash, returning her gaze to Ben with a stiff smile. "I'm just...putting it on hold for a while."

"Okay, then make me a promise, here and now." He sucked on the straw, savoring the chocolate bubbles. "If you promise to hold on to your dream of working in TV, I'll do the same with acting."

"Ben—"

"C'mon, you can't urge me to keep going and then ignore your own advice. Swear on that California wrappy thing."

She set her phone on the table. "So, you're going to stick with it?"

"Yeah, why not?"

Los Angeles...I'm envious. Riley's eyes crinkled in the corners, visions of swimming, sunshine—*freedom*—flashing through her mind. "Will you head back to LA?"

Ben scratched his eyebrow. "I think I'll stay in New York for a while. Someone's gotta say yes at some point. One good audition could change everything, right?"

Yes! He's staying... She nodded enthusiastically.

"So, come on, Hope—pinky swear you'll not give up on your dream either?" He offered his small finger expectantly. "Don't leave me hanging here."

Riley's shoulders slumped as she gave in to his demand, briefly locking her pinky finger with his. "Erghh, fine!"

They shared a smile and dug into their meals.

Come 2:30 a.m., both were slipping into carb comas. Ben insisted on paying for Riley's dinner as an apology for his behavior at the club.

BUZZZZZZZ. He pulled his phone from his pocket, his brows furrowing farther with each passing second. "Shiiiit!"

"What's wrong?"

"Hunter. He brought two—" He blinked. "No, *three* girls back from the club—perks of the job, I guess—and he's asked me to make myself scarce." He exhaled heavily. "I sleep on his sofa, so I'd have a front row seat…"

"Yikes!" Riley squeezed the takeout box containing half her wrap, tomorrow's lunch.

Ben slouched back, running his finger along the edge of his plate, dotted with cake crumbs. "I'll hang here, have another slice. Bet their breakfast is good."

Putting on her jacket, Riley toyed with what to do. *Should I offer?* A pack of drunk teens harassed a neighboring table for change, making fun of the man's accent and refusing to take no for an answer.

Ben looked over his shoulder and rolled his eyes. "Kids, eh?"

I can't leave him here—alone. "You could crash on my sofa? It's not very big—well, my whole place is claustrophobic, but at least you won't be bugged non-stop."

"You sure? Your fiancé won't like it."

"Ben, it's sleep, not an invitation for sex."

"But aren't you afraid I'll steal your spoons…eat all those peanut butter things you love so much?"

"I don't have any peanut butter cups or valuables worth stealing, and don't think you can try anything because I can taekwondo your ass with one hand tied behind my back."

"I don't doubt it."

"Okay, so get a move on, Benjamin. It's a one-time offer."

"Riley, what can I say? You're a real mate—thanks a lot."

She smirked and picked up her leftovers. They both rolled out of the diner, sleepy and uncomfortably full.

FIFTEEN

Ben eyeballed the shops along St. Mark's Place. *This place looks like Camden High Street on a bender. Great for going out on the lash, but...* He scrunched his nose. "Hope, this is your street?"

"Think I can't handle myself?"

"I bet you can, it's just..." *If you were mine, I wouldn't want you to.* "Really grungy."

Across the way, a disheveled old man in a torn coat rummaged in a recycling bin.

"Murray!" Riley hollered. The scraggly guy peered over the pile of bottles and waved a dirty hand. "You hungry?" She ran across the road, giving him the box containing half her wrap.

Did she just...? Wow.

Riley said good night and skipped back to Ben.

"That was your lunch and you..."

She shrugged. "Murray's a great guy. Piper and I make him sandwiches whenever we can. You should hear his stories about this neighborhood back in the day." She pointed at the bright yellow awning. "I live here."

Funky Town? Ben broke out into a huge grin and laughed through his words. "Oh. My God. You've got to be kidding. That song!"

"I know!" She stuck her key in the lock, shimmying back and forth while singing. "Funky Towwwwn! *Shrek 2* is hilarious."

"I've never seen *Shrek*." Ben's eyes tailed a taxi zooming past

"You've never seen *Shrek*?"

He shook his head.

"What kind of depraved childhood did you have?" She waved

him inside.

"I didn't really watch cartoons."

"What kid doesn't like cartoons? Are you for real?" She yanked open the stairway door. "If you haven't seen the movie, how do you know that song?"

"Ah, I have my ways."

They ran up the stairs and entered Riley's room, a wave of heat surging forward.

Woah. "Who turned on the sauna?" Ben took off his cap and fanned his face.

She tugged off her ankle boots and rushed over to the window, hoisting it open with a groan. "The heating needs to be fixed."

Ben removed his shoes and coat then yanked his hoodie over his head, sending hair tufts reaching for the ceiling. Dropping the two layers on the loveseat, he bent slightly, eyeing a bunch of library books scattered over the cushions. *What's she got here? The Art of Racing in the Rain, A Woman of Independent Means, 84 Charing Cross Road...* His fingers briefly tugged on a thin leather bracelet knotted on his right wrist.

Riley adjusted the curtain so no one could see in from the building across the street. "I'll leave it open, but if you get cold—" Shaking off her jacket, Riley turned around. Ben was reading the books' spines and flapping the bottom hem of his Police t-shirt, trying to cool down. He looked up, catching her raised eyebrows.

"Oh, don't worry." He straightened his posture, a cheeky grin brightening his face. "Nothing else is coming off. This stripper has hung up his G-string for good."

Riley bit her cheek, avoiding his eyes and diving for the mess on the cushions.

Aw, she's blushing! Cute! Let's see if I can make it worse. The smile fell from his face. "Actually, I'm disappointed. My final dance was supposed to be performed...completely starkers."

91

"Starkers?"

"Naked."

Riley juggled the books in her arms. "OH!"

His intense expression cracked. "Your face! Back of the net!"

"Yeah, yeah!" She smirked and squeezed around him. "Very funny!"

"Well, *I* thought so!" He laughed, smoothing down his t-shirt as he surveyed her place. On top of her drawers, a colorful collection of candy dispensers standing to attention drew a smile. "PEZ fan, eh?" He picked up a Snoopy.

"Um…" Her cheeks gave away her embarrassment—again. "When I was a kid, yeah. I'm not sure why I still have them…"

"You're nostalgic—nothing wrong with that." Taking in his surroundings, Ben flicked Snoopy's chin up and down and returned him to his perch. "You've made great use of space."

"Thanks. I can't afford anything bigger." She piled the books underneath her clothing rack, her eyes catching the red and white pattern on his green socks—candy canes. She stood up and bumped into him. "Um, sorry."

But Ben was distracted. "Riley…there's a…*spider*." He pointed a shaky finger at the wall.

"Eww!" She did a double take—Ben was pale and wide-eyed. "You're more freaked out than I am!"

"Spiders give me the willies."

"Well, I'm not killing Charlotte. It's bad luck!"

"But…how will you *sleep*…knowing it's…" Ben gulped and bent over, pulling a tissue from a box on the milk crate. "Don't… move." His hand flew at the wall and he scrunched the tissue quickly. "Oh, FUCK. It's wriggling!" He leapt to the open window and set Charlotte and the tissue free.

"My hero!" She teased. A dark blue design on Ben's inner arm drew her curiosity. "Hey, what's that?"

Ben's face relaxed. "My tattoo? He's from Pac-Man, a fright-ened ghost." He stretched out his arm, showing off the character, which was a little bit larger than a quarter. The top of its head was rounded with pink dot eyes and a squiggly frowning mouth, and its feet were three undulating waves.

"Pac-Man? You a gamer?"

"Not really. The café near school had a beat-up machine, and I'd play for ages. I always felt an affinity with the frightened ghosts, aimlessly wandering..." He chuckled. "Do you have ink?"

"No. I can never decide what to get."

"Hey, nothing worse than tattoo regret." His smile dissolved in-to an eye-crinkling yawn. *She probably wants to change, but with me here...* "Where's the toilet?"

"Oh, bathroom's down the hall. It's shared—hopefully you won't walk in on someone having sex in the shower."

"Hopefully not! Uh, you wouldn't have a spare toothbrush, would you? I know I'm British and people joke we have bad teeth, but I *always* brush before bed."

"Let me see." She pulled out a box from underneath her cloth-ing rail and lifted its lid, the cardboard packed with toiletries, in-cluding an unopened toothbrush. "You're in luck." She handed it over with a new tube of paste.

"Cheers, Riley."

"I'll leave the door unlocked."

Five hours ago, I thought I'd never see her again. Now, I'm sleeping over. With a smile, he slipped through the door.

Riley quickly changed into an NYU tee and a pair of shorts, catch-ing Josh smirking from a photo taped to her wall. *What? It's not like you don't have female friends.* She brushed her teeth at the sink and was hanging up a damp facecloth when a knock behind her head made her jump. "It's cool, come in."

Ben squeezed through the opening, careful not to hit Riley with the edge of the door. "Cheers." His fresh minty breath punctuated his gratitude.

"I'll just…" Riley pulled a fuzzy blanket from a storage box and snuck past to the loveseat.

"I'm so knackered, I could kip on a bed of nails." Ben followed, leaving the toothpaste tube on top of the box.

"Ahh, sorry—sold that on eBay last week."

Straightening up, Ben copped an eyeful of Riley's ass as she bent over.

"You'll have to make do with this." She unfurled the blanket on the loveseat.

"Um…looks *great* to me…" A nervous laugh broke through his lips as he backed away, inching toward the open window. He nudged the curtain and leaned sideways on the sill, ogling a vintage car parked outside. The frosty air prickled his warm skin, sending his hand on a mission, climbing…climbing underneath his thin t-shirt. The more he burrowed and clawed at his chest, the farther his threadbare tee crept up his stomach. "Christ! So itchy." His other hand squeezed his toothbrush, absentmindedly spinning it round and round.

Riley looked over her shoulder, catching a fleeting glimpse of letters spelling FCUK on the underwear band poking above his low-rise jeans. A breath caught in her throat, her eyes tracing over those four letters again. *Err, who's dyslexic now?* Guilt warming her cheeks, she expected to be caught out, but her below-the-belt peek remained a secret. Ben's attention was out the window, but his hand mindlessly skipped downward. The movement drew her eyes back down his chest and taut abs to hover below his navel where his hand stopped. *Do you know how hot you are? Why don't you have a girl-friend?* She pulled her gaze away. *Riley! STOP THINKING ABOUT*

BEN LIKE THIS!

Watching the street below, Ben winced, his thumb tracing where there had previously been a trail of hair disappearing into his underwear. "I have stubble where no bloke should ever have stubble. Not shaving *there* again."

Ben, can you NOT...! Riley gulped and kneeled down, smoothing the throw's velvety softness, its warmth slipping through her fingers as her mind scrambled to reel in her thoughts—thoughts that had stolen her breath back at the club when she realized the good-looking guy with the wild dark hair stumbling on stage was Ben. *Luggage-thieving, five-layer-wearing, cheeky Ben...stripping?! Half-naked!* Owner of strong shoulders, a defined back, sculpted pecs, and a narrow waist—lean like a swimmer's physique—*who knew?* He was beautiful, sexy, her physical ideal—and those adorkable dance moves? Ready to share, his open, toned arms an invitation...to explore *that* body.

Her mind shuffled, replaying the brief moment she'd felt his skin against hers, wrapped in an unexpected dance floor embrace. She had felt uneasy at first. *Am I being unfaithful?* But Ben's behavior had been respectful, self-aware, not presumptuous or handsy like Hunter was with Leia. No, Ben had waited for a sign—a smile, a nod—before tripping the light fantastic with her. He was a gentleman, not at all what she had expected. *He's cute and courteous. I bet he's been with a lot of women.* Good looks and decency would attract girls like a Black Friday sale at Sephora. *How many have peeled away all those layers: t-shirt, hoodie, jeans...sliding their hands, their lips along his ripped abs and slim hips while his mouth sucked and teased, his tongue sweeping over...* A dizzying warmth began to throb between her legs. *Fuck, he could cut my thighs with those cheekbones, the feel of stubble burn—*

"Hope? *Riley?*"

She shook her head. "Oh! S-Sorry?"

"You okay there, starin' off into space?" Ben's hand skimmed the top of his underwear before pulling away, allowing his soft t-shirt to slip down, kissing his jeans. He snickered and tapped the toothbrush against his lips. "You mumbled something about stubble burn."

A blush coaxed her cheeks into a slight smile as she pretended she wasn't flustered. "Oh, yeah…uh, strippers…so much stubble, shaving their chests…"

"That's not all they shave."

Okay then. "Uh…you can keep that toothbrush."

"Great!" He pointed it at the loveseat underneath her raised single bed. "So, off to Bedfordshire, then?"

Riley stacked cushions into a headrest and stood up. "Yep."

"This means a lot." He paused awkwardly, his arms lost, swaying by his sides like they needed a purpose. "Thanks, Riley…"

Is he going to hug me? I-I can't… Riley busied her hands, clasping the ladder leading to her bed. "Well, night." She climbed up and grabbed threadbare Puffin, hiding him under the duvet as she slipped underneath. She closed her eyes but knew sleep wouldn't come easy.

The springs in the loveseat below groaned then grew quiet. A few minutes passed. Unsure if Ben's tossing and turning was finished, Riley peeked over her bed's edge, careful not to give herself away. Ben's long legs and Christmas socks were hanging off the loveseat, but if he was uncomfortable, it didn't sound like it. His breathing was restful, quiet. *He IS still breathing, right?* She hovered on the edge for another minute, listening to him sleep and then returned to her pillow, her mind swirling with the pinky swear she'd made with a hot guy over a California wrap and a vinegar-soaked burger.

Sixteen

Munching away on a piece of buttery toast smothered in peanut butter, Ben leaned against the sink, flipping through the pages of Riley's *Lairds and Liars* calendar.

"Ben?" A sleepy voice wafted down from the suspended bed.

Shit, caught out. "Ah, Hope," Ben mumbled, fingers abandoning August to fly over his full mouth. "Morning!" He shifted to his left, plunging the lever of Riley's toaster. The two heating elements lit up, surrounding two slices of bread with an orange glow. He turned around, hands jammed in the pockets of his jeans and cheeks full of toast.

Riley scratched her bedhead. "Feeling at home?"

"Uh…" Swallowing the mouthful, he dipped his chin, his fingers escaping his pockets to twist the hem of his t-shirt. "Yeah, I got peckish and wanted to make you breakfast—to thank you, but…" His eyes swept the open shelves. "You don't have much in."

"Hello, student budget." She climbed down the ladder and smiled at the butter and open bag of sliced bread. "This is a first."

"What is?" *Jeez, she's even more adorable in the morning.* Gaze falling from her face, Ben momentarily lost the ability to form words. *Fuck, nipples—she's not wearing a bra under that t-shirt. Stop gawking!*

Joining him at the counter, Riley pulled at her t-shirt's hem. "A guy making me breakfast."

Focus, Fagan. Finish your breakfast…pretend she's wearing a parka—or just don't look at her at all. He picked up a knife, dipping it into the peanut butter. "Call off the trumpets, Hope, it's only toast."

"But I LOVE toast."

He smeared another blob of peanut butter on his breakfast.

"You really like that stuff, huh?"

"There's something about American peanut butter that's the dog's bollocks—*I mean*, it's awesome." He bit into his remaining piece, his eyes alive with childlike bliss.

Riley lifted a box of cereal. "You should try these."

Ben chewed quickly, the Reese's Puffs pulling his eyes back to her. "Peanut butter cereal?! Cereal is life, especially Frosties. I could eat it breakfast, lunch, and dinner. I'd love to try that, but your milk is off."

"Oh, really? Crap." She returned the box to its home. "So, meet any more spiders?"

A subtle burning smell tweaked Ben's nose and a twirling ribbon of smoke rose from the toaster. "Shhiiiiiit." *Is it ruined?* He dropped his breakfast on its plate and swooped, forcing Riley's partially charred toast to spring into view. "I'll make more—"

"No, it's fine—"

"Let me fix it." Ben chopped off a singed corner then stuck a knife into the butter, carving out a large curl. *I'll cover the rest, make it edible. Jeez, can't I do anything right?* He handed her the plate, butter pooling on the crunchy toast.

"Yum, thanks!" She sat down on the loveseat.

She's just saying that. Ben followed but stood, plate and knife in hand, looking at the pictures taped to the wall. A few postcards stood out: Strand Bookstore, London...*Puffins?* He paused at a photo of a rosy-cheeked guy in a green and white hockey jersey, helmet tilted up on his forehead and a 'king of the world' glint in his eye. *Someone thinks highly of himself.* Ben pointed the knife. "Is this the boyfriend?"

Riley looked up. "Yeah, that's Josh."

Several photos showcased relationship bliss: holding hands

while skating in Central Park, a selfie snapped at a parade, laughing hysterically at a gigantic SpongeBob SquarePants balloon hovering overhead. *Josh is definitely the center of her world.* With a long exhale, Ben moved on, skimming pictures of Erika and a few people he didn't recognize, including a male with wavy shoulder-length brown hair, intense green eyes, and a puppy tugging on a leash. "Is the guy with the dog your brother?"

"No, that's my friend Casey, pre-haircut. The dog is Erika's." Riley licked buttery crumbs from her thumb. "I'm an only child. How 'bout you?"

"Same." Ben didn't turn around, admiring photos of Riley in a bathing suit. "I feel like an island sometimes."

"I know how that feels. Good thing I know how to swim." Riley giggled and returned to her toast.

If only you'd swim out to me. My God, you're beautiful.

"All my friends have siblings. Piper has an older brother, Casey has three sisters, and Erika's family's practically a football team—so many kids!"

Ben motioned toward an image of Riley hugging an older brunette. "Who's this?"

She smiled. "My mom."

"Her hair color is different, but you look like her. She's got kind eyes."

"Mom's the best—"

CLICK! The lock on her door turned.

Riley sat up straight. "Hello?"

Ben flinched, pointing the butter knife toward the apartment door as it swung open.

"Wakey wakey, Rye!" Wrapped in her candy floss-colored coat and carrying a bulging plastic bag, Piper struggled through the doorway, a newly procured set of spare keys dangling from her hand.

Riley's tense stare dissolved. "You're early!"

Ah, yeah, this one's on the wall. Ben relaxed and the knife returned to his plate.

"No, you're late." Piper's teasing eyes flew from her best friend to Ben and back again. "And I approve! Breakfast together—this looks cozy."

"Pip!"

Piper dropped the keys into her pocket and the bag to the floor. "Oh my God! Did Riley pick you up at the strip club last night?" She beamed and extended her right hand. "I'm Piper."

Ben wiped his right hand on his jeans and met her confident grip. "Oh, I'm not a stripper. Well, actually, I *was*, but only for two disastrous weeks. I'm Ben—just a friend."

"You're English!" Piper let go of his hand.

"Scottish, actually."

"What?!" Piper's eyes lit up. "No way!"

"I was born there."

"Really? Me, too. Whereabouts?"

"Edinburgh."

"Me, too! High five!" Piper lifted her hand, which Ben gave a reluctant smack. "What part?"

Riley's eyes volleyed between the two Scots.

"Niddrie. I didn't grow up there."

"I was gonna say, your accent's *definitely* not Scottish. Your family must've moved to England when you were young, huh?"

Ben ducked her gaze. "Yeah, something like that."

Piper didn't pause for breath, whipping off her coat and hanging it on the back of the door. "I'm soooo into Scotland. We moved when I was a newborn. Dad was a diplomat, so we lived in France, got sent to Japan, which I adore! Love Japanese things—"

"Except Erika." Riley snickered, savoring another bite of toast. To borrow a phrase from Casey, Piper always said Erika was 'up herself'.

Piper smoothed down her black knit mini-dress. "—but my heart belongs to anything Scottish: shortbread, haggis, the Loch Ness Monster. I'm a total believer—Nessie's real."

Riley chuckled.

"She is!" Piper snapped her gum, the sound earning a fleeting grimace from Ben. "I also Highland dance, I love a flirty kilt, and I can play bagpipes."

Man, she talks fast. Ben nodded politely. "Bagpipes, eh? And your name's Piper?"

"I know! Funny, huh? My parents—wackos!"

"Piper's playing sounds like she's strangling a cat." Riley munched her toast, raising her eyebrows at Ben.

"A neighbor once called the humane society on me—fact. And I did fail my audition with NYU's Pipes and Drums band." Piper kicked off her boots. "Whatever. I swear I have tartan blood. Last night, I watched my people taking no shit on Netflix."

Ben crunched his crust and looked back at Riley, who chewed quickly. "I thought"—Riley mumbled through the mouthful—"you had a date? Some dude from work."

"Yeah, cinnamon cupcake guy!" Scratching her arm, she looked at Ben. "I work at Sprinkles. It's not exactly hookup central, but this guy stood out." She turned to Riley. "Get this: he owns Twister bedsheets—the most awesome thing ever! I was about to go d—" She caught Ben's peaked eyebrow and paused, swerving where her tongue was headed. "He...ah, he said, 'Don't freak out, but I think I have bed bugs.'"

"No way!" Ben shivered.

"Gross!" Riley joined his chorus of disgust. "God, you didn't bring any with you, did you?"

"No!" Piper scratched her hip. "I hightailed it, showered twice, then stayed up until three with *Lairds and Liars* and Mark Keegan instead."

"Mark Keegan?" Ben looked between Piper and Riley. "I know Keegs."

"What?" Riley did a double take.

"No! *Really?*" Piper skimmed Ben from head to toe, her sweep totally obvious.

"Yeah, went to drama school with him." He wiped crumbs from his mouth. "He was two years ahead of me."

"Are you for real?" Riley pursed her lips.

"That. Is. Crazy!" Piper squeezed his arm. "He's Riley's favorite actor." She motioned to the wall. "I gave her that *Lairds* calendar for Christmas."

Ben grinned. "Small world."

"But Josh gets jealous." Piper pulled a red binder from the plastic bag. "He hates Riley swooning over actors."

"That's silly." Ben met Riley's gaze. "Besides, they're eng—"

"So, Pip." Ben noticed a 'shut up' glare in Riley's eyes. She blinked and it vanished as she turned to Piper. "Are those the notes?"

Shit! Piper doesn't know? Ben looked at Riley. *Why hasn't she told her best friend?*

"Yep!" Piper dragged the bag along with her. "And I have candy—lots of it."

Ben walked to the counter, set down his crumb-speckled plate, and retrieved his hoodie from the armrest.

Piper plopped down on the loveseat, bouncing Riley and sending her toast sliding across the plate. "I took three pages of notes. Fuck, talk about coma-inducing. You had the right idea, working a sneaky shift while the rest of us were bored to tears…" She opened the binder. "You know how he loves to drone on about camera positions and shit."

I'm a third wheel now. "Erm." Ben scratched his chin. "I'm gonna head off."

Riley looked up from the page. "You don't have to—"

"Stay!" Piper rooted through the plastic bag. "I've got enough for everyone: Nerds, Pocky, Fun Dip—"

"Mmm, Fun Dip!" Riley licked her lips.

Fun Dip? Ben put on his coat and cap.

Piper flashed a rectangular package. "Check it! A new PEZ present for Riley. It's the one you wanted, right? Badtz-Maru from Hello Kitty?"

"Right, thanks," said Riley tightly. She snatched the penguin PEZ and stashed it under a pillow.

Childhood PEZ collection, eh? Ben laughed as he stuffed his feet into his shoes.

"C'mon, Ben, stay a bit!" Piper grinned.

"Cheers, but I've got stuff to do." *If only.* Ben backed up toward the door. "Thanks for everything, Riles, really."

Her grin lingered. "Anytime."

I hope so. "Nice meeting you, Piper."

"Be seeing ya, Ben!" Piper waved as he closed the door behind him.

"He called you 'Riles'! Kill me now!" Piper grabbed a box of Swedish Fish from her haul. "AND he's a total smoke show. If you're ditching Josh for him—"

"I'm not ditching Josh. Ben's just a new friend."

"Then why did you keep him secret?"

"I didn't. We met on the airport bus two weeks ago and I haven't seen him since."

"Until you got an eyeful last night."

Yeah, FCUK...

Piper bit her lip. "Mmmm, stripping, huh?"

"If you could call it that," said Riley. "He got fired and needed a place to crash, so I let him sleep on the loveseat—and before you ask, nothing happened."

"Well, if *you're* not interested—"

"Why would I be interested?"

"Duh! His socks, Rye! Funny socks on a hot guy? You LOVE that—or at least you said you did." Piper's eyes lit up. "And he knows Mark Keegan!"

"I guess…"

Piper abandoned the candy and grabbed Riley's phone from the milk crate, entering the security code.

"What are you doing?"

Piper scrolled until she found what she was looking for. "Texting myself Benjamuffin's number…oh! He sent you a Facebook friend request." She handed the phone back and flipped a page in the binder, scowling. "Okay, let's get this over with."

"Wait, I need to text Josh, confirm details for later."

"I can't believe you're flying to Minnesota for twenty-four hours. Why isn't the game in North Dakota?"

"The final is in a different city every year." Riley typed and hit send.

See you afterward outside the arena's restaurant. Lots of luck!

"Done with PuckHead?" Piper raised an eyebrow.

"Pip!"

"At least with you going there, you can't drag me to a noisy sports bar where I'd probably get a migraine."

Riley's phone lit up with a text.

Thx, baby! Super hyped! Scouts from the Wild here—guess who they came for? Luv ya.

Riley dropped her phone on her lap. "Just wait until you have a boyfriend or girlfriend…"

"Might be sooner rather than later if Ben goes out with me."

Piper playfully nudged Riley.

"Actually…" Riley bit the inside of her cheek. "Josh isn't my boyfriend anymore."

"What? But you're flying—"

"He's my fiancé."

"NOOO! You—!" Piper's jaw dropped. "I can't believe you said yes. I can't believe you lied to me!"

"I didn't—"

Piper raised an eyebrow.

"Okay, I *did*, but it's only because I wanted to tell my mom first in person."

"Did you tell your mom *why* you said yes?"

"No."

"Of course you didn't—she would've forced you to call it off." Piper met her best friend's eyes. "You don't have to be with him just to help your mom, Rye. Let's try a crowdfunding page. People do them all the time for medical shit."

"Those things never work."

With a pout, Piper flipped a page, then another, muttering under her breath. "But you'll marry fucking Josh…yeah, *that'll* work!"

"You can't stay mad at me…"

"I will if you actually go through with it. Until that happens, there's hope." She ran a finger down the notes. "Did you tell Erika? I bet *she's* thrilled."

Riley nodded. "Yeah, last night. She kept bugging me with wedding advice. I told her four times to drop it. I need to concentrate on finishing school."

"Yeah, you do." Piper returned to the binder. "So, where were we?"

Fifty minutes later, empty packets of Nerds, stray Skittles, and class notes littered the floor. Riley couldn't hold back a large tonsil-flashing yawn as Sia burst from her phone. She didn't budge from her sofa slouch until she squinted at the lit screen. "Oh, it's Mom!" With a lunge, she accepted the call. "Hi! What's up? Pip's here, going over lecture notes before I hop in the shower."

"Hi Piper."

Riley turned to her friend. "Mom says hi." Piper waved in response.

Maggie cleared her throat. "How was last night?"

"It was okay. Erika had a blast—"

Piper leaned in. "RYE LEFT WITH A STRIPPER!"

"I did NOT! He's just a friend I saw last night."

"Yeah, she saw A LOT of him last night." Piper laughed. "He stayed over, too."

"PIP!" Riley elbowed her.

"Stayed over?" Maggie's tone was concerned.

"Ignore her. She's gone way over her sugar limit and it's only ten-thirty. Ben's roommate was having a party. He sleeps on the couch, so he couldn't go home—"

"Unless he wanted to land himself in an orgy!"

Riley threw an empty box of Pocky at Piper and returned to her phone. "He's only been in New York for a few weeks and doesn't know anyone, so what was I supposed to do? Leave him in an all-night diner? And he slept"—Riley turned to Piper—"on my loveseat, *fully clothed* and alone. Nothing happened."

"Rye's loss is my gain, Maggie." Piper leaned into the phone again. "I'm gonna ask him out."

"Tell Piper I say good for her."

"Mom approves." Riley laughed.

"I'm glad you had fun with Erika…" Maggie's voice slipped into a breathy whisper.

"Mom?" A heaviness squeezed Riley's chest. "You okay? You weren't at the ER again, were you?"

"No, sweetheart, but…my results came through."

"Results…" Her eyes widened. "You weren't supposed to hear back until next week. They said—"

"Honey, the cancer…it's no longer responding to treatment. It—it's grown."

This can't be happening. Riley bowed her head and pulled her knees up to her chest, her body retracting into a ball. *No! Third time lucky, remember? Third time lucky!* A shaky hand met her mouth. "It's what…?"

Piper leaned into her best friend. "What is it?" Her normally loud voice was barely a whisper.

A lump grew in Riley's throat, stealing away her ability to answer.

"They called yesterday afternoon," said Maggie. "I didn't want to ruin your night out."

"I'm—" The rail of clothing across from Riley began to blur under a veil of tears. "I'm coming over." She choked out the words.

"Okay, but be careful. Roads are icy, sweetheart," said Maggie.

Riley hung up, collapsing into Piper's arms. Her tears told her best friend all she needed to know.

SEVENTEEN

"Courage is being scared to death but saddling up anyway."
– John Wayne

"Thanks for coming with me." Riley sniffed as they left the shoveled sidewalk on Arlo Road, their boots sliding through the icy slush on the walkway leading to her mom's apartment. The ninety-minute journey—a walk, a subway ride, the Staten Island Ferry, a bus, and then more walking—always felt much longer when she was in a hurry. "I'm sorry we took the wrong bus. My mind is…"

"Don't apologize." Shivering under her fluffy coat, Piper's eyes hopped across the snow-covered grass from one two-story dwelling to another. "I love the ferry. I always feel like Melanie Griffith in *Working Girl*, but without the crazy shoulder pads and hair sprayed to high heaven."

"It's a classic." Riley removed her sunglasses, tucking them in her parka's pocket. The tears had stopped, but her eyes remained swollen and red. "Mom says all her Staten Island friends looked like that in the eighties." Key in hand, Riley paused on the doorstep, taking a deep breath.

Piper leaned in. "It's going to be okay."

Riley unlocked the building's front door and led Piper down the hall to her mom's place, a one-bedroom apartment at the rear of the small building. She stuck the key in the lock and opened the door, the aroma of freshly baked cookies welcoming them in. Maggie sat on her sofa underneath a fuzzy, mocha-colored throw.

"Mom…" Riley dropped her backpack, yanked off her boots, and flew across the room, embracing her mother tightly.

Maggie mouthed, "Thank you," over Riley's shoulder.

Piper nodded. "I'm gonna head to that café down the street. The burrito I ate on the way needs company."

Maggie slowly pulled out of the hug but clasped Riley's hand, refusing to let go. "Piper, are you warm enough? Do you want a hat or mittens?"

"Aw, thanks, Maggie, but I'm good. Text if you want anything brought back, okay?" Piper slipped through the door, leaving the small apartment quiet apart from the upstairs neighbor's footfalls and the excited chirps of chickadees fighting over the feeder outside Maggie's window.

Riley's gaze focused on Maggie's hand wrapped around hers, warm and reassuring. Growing up, Riley always felt safe and content holding her mom's hand, but today she wanted to repay the debt accrued over her short lifetime, to take away the fear, the uncertainty—for both of them. If only she could hold it together. *Don't cry! Stay strong.* A creeping heaviness invaded her chest and climbed up her throat, constricting the release of breaths and threatening to unleash the flood of sobs churning below the surface.

Maggie swept Riley's hair off her forehead, looking into her eyes. "Piper's lovely, so caring and supportive. I don't worry so much, knowing you have a good friend like her."

What? Riley gulped for air. "Mom, stop talking like you're…" She couldn't say it; saying it would make it real. *Dammit! Don't cry, Riley, you'll upset Mom. Be strong. Don't cry!* She bowed her head, her bottom lip surrendering, trembling out of control.

Maggie squeezed her daughter's hand. "Oh, sweetheart, I'm not going anywhere."

"I want to know the truth, Mom." Shrugging free of her parka, Riley's eyelashes fluttered, trying desperately to stifle a further swell of tears. "Don't protect me—I need to know."

"Okay." Maggie took a deep breath, buying time. "The ovarian cancer has grown from Stage 3 to Stage 4…actually 4B because it's now inside my liver, but my oncologist says it hasn't spread to my lungs or bones. Only the liver's involved, which is *good*! It could be far worse. She's changing my chemo drugs and hopefully that will stop its progress."

Looking up, meeting her mom's eyes, the ache grew in Riley's throat. *How did we get here?* "Is it terminal?"

"No, she said it's advanced."

"But…isn't that the same thing?"

Maggie shook her head. "The oncologist explained that advanced and terminal are two different things. Advanced means the cancer can't be cured—"

"But if it isn't curable, how is that *not* terminal?" The words didn't make sense. They teased and twisted, a cruel riddle in Riley's mind…

The cancer can't be cured.

Mom can't be cured.

Riley burst into breath-stealing sobs.

"Oh, honey." Maggie wrapped her arm around her daughter and pulled a tissue from the box on the coffee table. Riley accepted it without hesitation. "I know it's confusing, but listen, it's *not* terminal. Advanced means the cancer won't go away, but I can live with it—lots of women do. I'll have more chemo, maybe enroll in a clinical trial for a new drug, and if the tumor gets smaller, surgery could be an option."

"But it could get larger." Wiping her nose, Riley's voice cracked behind the tissue. "Or spread more."

"It could, but here's how I'm looking at it. I have three scenarios: one, it could grow and spread; two, it stays the same; or three, it shrinks. Two out of three ain't bad! And I'm going to fight for those odds."

"But it could get worse at any moment. It's…lying in wait."

"You know I've never been a fan of inspirational quotes, but in this case, they're actually right. 'Tomorrow is never promised to anyone.' Soak up every moment, be generous with your love, and be thankful for those who love us back—rules we should all follow, right?"

"Yeah, I guess." Riley rolled her damp tissue into a ball and paused for a moment, stuttering breaths playing catch-up, delaying what she wanted to ask next. "So…when is cancer terminal?"

"When there's nothing more the doctors can do. When drugs and surgery can't halt the cancer, they resort to palliative care—pain relief, basically. They keep the patient as comfortable as possible until…it's time." Maggie's voice broke.

She's scared. She's trying so hard to hide it. Riley hugged her mom, but Maggie's sharp collarbone jabbed her throat. Her mother's tender softness, a comfort since childhood, was long gone, a souvenir of her many chemo treatments. *I can't lose her…I just can't.*

Tears slid down Maggie's cheeks, but she swept them away as quickly as they fell. She swallowed and took a deep breath, a quivery smile taking over her face, not that Riley could see it. A loving hand caressed her daughter's hair. "Hey, listen to me. Lots of people live for years with incurable cancer. We have to remain positive, keep moving forward. The new treatment might stop the cancer from getting bigger—it might even shrink it."

"Might shrink it? No, no, it WILL shrink it. It has to." Riley pulled back. "Third time lucky."

"Third time lucky." Maggie softly smiled. "And the doctor can give me painkillers for any discomfort."

"But you're already on painkillers…"

"They'll just increase the dosage."

"But what if we can't pay for it? The insurance copays…"

"Don't worry about that right now. First things first. I'll get better, then I'll deal with the debt once I'm back at work." A slight sigh escaped Maggie's lips.

She looks so tired. How will she get through this? Riley cleared her throat. "Mom—"

"Riley, I've come this far, and I'm not giving up. For one thing, there's a wedding next year." Maggie squeezed Riley's hand. "I'm not kidding myself. I know it's going to be hard, but life's boring without a challenge, right?"

She says that like she's about to learn Chinese or take up triathlons. Riley nodded. *I can't show how scared I am. I can't pull her down. I have to work harder to pretend everything is fine.*

"The new chemo cycle starts in four days, so until then, I'm doing whatever I want, which means eating ice cream, lazing in PJs, and binge-watching *The Crown* and *Lairds and Liars*. I could listen to their accents all day. I'd love to visit Britain and see everything for real."

"England and Scotland?" *Be positive, Riley!* "We'll go next year when you're feeling better! See where they film *Lairds*, visit the Queen, have fish 'n' chips with deep fried Mars bars...go see puffins!" Riley fell easily into an old game Maggie had introduced when she was little and feeling down, discussing the perfect—albeit imaginary—getaway: the places they'd go, what they would see, what they would eat. Anemic finances meant none of these trips had ever happened. Riley always hoped the day would come when the two of them boarded a flight to Europe, credit cards be damned— and today she felt it more than ever before. "We could channel Harry Potter and visit Platform 9 ¾ at King's Cross station, see the crown jewels, and pose with Big Ben." *Ben...* Her smile stretched a little farther.

"So many castles, so little time." Maggie laughed. "Will Josh come too?"

"No!" The smile slipped from Riley's face. "Girls only, right?"

Maggie got up from the couch.

"Where are you going?"

"I read that goals are more likely to be met if you visualize them every day." Maggie tore the 'Saturday, April 7' paper square from her small page-a-day calendar beside the telephone. She flipped the paper over, writing 'Hope for Britain 2019' in her elegant penmanship. Maggie's handwriting belonged in another era, all sophisticated swirls and delicate curves, drawing compliments from everyone who saw it. She pinned the paper underneath a purple and white NYU magnet she proudly kept on her fridge. "Done!" Her fingers lingered, tracing photos of Riley atop a large boulder in Central Park and on the Santa Monica pier in California. "You should be heading to the airport soon, honey," she said quietly. "Josh's big game—"

"I'm not going anywhere." Riley scratched her unwashed hair. "I'll text him after. He'll understand."

Maggie smiled softly at the photos and looked over her shoulder. "Should we text Piper? Get her back here for cookies and ice cream?"

"Definitely." Riley pulled her phone from her parka.

"Great! I'll get the bowls ready." Maggie disappeared behind the kitchen wall, taking Riley's grin with her.

It's okay to have dessert for dinner—or eat more than one slice of cake! (Just not every day, okay?)

Big dreams are never silly. They help soothe a bad day and give us something to reach for.

If you believe in nothing else, please believe in love. It can make miracles happen.

Eighteen

Sunday, Monday, Tuesday, and…Wednesday—and nothing from Riley. Ben had sent two texts—*How R U?* and *How was the game?*—over the past four days but both messages had gone unanswered, and she still hadn't accepted his Facebook friend request. Popping a chunk of a black-and-white cookie—a New York City staple—into his mouth, he stopped in the shade of an abandoned doorway on MacDougal Street, shoved up the long sleeves of his blue t-shirt, and slowly typed out another text.

Got 2 job leads 2day. Wish me luck.

Wiping perspiration from his forehead, he continued on his way, greeting the unseasonably hot April day with an optimistic grin. *She'll be chuffed for me.* He dawdled through Greenwich Village, glancing down at his phone every few blocks, but his latest message ended up like the others: ignored and relegated to text purgatory. His smile slowly evaporated as a nagging hollowness wrenched his gut. *She owes you nothing, Ben. Why would she answer you right away—if at all? You're setting yourself up for disappointment like every other time—you know that, right? FUCK!* He took a deep breath. *But…Riley's different…*

Careening around strolling tourists, Ben wanted answers, refusing to believe he and Riley hadn't forged a friendly connection, refusing to believe she was ghosting him, that he wasn't someone she cared about even a tiny bit. *Maybe something happened? Maybe her Josh bloke got injured?* Head down, forcing pedestrians to swerve around him, he typed slowly, but his spelling mistakes riddled the Google search bar. He jabbed the delete key, his frustration growing with each erased letter. Several tries later, 'ice hokcey championship', 'winner', and 'Josh' filled the bar. He hit go and slammed face-first into a rock-hard shoulder.

Shit! Ben spun 180 degrees on impact and his phone flew from his hand, clattering on the pavement. He winced, clutching his nose. "Fuuuuuccck!"

His victim, who could have passed for an Olympic weight lifter, didn't budge an inch, and neither did the steel dolly he was pushing, stacked high with heavy boxes of beer destined for the pizzeria behind them. Ear-splitting rap leaked from his massive headphones. The mountain of a man glared at Ben, clearly annoyed.

SHIT! This stonking bloke could snap me in half. "Sorry, mate. My fault...wasn't looking where I was..." Eyes watering, Ben's hand dropped from his nose. A streak of bright red blood coated his fingers, derailing his apology and leaving him speechless, shuffling backward in a daze.

"Hey!" The delivery guy let go of the dolly and lunged, grabbing a fistful of Ben's t-shirt, yanking him too close for comfort.

Ben flinched, lifting his hands to protect his face. "I'm sorry, okay?!" *Fucking hell, he's gonna hit me!* He held his breath and squinted, dipping his shoulder and twisting away so his throbbing nose was almost out of reach. He did a double take over his shoulder, his jaw falling slack. Only a few inches behind him, two metal hatch doors reached skyward, exposing a square hole in the sidewalk and a bone-breaking drop. Steep cement stairs led downward to the restaurant's storage cellar, cluttered with sealed boxes and bins of shattered glass bottles. *Oh...my God!*

"Jeezus guy, watch where ya walkin'!" The man's Bronx accent fought with Drake, still spilling from his headphones. He swept Ben to a safe corner of sidewalk and released his shirt, which was now stretched at the neck and speckled with red droplets.

Ben let a breath go and a searing jolt of pain exploded through his nose. *Jesus!* His watery eyes surveyed the drop zone. "Hey, thanks, mate. You saved me—"

"Tourists!" With a hairy wrist, the hulk mopped sweat from his unibrow and shook his head, seeking agreement from the cluster of people stopping to gawk. "This time, a broken beak. Next time, a broken neck—or worse, ya hands." He snorted, playing to his audience. "How the hell would ya walk and text then, huh?" Onlookers, including several tall, willowy women laughed, earning a crooked smile from Ben's sweaty guardian angel.

Everyone's a comedian. Cheeks burning red, Ben dabbed his bleeding nose with the back of his hand. "Cheers, mate." *As if I didn't already feel like a total pillock.*

"No sweat." Show over, the guy leaned on the dolly's handles and wheeled its cargo closer to the opening in the sidewalk.

Two attractive twenty-something women carrying modeling portfolios stepped forward, one handing Ben his phone and several tissues. "Aw! Poor you, are you okay?"

Would you two fancy nursing me back to health? A slight smile fought through his pain. "Hi."

"Eww, it's swelling!" The woman winced to her equally gorgeous friend. "A doctor might need to reset it. There's a hospital about fifteen—"

Hospital? He made a sour face. "No, it's fine, really. Cheers for the tissues." He plunged his nose into the Kleenex and escaped their scrutiny, rushing past Mediterranean and vegan restaurants toward Bleecker Street. Turning the corner, he headed east, his nose throbbing harder with each quickened step and pound of his heart. He carefully steered clear of the various metal hatches—open or closed—along the gum-stained sidewalk.

A few blocks later, an oasis in the April heat stood proud on a corner—The Red Lion pub. Ben slipped inside, craving a beer, air conditioning, and somewhere to clean up. He immediately felt at home. His favorite soccer team, Tottenham Hotspur, was playing

Manchester United on the numerous flat screens, and a red telephone box stood guard in the corner. Familiar names: Boddingtons, Newcastle Brown Ale, Strongbow—imported beers and ciders— called out from a framed board behind the bar. He removed the stained tissue from his nose and fled to the men's room, its mirror confirming what he'd suspected—he looked a bloody mess. Washing away the dried blood, he prayed his swollen nose wasn't broken. *Brilliant. How's this going to look at job interviews?*

Back at the bar, he ordered a Smithwick's and scowled at his shattered phone. New cracks joined old fractures zigzagging across its screen. He carefully opened the browser and selected the top search result, still waiting post-crash.

NCAA Men's Ice Hockey Final: North Dakota Fighting Hawks 3, Boston University 2. Winning goal scorer, Josh King...

Her fella wasn't hurt; he was the hero.

The rest of the article began to dissolve into a jumble of half-formed letters, so Ben abandoned it, selecting the images tab instead. *I bet Riley stayed in Saint Paul longer to celebrate. Makes sense.*

Photos of the players celebrating on and off the ice slid underneath Ben's fingers as he searched for Riley in the crowd or by Josh's side. *Nope.* He opened a YouTube video of the previous day's standing-room-only homecoming in their college rink. Riley's fiancé, all muscle and brimming with confidence, wearing the team's distinctive Kelly green and white hockey jersey, was front and center—the team captain, the game-winning goal scorer, adored by everyone. He took to the microphone and made a speech like he was born for it, thanking the coaches, team staff, and "the best fans in college hockey, as well as our families, who've always been there to drive us to practice at the crack of dawn. This celebration is for you, too!" Cheers rose from the crowd and the UND band's trumpets, tubas, and trombones erupted into an annoying tune Ben didn't recognize.

Mystery over, then. This is why she didn't text back. She has HIM. What could you offer her? His stomach pinched. *You're kidding yourself if you think she'd ever be interested in you in that way, Fagan. Josh is somebody. You? Nobody.*

He took a long swig of beer and stared at the football match on the screen, the ache in his nose morphing into a full-on headache. His phone buzzed on the bar—a text from Piper.

Hey! Wanna go out Friday night?

NINETEEN

Riley withdrew from the world, choosing to stay with her mom. She called in sick to Sephora and her BBC internship, temporarily vanishing from campus. Her swimsuit remained in her backpack, balled up and ignored, and unread notifications congregated in her social media accounts. More important tasks beckoned, like running errands to the pharmacy and bank, plus accompanying Maggie to her first revamped chemotherapy treatment. It hadn't gone well.

Maggie returned home more nauseous than usual, could barely eat, and was tormented by an angry red rash that had sprung up across her abdomen and back. Stoic as ever, she downplayed her discomfort and exhaustion, telling her daughter in no uncertain terms that with only a month left until graduation, she was jeopardizing her degree and she should "get her ass back to the East Village, pronto," but Riley wouldn't listen. The thought of returning to school, hoping no one would find her crumpled in the corner of a restroom stall crying her heart out, made her sick to her stomach. She needed to be by Maggie's side, making things easier any way she could. While her mom napped, she did laundry, cleaned the apartment, and prepared meals, trying to keep her hands and mind busy. Sitting still with nothing to do let the unthinkable creep into her thoughts, stoking the cold fear that grew inside her. But, once her mom was awake, Smiley Riley was back in action, boosting spirits and building a wall around her depression so no one, especially her mom, would be the wiser. Maggie knew, though. Moms like Maggie always did.

The only person Riley spoke to regularly was Piper, whispering underneath a blanket on the couch while Maggie slept. Sometimes after their chats, Riley would bawl in the shower or muffle her cries with a pillow, but later, puffy eyes and a swollen nose betrayed her secret. Messages and texts—including an angry email from Riley's landlord demanding rent—clogged her screen, remaining unanswered until Piper stepped in, dealing with Riley's super, and keeping Casey and Erika in the loop, allowing her best friend to focus on her mom.

Reaching her fiancé, however, had proved nearly impossible since North Dakota won the NCAA final the same day Maggie's news broke. Josh had sent her a text immediately following their victory and Riley spoke to him briefly, but she barely had three minutes with him before the media relations director whisked him away for the post-game press conference. A text followed the next day.

Sorry about yesterday, babe. They've got us booked for interviews and meet and greets, it's crazy! I'm sorry I can't fly home to be with you right now.

And that was it. Since that message—six days ago—Riley's calls, FaceTime attempts, and texts went unanswered by the team captain. His social media feeds, on the other hand, were updated with photos of ecstatic teammates sprawled on the ice with the NCAA trophy, images from the standing-room-only celebration on their home rink, and party shots—lots of boozy party pix, bleary-eyed and posing with people she didn't recognize. She knew the big win would come with unavoidable obligations this week, but why hadn't he spared a few minutes to get in touch?

Fuck it. She stopped folding towels in Maggie's living room and texted him.

I've changed my mind.

Josh replied within seconds.

What?

Riley shook her head. *Well, THAT got his attention.* She sent a

FaceTime request. It barely beeped before her fiancé answered, neatly dressed in a suit, Kelly green tie and a white shirt, the collar of which stood out against a purple bruise on the side of his neck. *Ouch!* Male voices joked in the background, but Josh ignored them, staring into the screen.

"Riley, what's going on?"

"You tell me." She squinted. "What happened to your neck?"

"I got whacked with a high stick on Saturday—"

"Josh got payback, though!" A deep voice, accompanied by a face Riley recognized—a freshman teammate—interrupted. "Fucking legend! Scored the winner while that asshole stewed in the box! Won us the whole freakin' thing!"

"Yeah, well…" Josh winced, scratching his playoff beard. "Give me a minute, bro." He shifted his phone so the camera captured him from the chest up as he started walking. "Rye—"

"KINGY!" Several teammates hollered as he rushed passed. Riley couldn't tell where they were. The pot lights, ambient music, and Josh's clothes suggested they weren't on campus. He turned a corner, entering somewhere quiet. His furrowed brows and the space's shadowy light made him look majorly pissed off.

"You've changed your mind?"

"Yeah, I think we should get married *this* year."

He slumped against a wall covered in golden wallpaper, his face softening into a grin. "Fuuck, you had me! I thought you were calling it off!" He laughed. "Can't wait to become Mrs. King, huh? Wife of a future NHL star? Yeah baby, lock me down—but why the change? Not that I'm complaining."

"It has to be this year because I don't—" Her breath hitched as the words got stuck in her throat. "I don't know if—" Tears stung her eyes. "I can't get married without Mom there."

"Oh, of course. Of course, baby, she'll be there. Tell you what, pick any date you want—as long it's not in early September when rookie training camp starts. When I'm home next month, we'll buy your ring and start planning, 'kay?"

Riley forced a deep breath into her lungs. "The ring, Josh...I can't wear something worth thousands when my mom can't afford her treatments." After the proposal, Josh had said he'd help with Maggie's bills, but Riley wanted confirmation. *Say it again. It needs to be at the forefront of your mind.* "I—I'd rather use the money to help her." She exhaled, waiting for the fallout.

"O-kay..." He paused. "But I still want you to have a nice ring—" A burst of voices rose off camera, drawing Josh's gaze. "Don't worry. I'll help with her bills."

"Really?"

"Yeah." His eyes returned to her.

She couldn't hold it in any longer. All the frustration, the fear—the dread of what her future might look like—bubbled up into a chest-heaving flood of uncontrollable tears. Worried Maggie might hear, Riley grabbed a freshly laundered towel and suffocated her sobs.

"Rye?" Josh looked pained. "Babe, please don't cry. Things will work out." He checked his watch. "Uh, shit." He toyed with his tie and glanced away, torn. "I have to go..."

"Where?" Riley lowered the towel and wiped her nose with her hand.

"An interview with *Sports Illustrated*." He tugged the knot of his tie. "But I'll stay if you want me to. The guys can do it without me."

His selfless words warmed Riley's pounding heart, but her belief in them quickly dissolved. Something lurked in his eyes. Josh had one of those faces; if you knew him well, you could read it instantly. *He's disappointed. Can I blame him?* It wasn't fair to hold him back from the rewards of his success. "No, I want you to go. You earned this, Josh. I'll be fine. I shouldn't be crying with Mom in the next room, anyway."

"You sure?"

She nodded and plastered on a smile. "Enjoy *Sports Illustrated*. You'll be great. I'm proud of you."

"Thanks, babe. I'm really sorry I can't be there, just too many commitments."

"I know."

Josh blew her a kiss and Riley tapped the disconnect button.

"Riley?" Maggie's voice entered the room a few seconds before she did.

"Hey, Josh says hi." She left her phone on the coffee table. "How you feeling? Are you hungry? I can make soup."

"I feel rested, not so itchy. Soup would be amazing."

Riley smiled and leapt up from the sofa, feeling hopeful for the first time in days.

TWENTY

Three days later

"Finally, bare legs!" Piper's huge oval sunglasses made her look permanently surprised. She perched on the steps of the fountain in Washington Square Park, smoothing her short skirt. "No more tights. Hello, spring!"

Casey squirted a blob of gel sanitizer into his hand and rubbed it in thoroughly before raising his grande iced coffee to his lips. "Spring? As if." He slurped the complex concoction featuring thirteen pumps sugar-free vanilla, fifteen pumps hazelnut, a heap of extra ice, twelve Splenda, and an inch of caramel drizzle. The name printed out on his cup, courtesy of the eye-rolling baristas, read 'Crazy' instead of 'Casey'. "We jumped straight to summer."

Piper reached across his lap, waving an open box of Insomnia cookies in front of Riley. "I'm happy spring's back but even happier *you're* back—because that means Maggie's feeling more like her old self."

"She is, but…" Riley squeezed her phone. "I hate not being there. What if she needs me?"

"If she does, you go." Piper's eyebrows rose above her sunglasses. "But sitting around her apartment when she's feeling stronger and graduation's only weeks away helps no one. I bet she kicked your ass this morning, am I right?"

Riley sighed.

"Don't feel guilty. You need to take care of yourself, too." Piper shook the cookie box. "C'mon, eat! I didn't buy them just to look at."

125

Riley yawned and chose a snickerdoodle cookie. "I missed these."

"Cookies are life—fact." Piper nodded.

Casey pointed to the box. "You sanitized your hands before rooting around in there, right?"

"No, I picked a booger and then fingered each and every one." Piper snatched it away, but Casey's reach earned him a chocolate chunk cookie anyway.

"Our Monday afternoon ritual isn't the same if you're AWOL, Rye." Casey leaned in, a buttery popcorn smell from his part-time job at a cinema lingering in his light jacket. His eyes chased the fountain's waterworks as they leapt into the cloudless sky. "Thank God you're back. Listening to Paisley here, waffling on about her latest sexual misadventure, was detrimental to my GPA."

"I heard that!" Piper scooted a smidge to her left, setting the box down between her and Casey. "I have needs, so sue me."

"And I'm happy you're fulfilling them." Cookie in hand, Casey shook his head. "I just don't need all the gory details—"

"Did you ask Ben out?" Riley's question got lost in the verbal volleys to her left.

"Case, I'm not going to apologize because I enjoy a good fuck," said Piper.

"You and Ben—?" Riley's eyes widened.

"They did." Casey snapped his cookie in half.

"Really?" Riley stiffened, her tone sharp.

"NO! Ben and I went *out*! We didn't have sex—Ben's a gentleman," said Piper. "We had a date Friday night. Sorry I didn't tell you, Rye."

Three days ago, and I'm only hearing about it now?

Piper lifted her sunglasses, nudging them into her hair. "It seemed like something that could wait, you know? After we talked about your mom and what you missed at school each day, you sounded exhausted."

Riley slowly nodded. Piper wasn't being secretive; she was being considerate as always. "How'd it go?"

"Okay, but poor Ben looked awful. Swollen nose, two black eyes—"

"W-What?!" Riley jerked forward. "What happened?"

"Broke his nose." Casey winced. "Collided with some bloke on the street, apparently."

"Yeah, two days before our date." Piper nodded. "The timing couldn't have sucked more. He had an interview for a job at a bakery *and* an audition today…"

Shit. Right. He texted me last week—the day of Mom's chemo. Too much was going on to respond.

"Singing on Broadway."

A knot tightened in Riley's stomach. "Singing? That's amazing." *You would've known the news first if you had returned his text.*

"I don't know if he got either job, though." Piper sighed, twirling a short piece of hair around a finger. "If he didn't, maybe he's too embarrassed to say anything, poor guy."

Piper seems interested…maybe Ben is too?

"His bruises might've turned them off. He looked rough—not that *that* ever stopped me!" Piper licked her lips. "I told him if those jobs didn't work out, he should join me at Sprinkles. I said it as a joke, not thinking he'd be interested, but he asked me questions about cupcake recipes and everything. Apparently, he baked with his mum when he was little! Super cute."

"Where'd you guys go?" Riley bit her cookie.

"That mac 'n' cheese place on First. He ate a huge portion of their four-cheese mac and *three* brownies." Piper giggled. "He stole a spoon, too. I think Ben's a bit of a klepto!"

"Just your type, Pip," said Casey.

She laughed. "Hey, I haven't shoplifted since freshman year! So, *anyway*—we went for a walk. It was so warm, everyone was out. Ben was like a bottomless pit, though, still hungry, so I dragged him to that cookie dough shop on LaGuardia."

Casey sipped his coffee. "I love that place, but it always has a humongous line."

"Yeah, it was crazy, so we had lots of time to talk Scotland, but for someone born there, he knows jack shit. Said he left as a six-year-old and never went back." Piper dug in the box, selecting a sugar cookie. "I mean, I left two weeks after I was born, but at least I've visited a bunch of times. He wanted to know all about my background, so I gave him the world tour. He didn't nod off into his chocolate milkshake or anything, so—yay me!"

"How many people can say they've lived in Edinburgh, Paris, Tokyo, Toronto, Chicago, and New York by the age of twenty-three? Of course it's interesting," said Riley. "You're interesting."

Piper chewed her cookie. "I guess being a diplomat's brat makes for good date conversation. Ben told me a bit about England. He moved a few times and lived in Windsor."

"Hmm!" Casey raised an eyebrow. "Windsor is home to the most millionaires in Britain, including the Queen when she's in residence at Windsor Castle."

"Why Google when you have Brit Twit?" Piper groaned.

"Wow, I had no idea Ben had royal neighbors," said Riley.

"Is he a toff?" Casey set his coffee down between his Harry Styles-influenced Chelsea boots.

"Toff?" asked Riley.

"Rich Brit. Privileged upper class."

Piper chuckled. "Doubt it. He wasn't flashing a platinum card. Our date was cheap and cheerful."

"I think he's as broke as I am." Riley's phone lit up, sending her heart surging into her throat. *Mom?* A hockey GIF from Josh filled the screen. *Ahh, thank God.*

Casey chose another cookie. "I guess he's never met the Queen, then. Stolen her silver teaspoons, maybe..."

"Ben knows someone even *better.*" Piper tilted her freckly nose into the bright sun. "Mark Keegan."

"Bollocks, he does!" Casey snapped the cookie in half.

"He does! Ben said Mark looked out for him at drama school, made sure he wasn't homesick, helped him learn lines. Can you imagine? Sweet, huh?"

"Yeah." Riley swallowed, trying to dampen the twinge in her chest. She was happy Piper was spending time with Ben but felt left out, hearing about his past secondhand. *Why didn't he open up about this stuff to me?*

"He hasn't spoken to Mark in a while, though. Ben called him last fall, but his number had changed," said Piper.

"Well, *that's* convenient." Casey snorted. "Knows him, my ass."

Piper rolled her eyes and continued. "Ben said they both auditioned for the role of Callum in *Lairds and Liars*, but he lost out because Mark's Scottish accent was better. That's crazy—born in Scotland and you lose to an Irishman."

"Or maybe Ben's a shit actor."

"Casey!" Riley glared. "Maybe Mark just had the look they wanted."

"Yeah, listen to the future casting director!" said Piper. "Ben told me about beating Mark for a voiceover job. It was a kids show—with puppets! I nearly died! Ben's puppet-friendly! That was all I needed—"

"Bloody hell!" Casey laughed. "You didn't make him watch your YouTube channel on your date, did you? I thought you liked this guy. No wonder you didn't get laid."

"If a guy—or girl—doesn't get me or my love of puppets, then good riddance. I'm going to become THE go-to person for children's television in LA one day, and my future partner will be supportive." Piper sniffed. "My puppet channel has over twenty thousand subscribers, so I'm doing something right."

"Did you show him?" asked Riley.

Piper beamed. "He complimented my storytelling and said my puppets looked like Muppets! That's the ultimate compliment."

"Your internship last summer at the LA workshop paid off in more ways than one," said Riley.

"I know, right!" Piper brushed crumbs from her skirt. "Intern now, CEO in ten years. I told Ben that and he said 'I believe it!' Aw, Benjamuffin! He's such a cutie."

"Benjamuffin?" Casey's face turned sour.

What's with the Benjamuffin? "He's definitely cute." A tight smile crossed Riley's face. Piper's gushing about Ben was stoking that pang in her chest again. She squinted into the fountain. "When are you going out again?"

"Oh, we're not. Ben's not into me, and you know—vice versa."

"What?" Riley's jaw relaxed. "Why?"

"Knew it." Casey nodded. "Piper plus puppets equals total boner killer—"

"It has nothing to do with my puppets. We had zero spark. There was no flirting, no kiss good-bye or hug. I dunno, maybe he's asexual? Or a germophobe?" She gave Casey side-eye. "It was like he was channeling you, C-3PO."

"Steady on!"

"He's totally yum, but he just doesn't do it for me," Piper sighed. "Unlike a certain woman with a gorgeous wild Afro…"

Riley leaned forward. "That girl at Peet's?"

Piper's face lit up. "Yeah! She always does a cool design in my latte. Remember the cat, Casey?"

He nodded. "Well, do the opposite of what I'd do then."

"What? Buy a *regular* coffee?"

"No. Ask her out." Casey was dead serious.

"I think she goes to Tisch," said Riley. "I overheard her say she's a dance major."

"Ooh, bendy, Pip." Casey raised an eyebrow. "Bet *she's* into Twister bedsheets."

Piper nodded. "A girl's gotta have *some* fun."

"Amen to that." Riley woke up her phone—still no messages from Maggie.

"The same could be said for the future Mrs. King." Casey elbowed Riley. "Before you vanish into the backwoods of Minnesota as Josh's child bride, apparently…"

Her heart dipped like a lead balloon. *Minnesota.* She lowered her phone to her lap. "Aw, Case, I *was* going to tell you—"

"Hey, it's okay, really, I'm just winding you up. You've been busy. I didn't mind hearing it from Pip." Casey protectively wrapped his arm over Riley's shoulder. "What you're doing for your mom is…" He took in a deep breath. "I just wish you didn't have to marry Josh to do it."

A sour taste rose in Riley's throat.

"It's a shame you won't be living the west coast life with Pip Pip Hooray here…" Casey squeezed Riley's shoulder and let go. "You know, it's not too late to bail."

"Guys—"

"Just…think about it," said Casey. "Josh will be off, pretending to be the new Grootzky—"

"It's *Gretzky*."

"Whatever." Casey huffed. "Josh will be leaving you alone in the middle of nowheresville with only deer and pine cones to keep you company. What do they do for fun out there? Do they even have THX in their movie theaters?"

"Saint Paul is a city, Case—Minnesota's capital." Riley briefly closed her eyes. "Look, I know you guys think this is some submissive move, but I'm not in the back seat. *I'm* the one driving this thing, being proactive about helping Mom. I'm not a victim. This is my choice."

Shaking his head, Casey reached for his coffee. "But do you have to marry him—"

"I do!" Her sharp tone drew stares from two stroller-pushing nannies. A tightness squeezed her chest. *Lower your voice, Riley.* "Things…things are so much worse…"

Casey paused mid-sip. "Worse? How?"

"Where do I start?" She sighed. "The scans, surgeries, insurance premiums, chemo and radiation treatments, drugs, transfusions, ER visits, transportation costs—they haven't taken a bite out of her savings, they've devoured *every scrap*. We had to sell her car, most of her furniture—where does it fucking end?"

"Aw, Rye." Piper leaned in. "I thought her place looked kinda empty."

"And she's one late payment away from losing her apartment. I can't stand by and watch her become homeless. I had to do something."

Casey squeezed his cup. "That's so wrong. Cancer patients have enough to worry about—they shouldn't end up bankrupt as well."

"Mom can't even *declare* bankruptcy—she can't afford the filing fees." Riley's breath hitched. "And I feel so…guilty…"

"Why?" Casey squinted.

"A year and a half ago, when she got cancer for the second time…" She diverted her eyes to her phone, sitting in her lap. "I've never told you, but I was going to withdraw from NYU."

"Seriously?" "What?" Piper and Casey's words tripped over each other.

Riley blew out her lips. "I've always paid my rent and expenses, and I contribute a bit toward fees, but even with my scholarship and loans, it's not enough. Mom pays what they don't cover, but with no steady income... I couldn't have her choosing to pay for college over heating her apartment or eating, so I decided to quit."

"Wow." Casey's jaw dropped.

"That didn't go down well. She tore up the withdrawal forms and said 'over my dead body.' She laid down the law *and* made a morbid joke." Riley bowed her head.

"Maggie's such a badass!" Piper smirked.

"She said savings were put aside for my college education and she'd never let her cancer stop me from getting a degree, but now she's sick again and I keep thinking, if I had just *done* it...if I wasn't here, I know she wouldn't be in debt."

Casey sighed. "And you're fixing that by marrying PuckHead."

"He gets what he wants...and I do, too."

"Ahh, true love? Who needs it! It's overrated, anyway," said Casey, bumping her shoulder.

"I don't think it's overrated." Riley looked weary. "And I do *care* about Josh. I did love him...once. Maybe I will again—" Her phone glowed with a text from Erika.

Rye! Check out this link for wedding invites—

She scoffed and turned her phone over.

"Ugh, let's hope not. Save your heart for someone who's worthy of it." Casey locked eyes with Piper. "Look, promise me once your mom's fine, you'll divorce Josh's ass."

Piper leaned forward. "Rye, we get it. You're doing what you think is best for your mom. We'll support whatever you decide to do, but make me a promise, too?"

"You guys and your promises." Riley smiled. "What? I use your mom as the divorce lawyer?"

Piper pointed at Riley's phone. "Text Ben."

"Why?" Casey scrunched up his face.

"I think he could help, you know, get your mind off things," said Piper. "He's not at Tisch and he doesn't know anything about Maggie. He's funny and he'll make you smile—God knows you need that kind of escape right now. Plus, he's basically alone here...I'm sure he'd like to hear from you."

A chance to escape. A flutter tickled the heaviness in her chest. "Okay. Maybe."

Piper giggled. "He wore Christmas pudding socks on our date. How cute is that?"

Casey raised his eyebrows.

What's a Christmas pudding? Don't ask Case. He won't shut up.

The three friends sat quietly for a moment, watching the fountain rise and fall, soundtracked by the 'oohs' of overheated tourists and giggly children.

"Oh, shit!" Piper rose quickly, discarding the empty cookie box on the fountain's edge. "I have my Pitching Stories lecture in five. I gotta run. What do you guys have?"

"Cinematography for Advanced Productions. My prof wants to see my doc." Casey snapped up the empty cardboard box.

"Library for me." Riley picked up her backpack. "Gotta catch up on my notes."

Piper swiped gloss over her lips then pulled Riley into a hug. "Don't pull an all-nighter, okay? Text me before ten; I'll bring you a bagel."

"Thanks, but I'll have escaped by then." Riley waved as she headed to the southeast corner of Washington Square Park and Bobst Library.

TWENTY-ONE

9:22 p.m. stared back at Riley from the upper right corner of her laptop screen. She could either power through for another two hours, risking burnout, or follow Piper's advice and text Ben.

"I'm sure he'd like to hear from you."

She picked up her phone. *But would he? I ghosted him—not on purpose, but still.* She paused, taking a deep breath. Responsible Riley, reporting for duty. She began typing.

Have you eaten?

An answer popped onto her screen within a minute.

Yes sweetheart. Have you?

Moms never change.

Yep, a salad. Just finishing at library. Heading home soon. x

Riley fibbed. The only thing she had eaten besides the cookies with Piper and Casey was an apple and some leftover heart-shaped Valentine's candy. Maggie would worry if she knew her daughter was skipping meals. Sometimes a little white lie was the only option.

Text me when you get home. Love you. x

So, her mom was doing okay…no need to rush to Staten Island tonight. Her narrative television project was coming along nicely… She chewed the end of her pencil. *Fuck it. No time like the present to grovel.* She returned to her phone.

Hey. I'm sorry for being a shitty friend.

Twenty-seven minutes and three pages of studio blocking notes later, her phone shined bright.

Riles!!!! Her name and the abundance of exclamation marks were followed by an emoji, the beaming face with smiling eyes.

Riley grinned back. Ben was alive and well—somewhere—and if there ever was an emoji that captured his smiling half-crescent eyes, that one was it. She dashed off a response.

Sorry I didn't answer last week. Busy = no excuse. How are you?

Riley returned to her project, figuring out where the studio cameras should go. A few minutes passed.

Apolgy accepted. The clapping hands emoji came next, forming a sentence with *4 Josh. Big win!! Fun?*

Her thumbs hovered over her phone. Piper hadn't said a word to Ben about her mom, so what to say about her disappearing act…anything? She hated telling people about her mom's cancer. It wasn't something she could easily drop into conversation. 'Yeah, I'd love to hang out, and oh, by the way, my mom has cancer—for the third time.' The fact that Maggie had been sick more than once didn't make the 'cancer talk' any easier. If anything, it had become harder.

Luckily, some people listened and offered sympathy or support at the first drop of the C-bomb, people like Piper and Casey. Neither one had gone through a serious illness with a parent—neither one knew anyone with cancer, but Riley didn't have to draw a picture of her fear or anger for them; they intuitively knew. Gestures both little and large—hugs, notes taken in class, a meal brought to her door, the willingness to listen 24/7—proved they got it.

But, some people didn't get it, and Riley always knew what was coming. It was just a matter of assigning jerseys for their respective teams.

The Downloaders: Friends who would ask personal questions she didn't feel comfortable answering. *Boundaries, people!*

The Bubble-Wrappers: Friends who would douse her with pity, treating her differently, like a delicate glass ornament about to shatter at any moment. *I don't have to be kept away from your party, you know. I won't burst into tears over the guac.*

The Fakers: Friends who would profess they understood, but their words and actions proved otherwise. Erika fit in here, going off on oblivious tangents about her mom interfering with wedding planning. *At least her mom will BE at her wedding.*

The Grim Reapers: A small percentage, but some 'friends' would tell stories about so-and-so who fought cancer, had chemotherapy, and then died. *Seriously, how does that make me feel better?*

The Ghosters: The worst of all. Friends Riley thought were reliable and empathetic who would hear the news and—*poof!*—vanish.

The most recent ghosting happened the previous November. A friend of Riley and Piper's had just moved in with her boyfriend and invited them over for a game night. They were getting ready when the call came through—Maggie was in the ER, doubled over in horrific pain. The doctors were running tests with plans to admit her as soon as a bed became available. Piper stepped in, calling their friend to cancel, and sat with Riley until morning when the heartbreaking diagnosis was made—a recurrence of ovarian cancer, Stage 3C.

A day later, Riley called their loved-up gal pal to apologize personally for the sudden cancelation. The girl insisted it was "fine, really" and promised to have Riley and Piper over another time, but months passed and a do-over never happened. In fact, no texts, no emails—nothing, not even a check-in to see how Riley or her mom were doing. Maybe the girl didn't know what to say, maybe Maggie's illness slipped her mind, or maybe Riley's situation brought up feelings about her own parents' mortality? Perhaps she just wasn't a kind person to begin with and Riley never saw it. Whatever it was, Riley had no clue. The girl's hasty exit from her life came at the most vulnerable time, leaving her feeling disposable, a burden, unimportant. No wonder she chose to shut people out or fake it, only sharing happy aspects of her life.

As she mulled over what to type, her phone woke up again.

You stayed 2 celebrate?

Ben clearly didn't know that she never made it to Minnesota or the championship game, let alone party with Josh post-win. *And maybe it's better that way...*

She typed quickly. *Yeah!* And paused. The less time embellishing the lie, the better. *Hey, how'd the interviews go? Bakery or Broadway?* She hit send.

The beaming face with smiling eyes emoji popped up on her phone again with *Broadway, baby!!!*

"YES!" She bounced in her chair, forgetting where she was until two guys at the far end of the wooden table cleared their throats loudly. Her fingers raced to answer.

CONGRATS! Tell me everything.

Three dots danced up and down on her screen—Ben was composing something.

Meet now?

Now? She paused. *Makes sense.* Most Broadway musicals were dark on Mondays. She typed and hit send.

Ok. Need to drop off my stuff @home first. Meet me at mine in 30?

His answer was immediate—the thumbs-up emoji.

TWENTY-TWO

"Shit!" Ben's shoulders met his ears. *Fuck, fuck, fuck!* He squeezed a small stone in his hand, trying to play it cool. The concerned stares of people strolling past on St. Mark's Place scorched his skin, the yellowy-purple bruises under his eyes surely adding a menacing backstory to his questionable behavior. *Don't look at me! Look at that bloke over there, pissing in the shop's doorway.*

He had one try left. *Hit her window. Make this one count.* He lobbed the stone into the air, but it fell short just as Riley appeared, nose to glass. She pushed her window open and leaned over the screen-free sill with a sudden intake of breath.

The bruises...I should've warned her.

A soft smile lifted her cheeks. "Forgot how to text, Fagan?"

"Forgot to charge my phone, and your door's buzzer doesn't work."

"Argh, sorry. I'll be right down."

Ben moved closer to her front door, watching late-night shoppers, bags bulging with collectibles, leaving the tiny comic book store across the street. Just shy of 10:30 p.m., the evening air had cooled considerably from the stickiness of the day, making a jacket—or in Ben's case, his purple hoodie—a necessity. He inhaled a deep breath, excited to see Riley. Within moments, she appeared in dark jeans, a t-shirt, and flats, her denim jacket hugging her curves.

"Hi." Closing the door behind her, the smile remained on Riley's lips but slowly abandoned her eyes. "Aw, Ben, your poor face. Piper told me."

"Yeah. Good thing purple's my fave color, right?"

"It looks sore."

139

"No, worst is over. Now I'm just ugly."

"Hardly!" With a hint of giddiness in her voice, the word leapt from her lips and stole Ben's breath.

Wait? Really? REALLY? Did she just...flirt with me?

Her eyes darted to the sidewalk and her fingers tugged the closure on her cross-body purse. *Zip zip zip!* Back and forth. She pulled her bottom lip into her mouth, biting it like that single word had said way too much and she wanted to reel it back in. "So, you hungry? Where you wanna go?"

"Anywhere we can have a drink and a chinwag."

"Okay! Let's go...this way." She swiveled to the right, leading Ben towards Second Avenue.

"How was uni today?" asked Ben.

"Good. Lots going on with graduation next month, but that's boring. Tell me about your job! Piper said you're singing on Broadway! Oh my God, BEN!" She squeezed his arm.

He smiled at her hand on his upper arm, his eyes hopping to hers. "Actually, Piper got it wrong. It's a singing waiter job ON Broadway. We serve food and perform musical numbers."

"That place at West 53rd?" Ben nodded and Riley's hand returned to her purse strap. "It's been around for *ages*. You're literally singing for your supper."

"I am!" He winced. *She thought I was in a Broadway musical.* "I know it's not a proper acting job..."

"Ben, it's a start—a good one."

"I hope so." He stared at a guy on a bike up ahead weaving back and forth on the sidewalk.

"What was the audition like?"

"Different, nerve-racking. We had to sing in the restaurant in front of the artistic director *and* customers. Luckily the diners seemed to like me."

"What did you sing?"

"I started with 'City of Stars' from *La La Land*, then did *Rent*'s 'Seasons of Love', but they cut me off—oh, careful." The cyclist, refusing to get off the sidewalk, increased his speed. Ben gently clasped Riley's arm, guiding her out of harm's way.

She glared at the speeding bike. "I hate when adults cycle on the sidewalk. I always try to force them back onto the road where they belong."

An amused smirk crinkled his eyes as he let go of her arm. "Your feisty is showing again. Like it."

She smiled at Ben. "So, why did they cut you off mid-song?"

"I was the fifth person singing that *Rent* tune, so they asked me to do 'Take What You Got' from *Kinky Boots*. It's a song two blokes sing in a pub. I had to do both parts."

"Ooh, I like that one! Sounds like typecasting was going on there—British actor, British character?"

"Yeah, they had a British bloke, but he took a job on a cruise ship. They didn't want an American doing a dodgy accent, so they were keen. I moved on to the restaurant and customer service job interview stuff straight after. By late afternoon, I got the call—job was mine."

"This is amazing." Riley leaned in. "You'll perform, be in the middle of everything. You might even serve someone who could help your career. Casting agents have to eat, too. I think it's great."

"Cheers, Riles. Hey, you should come by! They have amazing waffle fries."

"You had me at potato!" She giggled. "When do you start?"

"Thursday. Hopefully my bruises will have faded so I won't put diners off their chicken parm. My first five days will be training. By the third, I'll be singing, and on the fifth, I get my own serving section. It might be multitasking hell. God help me if I dump a sloppy joe in someone's lap. I really need tips—the wages aren't great."

"Turn on that cheeky British charm and you'll win them over

no problem."

"You think?"

"You'll become a favorite in no time."

She really thinks I can do this. "I don't want to blow it. I'm going to spend this week swotting up on all the Broadway songs I don't know."

"I'm happy you're staying." She smiled.

"Me too." His eyes lingered over her lips. *Riley, if you gave me a sign, I SO would...*

They strolled in silence past several stores and a crowd of chatty students leaving a bubble tea shop.

"I had a bit of a wander after my audition. I was too wired to head back to Hunter's, so I faffed around Times Square."

Riley flashed a sarcastic smile. "Yeah, 'cause Times Square is *relaxing.*"

"It was bonkers! I thought Piccadilly Circus was barmy with the screens and people darting everywhere, but Times Square..." He blew out his cheeks. "Total sensory overload, but cool, too." His hands settled in his hoodie pockets. "Oh! I got you a present."

"A present?"

"It's also an apology for *almost* spilling your engagement news to Piper." He pulled out a colorful wrapper folded in half.

"Fun Dip!" Riley laughed, clutching it to her chest. "I love this stuff. How'd you know?"

"That morning in your flat—you lit up like a Christmas tree when you saw it."

"We grew up with it. Tastes like Kool-Aid powder, but sour— in a good way. Did you try it?"

"You think my tongue is naturally blue?" He stuck it out then laughed. "The candy stick was the best part."

"I know, right? Thank you!" She rooted around in her purse, removing a small pink box to make room for Ben's gift.

"More candy?"

"Yeah, say hello to dinner." She shook colorful candies into her hand. "Want some?"

Ben squinted. "What are they? Pieces of chalk?"

"They're candy hearts. They're available around Valentine's Day. See? They have sayings."

He scrunched up his nose. "They look stale."

"The candy or the sayings?" She smirked and stepped around a row of wheelie recycling bins blocking the sidewalk. "Here." She grabbed Ben's hand, pouring a bunch into his palm. "Erika stocked up for her wedding but then found out she could custom order her own messages. She was about to chuck 'em."

"You should've let her." He nudged the candies with his finger, flipping them over. "We have Love Hearts back home. They're bigger, better looking. Riles, these are crap."

"Taste one!"

"Why would I pop something so hideous in my mouth?"

Riley giggled.

Ben looked up, flicking his hair from his eyes. "What?"

"I said that to Piper once, but it wasn't about candy…"

Ben broke into a laugh. *Should I go there? Yeah, go on.* "And despite that, you *still* said yes to Josh?!"

Scrunching her eyes, Riley burst into full-on laughter, giving him a playful shove. "Benjaminnnn!"

Still giggling, he picked up several hearts, reading the sayings aloud. "Nuts 4 U, 1 On 1, Pugs &…Kittens? What?! What the actual *fuck*?"

Riley laughed and traded the box for her phone, tucking the candy into her purse. "They don't say 'what the actual fuck'."

"Well, they should do!" He hid the hearts in the pocket of his jeans. "I'll find you the real deal, the British ones. Once you go Brit, you just can't quit…but tell that to Piper. I was probably her worst date since the bed bug bloke." He glanced across the road at a drunk guy yanking his equally wasted friend from a mound of leaky trash bags. A chuckle left Ben's lips as he swept the candy dust from his hands and with it, his conversation with Riley. Silence swallowed up the air around them. *Oh, shit. Did I cross a line?* He peered sideways, testing the temperature, but Riley wasn't shooting daggers or shaking her head in annoyance. She was staring at her phone. *Hmm.* "Riles?"

She turned her head suddenly, stuffing her phone in her jacket. "Uh, yeah?"

"It's not weird, is it? That I went on a date with Piper?"

"No. Do you feel weird?"

"No." He toyed with the strings dangling from his hood. "I just don't want you to think I was letchin' after your friends."

"Pip asked *you* out, Ben. If anyone was letching…" She cleared her throat.

"I hope I didn't hurt her feelings."

"As long as you didn't diss her puppets, she'll be fine."

Approaching the intersection of St. Mark's and Second Avenue, the flashing red 'Don't Walk' hand halted their progress. Riley fiddled with her purse's strap. "Can I ask you something?"

"Sure, anything."

They waited for a few cars to pass then ran across the street, a speeding taxi honking at their heels. Ben raised a protective arm, shielding Riley until she skipped over the curb.

"How can you work here?" She veered right, heading south on Second Avenue. "Do you have a green card?"

"I have an H-2B visa from an indie film I finished in LA two months ago." His eyes drifted to a homeless man up the street who was brandishing a squeaky-wheeled shopping cart, its metallic whine competing with a thumping synth-pop song emanating from a building up ahead. *I know this old song.* "The project wrapped early and my visa was still valid, so I stayed for pilot season and picked up an advert for crisps." *Got it! New Order, "Bizarre Love Triangle". Haven't heard this in ages.*

"Ben Fagan, potato chip pusher—I approve!"

Bobbing his head to the song's irregular drumbeat, a cocky smile lifted the corners of his mouth. "I'm a natural, me! All those prawn cocktail crisp sarnies—"

"Sarnies?" Riley scrunched her eyebrows.

"Sandwiches made with spongy white bread, tons of butter, and prawn cocktail crisps—*chips*. I lived on those things growing up."

"Prawn…like shrimp? Fish-flavored potato chips? That's your go-to?"

"I don't follow the crowd, Hope."

"Me neither. I'm a Funyuns fan."

"Fun-what?"

"Funyuns—onion-flavored rings. When I was tiny, I wore them like bracelets. Not exactly the most sophisticated of snacks, but I like them." Riley swerved around a half-eaten burrito splattered on the sidewalk.

"I reckon there's nothing cooler than liking what you like, doing what you want, even if the crowd thinks it's uncool. Be true to yourself, be your own person." The song's verse melted into a shimmering chorus and Ben slipped into a head bopping, close-eyed sway, his lips mouthing, "*Say the words that I can't say*"…until a honking taxi popped him back to reality.

Riley smiled. "Think you'll do more commercials?"

"No, I need a regular gig. That's a stipulation with this visa. You get it for a specific job for a specific timeframe. They're pretty strict about what you can do."

"So, that stripper job—you must've been paid under the table."

"So under I was practically lying on the floor!" He chuckled.

"Needs must, huh?" Riley raised an eyebrow.

"Exactly."

"How much time do you have?" Riley pulled her phone from her pocket again. "I mean, before the visa expires."

"Another month, but the diner manager is filling out the forms so I can get an extension. Foreign restaurant workers get this visa all the time. Hopefully, I can stay until mid-November, and if all goes well and the diner wants to keep me, they can request another extension. I still want to find proper acting work, though, and when that happens, the production would file for my next visa. Things are looking up!"

Riley peeked at the screen and tucked it away again.

Why does she keep doing that? It's like she's here, but part of her isn't. "You okay?"

"Yeah, yep." She smiled quickly. "So, let's celebrate!" She stretched her neck, angling for a better view down Second Avenue. "Somewhere fun."

Ben stopped in front of a café-cum-nighttime speakeasy. "Like this place? Shall we check it out?" A chalkboard stood sentry by the entrance with messily drawn daisies and *TONIGHT: CIDER WITH ROSIE* scrawled across its black enamel. He pulled open the door for Riley and followed her inside to a small bar with a cramped performance space. An earnest bohemian couple was mid-song and plucking tiny instruments, crooning something about a farm and its failed harvest.

"Jesus, lutes!" Ben's exaggerated look of horror matched Riley's scrunched-up face. They caught each other's expression, burst into snorting laughter, and tripped over themselves to make a hasty retreat.

"What the fuck was that?" Ben swept his hair from his eyes. "Did we step through a wormhole to the 16th century?"

Still giggling at their hurried escape, Riley's expression changed to concern. "Oh my God, I feel bad, though! Do you think they noticed us leaving?"

"No. They're too busy worrying about the bloody harvest."

They both creased up with laughter again.

She gets my sense of humor. God, she's cute when she laughs...

Once Riley had caught her breath, she pointed across the street. "C'mon. How 'bout that Mexican place?"

Ben jigged on the spot, succumbing to the retro-pop still vibrating from the building next door. "Or there?"

"You wanna go clubbing? On a Monday? They're playing my mom's music..."

His eyes traced the nondescript black metal door and its small square window. The light inside spilled out onto the pavement in streaky spears. "When's your first class tomorrow?"

"Not 'til four."

Yes! Ben pumped the air with his fist. "PERFECT!" He leapt over to the handle, tugging it with gusto, but when it didn't budge, his eyes shot to a torn note hanging from a single piece of tape inside the window. *PRIVATE PARTY TONITE* sneered back through glass dappled with a thousand fingerprints. *Nooo!* Ben's mouth, his shoulders—his whole body drooped. "Bollocks."

"Come on!" Riley grasped his hand and pulled him down the street.

TWENTY-THREE

Two shops down, Riley stopped abruptly outside an ajar door with *POST NO BILLS* stenciled in white paint, the scent of onions and burnt bacon creeping around its edge. *I hope this still works.* She turned to Ben and shouted over a surging song chorus. "Watch your step and duck your head!"

Pushing through the door like she owned the place, Riley led Ben into a dingy pocket-sized kitchen. A guy wearing a white uniform in need of a good bleaching fought with a bubbling deep fryer while another in a hair net flattened sizzling burgers into a charred grill. If they minded the invasion, they didn't say, and Riley didn't ask. She dashed through, dragging Ben around a cluttered steel counter, a yawning server texting on her phone, and towers of oversized pickle jars. They popped through a swinging door into a cramped corner, home to four chrome and vinyl booths that had seen better decades. The worn seats didn't faze the college-age clientele though; they sat shoulder to shoulder downing cheap beers and tapping away on Apple's latest must-haves.

Riley paused long enough for Ben to shout in her ear. "Snuck in before, Hope?"

"All through freshman year." She eyed the lazy legs and feet snaking out from the booths, blocking their escape route. "Glad to see the tradition continues."

Still holding hands, they stepped over the booth-bound obstacle course and through a fence of boisterous drinkers clogging the bar's nook, hitting the dance floor as the DJ sloppily cut off "Bizarre Love Triangle".

Dancers frowned and shouted obscenities. "Aw! What the fuck,

148

man?" "Not great, Bob!"

"Bob?" Ben chucked, his eyes flitting around the claustrophobic dive. "That's got to be the least showbiz DJ name ever." The impatient tempo of synth drums burst from the speakers and Ben froze, his eyes collapsing into smiley crescents. "No wayyyy!" He leaned in toward Riley's ear, his smile flirting with her hair. "That's my ringtone! 'Take On Me'…a-ha?! Bloody brilliant! C'mon!" He pulled her into the crowd and released her hand.

Jumping up and down, the impossible happened—the higher Ben bounced, the wider his grin stretched. He closed his eyes, shutting out everything but the urgent synth-pop, singing every word like his life depended on it.

Why is he so into this music? He wasn't even born when it came out. Riley danced tentatively by his side, more interested in watching her friend let loose than breaking a sweat of her own, although the floor was jammed so tight, perspiration already dampened her clothing. She checked her phone quickly—no texts from Maggie, all clear—and tapped Ben on the arm. "Thirsty?"

Eyes half closed, he shook his head. "Soon."

Once the song faded out, they zigzagged through the crush seeking celebratory drinks, but a rousing guitar calling all revelers snapped Ben back to the dance floor like he was tethered with an elastic band. "Oh, DJ Bob's on a roll! It's Billy-pissing-Idol!"

Riley laughed and rejoined the throng, mesmerized by Ben's endless energy for pogoing and flailing, letting loose…

"Dancing with myself, oh, oh!!"

…and shouting the lyrics as loud as his lungs would permit. *Ben dances like a little kid who's had too much sugar. He doesn't care what anyone thinks…*

"Hope, c'mere!"

Screw it! I don't care either!

Riley joined in, swaying her hips and tossing her hair. Ben

laughed and clutched her hands, encouraging her to jump higher, to sing louder, his smile bright and reassuring. "Go on, Riles!"

She jumped and giggled, breathlessly shouting the chorus with Ben, letting their inner goofs rise to the surface as their cheeks ached with glee. "Dancing with myself, oh, oh, oh, OH!" They howled with laughter, playfully punching the air as they shook their heads until the room was a blur of colorful twirls and swirling light. If students were staring, the pair had no clue—and they didn't care. A few times they stumbled and bounced off each other, releasing more giggles and leaping about.

I am dying, but this is FUN! Riley fought for breath and grabbed Ben's hand. *My legs hurt and my lungs hate me, but I haven't laughed this hard in so long!*

The song was building to its sweaty finish when DJ Bob abruptly plunged into Cyndi Lauper's "Time After Time". Most people groaned and stomped off the dance floor while a few drunkenly fumbled and paired up. The couple at Ben's shoulder began devouring each other's faces, their roaming hands getting as much of a workout as their mouths.

A twinge of heat flooded Riley's chest. Normally, she wouldn't react at all, but normally Ben wouldn't be stroking her hand with his thumb. *He hasn't let go.* Adorable Ben with the unruly hair and stupid Christmas socks and stubble where no guy should have stubble. The warmth of his finger caressing her skin quickened her breath. *Riley, you're just lonely. Let go.* Releasing her grip, she gave him an exhausted smile. "Get that drink now?"

"Yeah, I'm parched." He smiled back.

They inched their way over to the bar, which was a no bigger than a kitchen counter, and joined the thirsty swarm. Their talk skirted what had just happened, tackling the weather, Piper's puppets, and favorite alcoholic beverages (a sidecar for Riley, Stella for Ben). After what felt like the longest five minutes of waiting in her

150

life, Riley ordered a soda for herself and treated Ben to a bottle of his fave brew, the grin returning to his face when she pressed it into his hand.

"It's been too long."

"Since your last Stella?" She took a quick sip of her soda, walking a few steps over to a claim a sliver of ledge on the wall for their drinks.

"No, dancing like that." Ben wiped his face with his forearm, removing beads of sweat but not his beaming smile. "Surrendering to the music, forgetting my problems."

I actually forgot too...about cancer, about Josh. Riley stared into her drink.

"You having fun, Riles?"

"I am." Her chin lifted along with her voice.

"Really? You don't have to pretend—"

"No, I am—really! I can't remember the last time I danced...or went out on a Monday. It's nice to escape for a bit."

He took a large swig of beer. "I think we should make this the rule and not the exception."

"Clubbing on Mondays?"

The smile refused to abandon his face. "No, doing things we've never done—or rarely do. We could even make it a competition. You up for it?"

Riley hated being pushed out of her comfort zone. "Depends on what those things are."

"Nothing illegal—mind you, I wasn't the one who snuck in here without paying cover, so that's on you, Hope."

Nothing illegal, says the charming kleptomaniac.

He set down his beer and took off his hoodie. His t-shirt—a damp Duran Duran concert tee—tucked into the front of his jeans, drew a grin to Riley's lips.

"Is that one of those retro tees from Urban Outfitters?"

"Blimey O'Riley! What do you take me for? A bandwagon-jumping millennial? This shirt was born in 1984!"

"Wow, it's in pretty good shape for a relic." She laughed. "I like the colors. So, what's with you and the eighties, then? The Pac-Man tattoo, this place—you were wearing a Police tee the other night. You weren't even born in the eighties."

"The shirts were my uncle's. Mum kept them in an old trunk." He folded his hoodie, piling it behind him on the ledge. "Mum grew up in the eighties, so—"

A drunk dude bowled into Riley, slopping her soda. "Ow, shit!" Ben swung back around. "Riles?"

"Hey, gorgessssssssss!" the wasted guy slurred, a wobbly hand headed towards her cheek.

Riley smacked it away. "Don't fucking touch me!" The sudden fury in her eyes deflated the drunk's bravado.

"For fuck's sake, mate! Bugger off!" Ben pushed him away and moved closer to Riley, his eyes concerned. "Did he get you?"

"I'm okay…just sticky." She shook her soaked hand, which was dripping with soda, but her clothes had escaped unscathed. Leaving her empty glass on the ledge, her eyes pored over Ben. He was untouched, too.

He picked up his hoodie. "Use this to dry off."

"No—"

"It's old and ratty. Go on, it's fine." He placed his hoodie in her hands and shot an annoyed look at the drunk bouncing off people like a loose pinball. "I'm glad he didn't stain your top."

"Or yours. That's a family heirloom." Riley reluctantly did a quick cleanup and handed back his jacket. "What were you saying about your mom?"

"Oh, yeah, this music." Ben stuffed his hoodie on the ledge and picked up his beer. "Mum played it all the bleedin' time growing up. My strange obsession with a-ha is her fault—I even had their first album on vinyl—but in all honesty, I think old music sounds better than the crap that's out today." He tilted the beer to his lips then thought better of it, pulling the bottle away. "I know some people think eighties music's cheesy, but it's fun and heartfelt. Listen to the lyrics—there's a lot of truth there."

"My mom likes it. She calls it memory music."

"Yeah, exactly. I think the music you're into at our age kinda stays with you..." Ben swigged his beer and glanced back at the bar. "Want another?"

"I'm fine, thanks." Riley didn't want Ben treating her on his celebratory night out, and she had already blown most of tomorrow's grocery money on their drinks. "Some eighties songs are okay, but I don't really feel a connection."

"I bet I can find an eighties song that speaks to you."

Riley laughed. "Good luck with that."

"I love a challenge, Hope." He surveyed the room. "You do too, I suspect."

"You think?"

"Yeah! Making TV programs to help people feel good? Can't be easy to create happily ever afters, but I bet you'll be great at it."

"Aw, thanks. It comes from an honest place—so many times, I wish *I* could escape."

"Tell me about it!" A whistle pierced the bar's speakers and Ben's ears pricked up. He pointed at his shirt. "Ah, Duran Duran! 'New Moon on Monday'—one of my mum's faves."

"Ha, one of my mom's, too. Our moms would get along famously," said Riley. "You must miss your parents, being so far from home."

"I miss *her* a lot, but I talk to her all the time. The old man left when I was a year old."

"Oh, you don't see him?"

"Nope. He was a rat-arsed bastard back then and probably still is now, if he's alive. I have no clue." He raised his beer and paused above the rim. "And I don't care."

"I'm so sorry."

He gulped a large mouthful. "Don't be. I'm better off rid. He drank, did drugs, sponged off benefits. Never married Mum. She was the earner. She worked damn hard in a biscuit factory—with the hairnet, blue smock, the whole deal—early mornings, extra shifts, but could only afford a bedsit—a one-room rental—in a rough area of Edinburgh. We'd often get meals from a local food bank, but she did her best for me." Ben picked at the label on his bottle. "He was supposed to look after me while she worked, but one day Mum came home and found me alone in my cot, wailing with a soiled nappy. I'd been left there all day. Apparently, he used the cash Mum saved for baby food on drugs. Anyway, the asshole never came back, so good riddance to bad rubbish." Raising his beer to his lips, he downed the lot.

"You don't call him Dad?"

"He doesn't deserve to be called Dad." The bruises around Ben's eyes added a sinister feel to his words. "To me, he's a sperm donor." He stifled a hiccup. "Do you get on with yours? You only mention your mum."

"He's out of the picture."

"Dead?"

"Might as well be."

Ben raised his eyebrows.

"Sorry, that sounds crass." Riley winced. "We were insepara-ble, once. I used to be a total daddy's girl, but not in a princess-y way. It was sports. Dad was all about sports and put me in hockey and taekwondo when I was three, but hockey was my thing. I loved the sounds: the *ksssh-kssh-kssh* of skates carving the ice, the crack of the puck striking your stick"—her smile stretched with each memory—"and my favorite, the puck ringing off the crossbar with a

CLINK! There's a freedom with hockey that you don't get with other sports—flying over the ice, your lungs full of cold, crisp air—ahh, the best." *I miss it.* A burn rose in her throat. *Don't...* She blinked and looked away, pausing to swallow the bittersweet memories, then turned back to Ben. "He also taught me how to scale the rock walls at his gym when I was five."

Ben's eyes widened. "Five?"

"I know, right? I must be part monkey or something. Once I mastered that, we moved to the boulders in Central Park. Bouldering is such a rush."

"Wow, who *are* you?" He chuckled. "I was probably eating dirt in the park at that age."

"I swam, too."

"Part mermaid, part monkey—a *mer-monkey*, that's what you are!"

"You're got more monkey in you than me! All long arms, skinny legs—"

"You know, that's really weird 'cause sometimes I do fling my poop at people I don't like."

"Ben!" She grimaced, playfully punching his arm.

"Okay, I'm a monkey, but I'm cute with it, right?" He winked.

Riley felt her heart leap. *So cute.*

"So, you swam competitively?"

"No. Mom almost drowned when she was nine, so she made me take lessons." She pressed her lips tight. "But sports was our thing—me and Dad, but then he got promoted and we barely saw him."

"What was his job?"

"He worked at an ad agency, their TV broadcasting division. He often had late edits or sometimes he'd be out schmoozing clients. That's how he met Mom, at a work party in '93. She was the creative specialist in the ad department for Barnes and Noble."

"So, you inherited your love of TV from your dad and books from your mom."

"Yeah. I think Mom hoped I'd become a writer, but as long as I was doing something that made me happy, she cheered me on. Dad was determined that I'd end up with the USA women's hockey team, but I made sure that wouldn't happen."

"Why?"

"It's a long story." Riley fussed with her purse.

"I've got time."

"Well…" Riley looked up. "Mom hurt her back when I was nine and had to take a leave of absence from work. Dad wasn't around much to help—working on budgets, lots of late hours."

Ben shook his head.

"Turns out he wasn't just on top of budgets but also a coordinator named Clarissa. He left us a few months later, divorced Mom, and married Clarissa when I was eleven."

"Shit."

"Yeah. I was devastated. He tore our family apart. I skipped their wedding and rebelled by dumping his last name a week after he remarried. I've gone by Mom's ever since."

"Hope is your mom's maiden name?"

She nodded. "I also quit taekwondo and hockey because they reminded me of him."

"But didn't you miss it—hockey?"

"Sometimes. I'd still skate with Josh, practice shots in his backyard, and have pick-up games with friends, but I wasn't part of a league anymore. I didn't want to make Dad's dream for me come true after what he did."

"Makes sense. You've known Josh forever then, eh?"

"Since I was eight. We met playing hockey at the community center, went to the same schools, but didn't date until the summer after freshman year of college. I bumped into him, he asked me out, and the rest is history…" *I gotta move this away from Josh. No engagement talk—I can't stomach it.* "So, yeah…Daddy dearest let us down."

"Does he still live in New York?"

She shrugged. "I cut ties after he married Clarissa and told Mom I wanted nothing to do with him. I probably have half-siblings, but I wouldn't know them if they were sitting beside me on the subway. Broken families—fun, huh?"

They both stood in silence for a moment, Nik Kershaw's "Wouldn't It Be Good" blasting through the speakers.

Riley laughed. "Now that DJ Bob and I have bummed you out…"

"No, it feels good sharing this stuff with someone who understands."

"It does…yeah." Riley smiled.

DJ Bob chopped off Mr. Kershaw, leaping into Prince's "Let's Go Crazy".

"I LOVE this one!" Ben shouted, his eyes wild. "You in? Real life can wait four minutes, yeah?"

"It can wait all night, Monkey!" Riley laughed and raced him to the center of the dance floor.

TWENTY-FOUR

Lit up by the jaundiced yellow glow of the Funky Town awning, Riley fished her keychain from her purse. "I'm gonna feel it tomorrow. My only exercise is swimming, and I haven't been in weeks."

"See?" Ben crammed his hands into the front pockets of his jeans, his fingers reuniting with a few candy hearts. "Not only am I expanding your social horizons but your physical fitness ones, too! And coming from me, Tragic Mike, that's saying something."

"It is." She laughed. "I'm sorry I couldn't buy you another beer."

"Riles, I wanted your company and a natter more than booze."

The smile lifting his whisper made her blush. *Adorable. Charming English guys like you don't stay single long.* She pointed her key at the door, her puffin keychain poking out from her palm. "Well, it's almost 2 a.m. I should get…"

Ben's eyes left hers, dropping to his sneakers scuffing the sidewalk. "Yeah, I have songs to learn tomor—today, actually. Can't show up and forget the words." He looked up, running a hand through his hair. It was even wilder than usual from his uninhibited dance floor acrobatics. The memory made Riley giggle, and Ben chuckled like he was in on the joke, too. "I had a good time. Thanks for hanging out."

Riley nodded. "Thanks for getting me out!"

"Anytime." His eyes traced her mouth, all hilarity vanishing from his warm gaze.

Riley felt every second of his stare, her mouth going dry. *I can't help but wonder what he'd be like, how he'd taste…* She glanced down the street. "You okay getting back to Hunter's?"

"Yeah, I'm good." He pulled the strings dangling from his hood.

"Good." Riley weaved on the spot. *Should we...hug? I always hug my friends goodbye, but...he didn't hug Piper. This is awkward!*

Ben rubbed his nose, dampening a nervous chuckle. "Well, 'night." He rolled back on his heels, stuffing his hands in the pockets of his hoodie. "I'll text you, yeah?"

"Yeah." Riley gave a kind smile, her final goodbye. "Get home safe."

Ben backed up, lifting his hand in an overly enthusiastic wave. "You too!"

Riley turned, hiding her giggle as she unlocked the door.

Staring skyward, Ben picked up speed along St. Mark's Place, his face and neck burning up from the inferno of embarrassment sizzling under his skin.

Fagan! You absolute muppet!! "You too!" What kind of goodbye was THAT? What's she gonna think? And I should've hugged her. I have no problem shagging a girl within an hour of meeting her but didn't move in to hug Riley good night? It's just a hug, idiot! Why does that scare you so much?

Stepping off the curb at Third Avenue, a taxi's horn screamed and Ben leapt back to the safety of the sidewalk, the red 'Don't Walk' hand scolding him to play it safe.

TWENTY-FIVE

A bellyaching laugh rose from Maggie's couch. "Oh, Sue, you're killing me!"

Setting a bag of frozen blueberries on the counter, Riley broke out into a smile. *It's good she's enjoying something.* Maggie hadn't had a lot to laugh about recently, but this call from a former work colleague was brightening her Tuesday afternoon considerably. As much as mother and daughter liked to swear by 'third time lucky', this cancer fight was taking its toll on Maggie's body as well as her spirit, so any little distraction—a new release on Netflix, a bag of donut holes, or a phone call from an old friend now living in Kentucky—was celebrated and very welcome.

Maggie's favorite distraction sat beside the blender on the kitchen counter, her birthday gift from Riley—a 'book of the month' subscription box, which she worked double shifts to pay for. Just two months into the program, bookworm Maggie was already addicted to the mid-month deliveries, giddy for the next book to be devoured. She couldn't have asked for a more thoughtful gift from her daughter, but for Riley, the present was something more. The yearlong purchase was an act of faith that said, *You're going to be here a year from now, Mom.*

Riley pored over the recipe on her phone one more time. *Blueberries, lime juice, balsamic vinegar...* Since Maggie's chemo regime had changed, her taste and smell were off, making eating unpleasant, sometimes impossible, and yet, she'd developed weird cravings for limes and raw snap peas. She couldn't afford to lose any more weight, so Riley was following the advice of the cancer clinic's nutritionist, making healthy but easy-to-tolerate smoothies and snacks, like blueberry yogurt parfaits. The ingredients had cost more than her mom had given her, but Riley covered the shortfall without saying a word. Skipping lunch was a small price to pay if her mom felt a little better.

A text invaded her screen. Josh again, fifth text within twenty minutes—another video. Slick with sweat and grunting, he was doing CrossFit handstand pushups against the wall of his college's gym. His soaked tank top had slipped down exposing his rock-hard six-pack. Someone was whooping and clapping in the background.

Riley couldn't deny it: Josh, in his flimsy exercise shorts that flaunted every bulge and outline, looked mouthwateringly hot. If she had received these messages last year, she would be texting back, craving a FaceTime rendezvous as soon as she was somewhere private. But, today, his horny onslaught wasn't turning her on; it was testing her patience. She had already texted back three times, telling him she couldn't hook up over FaceTime, not with Maggie in the next room and a mandatory four o'clock lecture just hours away. If he kept this up, she'd have to mute her phone.

She set it down and reached into a cupboard, grabbing the sugar. A sharp twinge rippled through her upper back, her wince morphing into a thankful giggle. The outing with Ben, complete with awkward goodbye, had left her with a souvenir: pulled muscles from their flirty dancing during Salt-N-Pepa's "Push It". She felt immediately nostalgic for the night before. The cheesy eighties disco had proven to be a lift she so desperately needed, even if the fairy tale faded as soon as the gaudy awning outside her apartment came into view. Ben was a fun and willing sidekick, and best of all, the words 'cancer', 'debt', and 'poor you' never once fell from his lips. Maybe that was the life hack? Don't share your greatest fears or worries with your friends, and you too can forget they exist—for a few hours at least. What better way to play make-believe than with an actor, and a hot one at that.

161

The bottle of lime juice lit up, illuminated by her nearby phone. Another text. Her shoulders fell. *Josh?*

Ben.

Ben! A jolt of electricity shot through Riley's veins. She read his message.

Riles!!! Mission accmplished!!!!

That was it. Ben's excessive use of exclamation marks and dyslexic spelling were a far cry from Josh's bulging muscles. *Hmm.* With an eye on her phone, she poured the berries into a saucepan. Would Ben elaborate?

DING. An attachment arrived—a Spotify playlist simply titled '4 Riles!!!'

She opened it, finding "The Sun Always Shines on TV" by a-ha and nothing else. *Great title. I like!* Parfait-making could wait. She bent down and pulled her tangled earbud cords from her tote.

The song began slowly with tentative synthesizer chords and the singer's falsetto vocals soaring over top. Riley scratched her eyebrow. *Where is this going?* But then the song shrugged off its intro and built up and up and up into a crash of electronic drums and racing guitars, a circus of urgency. Rallying her attention, its keyboards pulsated with reckless abandon, but it was the song's evocative lyrics that took her breath away. They sounded like thoughts she had jotted down in her journal—now abandoned—six months earlier...

November 10, 2017

It's not just feeling sad about Mom. There's more to it than that.

I look deep within, desperate to find something to lift my mood, but my search is for nothing. All I see inside is emptiness, fear...darkness. I feel so down, sometimes I don't recognize who I am anymore.

The worst part...I can't articulate what's gone wrong. It's like my brain has the reason locked away somewhere and I don't have the key. So instead I get dragged down when all I want is to find out why I feel like this—so I can climb back up, be myself again. Then maybe I can feel happy, even for a little while.

I wish life was like it is on TV—love conquers all, problems fade away, everything's perfect and everyone gets their happily ever after.

A lump grew in Riley's throat. *My journal matches this song. It's so true, so...me.* The rawness, the familiarity—someone else had written the song's words, but they spoke to her heart about *her* fears, her hopes. Depression was always lurking over her shoulder, but maybe one day she'd have the power to look it in the eye and defeat it for good—or at least be better at taming it.

Don't let Mom see me like this. She wiped away a tear, thankful Maggie was on the other side of the wall, merrily chatting away on her phone.

Ben's adorable English accent played in her head. *"I bet I can find an eighties song that speaks to you."*

Mission accmplished, Brit boy. Mission accmplished.

"What class do you have this afternoon?" A small amount of blueberry yogurt parfait remained in Maggie's tall glass.

"The senior colloquium."

"That's lectures, isn't it?"

"Yep. I have to stay awake for this one. The speaker is an assistant director at Warner Bros., and she's talking about working with actors and procedures on set in Burbank."

"Sounds right up your alley." Maggie licked her spoon. "If you have to leave now, sweetheart, I'll be fine. I can't wait to dive into my new book."

"I can stay for another forty minutes. You can't get rid of me that easily." Riley's chuckle quickly retreated along with her smile as her spoon dug around her glass of yogurt and granola, a weighty silence settling over the table.

"Honey…" Maggie bit the corner of her lip. "Is something bothering you—"

"No."

"Riley." She covered her daughter's hand with her own. "Don't shut me out. Talk to me. Something's up…"

Shit. Riley stuffed a spoonful of granola in her mouth. "I'm fine." She mumbled while chewing. "There's nothing to talk about."

Maggie sighed. "I should've made you go back."

"Go back? Where?" Riley swallowed. "My apartment?"

"To therapy—when you were in high school."

"W-What? Why?"

"You seemed happier." Maggie's chin quivered. "But it didn't last and I didn't do anything about it. I let you down."

Riley's eyes widened. "No, you didn't. You had just been diagnosed with cervical cancer."

"Cancer doesn't erase parental responsibilities."

"You make it sound like I went without food or shelter. Mom, you were in agony, recovering from surgery, dealing with radiation, chemo. Your hands were more than full! And I did okay, didn't I? I still made honor roll, volunteered at the shelter, kept my part-time job."

"And I was so proud of you! But if you'd kept up your sessions, maybe your depression wouldn't have recurred. Maybe you wouldn't be feeling like *this* again. Riley, we need to talk about it. We need to deal with it, properly. It's nothing to be ashamed about—"

"There's *nothing* to talk about. Everyone gets sad sometimes.

That's life."

"But this is more than being sad, sweetheart."

It is, but... Riley chipped at a cluster of almonds and oats with her spoon.

Maggie ducked her head, trying to see past Riley's hair. "It's Josh, isn't it? The engagement."

Riley's body tensed. CRUNCH. The spoon broke through the chunk of granola. *Crap.* Her eyebrows lifted innocently. "Josh? No." A half-smile fought her stiff cheeks.

Maggie squeezed her hand. "Riley, you can call it off."

She avoided her mom's gaze, her throat tightening, refusing to give in. "I don't *want* to call it off."

"If you're happy and want to spend the rest of your life with him, I'll support your decision, but if you're unsure, feeling pressured, or scared about breaking up with him, you can tell me. I'll listen and we'll work through it together."

"I want to marry him." *Why isn't she buying it?* Riley met her mom's eyes, her voice flat yet determined. "Why do I have to justify my decision?"

"When you talk about it, you don't look happy—and that scares me."

Riley scoffed, pulling her hand away. "What you see is exhaustion, Mom. I'm scrambling to complete everything before graduation and I haven't slept well for weeks. My apartment is hell on wheels—it's boiling and sweaty and I'm lucky if I can catch four hours a night."

"And my situation isn't helping." Maggie adjusted the pretty blue scarf on her head.

"I'd worry about you even if you didn't have cancer. You're my mom, and I love you more than anything."

Maggie smiled softly.

"Things will be better after graduation." Swirling the last pieces of granola around her glass, she leaned forward and swallowed heavily, but the lump in her throat wouldn't move, lending a stilted quality to her words. "The stress will be gone."

"I remember the therapist saying a recurrence can be triggered by a major life change—"

Riley nodded. "Like graduation."

"—like an engagement," said Maggie, their words clashing.

Riley dropped the spoon in her glass. "The engagement has nothing to do with it."

"I wish I believed that. *Look* at me, honey. If that's the truth…"

I can't. Riley picked at her fingernails.

"Oh, sweetheart." Maggie wrapped a loving arm around her daughter, pulling her in. "You're young and your life is opening up to so many possibilities. Why get married now? Why rush?"

I can't tell her why. Make something up. "B-Because we've already spent three years apart and we can't do it any longer." Tears stung her eyes for the lie that was leaving her lips and for the fear that her plan was about to fall apart. She couldn't fail her mom.

"But what's another year? Have a long engagement. Give yourselves time to settle into your careers, and *then* set a date. So much is changing for you both, and you've worked so hard at college. Don't let everything you've learned go to waste. Josh will be following his dream—you should follow yours, too."

Don't. Don't cry…stick to the script. "I want us to be together."

"But your life—your happiness—isn't defined by sharing the same carpet, Riley. How will you thrive if you're disappointed, resentful? It's hard watching your husband do what he's always wanted while your dreams stay on the shelf. Trust me on that."

Riley's eyebrows peaked. "You and Dad?"

Maggie nodded slowly.

"What?" Riley eased back. "I thought—"

"Marketing was my calling? Honestly, is it anyone's?" Maggie chuckled. "No, my dream was to own a little bookshop close to home. I planned to have a counter selling fresh coffee, muffins...it was going to be a comfy hangout that celebrated a love of good books."

"Sounds incredible."

"Yeah, but the idea faded, lost somewhere between your fourth birthday and Bradley leaving us."

"How come?"

"We got turned down for a loan. Bradley said we'd apply again once he got the promotion he was promised, so we both kept working and saving. A couple years passed, still no promotion. I figured if we weren't going to try for another loan right away, we should try for a baby. You were growing up so quickly. I wanted to give you a brother or sister while you were still little, but Bradley wanted a bigger house first. So, a new house and a baby were added to the 'when Bradley gets a promotion' list. Then he finally got the promotion in 2003—and a year later, he was on the Upper West Side with Clarissa."

"Oh, Mom."

"He went for exactly what he wanted. I waited for my turn and it never came. Goodbye dream, goodbye new baby...hello divorce. After he left, I saved and planned, and a few years later, I was approved for a loan, but then it was cancer's turn to put an end to the bookshop."

Riley's eyes teared up. "Mom, I'm so sorry." She leaned in. "Why didn't you tell me?"

"You were so mad at your dad, and I didn't want to throw more gasoline on that fire. I didn't want anger to hold you back, especially when you were diagnosed with depression. You've been through enough. You know I'd do anything to keep you from getting hurt."

And I'd do anything to keep you from losing everything.

"All I'm saying is: don't wait for your turn. If Josh loves you with all his heart, he'll be cheering you on in LA, knowing that when the time is right, you'll be by his side as his equal, not his shadow. You've never been anyone's shadow—why start now?"

"So, I shouldn't move to Minnesota?"

"I can't make that decision for you, sweetheart." Maggie reached over, her thumb drying a stray tear sliding down Riley's cheek. "But I just…wish you'd put yourself first. No one else will. I know what it's like to love someone so much you'll do anything for them, but you can't lose who you are in order to do that. It's not worth it. You'll always wonder about the what-ifs? Stay true to yourself, Riley—always. Promise me?"

Riley licked her lips. "But what if staying true to yourself means you'll hurt other people?" *Josh…you…*

"Hopefully they'll understand. The people who really love you will *always* understand." Maggie kissed her daughter on the temple like she had done a thousand times before when easing the pain of a scraped knee, a hockey loss in overtime, and all the other heartaches Riley had faced growing up. Her mom smiled and returned to her parfait.

Turning back to hers, Riley's stomach dipped.

Kiss and make it better? If only that would work this time, Mom.

TWENTY-SIX

Hunter looped his arm through a mountain bike frame and picked up a box of handlebars, clearing Ben's path to the corner kitchen, open to the one-bedroom's living room. "Sorry, man. I promise this crap will be outta here tomorrow."

"Bike courier biz, eh?" Ben snatched a glass from the drying rack on the counter and stuck it under the tap, filling it with cold water. "It's really happening?"

"Yup. Can't afford to live here without a second job. I've been an English-as-a-second-language tutor, dog walker, even worked a dosa cart in Washington Square Park, but I've always wanted to be my own boss."

Ben slipped past a tower of fat tires and several fully built bikes then sat on the sofa, his knees inches away from Hunter's laptop on the coffee table. He flicked the trackpad, scrolling through a song lyrics website. "It's been ages since I rode a bike."

"It's like sex, man—you never forget." Hunter looked around his cramped apartment. "And what better way to make money, work out, and be outdoors? The guys I've got on board have experience, know the city inside out, and brought me clients—it's all good." He dumped his supplies on top of two boxes of pedals. "I'm desperate for cash. I'm still waiting for my next donor check to roll in."

"Donor?" Ben raised the glass to his lips. "Blood—"

"Sperm."

Ben choked on his water. "Wha—you're kidding?"

"Nope! My swimmers make me an easy fifteen hundred a month."

"Seriously? How often do you…"

"Twice a week. Hey, if I'm going to rub one out, I might as well get paid for it! I've been doing it for over a year, but checks don't arrive until you're six months in. FDA rules. Your jizz has to be frozen and tested for diseases before it's added to their catalogue. Hey, you interested?"

Ben set down his glass. "Erm, me? Donating my...uh...?" A text lit up his phone. Spotting the sender's name, he greeted it with a smile.

Hey! In a lecture break. Love that a-ha song. The mission WAS accomplished!

Ben sent her the wink emoji.

A second text nudged Riley's first message up the screen. *My turn!* was typed above a link to a playlist titled '4 Benjamin'. With one swipe, Sting's "An Englishman in New York" stared back. *Classic!* He looked up at Hunter. "I feel for the kids, though, having a sperm donor for a dad, never knowing him..."

"You don't miss what you've never had," said Hunter.

A third text bounced onto Ben's screen. *I didn't insult you, did I? Couldn't find any Scots in NYC songs. And you do sound English.*

He typed carefully, chuckling under his breath as he hit send.

Insult me? Impossible!!!

Hunter dug through a ripped box of seat posts. "Not all donations are anonymous. You can be an open donor if you want to know your kid. It gives them the option of contacting you when they turn eighteen."

That's more than I got from my father. "You doing that?"

"No way. I value my privacy too much."

"Privacy? You dance bollock-naked on stage!" Ben laughed and returned to his phone. "I would hate to have a kid somewhere wondering who I was, why I wasn't in touch."

"Well, bud, if you change your mind, I'm sure lots of New

York ladies would love to have a British baby daddy."

"I can't even commit to a girlfriend, let alone a kid."

"Just think of the easy money," said Hunter. "You could be 'wanking' all the way to the bank."

"Who knew philanthropy could feel *so* good?!" Ben chuckled and hit play on the song Riley had sent him.

Be wary of falling for someone who wants to change who you are, because thats not the person you are meant to be with.

I want you to try new things whenever you can. If you feel nervous, that's good! It means what you're doing matters to you.

Always be open to new friendships. The person you chat with in line at the supermarket might become your best friend, or even your soul mate.

TWENTY-SEVEN

Three days later

"Thank fuck it's Friday!" Piper, wearing a thin black sweater and a flouncy champagne-colored tutu, did a pirouette in the middle of the crossing at Third Avenue and St. Mark's Place. "Now, let's come up with a scheme to get out of dinner with Casey's family after his documentary screening. Did he tell you what he did?"

Riley finished typing a text to Ben.

That noisy, huh? I'm glad your 2nd day's going well—despite the headache. I'll stop by Sunday. She hit send and squinted into the warm sun. "You only have to pretend for one night. If they think you're his girlfriend, they'll stop bugging him to find one."

Piper hopped onto the curb, pulling her MoMA tote into her waist. "What should I fake to get out of it? Pick one: strep throat, a raging UTI...shingles?"

"What *is* shingles?" Riley's ponytail bobbed and swayed as she stared into her backpack, her hand pawing past books, her wallet, a phone charger...

"I don't know, but I've got it bad."

"We can't bail." Passing the piercing place on St. Mark's, Riley met Piper's eyes before diving back into her bag. "Tell you what— I've got half a bottle of gin in my apartment. I'll bring it along for Dutch courage."

"You never buy gin."

"Josh does. It must've rolled under my loveseat at Christmas. Shit! Where *are* my keys?!" Riley upended her laptop, digging...

"Well, tickle my tits 'til Tuesday. You can enjoy that gin together...fucker." Piper glared over her sunglasses and bumped Riley with her tulle-covered hip.

"Huh?" Nose deep in her backpack, she looked up. Head down, scrolling on his phone and brandishing a cheerful bouquet of red roses that popped against his black Fighting Hawks t-shirt, Josh stood steps away in front of her building. *He's here? NOW?* For a split second, she felt like she was floating, teetering atop a massive rollercoaster before the breath-sucking plunge. *Shit.*

Her silence drew a smirk to Piper's pale lips. "Be quiet, little rabbit. We can turn tail and run for the hills?"

Lowering her backpack, Riley's eyes slipped from the garment bag flung over Josh's shoulder to the duffle bag at his feet. "He's not supposed to be here for three more weeks."

Josh glanced up, his eyes skating down Riley's dress to her bare legs, a loved-up grin rising through his scruffy beard. "Hey, baby girl!"

Riley gave him a tight smile. "Hey! What are you doing here?"

"I came for the weekend. I couldn't wait 'til your graduation." He stuffed his phone into his khakis, his eyes jumping to Riley's left, all joy evaporating. "Piper."

"PuckHead." Piper wrinkled her nose and tilted her head away, planting her hands on her hips. She knew he hated that nickname.

Josh ignored the defiance radiating from Piper, his smile returning as he proudly laid the bouquet in Riley's hands. "So...surprise!"

He never buys me flowers. "Wow. They're beautiful." Piper snapped her gum. "Thanks." Riley wrapped her arm around his neck, drawing him close. Pressed between their chests, the roses' cellophane crinkled, but Riley squeezed Josh tighter, ignoring the thorns lurking beneath. She met his lips, their teasing warmth and the loneliness in her heart urging her to go deeper. Josh obliged, his tongue beckoning, slow and tender. His hand traced her hip, up the back of her black and white floral dress and into her hair, his fingers gently tugging.

Piper gritted her teeth behind a plastic smile. "I'm still here, you know."

Pulling away, Riley peered over her shoulder, tucking a piece of hair behind her ear that had escaped her ponytail. "Pip, *sorry*. Tonight—"

"What's tonight?" Josh squeezed the handle of his garment bag.

Piper ignored him. "Nah, forget it. My shingles are a bitch."

"Call you tomorrow?"

"You better." Piper swiveled in her flats, her tutu bouncing around her hips with each stomp down the street.

Josh whispered in Riley's ear. "You're mine—finally."

Backpack landing with a thud, Riley flipped off her flats and shoved her long sleeves up to her elbows, the cellophane-wrapped roses crunching in her arms with each shift of her body. "I wish I knew you were coming. Casey's documentary screening's tonight, and I'm scheduled to work tomorrow…" Mid-frown, she eyed the Fun Dip packet from Ben on the counter, triggering a memory. *Ben's blue tongue…*

"Can't you say you're sick or something? Babe, I'm only here for two nights." Josh hooked the garment bag on the back of her door and yanked his t-shirt over his head, lobbing it past his duffle, a pool of black settling on the fluffy rug. "Jesus, this shitbox is even smaller than I remember—hotter, too." Storming past Riley, the floor squeaked under his pounding size twelve Nikes. He swatted the curtain away and gripped the bottom of the window, his naked back muscles flexing impressively as the weighty wood and glass stuttered upward. No grunts or heavy exhales escaped through his lips. *Typical Josh.* Impatient, overtly physical, dominant—all words that could also describe him between the sheets. "This weekend will be one of the last we spend in this sauna. Good riddance…although it does have one advantage." He scratched his patchy facial hair.

Exasperated, Riley set down the flowers and tugged the V-neck of her dress. "What's that?" She took her phone from her pocket and texted Casey.

Josh here. Don't hate me—can't make it.

"You're always half-naked." He turned around, his heated gaze sliding down Riley's body. "Take it off, babe. Let me see you." His hand skimmed over the bulge already pressing through his khakis, triggering a sharp inhale.

Riley pressed her lips together. *I've missed being held, touched, but…will it be different this time? What if it's not?* There was only one way to find out. She slipped her phone in a pocket. "Let me see *you.*"

His hurried hands flipped open his belt as he moved closer, en-raptured by his fiancée, hands aloft, untying her hair. She scooped up handfuls of it, teasing and coaxing. *Come closer, closer…*

Josh kicked off his khakis, his flimsy boxers giving Riley an eyeful of how eager he was.

She held up her hand. "Wait." For once, he obeyed.

An ache throbbed in her chest. *Show me, Josh. Show me I'm right, saying yes. Show me you'll always be here for me—that you can be tender.* Her fingers skated down her dress, meeting the swell of her breasts and the line of buttons trailing down toward the skirt. One by one, she set them free, letting the soft cotton fall away, opening herself up. His stare grew heavy and wanting like he couldn't wait to slide his hands beneath her bra, hungry to caress the silky skin of her breasts and feel her stiffen under his touch. *You want to lose yourself in me, don't you, Josh?* She skimmed her fingers over her black satin bra, feeling her nipples respond. Would Josh take his time, be attentive like he used to be?

An appreciative grin grew across his cheeks as she lifted the hem of her dress…

BUZZ!

The raised pocket twitched against her bra. *Shoot! Phone.* "Oh! I need to check…"

Josh's smile collapsed.

She dropped the material and fished out her phone, the screen lit with a text from Piper.

You HATE roses! Three years and he still doesn't GET you!

The words kicked her under the ribs. Riley smiled tightly and cleared her throat, turning off the phone and tossing it onto the counter.

"Who was it?"

"Wrong number." She lifted her dress and tugged it over her head.

As it fell to the floor, Josh claimed Riley's shoulders, pressing her against the ladder leading to the bed. Her fingers trailed down his six-pack, sparking memories of unhurried trysts early in their relationship. She smiled. "This reminds me of—" But the words barely left her lips. Josh's mouth sucked her neck as his hands yanked down her panties. She gasped and let them fall, her hands pulling at his underwear and taking control of his arousal, sprung free from his boxers. She wrapped her hand around him, tightening her grip. "Josh, slow down…" His lips leapt to hers and Riley rocked into him while he tore at her bra, fighting with the clasp until it gave way and the straps fell down her arms. Letting him go, Riley dropped her bra to the floor.

"Baby…" He panted. "Take me in your mouth."

She shook her head. "No, let's—"

"I'll get a condom." Josh kneeled down, rifling through her toiletries box, tossing soap and makeup aside until he spotted a square wrapper.

Riley's chest rose and fell, her hands curling around the ladder behind her back as he put on the condom. *Prove it to me, Josh. Prove I'm doing the right thing. Prove we can get back to old Josh, old Riley, like it used to be…when I loved you…*

Josh stood up, taking Riley's face in his hands. "I want you so bad."

She let go of the ladder, tugging him closer, her hands reuniting with the curves of his hard triceps. "I want to kiss for a bit…we've got all night."

He pressed tiny kisses down her forehead and nose, slowly, lovingly, reaching her lips, which were parted in anticipation. Staring into her eyes, his hands swept down her neck to her breasts, his breath quickening the farther they traveled.

This is more like it. Riley leaned into him, wrapping her leg around his hip.

"I love you, Rye." His left hand took a detour, curling around her ass as he pushed inside her, hard.

Riley cried out and clutched his back, riding each deep thrust and roll of his hips. She was determined to make their physical passion for each other mean something more, but would her heart listen?

I can't budge. I'm trapped. "Josh?" Riley whispered. "You're asleep—*already?*"

Face down in the nook of her neck, he answered with a long rumbling snore that tickled her skin.

"Damn." Crunched against the wall, she wriggled, but she couldn't shift the weight of his 215-pound body pinning her to the twin mattress. *The only way is up.* One-handed, she shoved a sculpted shoulder off her chest. Josh stirred, his snores cut off by a sharp snort, but even with a little breathing room, Riley had no space to shift. *Thanks, wall!* She lowered him back down. Even if she could push him off, there was nowhere to go. The bed wasn't made for two adults, especially when one of them was a six-foot-two, broad-chested hockey hunk—one who was lying like a starfish with a muscled leg dangling over the edge of the mattress—and waking him…no. She could feel a throbbing hardness against her thigh. It didn't take much for Josh to get turned on, even in his sleep, and if she woke him, he would be raring to go. At this hour, Riley didn't feel like having an argument or an orgasm; she just wanted sleep.

The raucous shouts of early morning drinkers burst through the open window, and a slight breeze ballooned the curtain before sucking it back into the frame. She dipped her chin, catching a glimpse of Josh's face tucked into her neck. He looked peaceful, almost smug. *I wish I could fall asleep satisfied.* Sex with Josh was always athletic, like he had something to prove. They'd done it twice, both times standing up—Josh's go-to position. The first sesh wasn't pleasurable or comfortable, and if the ache was anything to go by, bruises from the ladder were already blooming across her back and ass. Their encore was better. Off the floor against the coat and garment bag-covered door, arms and legs wrapped around him, Riley held on tight as Josh thrusted away, his hazel eyes darkening as his breathing became more labored. Anyone passing in the hall would've known exactly what they were up to. Josh's momentum made the door creak and whine, and he groaned loudly when he came. And—surprise—Riley came, too. *When was the last time he made me come? Months…last summer, maybe? Maybe longer.* She always felt closer to him, more connected—meant to be—in those vulnerable moments after the waves of shared pleasure washed over them, tangled in a heap of arms and legs, hurried breaths and whispered promises…but moments like tonight were mostly in the past, before post-graduation possibilities beckoned, before the distance grew both physically and emotionally. Their lives were changing quickly, creating obvious cracks in their relationship. These fractures were becoming more pronounced, turning into fissures filled with new hopes, old dreams, and renewed fears about growing up. Riley's gaze left Josh and landed on the ceiling, inches away from her nose. *Will marriage repair the rift? Or make it worse?* Shuffling through the night's events, Riley bit her lip. *Maybe, maybe...not?* If she couldn't sleep, she might as well work through this...

Negatives
Josh was chasing his orgasm the first time and didn't wait for me to reach mine, so I faked it.
He didn't last long either time. Same old position, rough and hard. No tenderness.
Didn't offer to go down on me (never does), but asked for a blow job, which I refused.
Fell asleep immediately after. No cuddling. Was going to take me out for late meal but...
Positives
Josh showed up here out of the blue. He came all that way, for me.
Brought me flowers (He never does! Always blames his allergies).
Made sure I finished the second time. Felt good.
Says he has several surprises for me tomorrow. Hmm.
Score
Negatives 4, positives 4—a tie. Looks like we're headed to overtime.

Unable to move, her eyes gently closed. *No matter the final score, you have to think of Mom. You'll marry him because he loves you, and because it's the only way you can help her.* A tear escaped her lashes and slipped down her cheek.

TWENTY-EIGHT

Ben stared upward, counting a cluster of glow-in-the-dark stars peeling off the bedroom ceiling. *This would be cool if they were constellations, but they've just been thrown up there, all wonky.* Swallowing again, a bitter taste tortured his tongue. *Next time, don't waste two days' tips on cheap beer...* A soft moan pulled his eyes away. Across the pillows, a brunette smiled in her sleep, a mumble of giggly nonsense slipping past her smudged lipstick. *Or on girls you've just met.* She flipped onto her back and bent her knees, tugging the bedsheets off her chest, which Ben had feathered with kisses an hour earlier.

What am I doing? She's a laugh, but the whole time I was thinking...of Riley...how she would taste, what sounds she would make, if she would lie in my arms after. Christ, I want her so bad.

Laughter accompanied by a blast of music from a just-switched-on TV crept under the crack of the bedroom door. *Roommates? Does, erm...shit, I can't remember her name!* Ben scratched his chin. *Did she even tell me?* He rolled onto his side, the shift causing something to jab the skin underneath his regrown happy trail. *Aah!?* A skim of his hand and...the condom wrapper. He balled it up in his fist. *Riley would never be just a one-night shag. I'd want more. I'd want to be with her, properly...* He frowned. *Jeez, these things I'm thinking, I used to laugh at. You do like to torture yourself, don't you, mate?*

He pulled up the sheets, covering the girl who continued her sleepy soliloquy.

It's better this way, Riley being with Josh, me fucking around— I don't DO relationships. The minute you care about someone, you get hurt. Simple as that.

Ruffling his hair, he checked his phone—2:36 a.m. *Shit. Gotta work in four hours.* He lowered one foot to the floor and eased out of the bed slowly, careful not to bounce the mattress and wake the nameless woman. His other foot landed on something small and sharp. *Oww! What now?* Using his phone, he shone a light on the floor, the glow illuminating three small candy hearts. *Riley's naff American sweets—must've been in my pocket.* A tightness squeezed his chest. *Get over it, mate. Sometimes the heart wants what it can't have.*

Quiet and quick, he threw on his clothes and returned the candy to his pocket. He felt around for his shoes and, without tying the laces, grabbed his hoodie then slipped out the bedroom door.

TWENTY-NINE

Riley's heart melted as quickly as the vanilla ice cream collecting in the holes of her warm Belgian waffle. "I can't believe you brought me here." Her eyes climbed the twisty trunk of a real African acacia tree looming overhead. Its branches and leaves stretched towards the high ceiling, mingling with the other trees to create a magical forest canopy inside The Garden, the Four Seasons Hotel's restaurant. *This place is otherworldly and so expensive. Josh hates places like this. He's trying...he's really trying!*

"I want today to be memorable." He pointed his fork at the enormous trunk next to their table. "I wonder how fast those trees grow? Bet Erika knows."

Riley held her breath. "Is she here?" With her recent promotion, Erika had been working more weekends to make herself as visible to upper management as possible. "Did she arrange this reservation?"

"You kidding? She'd show up and talk non-stop about *her* wedding. No way—today is about us."

Thank God. Riley exhaled quietly. *I can do without Erika spazzing out.* She cut a bite-sized chunk of waffle and swirled it through the merging pools of ice cream and maple syrup on her plate, catching an eyeful of her sunny yellow Kate Spade dress. Even though it was secondhand, it was the most expensive piece of clothing she owned. *I'm glad I dressed up.*

Fussing with his tie, Josh nodded at her plate. "Make sure you eat up—you'll need lots of energy for ring shopping *and* for what I have planned later!" He dug into his egg white frittata stuffed with spinach and broccoli. Grilled turkey bacon and a bowl of steel cut oatmeal sat in reserve alongside his coffee. He reached into his jacket pocket. "I was going to make you wait, but…"

"But?"

He handed over his phone, a grin creeping through his scruff. "Check out this email."

Another surprise! Without hesitation, Riley began reading.

Dear Josh,

Please thank Riley for her interest in KMIN-TV. We're pleased to inform her of an upcoming production assistant vacancy in our sports department. The position is a maternity leave fill and will commence September 4th for the period of four months.

We have scheduled an interview with Riley at our office on June 21 at 1 p.m. To confirm, please ask her to call 952-555-7623 ext. 2671 or email me at…

He didn't… The hot chocolate in Riley's stomach curdled. She read it again quickly. *Yep, he did.*

"Pretty cool, huh?" Josh leaned over his breakfast. "I got chatting with this TV guy after the championship and when I said my fiancée was into hockey and graduating from Tisch, he told me about this job. He says the interview is a formality. Job's yours!"

Yeah, a job YOU want me to have—in Minnesota. Her smile waned.

"Your degree can be put to use right away. I told you, didn't I? I got this, babe. I'll take care of everything."

"You did." She set his phone down on the table. "But you shouldn't have gone to this trouble."

"Oh, it was no trouble." He smirked, picking up his coffee. "It's who ya know, not what ya know!"

She lifted her fork and batted a blueberry around the flooded waffle. "But being a PA in a news department—"

"It's sports, Riley." Josh's eyebrow peaked along with his tone. "You *love* sports."

"I do, but it's the sports desk in a *news* department. It's a great job...for someone else."

"What?" He frowned, resting his cup on the table. "You're turning it down?"

"Josh, I've spent four years preparing to work in *production* making sitcoms or dramas. This job's in sports television—that's *broadcasting*. Production and broadcasting are two different things."

He jabbed his fork into his frittata. "Well, you have to start somewhere."

"I know, but this job is starting at the other end of the spectrum. It's like I've been studying German and you're expecting me to speak Chinese."

"I think you're exaggerating. He knows you're clever. An NYU graduate? Come on! He said what you don't know, you'll learn on the job."

"It's not a question of learning—of course I'd get the hang of it—but it's not what I want. I told you ages ago, I want to try California."

Josh dropped his fork, his head tipping back as he closed his eyes. "Ryyye! You're expecting me to walk this back? Do you know how bad that looks for me? This guy will be covering my career from day one."

"So that's what this is? I'm supposed to take this job to make *you* look good? I didn't ask you to do this—you went behind my back!"

"Rye—"

"This is exactly what I was worried about—my career taking a back seat to yours—and now you've proven me right." Maggie's words ricocheted in her head. *"It's hard watching your husband do what he's always wanted, while your dreams stay on the shelf."*

"That's bullshit and you know it. I wanted you to have something of your own when we moved to Saint Paul to keep you busy, so you wouldn't feel homesick or lonely. That's it! Jesus, you make me sound like a manipulative asshole."

If the shoe fits... Staring back at him, she crossed her arms. "For TWO years, I've talked about finding a production job in California. Nice to know you listened."

"Look, can we discuss this later?" He picked up his cup, lowering his voice. "I don't want to spend today arguing."

"I don't either, but you can't expect me to do cartwheels about a job I would never apply for in the first place. TV jobs might all sound the same to you, but they're not. It's like me drafting you to play goal when you're a center!"

"Okay, okay, I get it." He gulped his coffee and returned it to the table, his tone conciliatory. "He won't be in the office again until Monday, so...forget it for now. I'll take care of it."

Fork aloft, he leaned forward, stabbing a slice of bacon. His follow-through bumped his coffee, tipping it over at the table's edge and spilling its milky contents into the lap of his suit trousers. "*Shit!*" The restaurant's attention fell on Josh, his cheeks reddening above his clenched jaw.

Oh, great. Riley leapt to her feet and leaned across the table, using her napkin to prevent more coffee from slopping onto his lap.

Their waiter rushed over without hesitation. "Sir, may I help?"

Standing up, Josh slapped his soaked napkin on the table. "Where's the restroom?"

"Follow me." The waiter led Josh and his frown away.

Riley smiled tightly at the next table, waiting for them to mind their own business. She toyed with the blueberries on her plate, piling them into the soggy holes of her neglected waffle, and flipped over her phone. Several texts waited. Maggie's was first.

All good for tomorrow lunch? Will be nice to see Josh. x
She typed quickly, hitting send. *We'll be there around noon. x*
The second text was Ben's, another '4 Riles!!!' playlist attachment. She opened it, finding "The Sun Only Shines on TV" and "Dancing with Myself" by Billy Idol. An amused giggle erupted from her throat, drawing disapproving stares back to their table. *What?* Riley side-eyed the nosey diners then stared at Josh's abandoned breakfast. *Ben texts and I laugh. When was the last time Josh made me laugh out loud? I can't remember.* She slouched, shame pulling her down. *He's your fiancé, Riley...get it together.* She left her phone face down and cut into her waffle.

A phone buzzed again. She flipped it over, but the screen was dark. *Oh, it's Josh's.* She sat back, ignoring it, but it erupted into the full operatic chorus of Queen's "We Are the Champions", drawing more indignation from nearby diners. *Shit! Make it stop.* She reached across the table, spotting a number she didn't recognize.

"Hello? Josh King's phone."

"Hi...who's this?" asked the male voice.

"Riley, Josh's fiancée."

"Riley! Hi! It's Mitch Quindry, Josh's agent?"

"Oh, hi! Sorry, I didn't recognize the name."

"Yeah, I lost my phone so I'm using my wife's. Listen, can you give Josh a message? Can you let him know we're all systems go for the interview tomorrow? It's the NHL rising stars piece."

"Rising stars, cool."

"Yeah, *Sports Illustrated* will add it to their NHL preview before rookie training camp." Mitch's smile was apparent even over the phone. "It will raise Josh's profile at just the right time."

Sports Illustrated—again? Riley nodded enthusiastically. "Wow, it's amazing they want to interview him again."

"Again? No, it's the first time."

What? Riley blinked. "I thought he spoke to them after the championship."

Mitch snorted. "Hell no!"

Josh...lied? Riley's stomach pulled into a knot.

"All press engagements wrapped the night of the win, which was a good thing." He chuckled. "I wouldn't have let press anywhere *near* them with the state Josh and the guys were in down in Vegas!"

Vegas? Josh was in VEGAS—when I was looking after Mom? He said he couldn't fly home! His words from FaceTime bubbled up. *"Sorry I can't be there...too many commitments..."* Commitments? *Yeah, drinking, gambling, and God knows what else.* She tried to swallow, but the lump in her throat wouldn't budge.

"Riley?" Mitch's phone crackled. "We're about to go through the Holland Tunnel. So, you'll tell Josh—1 p.m. tomorrow, Chelsea Piers?"

"Yep, got it." She spat out the words and slammed Josh's phone onto the coffee-stained tablecloth.

"Can you imagine—me in *Sports Illustrated?* How crazy is that?"

It took every inch of Riley's restraint not to kick the coffee-colored bullseye on Josh's crotch.

Crossing Madison Avenue in silence, she didn't budge from her path on East 57th Street, her pinched eyebrows and determined stride forcing oncoming pedestrians to veer around her and Josh. *Yeah, get out of my way. I am NOT being pushed around today.* She gave Josh a slip of side-eye behind her sunglasses and wrapped her arms around her waist, hiding her clenched fists. *Do you think I'm THAT stupid? I wouldn't remember you mentioning* Sports Illustrated *last month?* Her pulse, spurred on by adrenaline, pounded in her ears, each word leaving Josh's lips fanning the heat rising in her chest.

"Thanks for taking Mitch's call." He glanced down at his trousers, pulling her Strand tote over his crotch. "And for letting me use your bag—hide this damn stain!"

Her smile was tight, barely opening to release her statement. "You're good at that."

"What—hiding stains?" He chuckled.

"Hiding *things*." She stared straight ahead.

"Huh?"

Riley grabbed his arm, tugging him through the busy foot traffic into the quiet alcove beside the mammoth Tourneau Time-Machine store, the large Rio de Janeiro clock's second hand clicking over their heads. "Why didn't you tell me about Vegas?" *You lied to me!*

"Vegas?"

"Mitch told me—on the phone. You went to Vegas after the NCAA win. I thought you were in Grand Forks. You lied!"

"Aw, Rye, I didn't lie." He winced. "I just didn't...tell you."

"Bullshit. By not telling me, you lied. Same diff." As the words left her mouth, guilt pinched her gut. *I haven't told him about hanging out with Ben, but...what's there to tell? We're friends, that's it.*

"I guess, yeah, but it was spur of the moment. You know what the guys are like! They get an idea and..." He shrugged. "Before I knew it, we were on the plane, drinking and celebrating, and as soon as we landed, it was casinos non-stop."

Riley crossed her arms.

"Babe, it was *just* the guys." His sheepish grin belittled Riley's annoyance. "I'd never cheat on you. You know that."

He's not taking this seriously. "This isn't about cheating!"

"Then, what *is* it about?" Tilting his forehead back, he wound his arms around her waist. "Look, I'm sorry I went away—"

"It's not that you went away. It's that you didn't come *back*." She batted away his embrace, raising a confused look on his face.

189

"You chose to stay in Vegas instead of flying home to support me! Mom got devastating news and what? You thought, she's been diagnosed three times before, Riley's an expert at this by now. What the FUCK, Josh?!?" Her raised voice drew furrowed glances from people walking past. "Why didn't you leave?"

"I didn't leave because...because..."

"Because, because—WHAT?!"

"All the guys were there and...I don't know! It was our last chance to party as a team." He shrugged.

She threw her hands up. "You're so unreliable and selfish. You only care about what Josh wants, what Josh needs. Vegas, that stupid TV job—it's the same old story."

"Come on, that's not—"

"I was crying my heart out and you weren't there for me. You could've come home but you didn't. Drinking and gambling with the guys was more important to you."

"Babe, I made the wrong decision, okay? I can't undo what I've done, but you have my word, it won't happen again." He glanced over his shoulder toward East 57th Street. "I thought...I'd be in the way. I'm not comfortable with hospitals and talking about health things like you are."

"I wasn't going to ask you to insert a catheter, for fuck's sake. If you really cared about me, you wouldn't ghost me when I need you. My dad did that to Mom and I can't—I *refuse* to follow in her footsteps."

"Baby, you won't. Come here." He pulled her into a tight hug. "I'm sorry. Look, how about we surprise your mom with the ring *tonight*? We'll get takeout, have my parents over, make it just family—how's that sound?"

Riley tensed in his arms.

"Okay?" He eased the embrace and smiled. "Come on, let's go get your ring."

Returning to the bustling sidewalk, Josh rambled on about diamond clarity and color grades, but Riley wasn't listening.

Showing up unannounced with a massive bouquet of flowers...

Splurging on breakfast in a fancy hotel...

He wants to surprise Mom with the ring...

Lovely gestures...but they're not selfless acts of love. They're manipulative strategies to keep me complacent, to get me to do what HE wants. This is a losing battle. I'm swimming against a riptide. As the reality of his actions sank in, Riley's throat closed, her stunted breaths making her woozy, unstable. She stopped, frozen in place.

Josh turned around. "Babe?"

"I-I can't." A tornado of fear and doubt whirled in her stomach, tearing apart everything she had planned.

He looked confused. "Can't...?"

It was like Riley had pulled a thread and everything started to unravel. "I can't do this. The ring..." Her vision began to blur. *I can't look Mom in the eye wearing a $25,000 lie on my finger.*

"You okay, Rye? You wanna go another time?"

I'm sorry, Mom. I can't pretend, I can't do this...even if...if it means...oh, God! A sour taste rose in her tight throat. "Josh, I'm calling off the engagement."

"What?" His jaw dropped. "Babe, I know you're upset about Vegas but—"

"It's more than that." Her words had a life of their own, each one fighting to be heard and tearing her heart in two for her mom, for herself. "I don't want to move to Minnesota. I don't want to give up my dream. I've worked too hard—"

"Babe, we'll talk about the job and everything will be *fine*. We'll work all that out—"

"It's not enough. I don't..." She bowed her head, holding back, but her truth had its own momentum and wouldn't be silenced—not anymore. Grabbing fistfuls of her hair, Riley met his confused stare. "I don't love you anymore." The words, once released, didn't make her feel any better. She had escaped one cage but wandered into another—alone with Maggie.

His jaw clenched like her words had smacked him across the face. "Jesus. Are you fucking kidding me? Where's this coming from?"

"I've felt it...for a while. We've been drifting apart, arguing—you *know* we have."

"Yeah, because we're *apart* all the time—that's the problem! Who wouldn't start to have doubts? But once we're together again, it'll be just like old times."

Shaking her head, her fingers rubbed her brow. "The distance isn't just physical. It's emotional."

"What?" His eyes narrowed. "There's someone else?"

"No...I mean, yes." She laid her hand over her heart. "Not a guy, Josh—*me*. I need to be honest with myself. I've been pretending everything's fine for months now, pretending us getting married is what I want, but...it's what *you* want." She gulped a breath. "I'm exhausted and worried about Mom, stressed about life after graduation. So many things are changing all at once. I guess that's part of growing up, but I feel like I'm going to lose it at any second."

"I know things are scary, and I'll help you through it. I know I haven't been there for you as much as I should've, but I'll try harder." He clasped her hand. "I will. I really will."

She shook her head. "Josh, we want different things in different cities. And you deserve to be with someone who loves you. I'm sorry, but that's not me anymore." She pried her hand away, hiding it in a pocket, out of reach.

"Look, let's talk about this at your place..."

I know how this will go. He'll stroke my hair, talk about when Dad left, how he was there for me—but that was then, and this is now. So much has changed and it's too late to go back! Riley met his pained gaze. "Josh..."

"Forget the engagement." He nodded quickly. "We can take it slow, just *date...*"

I never wanted to hurt him. "No, Josh! Please...*it's over.*"

Those two words woke him up like smelling salts at the ice rink. Blinking, he swallowed slowly, the realization sinking in. "Wow...so you...there's nothing I can say to change your mind, is there..."

She fought back tears. "I'm sorry."

"I'm just..." Josh cleared his throat and looked away, his hand skimming his beard. "Well, I'll...need to grab my shit from yours, then."

Riley nodded, waves of nausea making her hesitant to move an inch.

Josh didn't linger. He strode toward Fifth Avenue and hailed a taxi.

THIRTY

Saturday at lunchtime, Ben performed for a New York audience for the first time.

While diners tucked into French toast and steak and eggs, he teamed up with two servers for the "Greased Lightnin'" portion of the *Grease* medley. His brief sing-along earned applause, starry-eyed swoons from a table of teen girls, and a generous ten-dollar tip from a retired British couple, but he barely had time to breathe, let alone savor those moments. The restaurant was slammed with people, and vacated tables didn't sit empty for more than a minute thanks to a growing line of hungry customers looping around the block. Once inside, guests were swallowed up in a Broadway musical on steroids. Back-to-back performances, all sung with microphones cranked up to maximum, made normal conversation impossible, but the tourists ate it up.

Shadowing one of the diner's veterans, Ben picked up the slack with a smile *("Always a smile!")* and dashed to the kitchen to collect burgers, chili-smothered tater tots, and milkshakes.

"Doing great, Ben!" Stavros, the diner's manager, hiked up the waist of his trousers. "Listen, one of the guys called in sick and we're splitting his section. How 'bout you take two tables? Think you can cope?"

"Yeah." Ben's stomach growled, not that anyone would hear in the noisy restaurant. He nodded, eager to make a good impression.

"Cool. Table six is finishing up and table seven—the corner booth—just arrived."

Ben leaned in. "Pardon?"

Stavros pointed to a blue and red striped booth stuffed with four kids and a middle-aged dad. "Dive in, buddy!"

Don't fuck this up. Ben took a deep breath and filled his arms with menus, waiting for the performance of *Wicked*'s "Defying Gravity" to end so he didn't have to yell over the vocals. *Make it quick before the singing starts again.* "Hello! I'm Ben and I'll be taking your order today."

"You talk funny." A boy, around seven years old, scrunched up his freckly nose and whirled a fidget spinner on his finger.

"I'm from England." Ben set a menu down in front of the little guy as well as his tween-age sister who scrolled non-stop on her phone, his three-year-old twin siblings—a girl and a boy, dressed up as Elsa from *Frozen* and Spider-Man—and their dad, phone glued to his ear. The whole family was golden-haired and looked like they had stepped out of Central Casting. "Do you know where that is?"

"Don't care." The kid pouted and spun his toy again. "I want nachos!"

Ben glanced at the dad, still yapping on his phone. "The kids meals are on page five—"

"I want *nachos!*"

Ben's eyes circled the table. No one was paying attention. "I'll give you time to decide." Turning away, orange-stained fingers from table six grasped his elbow.

"I've been waiting ten minutes!" A chin popped out of a turtleneck sweater, its owner squeezing Ben's arm and shoving her plate of untouched carrot sticks and decimated chicken wings to the table's edge. *Urgh! BBQ sauce fingers!* "Take that back and bring us soda refills." She 'tsked' at her husband, whose nose was stuck in a newspaper's sports section. "And get us our check." She let go of Ben and pushed her husband's half-eaten burger and fries towards him.

With a forced grin, Ben flipped through his notepad and tore off their bill, leaving it on the table. He picked up their plates. "I'll be right b—"

"I-I need…!" Little Spider-Man at table seven was hopping across his banquette, clutching his ass. "I-I-I need go POO!"

Shit! Ben's eyes flitted from the kid to the dad, who was more interested in his phone than his panicked son's wails, and back to BBQ sauce lady. "Ah, I have to make sure Spider-Man doesn't hurt himself first." *Or with my luck, shit himself—whatever comes first.*

"You're gonna make *us* wait again?" Like a magnet, her bellow dragged the manager over.

"Everything all right, Ben?"

"We *only* wanted refills." Eyes bulging, the woman picked up a napkin and fanned her scowling face, her whining on a loop. "The service here is—"

"POO. I need, I need, NOW!"

Ben fought back a laugh. *Great timing, kid.*

"I'll get the drinks." Stavros turned to Ben. "Make sure that kid doesn't fall, 'kay? Don't need a lawsuit."

Hands full of dirty plates, Ben returned to the family's booth. "Hey, Spidey, take a seat and I'll get you some crayons—"

"We don't want crayons!" the seven-year-old interrupted, knocking baby Spider-Man closer to his social media-addicted sister. She was sitting on the edge of the booth, embarrassed to be seen with them. "Find my fidget spinner—I lost it!"

"I NEED POOOOOO!" Spider-Man wriggled. Flushed cheeks and a tight frown screamed, *Now!*

I can't take kids to the loo! Can I? Eyes sweeping over father of the year, still glued to his phone, Ben pointed to the far side of the restaurant. "The restrooms are—"

"He can't go on his own!" The tween rolled her eyes and dropped her phone on her unopened menu. "*I'll* take him!" Shooting daggers at Ben and her dad, she slouched her way out of the booth, grabbing her squirmy baby brother under his arms.

With Spider-Man and his older sister gone, their dad's mind elsewhere, the seven-year-old slowly slipped—first his chest, then his head—out of view, disappearing under the table. 'Elsa', all big blue eyes and button nose, hid behind her dad's right arm and peeked at Ben.

"Um, sir..." Ben bit his cheek as one of his co-workers launched into "New York, New York" a few tables away. Fighting her vocals, he shouted in the quietest way possible. "I think your son is under the tab—"

"Hold on, Gene!" Furrowing his brow, the father acknowledged Ben for the first time, pointing at his own ears. "I can't hear...look, it's my divorce lawyer. Could you just—?" Without waiting for Ben's answer, he vacated the booth and pushed past servers and customers until he reached the diner's vestibule.

Right. Ben exhaled heavily and set down the dirty plates, crouching down to join the boy under the table. Padding over lost straws, forgotten fries, and dirty lemon wedges, Ben spotted something shiny. He reached out to grab it as a small swinging sneaker clunked him in the temple. "Oww!" *Cheers, Elsa.*

"Ben?" The scuffed shoes of Stavros stood pigeon-toed in the aisle.

The little boy scooted out into the light. "He took my toy!"

You little shit! Climbing out, a blush rose on Ben's cheeks as his stomach let out a protracted growl. He stood up, his hands sticky and the knees of his black trousers gray with dust and crumbs.

The manager frowned. "What are you doing?"

"Finding *this.*" Ben handed the kid his toy and glanced at the princess sitting alone at the table, drumming a chicken wing bone against the ketchup bottle then lifting it towards her mouth... "No, don't—"

"Where's Dad?" The tween pushed past with Spider-Man in tow.

"I'm here." The father grinned. "Let's get some nachos." Prying the chicken bone from Elsa's grip, he picked up a menu and flipped through, stopping to read the kids options to her. Spider-Man fought over his dad's phone with fidget spinner kid and the tween lolled her head against the booth, looking like she wished it would swallow her up.

Stavros shouted in Ben's ear, "You've been on the floor—wash your hands before picking up orders, okay?"

Yeah, I know, mate—I wasn't born yesterday. Ben pursed his lips and reclaimed the dirty plates, avoiding any eye contact with...

"Hold your horses, sonny!"

Pain in the arse at table six—for fuck's sake, what now?

"Get them to sing something good." Sauce-stained fingers crept up her straw as she slurped her soda refill. Like 'Memory' from *Cats*."

A tight smile crossed his face. "Sorry, we don't take requests."

"What *do* you do?" She pounded the empty glass on the table. "It certainly isn't your *job!*"

If I wasn't broke, I'd tell her where to stick her request.

She rose to her feet and pushed past, her weary hubby offering a withering smile.

Ben collected the check and their cash. No tip. *Fuckers.* He frowned, stuffing the coins and bills into his waist apron then stormed off to the garbage bin, hidden away behind a half wall. *No one's watching, right?* He pinched a few fries, stuffing them in his mouth—the first food he'd eaten in almost twelve hours. *Ahh, so good!* Chewing quickly, he grabbed a few more and scraped the rest into the trash before visiting the restroom to wash his hands.

Okay, what's next? He took the family's order and waited for another server to finish on the computer touchscreen. Hugging his snarling stomach, he watched co-workers rapping a tune from *Hamilton* atop the narrow catwalk snaking between booths. *So cool!*

"All yours, Ben."

"Cheers." Punching in his employee code, the tip of his tongue slid across his lips, his brain struggling to concentrate. Two co-workers chatted behind him, snickering about menu items they would never eat. Ben smirked, reminding himself never to try the pot pie.

Twenty minutes later, his orders were ready. *Sirloin steak for the dad, mac 'n' cheese sliders for Spidey, nachos for fidget spinner kid...*

In two trips, he delivered the family's meals. "Careful, plates are hot." He set down their dishes with an oven mitt and a relieved smile. "Can I get you anything else?"

"Hold on." Clenching his jaw, the father wiggled his index finger for Ben to lean in. "I *told* you I was vegetarian. I ordered the lentil soup and gluten-free chopped salad. I can't eat *that!*" He shoved away the sizzling steak. "What's wrong with you?" The entitled snark accompanying his sneer suggested he'd have no problem reporting Ben's error to Stavros.

My fucking brain! A knot tugged in Ben's stomach. "Oh, sorry about that." Leaning forward, he picked up the meat, his eyes darting to the kids, wide-eyed and silent. "I'll fix this." Words flying from his lips, he turned quickly, weaving around dillydallying customers and stressed waiters. He stopped at the garbage bin and stared at the New York sirloin, mashed potatoes, and veggies hovering over the point of no return. His mouth watering, he picked a carrot off the plate. *I'm so hungry—*

"Ben!"

Fuck. Busted.

"Table seven was complaining. I fixed his order." Stavros hiked up his trousers again. "His soup should be ready in five."

"Thanks. Really sorry about that." Ben flicked the carrot into the bin, his stomach crying out in anger. "So, this gets tossed? It's steak..."

"Yup, doesn't matter. Can't serve it to anyone else." He slapped Ben on the back. "Don't feel bad. All newbies make mistakes. You'll get the hang of it."

"Right." *But will I? My dyslexia fucks up my concentration. I entered what I heard around me: 'The steak tastes like an old boot,' and I entered...steak. I can hide behind the new guy excuse now, but what about next week—if I last that long...*

Stavros swiveled back. "Oh, when you're done, grab the mic. You're up next!"

Fuck! "Great." Ben smiled through gritted teeth and dumped the steak in the trash.

THIRTY-ONE

Piper and Casey were unmissable. Devouring homemade ice cream, their exaggerated pleasure-filled moans from the benches outside Sundaes and Cones turned heads at the corner of Third Avenue and East 10th Street. Even nose-deep in her black sesame ice cream, Piper kept scanning the crowds for her best friend. "Rye!" She leapt to her feet, her lopsided waffle cone threatening to topple.

Riley barely raised a smile. It wasn't just her backpack and tote weighing her down.

"You okay?" asked Piper. "I couldn't believe it when I got your texts…"

"That's a lie." Casey lowered his cone, smirking over his hazelnut double scoop. "Don't deny it, you've been hoping—"

"I know!" said Piper through gritted teeth. "But you don't have to mention that *now*."

Sitting down beside Casey, Riley set her backpack by her feet and checked her phone, still waiting for a response from her mom. "It's okay. I know you guys weren't his biggest fans."

"But are *you* okay? You did the right thing, you know." Piper joined them on the bench as Casey chomped into his ice cream. "Would you stop doing that?" She winced across Riley. "You make my teeth throb!"

He took another huge teethy bite. "Feel the pain, Paisley!" The garbled words barely escaped his mouth as he gently elbowed Riley, trying to make her smile.

Sandwiched between her friends, Riley hugged her tote and grinned for the first time since breakfast. *I couldn't love these guys more.* "Case, how'd it go last night? I'm so sorry I missed it."

"Ah, it's okay. No one's watched it more than you have." He smiled. "Last night was good. Fifty people showed, nobody walked out, and my parents bought it—they think Pip's my girlfriend. Gets 'em off my back for now."

"And guess who turned up?" Piper beamed over her cone. "Cicely."

Riley sat up. "The girl from Peet's?"

"Yep! We're going on our first date next week."

"Aw, Pip!" Riley smiled. "I'm so happy for you!"

"I'm happy for *you*. PuckHead is his-tor-y!"

"Josh isn't a bad guy, a little selfish sometimes, but he never cheated, never—"

"Supported you." With a dismissive flick, Piper smoothed her cropped black capris. "I think he used your depression to manipulate you. He never listened, never put you first…"

"Yeah, I know. He wasn't reliable, and the engagement only made it worse…"

"I swore a blue fucking streak when I saw your text about that TV job," said Piper.

Casey tsked. "Another Starbucks we're banned from."

"His assumption that you'd just blindly take a job you had no interest in like a good girl? That shows *exactly* how much he didn't get you!" A river of dark ice cream crept down Piper's hand as she leaned in.

"Pip, you're like a four-year-old with that cone." Casey's free hand rooted around in his messenger bag and reappeared with hand wipes. "You're a germy, gooey clusterfuck." A wipe sailed over Riley's lap, landing on Piper's thigh. She quickly mopped up the sticky dessert.

"I wanted to help Mom so badly…but sitting in that fancy restaurant, I couldn't block it out anymore. I was using him, and it made me sick to my stomach."

"Don't beat yourself up. It's not like you were doing it for selfish reasons," said Casey.

"If Mom knew what I'd been thinking, she'd be livid. I had to let him go, even if I hurt him—and I really didn't want to hurt him." Riley's nose began to tickle. *Don't cry! You've held it together this long.* She pulled a tissue from her tote. "Ah, God, I feel even more lost now."

Piper sighed. "Breakups suck."

"I have to live with it: I stomped on Josh's heart *and* I've destroyed the only financial lifeline we had. The medical bills aren't going to stop just because I did the right thing." She shook her head. "I came this close to buying a lottery ticket on my way here. Can you say 'desperate'?"

"Where's Josh now?" asked Casey.

"Headed to his parents. He'll stay with them until he flies back Sunday night. He's got an interview with *Sports Illustrated* first—"

"Does he now? Well, someone won't be sitting in his old bedroom crying all weekend, then." Casey sneered. "Privileged prick. I hate jocks."

Riley glanced at Piper, ice cream trickling over her cone's edge again, eyes scrunched in thought. "Hey, we're dissing Josh, your fave pastime—why so quiet?"

"A crowdfunding page, that's still an option," said Piper.

"Asking strangers for money is so...I'm not sure Mom would like me advertising her illness or money problems on the internet. Plus there's that study I found—ninety percent of campaigns don't meet their goal. Lots don't receive *any* donations. If Mom's page had a big fat zero, it would break my heart."

Casey crunched through his cone. "I've seen lots of pages racking up donations."

"Yeah, from the arts crowd—for your friends' documentaries," said Riley.

"Not just that. A friend of a friend's dad"—he chewed quick-ly—"he needed money for stroke therapy and raised thirty thousand dollars. It's possible, you know. What do you have to lose?"

She shrugged.

"You don't ask, you don't get." Casey popped the last chunk of cone into his mouth.

"I guess. What would I have to do? Will you guys help me?"

Her friends spoke simultaneously. "Yes!" "Shit, yeah." Piper flung her ice cream into the bin beside the bench.

Casey pouted. "There's half left!"

"One word: diabetes," said Piper.

"God, you're not becoming *diabetic*." Casey scoffed under his breath. "Delusional, yes. Diabetic, no."

Riley's phone vibrated in her lap with a text from Maggie.

Sweetheart, come home. I've got hugs & smiley face potatoes. x

"I should go. I'm staying at Mom's."

"All weekend?" Piper licked her fingers.

"Just tonight. I'm supposed to visit Ben at work tomorrow."

Casey's eyes darted between Riley and Piper. "So, when do I get to meet the mysterious Ben?"

"When you stop pretending to be British," said Piper. "Us Brits find it irritating."

Riley changed the subject. "Case, you working tomorrow?"

"Yep." He nodded. "Popcorn for dinner again."

"Popcorn can count toward your five a day," said Piper.

"That's a stretch." Casey chuckled. "I'm hoping they've fixed their claw machine. The rescue needs more toys for the dogs."

Riley hugged him then stood up. "You'll score a bunch—you always do."

"Text if you need me and give Maggie a hug." Piper rose to her feet and embraced her friend. "You did the right thing."

"Keep telling me that until I believe it." Chin hovering over

Piper's shoulder, Riley met Casey's eyes, his kind expression unable to soothe the worry fluttering in her stomach.

Sunshine danced across the gentle waves of New York Harbor as the orange ferry carried tourists and locals toward Staten Island. With every passing minute, Lower Manhattan receded a little farther, but the watery gulf did little to distance Riley from her decision; she feared its ripples would affect her and Maggie for months to come. *I can walk away from Josh, but the fallout is impossible to outrun.* Sunglasses hiding her tears, Riley slumped on the railing, the wind whipping her hair and thoughts into a tangle.

What have I done? Failed Mom. Hurt Josh.

Beside her, a cluster of merry Italian tourists snapped selfies with a distant Statue of Liberty, torch thrust confidently into the cloudless April sky, her promise of enlightenment, freedom, and hope all on Riley's wish list. One of the group, a raven-haired woman wearing an 'I Heart NY' t-shirt knotted at her waist, held her hands just so, making it look like Lady Liberty was balancing on her palm. With a laugh, she kissed her tanned male companion and sank into an embrace, their eyes never leaving each other.

Josh and I were like that once. Just because you no longer love someone doesn't mean saying goodbye won't hurt. We shared memories, secrets…the pain and sweetness of the past, the fears and hopes for the future. If I did the right thing like Piper says, why does it hurt so much?

Her phone buzzed in her hand. She guessed who it was before looking at it. *Erika.* What was it this time? A list of bands for her and Josh's reception…photo booth vendors? Even before she had called off their engagement, Riley had grown sick of these continual nudges down the aisle, and the nauseous feelings were rising again. She wiped away her tears and tapped the call button. *Get it over with.*

Erika picked up two rings in. "Rye! So, whadya think? Aren't the hockey player cake toppers adorable?" Her words rolled fast and furious. "If you tell them Josh's uniform colors, they'll custom paint his figure. He'll LOVE—"

"Eri, it's over. I broke up with him—"

"WHAT?!"

"—this morning, so no need for cake toppers or bridesmaids...or anything else."

Holding back tears, Riley told Erika everything and tried to wrap up the call three times, but Erika kept lobbing questions. When Riley's answers weren't satisfactory, the bride-to-be shifted to advice for fixing the unfixable. They were going around in circles, their conversational carousel heading nowhere quickly.

"But Rye, you're giving up so much..."

Riley stood her ground, choking back tears.

"Fudge!" Erika huffed. "Gotta go. Stanley's using our new leather sofa as a chew toy. Talk later?"

Call over, Riley couldn't hold back any longer. Warm tears chased down her cheeks as melodic Italian accents happily sailed along the breeze. Carefree and reveling in their ferry adventure, the smitten couple glanced at Riley and looked uneasy. They shifted down the railing as if her heartbreak was contagious.

I'm not kidding myself. I know Josh's money couldn't guarantee a cure, but it would've alleviated some of Mom's stress, erased the fear of losing her apartment. Pitching in on her medical expenses was the ONE thing I thought I could help her with, and now I can't even do that...

As she stared into the water, the skirt of Riley's sunny yellow dress flirted with the light wind. She spun her mom's moonstone ring around and around her finger, wishing for a miracle.

THIRTY-TWO

"Sweetie, you sat inside all day yesterday. It'll do you good to get some fresh air this afternoon." Maggie set down her fork in her spinach salad—her most recent craving. She had already devoured its strawberries and walnuts. "And your friend Ben is from England? That's exciting."

Riley pushed up the three-quarter-length sleeves of her New York Islanders t-shirt and slumped back in her chair, taking a walnut from her salad with her. "Ben's working."

"Well, go meet Piper."

"She's making puppets after work."

"Does she need help?"

Riley laughed. "She's a grown woman making puppets—what do you think?" She rolled the nut between her fingers.

"Is Casey free? What's Erika up to?"

"Mom, you're trying to get rid of me?"

"I'm not! But at least your friends will keep you busy. Better than sitting here..."

I'm so down, I just want to hide. "I feel awful. I hurt him, Mom."

"Honey, he'll be fine. In time, he'll realize it was for the best. No one should be with someone who doesn't love them."

"I know, but..."

"Besides, he'll be so busy with graduation and prepping for the NHL, he'll barely have time to think—and if I know his parents, they'll be popping champagne corks over your breakup."

What?! Riley scowled.

"You know what they're like—God forbid Josh blows his

207

chance at the NHL. I was dreading the day he ended up in the minor leagues and you got blamed."

"Mom!"

"Well, they wouldn't blame *him*, would they?" She nibbled on a spinach leaf. "I spoke to his mom on the phone two weeks ago."

"Why?"

"I haven't talked to her since their Fourth of July barbecue two summers ago. I thought with your engagement I should say hi, welcome to the family, that sort of thing, but she had a few choice words to say about him proposing."

"Really? But Josh said—"

Maggie shook her head. "She thought Josh was getting too serious too quickly. They were worried he was becoming too dependent on you, always mentioning you and Minnesota in the same breath like he couldn't imagine moving without you. She called you 'his security blanket'."

"Nice! I'm no better than an old stuffed toy." Riley abandoned the walnut on her plate. *But...he was hell-bent on me going with him.* Her tight expression loosened. "Actually, she might have a point. I know he loved me...and he worked harder than I did to save what we once had."

"I'm sure he loved you, honey, but he wanted you to be something you're not and you just grew apart. It's sad, but it happens all the time. That doesn't mean you're not allowed to feel a sense of loss. At the end of the day, you did the right thing—for both of you. It takes a strong person to walk away. I'm proud of you, sweetheart."

"He's always been in my life."

"I know, but this is for the best. There's nothing you should feel guilty about."

If only.

Maggie stole the walnut from Riley's plate.

Thank God Mom's eating. Every meal was hit or miss. A text from Piper lit up Riley's phone.

On break but wanted to share what Case and I wrote for the crowdfunding page. Let us know if it's okay. Also sending Maggie pics for approval. If all good, we'll post. Luv ya.

Lowering the phone into the lap of her jeans out of Maggie's sight, she quickly read the call to action. It was to the point and up-beat without getting too in-your-face personal with information or emotion that would make Maggie cringe. Riley glanced up. Her mom was blissed out on gorgonzola and spinach, chewing with her eyes closed. If she mentioned the donation page, Maggie would probably say no. It was her last hope. Riley's thumbs flew over the screen.

Post it. Share it.

A white platter heaped with crispy waffle fries and dinosaur-shaped chicken nuggets bumped a plate of cheese-swamped nachos on a table set for two.

With a Disney-worthy smile, Ben delivered his best server's spiel. "Enjoy your meal, and if you need anything else, my name is Benjamin!"

Nuggets shaped like dinosaurs! A real grin fought past the fake one Riley had painted on since leaving her mom's. *He remembered.*

He leaned in close so his words could be heard over Beyoncé blasting through the speakers. "My treat."

He didn't have to do this. "Wow. Thank you!"

"My shift's over in ten minutes—"

"Ben! Now!" A server twice his size rushed past with a frus-trated scowl and two large platters crowded with club sandwiches.

"Yeah, coming." Ben stifled a laugh. "I'll be back before you know it." He made a funny face and dashed after his co-worker.

Cute didn't even begin to describe how adorable he looked.

Riley exhaled, taking in the generous portions in front of her. She'd barely touched her salad at her mom's and if she was going for a walk with Ben after his shift, she'd need protein and carbs to calm hungry, flighty feelings. Her mouth salivated, the plates crowded with the perfect comfort food. Fingertips poking into the fries' deep ridges, she took her first bite. *A little greasy, but sooo good.* She nibbled on a chicken Tyrannosaurus Rex and checked her phone, opening a link Piper had sent to Maggie's crowdfunding page. Scrolling down, three donations appeared: $20 from Piper, $20 from Casey, and—*bless her*—$200 from Piper's mom in Chicago. Only another $14,760 still to go. She closed the page quickly so Ben wouldn't spot it. Her mom's health, the news about Josh— she wanted to keep Ben in the dark as long as she could. He was her only escape, her island.

Hiding her low mood, she swayed to Beyoncé's "Single Ladies" and took a detour through Instagram and Facebook. Piper had posted a new puppet video and Casey was promoting dog adoptions. Queen Bey's empowering lyrics began to fade, replaced by a taped music bed of strumming guitar. An enthusiastic male voice joined in, prompting Riley to look up over her shoulder. *What? BEN?! On top of the banquettes!* Her heart froze before leaping into a sprint. *He's performing RIGHT NOW!*

Strutting atop two back-to-back rows of seats, Ben's signature confidence was on full display as he traded vocals with a tall, good-looking black guy with charm to spare. Riley recognized the celebratory song immediately—"Everybody Say Yeah" from *Kinky Boots*. His blue eyes sparkled, full of excitement, and his voice…

Wow, his voice! Her jaw dropped mid-chew.

It was a revelation, rich with emotion, yet straddling that fine line between professional polish and over-the-top fun. High above customers chowing down on burgers, Ben and his singing partner swiveled their hips and bobbed their shoulders, their infectious interpretation of the Broadway favorite encouraging most diners to drop their cutlery and clap their hands. Two tables of rapt twenty-somethings danced in their chairs, singing along, while several teens slouched in a nearby booth perked up and raised their phones, capturing every perfect note and PG body roll. A trio of little kids leapt into the aisle and jumped around, adorably out of time with the beat, their parents' attempts at corralling their offspring thwarted at every wiggle.

Riley bounced to the rhythm, her smile refusing to budge. *He can really sing! And dance! Tragic Mike, my ass!*

Ben caught her eye and winked, jumping back into the song for the rousing chorus before he hopped off the banquette's back rest and vanished somewhere in the rear of the restaurant. His moment in the spotlight may have been less than four minutes long, but his happy-go-lucky demeanor and heartfelt performance left Riley feeling upbeat and impatient to congratulate him.

Several minutes later, he reappeared, his blue diner t-shirt, black trousers, and server's waist apron replaced by an a-ha concert tee and low-slung faded jeans. His dark tangle of hair had a mind of its own.

Permanent bedhead. Riley couldn't stop staring at it.

"Hey!" Ben slipped into the chair across from her, his smile collapsing. "Oh, something in my hair?" He pawed a hand through it.

I'm that obvious? "Uh, no, nothing!" She dropped her gaze to his chest. "Hey, nice t-shirt."

"Ah, cheers!" His eyes flitted to the faded logo spread across her breasts and leapt back to the safety of her face. "Nice Islanders top. That's ice hockey, right?"

"Right! We'll make a New Yorker out of you yet."

Ben grinned. "I feel like celebrating. I haven't spilled anything on a kid or tripped over my own feet all day."

"Never mind that—Ben, you were amazing up there!"

He ducked his head, a bashful smile—one Riley had never seen before—brightening his cheeks. "Cheers, Riles." His eyes bounced to the plates. "Aw, not hungry?"

She nudged the half-eaten meal forward. "I saved you some dinos."

"Mmm, nachos, too." Ben snatched a chip, the mozzarella playing tug of war with the plate.

"You like nachos but not pizza? Weirdo."

Ben's eyebrows scrunched as he ate. "How'd you know that?"

"You told me at the bar...the strip club? I suggested pizza and you—"

"Oh, right." He eyed her untouched water. "Can I have a sip?"

"Go for it."

He sucked on the straw. "Yeah, it's the sickly-sweet tomato sauce I don't like."

"Seems funny now, but I kinda thought you didn't like *me* that night." Riley's mouth twisted. "It felt like you were trying to get rid of me."

Ben abandoned the straw and took a massive gulp of water. He cleared his throat. "Erm, I forgot about that. Yeah, I was being careful..."

"About what? Cheap pizza slices? Yeah, they're deadly—"

"About *us*...ah, this is awkward." He set the glass on the table and shifted in his seat, avoiding her gaze.

Us? "Awkward?" Her expression pinched.

"Riley..." He lifted the straw and plunged it slowly into the water, stalling. "When we first met at the airport...I really fancied you."

"And now I'm hideous?" Eyebrows aloft, a nervous laugh escaped from her throat. "Thanks a lot!"

"That's not what I mean…" Ben glanced over his shoulder and pulled his chair closer, his long legs bumping her knees. "Oh, sorry!" He awkwardly peered under the table, wasting more time before reuniting with her eyes. "I thought…I thought you might be a snog…or a shag."

Riley raised her eyebrows.

"I know, it sounds awful." His eyes fell to the food on the table. "But that's just what I'm used to. I don't really DO relationships—too messy, and they never work out anyway."

Oh God, he's a fuckboy?! Is that why he doesn't have a girlfriend? "So, when was your last relationship?"

"Drama school. It didn't go well so…" His fingers balled up the discarded paper from her straw. "I…I hook up instead." He winced.

Erghh! Well, at least he admits it!

"I'm sorry I was a jerk that night. I wasn't in a good place. I was embarrassed about stripping, about being fired—lots of stuff. I was in self-preservation mode." He shrugged, dropping the twisted paper. "And seeing you again…I still thought you were pretty and everything, but I knew you had a bloke so I wasn't going to try anything. You were different from other girls, though…the way you spoke to me, the way you acted—you were kind, and I thought, 'I could be mates with this girl.' Truth be told, I don't need another shag. I *need* a friend." He shook his head. "Lucky for me, you weren't having it. You didn't walk away. You wanted to be a mate even when I was being an arse."

"I did…I still do."

"I know, and that means a lot—really, it does. I appreciate it…and I appreciate you saving half your lunch!" His eyes brimmed with mischief as his hand flew back in for more nachos. Mid-bite, he looked up and clocked an attractive brunette three tables away, his gaze lingering before returning to the cheesy snacks.

I'm different from other girls—yeah, like that one, a girl he wants to shag. Her stomach twisted. *I feel kinda insulted, but at least he's honest.*

"You're starving, huh? After all that"—she lurched forward, swatting his arm—"dancing! You had moves all along, you big liar!"

"Yeah, turns out I dance better with my clothes on. Who knew?" He winked as he liberated two nuggets. "Just keeping you guessing, Hope."

THIRTY-THREE

"You've never done this before?" *This is so cool!* Looking at his phone, Ben backed up toward the curb.

Riley shook her head. "I didn't even know it was here." She squinted behind her sunglasses at the massive thirteen-foot-tall red sculpture—an HO sitting atop a PE. The pop art landmark hogged the corner of Seventh and West 53rd, and it was the sister sculpture to the LOVE design a few blocks away on Sixth. Her knotted brow released into a grin.

Ah, there's that smile! Ben's face lit up as he composed the perfect shot. "Say Funyuns!"

Riley laughed.

"Want a peek?" He showed her the image on his cracked screen.

She wrinkled her nose. "Not bad."

"Not bad? It's a masterpiece!" His smile grew as they continued north up Seventh Avenue, his head constantly swiveling, taking in the tall buildings and traffic heading in the opposite direction. "So, where are you taking me?"

"Central Park."

"Ooh, nature!"

"I'd take you up the Empire State Building but..." She adjusted her tote on her shoulder. "I'm kinda broke right now." Her voice faded away on the breeze.

You and me both. "Ah, no worries. I'm skint, too. I donated blood last week to get cash for my mum's birthday flowers. Have you ever done that? It's easy money."

"No. I'm scared of needles."

215

"Ahh, okay! That's why you don't have a tattoo."

"Partially, yeah."

"Hunter suggested I donate sperm for cash."

Riley shot him a wide-eyed look.

"I didn't!" Ben laughed. "Wanking on demand over a porno vid? At least take me out for drinks first!" *Why isn't she laughing?* "The blood money saved me, though. I won't get paid for another two weeks, and tips are thin on the ground. I made thirty bucks but blew most of it already. I need a second job."

"Ben, you shouldn't have bought me lunch."

"I wanted to."

They stopped at the intersection of Seventh and West 54th, their conversation halting along with the southbound traffic. *Hmm, maybe New York is like London—no fun when you're broke?* He did a second take. *Shit! Is her lip trembling? She's fighting it, but she looks like she might burst into tears.* Ben scratched his chin. *I think I insulted her at the diner. I pretty much said she's not shag-worthy, which actually couldn't be farther from the truth! Fuck, Fagan. Fix this. Be kind. Be a friend.* "Lunch was my thank you for letting me stay over *and* for going dancing. Most fun I've had in forever. I swear all the blokes were checking you out, and I felt like, 'Yeah, she's with me, suckers!'"

A tight grin flashed his way and then vanished, lost amidst the crowds crossing the street.

She keeps slipping away. Fuck, I DID insult her. "Riles, is everything okay? Did I do something?"

"You? No!" She nudged her sunglasses up her nose as they stepped underneath metal scaffolding erected around a building undergoing a facelift. She cleared her throat, but scratchiness clung to her voice. "I'm just stressed about graduation, life after..."

Phew! I didn't hurt her.

"The pressure to find a job, pay back my loans...the future—

it's getting scary."

"That's why I like acting. I can pretend to be someone else for a while."

She hugged her middle, but the comforting gesture didn't erase the tremor in her voice or the unwanted tears collecting behind her sunglasses. "I feel like I'm about to be shot out of a cannon without a safety net."

"I think that's normal. We've all felt it—I still do."

"I read about arts cuts, and it makes me worry I'll never find a job. Even if I *do* find one, the salary will be pathetic. Mom will worry, I'll get further in debt..."

"But won't your internship turn into something? Didn't Piper's?"

"Yeah, she's headed back to LA in October, but for me, there's no guarantee. Everyone wants to work at the BBC—you should see the resumes my boss gets." Her hands shifted away from her waist, her fingers spinning the ring on her right hand. "I thought I knew what I was doing but...I feel like I'm questioning everything."

"I'm always questioning everything. I don't think that's bad. It keeps you on your toes." Ben hung back for a moment, allowing a woman with a toddler to pass. *Riley's really fidgety. There's more to this. Something isn't right.* "Riles, did something happen this week?"

Crossing her arms, she looked away. Her fingers dug into her sleeves.

"Monday, you were telling off sidewalk cyclists and drunken pricks. Where'd that Riley go?"

She swallowed a sob. "I called off my engagement—Josh and I broke up yesterday."

Seriously? Holy shit! A spike of adrenaline made Ben straighten up. His eyes widened. "Jesus, what happened?"

"We've been drifting apart—well, me more than him. I fell out of love with him…months ago."

Fell out of…months ago?! Ben's heart clenched. *She's single…*

The pavement grasped Riley's attention. "I thought my feelings would change with the engagement, but they didn't." Her fingers flew under her sunglasses, dabbing away tears before they could fall.

Aw, don't cry. He reached out to console her but pulled back before making contact. His hands didn't know what to do. "You gave it a proper go, though, right? When you feel something in your gut…" *Like I do! Oh, Riley, why didn't you say something over lunch? Before my 'I need a friend' bollocks.*

She sniffed and wiped her nose. "Yeah, but I was afraid to admit it."

"At least you're admitting it now, before it's too late." *Fuck, should I…? Riles, give me a sign.* His fingers gripped the leather bracelet on his wrist.

"That's what everyone keeps telling me—except Erika. She thinks I'm making a huge mistake. Mom was relieved more than anything, I think."

"Why?"

"A bunch of reasons. She thinks I'm too young to get married, and Josh wasn't the most supportive. Everything was *his* career, where *he* wanted to live…"

"That sucks." *So does this. She took my stupid friends speech at face value. It's out of my hands. She's not interested in me. Dammit!*

"I don't know why I'm crying. It's so…stupid." Riley scrunched up her face and swiped away stray tears. "Look, can we talk about something else? Sorry, it's…"

"Yep, absolutely! Fire away." *And shoot me now.*

"Tell me about England and Scotland."

"Oh, sure. What do you want to know?"

"What's Scotland like?" They shifted around a vendor's table piled high with knockoff designer purses.

"Beautiful. Old. Cold, but the people are warm. I don't remember much about Edinburgh—we moved to England when I was six." His eyes drifted to a cart selling hot dogs and large pretzels. "Oh, hang on. Sorry, still peckish." He dug in his pocket for change and smiled at the seller. "Want one, Riles?"

She shook her head.

"A pretzel, please."

The vendor stared at him. "Five bucks."

"Five?! Nice try, buddy!" Riley glared. "Just because he's got an accent! Ben, it's two bucks."

"Shit, is it? I've paid five every time." Ben exchanged money and snide looks with the vendor. He took his pretzel and they walked on, Central Park's leafless trees poking the blue sky ahead.

"When you moved, was it just you and your mom?"

"Yeah, down to Slough. It's west of London."

"Piper said you lived in Windsor…?"

"Yeah, but later, briefly." He offered the warm pretzel. "Salty goodness! Go on, have a bite!"

She waved him off. "No, I'm good. So, why Slough?"

"Mum heard Ben Sr. had quit drugs and moved there. She wanted me to have a relationship with him, so she packed us up and down we went."

"Based on what you said before, I guess it didn't go well?"

"Nope. He wasn't easy to find, and when she finally did track him down, he was living with some woman and their kid. He was working at the Mars factory and I got really excited—free sweets!—but I never got a single Milky Way. He never came to see me." Ben bit the pretzel and chewed quickly.

"Did you ever meet your half—"

"Brother." He swallowed so he wouldn't be talking with his mouth full. "No. He's called Ben Jr. Nice, eh? I literally got re-

219

placed with a newer model."

"Oh God."

"Yep." Reaching into the bag, the pretzel's salt stung his finger. *Ow! Papercut.* "As if being a little kid with a weird Scottish burr in England couldn't get any worse. I had no dad, couldn't spell or read well—this was before my dyslexia was diagnosed. Kids picked on me." He sucked on his finger, washing away the salt. "My no-name secondhand PE kit didn't help me fit in either. In my school, if you weren't sporty or didn't have the latest Adidas trainers, forget it. Social Siberia."

"That's terrible!"

"Yeah. I'd hide behind the old church next door or in the library stacks, waiting for playtime to finish. A year or two on, things were still bad, so I changed what I could. I'd never own a pair of new Adidas or have a dad, but I could lose my Scottish accent. Took a while, but I did it."

"Oh, Ben. I can't even imagine…"

"Slough was more expensive than Edinburgh. Mum couldn't afford a babysitter after school, but there was a widowed OAP—"

"OAP?"

Ben's fingers broke up the pretzel into bite-sized pieces. "Sorry—old age pensioner, a senior citizen."

"Ah, okay."

"Mr. Chamberlain—he lived in the flat next door. His wife died three years before we moved in and he didn't have family. He must've been lonely. Mum arranged for me to stay with him until she got home from work. We'd watch TV and Mr. C would peel apples for me to snack on. Mum's cable was always on the blink and we'd usually end up watching her old VHS tapes, so telly at Mr. C's was a treat. He liked game shows and we'd sit and watch old American series like *Diff'rent Strokes, The A-Team*—"

"Mr. T!" Riley chuckled. "*I pity the fool!*" They both laughed.

"Retro TV shows, gotta love 'em! Everything worked out well by the closing credits."

"Everyone's happy, everyone's loved. Imagine if real life were like that?" said Riley.

"Yeah..." Ben sighed. "But my fave program was from the nineties, a cheaply-made British sci-fi show called *Equinox Ten*. Did you get that over here?"

Riley shook her head.

"Really low budget. It had spaceships made of tinfoil and cardboard, but I loved it! I would mimic their accents over and over again, copying the way they talked, and it kinda stuck. I sounded English, eventually."

"That's so sad." She pushed her sunglasses on top of her head. "I bet your kiddie Scottish accent was adorable."

You're adorable. Ben wistfully smiled at her. "If only I had known you then. One friend would've made all the difference." He dropped his eyes to his salty street treat and cleared his throat. "Actually, Mr. C was a good friend. Not like we'd ride bikes or play console games or anything, but he was super messy, which I thought was really cool. No one made him clean up *his* room! Looking back, he may have been a borderline hoarder, actually. He had piles of clothes, bags of empty takeaway containers, and stacks of dusty books. I'd flip through atlases, old books about space and stars, dreaming of big adventures..." He laughed. "Some things never change."

"He sounds like a really cool grandfather."

"Yeah, he was. I never knew my real granddad. Mum was adopted—"

"Really?"

"Yeah, so Mr. C was the next best thing. I had a great time there. He always remembered my birthday. Every year he gave me something: a Slinky, a Rubik's Cube, that old Operation game with

221

the tweezers—all stuff he found buried in his flat then wrapped up."

Riley raised her eyebrows. "No kids...but he had children's toys?"

"Oh, he wasn't some dodgy Child Catcher bloke! Him and his wife had been foster parents twenty years earlier and they never tossed anything. When I turned ten, he gave me an old telescope. I thought it was the coolest thing I'd ever seen."

"Are you still in touch with him?"

He exhaled heavily. "He died a few months after that birthday."

"Aw, I'm sorry."

"I came home from school and he didn't answer the door. It was weird because he was always there waiting for me. I sat outside, thinking he must've gone to the shops, but an hour later the cops came 'round, carrying his shopping bag full of apples and sweets. They were looking for next of kin. Mr. C had popped his clogs in the cleaning supplies aisle at Tesco—a heart attack."

"Oh no." Riley's shoulders drooped.

Shit, you've made her sad again. Fix it, Fagan. "I mean, what was he doing there? In the four years we knew him, I never saw him dust or use a Hoover. His flat was choked with stuff. So, was it the thought of cleaning up all that crap that finished him off? We'll never know."

Riley pushed him, stifling a laugh. *"Ben!"*

"It's *true*, though! I tell ya to this day, I can't see a dustpan without getting the willies."

Riley couldn't hold back and burst out laughing.

Job done. "If you can't laugh, right?" Ben winked and popped a piece of pretzel between his lips.

THIRTY-FOUR

"I can't believe I let you talk me into this. Oh, bugger!" Ben hugged his knees and refused to look down from his perch on the huge black boulder rising from Heckscher Playground in Central Park.

He's such a joker. Riley dusted off her hands as several little kids, all giggles and dirty knees, scrambled past on the forty-by-fifteen-foot rock. "Isn't it great? Don't you feel invigorated, climbing up here?"

"Invigorated—no. I think I might see that pretzel again."

"Ben!" She adjusted her sunglasses on top of her head. "Come on, the view is better higher up."

"Higher?" His Adam's apple bobbed as he swallowed. "No, I'll wait here, Hope."

"We're barely off the ground. This is nothing compared to what I used to climb…"

"Showoff." His voice cracked.

He's not joking. Shit, he's freaked out. "Aw, Ben, I'm SO sorry! If I had known…" She put her arm around his shoulders. "Look, we can go—"

"Got ya!" He laughed, leaning into her. "I'm not scared of heights. Spiders? Hell, yes. Heights, nah!"

"You goof!" Riley gave him a friendly shove.

"See? I AM a great actor! I'll be an Oscar winner in no time."

"I believe it." She laughed, her eyes sweeping over the playground's splash pad at the foot of the rock. "Ah, I have so many memories here."

"You really love this, eh?"

"Yeah. I learned a lot climbing these rocks."

"What, like it hurts to hit the ground?"

"Smartass!" She picked at the tear in the knee of her jeans. "When I was eleven, Mom and I came to Central Park for a free summer concert. Such a weird day. Dad was marrying Clarissa that afternoon, so Mom brought me here for hot dogs, the zoo, a boat ride. None of it cheered me up, though. I was angry...heartbroken, like why bother? We were headed toward the subway and I spied this big old guy, Rat Rock." She patted the dark stone.

"Rat Rock?" Ben's eyes bulged. "Do I even want to know..."

"Its official name is Umpire Rock, but climbers christened it Rat Rock because it used to be crawling—"

"With rats. Ugh." Ben cringed and closed his eyes. "Now I really do want down!"

She squinted into the sun. "I hadn't climbed for, jeez, maybe two years? Bouldering was something I did with Dad, but when we walked past, this crazy urge grabbed me. Mom paused to check her voicemail and I went for it, clawing my way up the steep north side. I've never seen her get off her phone so quick. God, she was mad— I guess it *was* a stupid thing to do. That side is like a wall, and I didn't have chalk or a crash pad in case I fell."

Ben shook his head. "Chalk?"

"Climbers use chalk to keep their hands dry, for a better grip. Mom was yelling at me—*'Get down here right, now!'*—but I ignored her." Her fingers traced the rock, the touch quickening her pulse. "It all came back to me—which creases were the right size for the toes of my sneakers, where to stick my fingers. I hoisted myself up halfway, a good five feet, then I slipped..."

"Jesus, Riley!"

"Mom freaked, people stared. I was dangling by one hand. I wasn't scared, though—I just remember feeling *angry*—angry at Dad for hurting Mom, for leaving us both, for marrying that stupid woman. I think there was a moment where I wondered, *What hap-*

pens if I just let go right now?"

Ben's eyes widened.

"And you know what I realized? I'd be letting him WIN. He threw us both away like we weren't good enough, and if I let go, I'd be proving him right, proving I was a loser and didn't have it in me to climb to the top without him there. So, just as some guys said they'd catch me, my adrenaline kicked in and I shouted at the top of my lungs, '*FUCK YOU, DAD!*' I used every muscle I had to reach up and across, got my hand into a crevice, and then I got my feet back in place, made it all the way to the top."

Ben smiled. "I so wish we'd been friends as kids. We could've bonded, swearing about our shit dads."

"Oh, I didn't get away with that. I was grounded for a month. Mom threatened to wash my mouth out with soap. Never did, though."

"So," said Ben, patting the rock, "right here is where the *feisty* was born."

"Maybe, but sometimes I need a reminder." She smiled softly. "Thanks for being a good sport, Ben, climbing up here."

"No probs. I think I'm gonna win our game of Never Dunnit—I deserve bonus points for risking life and limb today, just sayin'!"

She laughed, noticing a loose shoelace. "I still don't believe the eighties club was the first time you've ever snuck in somewhere without paying."

"Believe it. It's true."

"So, was the climb up here your favorite part of our Central Park tour?"

"Nope. That big lake with the turtles!" His playful grin was so infectious, Riley's smile grew, too.

Turtles? Aw, bonus points to the cute Brit for loving turtles.

"And those arches with the tiled ceiling near the fountain. That was pretty cool."

225

"Bethesda Fountain?" She tied her lace. "Yeah, it's beautiful."
"What's your favorite?"

"The walk along the Mall." Her eyes jumped to his socks. A face was peeking out between his jeans and sneakers. *Is that...Santa Claus?* The smile on her face reached for her ears. "I love how the benches face each other under the canopy of trees. It's so peaceful and calm—right in the middle of the city, you can just stroll, eat ice cream, check out the artists and street performers. I love it."

"Fancy an ice cream now?" Ben squinted into the sun. "I'd kill for an ice lolly."

"You just want down."

"No, don't call the fire brigade yet. Give me twenty minutes, I might go full-on Spidey, clambering all the way up."

"Bravery, thy name is Benjamin!" Riley snickered. "Well, while you plan your ascent, I'll go grab us ice cream. What do you want?"

"Surprise me. Something silly."

"Oh, you'll regret saying that!" Riley laughed and slid down the rock, joining a bunch of squealing kids at the bottom. *I'm so glad we're hanging out.* She jogged over to the vendor's cart, her wait a lengthy one if the messy line of excitable children and their parents was anything to go by. Pushing up her sleeves, she smiled at Ben and shouted, "Don't go anywhere!"

Watching her, he stretched out his legs and fished his phone from his front pocket, his Facebook app flagging a rare notification. With a finger tap, a post opened featuring a photo of Riley luminous in a sunny yellow dress. Her arms were full, hugging her mom and a retriever, its pink tongue lolling out the side of its mouth as it leaned against her. Below their loving embrace, a single sentence:

Click here to support Help Maggie's Cancer Fight, organized by Piper Paisley.

THIRTY-FIVE

Cancer?! Riley's mom has cancer?

Ben's stomach swirled with nausea. "Fuck no." Brows peaked, his eyes dropped to the vendor's cart. Still a dozen or so people ahead of her, Riley talked with a mom cradling a sleepy baby against her chest. With a heavy heart, he clicked on the link and read slowly and carefully.

My friends, Maggie and Riley Hope, are facing the most difficult challenge of their lives, and they need our help. Less than 6 months ago, Riley's mom, Maggie, was diagnosed with cancer for the third time in 5 years. Maggie is only 48.

Oh, sweet girl. Oh, Riles... Ben's lips pushed out in a reflective pout. *I can't believe...how...?* He read on.

In 2012, she was diagnosed with cervical cancer. Maggie underwent invasive surgery and multiple cycles of chemotherapy and radiation, putting cancer in its place. She enjoyed 4 happy and healthy years until the fall of 2016 when the cancer returned. This time, it was ovarian cancer. Another surgery followed along with more chemotherapy, and once again, Maggie showed cancer who was boss, but the all-clear only lasted a few short months.

Not satisfied with taking Maggie on twice, cancer came back for a third time 6 months ago in November 2017 as a recurrence of ovarian cancer—Stage 3. But in the months since then, it has

227

progressed to metastasized ovarian cancer, Stage 4 involving the liver.

Cancer—of the liver? Stage 4...oh no! Ben chased his breath. *Can people survive that?*

A cheeky laugh caught his attention. Riley was sharing a joke with the ice cream vendor, their hilarity echoing across the playground. She glanced back up at him, sticking out her tongue.

Um...wave at her! Pretend everything's normal. He raised his hand and gave her a smile until she turned away. *Read faster. I don't think I was supposed to get this.*

Maggie is currently undergoing more chemo to shrink the cancer and hopefully halt its progress. Right now, no other organs are affected, and Maggie continues to lead a vibrant and active life, but she needs our help. Her health insurance doesn't cover most of her costs and due to her multiple bouts with cancer, she's been unable to work for almost 2 years. In the past 6 years, bills for scans, surgeries, insurance premiums, chemo and radiation treatments, pain medications, blood transfusions, ER visits, and transportation costs have continued to mount. She recently had to sell her car and most of her belongings in order to keep her apartment at a time when she needs comfort and compassion the most.

A single mother to Riley, a senior in college, Maggie wants nothing more than to spend more time with her daughter, walking shelter dogs, baking, and reading.

I have created this crowdfunding page to help Maggie achieve 'third time lucky' and beat cancer, once and for all. No donation is too small, and each one is greatly appreciated. Please

help Maggie's fight with a donation or by sharing this message with your friends and family. Thank you.

Ben felt a wave of regret and sadness wash over him. His thoughts flashed back to just a few hours earlier, and their walk up Seventh Avenue. *Were you trying to tell me? Fuck! You must feel so scared, lonely...that lost look in your eyes, talk of escaping—it all makes sense now.*

He spied the crowdfunding donation list. A goal of $15,000 was set with only $840 raised so far—$20 each from Piper and Casey, $200 from a Mrs. Paisley—*Piper's mom?*—plus $100 from Leia and $500 from Erika. That total probably wouldn't pay for a ride in an ambulance.

Looking up, he saw Riley skipping along the pavement, ice creams held high. *What do I say?* Ben swallowed heavily and tucked his phone away.

THIRTY-SIX

"Look at this! It's a party on a stick!" Riley tore the wrapper off her birthday cake ice cream bar. *The crunchy rainbow coating is just like I remember!* Her smile grew as she took a bite and slid it against the roof of her mouth with her tongue. The sweetness melted faster than she expected, freeing her to speak. "Like yours? I was *this* close to getting you a SpongeBob one but thought that was more fitting now that you're a climbing pro!"

Ben stared at the unopened Spider-Man popsicle in his hands. "Riley, I have to tell you something…"

"Ooh, a confession?" *Is he kidding around again? Just play along.* "Oh, shit! Spider-Man! Your weird-ass cartoon phobia and SPIDERS, *right*." She nibbled the crunchy bits on the corner of her bar. "I'll run it back real quick, swap it for—"

"I know." Under his breath, he cut her off.

Woah. He's not kidding around. He looks upset.

"Riley, your mom…I know about her cancer."

Wait, what?! He knows about Mom? How?? A sinking sensation, like the one she'd felt from slipping down the rock, overwhelmed her stomach—only her jeans weren't sliding over stone, her sneakers weren't racing to the ground. Staring at Ben, she lost the ability to blink, and she had seemingly yanked his heart down with hers—his usually sparkly eyes peered back, dimmed with anguish and sympathy. She swallowed thickly. The sweet taste left behind on her tongue turned sickly, a cruel reminder that ice cream rainbows and carefree sunny days were meant for other people, not her.

He set down his popsicle and scooted closer. "I saw a crowdfunding link on Facebook just now—from Piper. I'm so sorry…"

She must've friended him…oh God, I should've thought of that. Losing focus, her eyes abandoned his face, searching the park without purpose. Kids continued to laugh and scamper nearby, but Riley heard only her heartbeat thrashing through her ears. *He was my island, my one friend who didn't know, didn't ask questions, didn't see me like he's seeing me now—someone to pity, someone to coddle…and maybe avoid.*

"Riles? *Riley?*"

A cold wetness—ice cream dripping on her jeans—jolted her back, but her eyes wouldn't settle. "I don't really want to talk about it. It's not…I…" The melting treat slipped from her fingers, landing on its wrapper.

"And we don't have to, not if you don't want to, but I know you must be at your wit's end, worrying about her." His tone was gentle, quiet. He leaned closer yet kept a polite distance, waiting for her to let him in. "Is…is there anything I can do? I'll donate some money, of course, but besides that? I want to help."

Her eyes began to sting. *What team will Ben join? The Downloaders? Bubble-Wrappers, Grim Reapers?* His frightened ghost Pac-Man tattoo on the inside of his right forearm caught her attention. *Ghosters. Didn't he say something about 'quick exits' on the airport bus?*

"I'm a good listener. If you want to talk or vent…I'll listen. People say it helps, having someone who'll listen."

You say that, but… She bowed her head and hid behind a curtain of hair, blinking rapidly. *Don't cry—not in public, not in front of him.* Still, her tears persisted, blurring her view of the colorful river of ice cream trickling down the rock. "It gets old really quick."

"What does?"

"Being friends with someone stuck on the cancer hamster wheel." In her bag, her hand scrambled for a tissue. "Trust me, I've seen it. People bail."

"Well, trust *me*—those people are arseholes." Tentatively, he reached out, softly laying a hand on her knee, careful not to touch the pale bare skin teasing through a tear in the denim. "So maybe not all our hanging out will involve chicken dinos or eighties clubs, but that's fine by me. It's the quiet moments—being there, listening...that's what makes a friendship. Riles, I won't bail." He squeezed her knee. "I promise. You don't have to face this alone."

She whisked away her tears, giving him a fleeting glance. *That look in his eyes—I think he really means it.*

"And if you're not ready to talk, if you just want company, I can wait. I'm not going anywhere." He looked down. "I mean that *literally*, by the way. The thought of letting go and climbing down this bloody mountain...I might wee myself—or worse!"

A ghost of a grin raised her damp cheeks.

He chuckled then pulled his smile back, a thoughtful tone imbuing his words again. "Riles, if you need me to be that guy who cheers you up, I'm still here. Just...please don't feel like you *have* to pretend. Not with me."

Pretending...it's become second nature.

A wasp, tantalized by the fruity scent of the melting Spider-Man, hovered beside Ben's thigh, but he remained focused only on Riley—and she noticed. Her eyes traveled to his hand, his thumb slowly grazing the denim—back and forth, back and forth—each light sweep erasing her hesitance to share...to bare her heart.

"Sometimes it's just easier to smile and get on with it, look happy." Several tears fled through her eyelashes.

Watching them slip toward her mouth, Ben's eyebrows creased.

"I keep up appearances at school, at work. I don't let the cracks show, and it's a full-time job." She sniffed. "So, I post happy photos on social media, lie about how I'm feeling, and push on. Truth is, I feel drained. I feel like a fake." She wiped away more tears. "I haven't been happy for a while."

His thumb paused then continued to stroke her knee. "But that's understandable…with your mom…"

"Yeah, that's part of it, but I had times like this when I was a kid. Before Mom was sick, maybe even before Dad left. I don't know, maybe I sensed something wasn't right between them? But it's weird. Sadness sometimes twists into loneliness—even when I'm with friends. Things I love don't interest me or cheer me up. Sometimes the dark clouds last a day, sometimes for weeks. And then, I get angry for feeling this way, but I can't climb out. It's like quicksand." She inhaled a stuttering breath. "So, I do the next best thing—pretend, and I think if I pretend hard enough, something will click into place and I'll feel happier. It rarely works, though…"

"Do you talk to your mom about it?"

"Sometimes. When I was a teenager, she made me—" She bit her cheek. *Am I rambling too much?*

"You can tell me, Riley. I won't judge."

She took a deep breath. "I saw a psychologist. He diagnosed me with smiling depression."

Ben's eyebrows disappeared into his hair. "Smiling…?"

"I know, right? Sounds like a joke, but it's real—smiling on the outside when you're lost and crumbling inside."

"Smiling depression…wow." His hand left her knee, drifting to his chin, where it scratched aimlessly. "I've never heard that before."

"Seriously, Google it." She sniffed and tucked the used tissue in her tote. "I don't like talking about it with Mom—she has enough to deal with. I don't want her more stressed, worrying about me. I have to be strong for her." Her eyes drifted to three sparrows sunbathing on the rock, falling silent for a beat. "I don't get into it with my friends, either. I mean, Piper and Casey know, but that's it."

"Not Erika?"

Riley shrugged. "It's not something you share openly in high school. I felt embarrassed, I guess…kinda still do. Erika's my oldest friend, but…"

"Not necessarily the closest?"

She nodded. "She's more of a *good-time* friend, you know? The one who's there for shopping, parties, meeting guys…but she isn't the most reliable when things turn sour."

"So, why tell *me*? I mean, I'm glad you did…"

"I don't know. Maybe because you know what it's like to feel a bit different from everyone else with your Scottish accent, your dyslexia…" Her eyes roamed the cloudless sky. "Sometimes it's easier to talk to someone who hasn't known you forever."

He smiled, his gaze slowly traveling from her eyes up to her hair and back again. "Well…thank you."

"For what?"

"Trusting me with something so important. It means a lot." He leaned forward, zipping his lips. "I won't tell a soul."

"You don't *know* anyone." She smiled, watching the sparrows chirp and flutter, dipping their beaks in the ice cream puddle. "Oh…except the Eggplant."

"And public nudity aside, he's a very private and discreet bloke!" Ben laughed. "But I mean it. I think it's brave, you telling me."

"Oh, you want *brave*, you should meet my mom."

"I'd love to. She sounds brilliant." He squinted into the sun and turned back to her. "So, your dream of working in California…you're not going with Piper, are you? Not yet. Your heart's here—with your mom."

He sees me. She nodded. "I'm not going anywhere until I know she'll be okay. She's my best friend—she's everything to me. It's always just been me and her against the world. I can't lose her, Ben, I just can't…" Fresh tears threatened her lashes, but she held them at bay. "Third time lucky. She's strong. She can beat it. It's just so unfair that she has to go through it all over again."

Ben blew out his cheeks. "You've really been through a lot."

He gets it. "So have you. We've all got scars."

"Yeah, I guess. I think sometimes the scars you can't see are a lot worse than the ones you can, you know?" Running a hand through his hair, he paused on the back of his neck. He sighed heavily, sinking into silence as his shoulders and chin dropped.

"You okay? Thinking about your dad?"

His eyes were soft, distant. "No. Cancer..." His fingers traced shapes on the rock. "My mum," he said in a whisper.

No! Your mom has cancer? Riley's hand shot to her mouth. "What?! Ben! How is—"

"No, no—it's okay!" he answered quickly, laying his hand on her knee again. "She beat it—years ago. It was breast cancer. They caught it early." He met her eyes with a soft smile.

"Oh, thank God!" She exhaled heavily, her relief palatable. *He's been through this. He knows what it's like.*

"And listen, Hope—your mom will beat it, too. You've got to believe that, okay?" He squeezed her knee. "She's a *fighter*, right? She sounds strong, just like you, saving yourself from falling"—he patted the rock—"when you were a kid. If anyone can fight this thing, and pull herself back to the top, she can. Third time lucky, right?"

"Amen!" *He's been so kind, and a really good...friend.*

"I'm not religious, but okay." He chuckled. "Although I might need a prayer to help me get off this bloody thing."

"You don't need a prayer, you just need me. C'mon, gimme your hand, you big wuss." Riley reached out, and Ben accepted.

Thirty-Seven

Three and a half weeks later

Riley's door flew open to a flash of dark tartan. "Are my roots showing?" Cheek bulging with a lollipop, Piper skulked inside, her fingers crawling through her pixie cut.

"Only slightly. You'll have your cap on, anyway." Riley scrunched her nose, sunburnt from NYU's all-university commencement ceremony at Yankee Stadium two days earlier. She clamped her hair straightener closed, ironing out a kink in the skirt of her blue wrap dress. In three hours, they would be wrapped in their graduation gowns again, taking part in Tisch's "Salute" ceremony, a special send-off just for the School of the Arts.

"But what about the traditional cap toss? Wednesday, I was one of 9,000 so no one saw there, but at Radio City, there's only—"

"One thousand four hundred graduates, Pip." Dewy perspiration collected on Riley's forehead, a souvenir from the hazy morning humidity. "The Salute will be packed too and the hall will be dark. No one will notice—everyone's too exhausted to notice!"

"Yeah, I barely slept this week. Exams, final assignments, packing to move—I'm beat." She pointed at the suitcases by her feet and widened her baby blues at Riley. "The bags under my eyes are just as big as these."

"I think you look gorgeous, Piper!" Maggie beamed from the loveseat, which was doing double duty as Piper's new bed. "That dress! What's the tartan called?"

Piper perked up, posing in front of Riley's overworked fan, its weary blades pointing down from its wall-mounted perch. "Royal

Pride!" The breeze made her flirty short skirt surf over her thighs. "It was created to celebrate Will and Kate's wedding—so Brit Twit tells me."

"Casey probably just Googled it." Riley smiled, smoothing her dress.

"I would've worn my Paisley family tartan, but the green and red would've clashed with the violet graduation gown." Piper's lips surrendered the yellow lollipop as she checked her phone. "Ah, Casey says his family is there and…YES! Grabbed seats on the orchestra level. Thank God! Can't see my mom scaling the nosebleeds wearing five-inch heels."

Riley's eyes locked with Maggie's, her lips mouthing, *"Five inch?"*

Tap, tap—tap. Something tiny and blue skipped across the hardwood floor and settled in the fuzzy area rug.

Riley unplugged the straightener, leaving it on her counter. "Drop an earring, Pip?"

Her friend stuck her lollipop in her mouth and grabbed one lobe then the other, shaking her head as a bright pink pebble clinked against the sill and fell by Maggie's feet. "A stone—?" She leaned forward. "Candy hearts?!"

"Oh!" Riley squished past and stuck her head out the window.

Underneath a crooked bike helmet, Ben smiled up from the sidewalk. Tidy in a shirt, dress trousers, and polished shoes with a small gift bag swinging from his forearm, he straddled a red bicycle that looked like it was one flat tire away from the trash heap. "RESULT! Got two inside your flat, Hope. What do I win?"

"Since when do you ride a *bike*?"

"Since an hour ago."

"Got a lock?"

"Er, no, not yet."

"Carry it up. I'll buzz you." She swerved around her mom's

feet and a primping Piper then buzzed him in, leaving her door ajar. "I forgot to tell him the buzzer's fixed." Riley doubled back, picking up the chalky hearts from the floor.

"Ben's got a bike?" Piper grimaced. "Ew."

"I finally get to meet your British friend!" Maggie's hand passed over her head scarf, ensuring it was straight. "It's great he could use the spare ticket."

"He's fun and totally delish." Piper sucked on her lollipop. "Wait until you hear his accent, Maggie—you'll LOVE it. He's such a Benjamuffin!"

"Pip!" Riley left the candy on her counter. "Stop calling him that!"

The hallway creaked under approaching footsteps. A front tire entered first, followed by Ben's playful whisker-free smile and pink cheeks, flushed from his ride over. "Hey, you look amaz—!" His eyes landed on Maggie then darted to Riley, his mischievous expression sinking fast. "Oh."

"Oooh, *Benjamuffin*." The sucker popped from Piper's lips. "That bike helmet is très sexy!"

He removed it and leaned into Riley's ear, lowering his voice, but the small room made privacy impossible. "Sorry, if I knew—I wouldn't have thrown..." The knuckles on his right hand turned white as he squeezed the handlebar.

"It's okay. She's early," she whispered behind her hair, taking him in. *And you're handsome.* Her hand pressed the middle of his back. *Firm, warm muscle...* She swallowed thickly. Underneath her fingers, his white long-sleeved dress shirt stuck to his skin—the humidity and his exertion to blame—but the cotton also felt stiff. Her eyes crawled up his skinny black tie, inch by inch, her smile growing wider and wider. *New purchases? You did this for me?* "Come say hi."

He leaned his bike against the counter and sink, its frame filling most of her space. Ben's tense brows peaked into an 'I'm sorry if I embarrassed you' wince, but Riley replied with a quick, reassuring squeeze of his elbow. "You look really nice."

"Cheers," he whispered back. "So do you."

They slipped past the bike and Piper, but Ben's usually wide, carefree stride was short and stiff as he clutched the helmet to his abdomen like a shield. Riley cleared her throat. "Mom, this is Ben."

Maggie stood with a smile. "Hello, Ben! Riley's told me so much about you."

He extended his hand. "Same here, Ms. Hope."

"Maggie, please." She clasped his hand, giving it a welcoming squeeze. "How was the bike ride?"

"Good. Quick. It was my first time, but won't be my last…" He let go of Maggie's hand and glanced at Riley. "I'm joining Hunter's courier business."

"Oh, that's great!" She bumped him with her shoulder. "You said you wanted a second job."

"How will you find time for auditions?" asked Piper.

He shrugged. "Gotta earn, otherwise…"

"Good things come to those who try." Maggie nodded.

"I hope so." His eyes found Riley again and he pulled the gift bag from his wrist. "I got you a graduation something."

Riley blinked. "Oh!" *He can't afford this.*

Piper leaned in, tapping the sucker against her lips. "Sweet!"

"That's so kind." Maggie sat down.

Riley pulled out a small box and lifted its lid. Nestled in pale blue tissue, her fingers traced a saddle brown luggage tag with a quote—*If you have a dream, chase it. You might end up with a fairy tale.*—burnt into the leather. *It's lovely.* Riley stared at it, her heart warm and full. *He sees me. He gets me.*

Ben hugged his bike helmet. "I broke Riley's luggage tag when we first met, so…least I could do." His gaze danced between Maggie and Piper.

"Yeah, but it was a cheap one, not like this…" Riley flipped the gift over. Ben had customized the back with her name and phone number. *"This* is gorgeous!" *Practical and pretty—too pretty to use!*

He broke into a smile. "I saw it online and thought with your LA dream—"

"I love it!" She threw her arms around his shoulders, barely giving him time to shift his helmet out of the way. "Thank you," she whispered in his ear.

Ben let out a breath, his free hand grazing her back like he was mindful that the room was watching.

Riley squeezed him tighter. *He's being shy 'cause of Mom. I bet his cheeks are pink.* She pulled away. *Yep!*

She met his eyes. "You shouldn't have, but I'm glad you did!"

"I'm glad you—*I mean…*" He chuckled, regaining control of his response. "You're very welcome."

"Can I see it, Riley?"

Riley handed Maggie the box and shimmied past, tugging the window closed. "Should we go early and meet up with Casey's family?"

Ben pointed over his shoulder. "Riles, I'll just run to the toilet quick…"

"Sure." She reached up and turned off the fan.

Once Ben was out of earshot, Piper lit up. "Isn't he *hot*, Maggie? So much better than Josh!"

"Pip!" Riley threw her a killer glare.

"Oh, come on. You can't deny it, Rye." Piper crunched her dwindling candy, pulling the bare stick from her lips.

"Fine, he's hot. Happy now?"

"He seems lovely." Maggie handed back the tag.

Riley fussed with the box's lid. "We're FRIENDS, people!"

"If I had my way, Riles and Benjamuffin would be a thing."

"And if you had your way, Piper, Netflix would be nothing but puppet shows. Doesn't mean you're onto something."

"Yeah, yeah. Doesn't mean I'm way off, either!"

THIRTY-EIGHT

Radio City Music Hall was almost full by the time Riley, Maggie, Ben, and Piper arrived. Salute-ready in their violet caps and gowns, the best friends waved 'bye to their loved ones and scurried off to join Casey and their fellow graduates backstage.

Ben's foot tapped nervously on the floor. *I don't usually do well alone with parents.* He flipped through the Salute program, hoping the festivities would start soon. "Oh, look! Piper will be chuffed—the opening ceremony includes bagpipes."

"She's a proud Scottish lass." Maggie smiled. "Riley says you were born there, too?"

"Yeah, Edinburgh."

"Your mom must be so proud, her son acting in America."

Shit! Guess Riley didn't tell her I'm just a waiter. His jaw and shoulders tensed. "Actually, I haven't had much luck so far. LA didn't work out, and my Broadway gig…" He swallowed and squeezed his phone, avoiding eye contact. "I'm a singing waiter."

Maggie shook her head and smiled. "Nothing wrong with that, Ben. You're earning money, practicing your craft. You'll get there."

Bless her, she's sweet. He met her eyes. "I'm barely scraping by, but that'll change with this bike courier job. No more living off cereal."

"Cereal! You sound like Riley." Maggie leaned in. "But I remember those days, starting out, hungry for experiences, fun—a good meal." She grinned. "It's a rite of passage."

No judgment at all. She's lovely—like her daughter. He shifted in his seat and his shoulders relaxed, but his foot kept jittering out of sight.

242

"I worry about her, though. The rent she pays for that shoe-box...but she needed to be near campus, and I didn't want her missing out on the social aspects of college. It's important." She paused, her smile rising from a memory. "She saved all through high school—every cent she earned babysitting and from her part-time job went into her college apartment fund. She wouldn't buy clothes or go out. Did she tell you NYU wasn't her first choice?"

Ben shook his head. "No."

"California was—UCLA, their school of theater, film, and television. Made sense, too. Working in California post-graduation has been her dream since forever, and she would've made great contacts during college. She got accepted, but..." Maggie's gaze fell to her lap.

You were diagnosed with cancer, and Riley wouldn't leave you. Ben stopped fidgeting, invested in Maggie's response.

"She chose NYU instead." She looked up at the vacant stage. "I told her I'd be fine and she should go to UCLA. She had worked toward it all through high school, but she's stubborn."

"You must be really proud of her."

"So proud my heart's about to burst. She's had so much thrown at her, but she never complained, worked hard, and here she is— wearing the gold tassel on her cap, graduating as an Honors Scholar...and she's still the kind, compassionate person I always hoped she'd be."

Ben nodded in agreement. His phone glowed with a backstage text from Riley: '4 Benjamin'. He tapped it and a new eighties song popped up: "Lucky Star" by Madonna. *You know it!* A soft grin lingered. "You raised a good one there."

Maggie smiled. "Did you go to college?"

"I did, yeah—Guildhall School of Music and Drama in London. I was the first one in my family to go to uni. Mum was adopted and they left her some money—she put it aside for my education. She saved like mad, too—with what, I have no clue, because we weren't exactly rolling in it." His eyes swept the art deco hall. "She never went out or spoiled herself. I think that's why she was kinda stuck in the eighties when I was growing up. She made do with what she had, and it's rubbed off on me—I love eighties stuff. Riley takes the piss. She's like, 'You weren't even born then!' but it's just what I like."

"And it bonds you and your mom. She sounds like a wonderful woman—with great taste in music." Maggie's finger looped around her ear as if she was trying to tuck hair behind it, but the only soft-ness she felt was her scarf. Ben stifled a wince as Maggie's wide smile faded. Her hand dropped to her lap. "Oh! I keep doing that. Old habits—"

"Ladies and gentlemen." A confident female voice emerged from the speakers. "Welcome to the Tisch School of the Arts Salute. The class of 2018 will enter in a processional, appearing in the order in which their departments were founded." Underneath her an-nouncement, "Pomp and Circumstance", the traditional song for graduation ceremonies, filled the hall.

"Where does the time go?" Maggie sighed. "I can't believe Ri-ley's graduated...oh! There's Casey!"

He entered from stage right carrying the purple 'Film and TV' banner. Behind him, a single-file procession of happy graduates waved, smiled, and snapped selfies.

"The Maurice Kanbar Institute of Film and Television." The woman's announcement was met with applause and cheers from the audience.

"This is pretty cool." Ben's eyes searched for his friend.

Maggie lifted a digital camera to her nose. "Oh, there she is!" She blinked back a tear and beamed, snapping a burst of photos as Riley walked behind Piper, the two women waving and laughing until they reached the steps leading down from the stage.

Ben raised his phone and pressed the red record button, following Riley until she disappeared into the darkness of the hall's orchestra seating.

A pint of Rolling Rock rose toward the ceiling. "To *our* class of 2018…" The Scottish brogue of Piper's father rolled over the long communal table in Hudson Malone, a gastro-pub on East 53rd Street. The watering hole, celebrated for its old New York charm, featured libations favored by Marilyn Monroe, Ernest Hemingway, and Audrey Hepburn. "Long may they keep us entertained!"

"To Casey, Riley, and Piper!" The party of eleven clinked their sodas, beers, and cocktails, their rush upward enticing the rustic table's candles to bow and flicker.

Riley smiled at Maggie, busy across the table sharing a memory with Piper's mom. *So far, so good. She doesn't look too tired.*

"Ahh, that tastes like heaven." Ben nodded to Piper's dad and wiped his lips, sweeping away foam left behind by his perfectly pulled pint of Guinness.

"Born in Scotland, raised in England, loving Irish beer…" Riley nudged his right arm and sipped her water. "Living in New York!"

"He's an international man of mystery."

Ben and Riley turned, following the male voice. Casey hovered over their shoulders, an iced tea in his hand. "It's about time we met, mate. I'm Casey."

Rising to his feet, Ben caught Piper's eye roll over Riley's shoulder. "Hey!" Casey, always wary of shaking germy hands, offered his fist for a bump. Ben complied. "I've heard so much about you."

"All good I hope?" Casey chuckled.

"Of course. And congrats—Riles says you're headed back to NYU to get your master's."

"And I hear you just made an indie film in LA—*and* you're bezzie mates with Mark Keegan."

"Er, I wouldn't call us *bezzie* mates." Ben's eyes dipped to Riley and Piper, who were listening intently. "He's a good friend. I haven't seen him in a while, though."

"Oh, like since uni?"

"Oh no, I last saw him...a year back? April, I think. Yeah, we went for a quick pint in London. He's never home, the bastard." He glanced over at Maggie. A smile lit up her face. "His career has exploded, makes staying in touch tricky."

"*Right...*" With a barely visible squint, Casey lifted his chin and nodded knowingly.

"I lose track of where he's filming these days."

Riley tilted her head. *Hmm. Doesn't sound like they're close.*

Casey played with his straw, plunging the ice in his drink. "I thought I saw something about him joining *Full Throttle 3*."

"I saw that, too." Piper jumped in. "Filming starts in August."

Ben nodded. "Ah, well, like I said, he's never in one place for long these days."

"I hate-watch that franchise. Car chases are so dumb." Piper chewed her martini's olive. "But with Keegs? Sign me UP."

Casey grinned as servers arrived with food for their table. "Ah, better get back to the folks. Just wanted to say hi."

"Thanks, mate. Good to meet you." Ben sat down and Casey returned to his parents at the far end of the table.

Okay, now that we're on the topic—how well does Ben know Mark? Riley smiled. "Have you met Mark's girlfriend?" *If they're close, you'd think Ben would've met her.*

"Alice? No, I haven't, actually."

Alice? "No, I think her name's Alex—she's a playwright? But there were rumors on social media they broke up, so—"

"Oh, nice one!" He leaned away from her, allowing the server to place a smoked turkey panini and fries in front of him. "Thanks. Mmm, this looks *gorgeous!*" He shifted the plate toward Riley, their plan to share the meal and its cost.

Well, Ben did say he's not best friends with Mark, and guys don't take their girlfriends with them everywhere. Riley smiled at him.

"I'm just gonna nip to the men's room." Ben stole a fry and excused himself from the table.

Maggie watched Ben disappear up the stairs and leaned over her small salad. "Sweetie, he's lovely! We had a nice chat earlier."

"He said you talked eighties music. He's such a goof." She giggled, glancing sideways at Piper.

"Must be hard being away from family." Maggie unfolded her napkin. "I'm glad he came out with us."

"Yeah, give him a pint, fries"—Riley picked up her half of the panini—"the promise of cake for dessert and he's a happy guy."

Maggie checked the stairs, ensuring Ben wasn't in sight. "I think he likes you."

Half-listening to Casey's sister, Piper jumped in, lowering the fried calamari skewed on her fork. "Yeah, get on with it, will ya?"

"Get on with it?" Riley mumbled, staying quiet so Casey's sister couldn't hear. "How about you and Casey get on with it?"

"Ew! I'm *eating* here." Piper lost her chin.

"Well?! It's no different. We're just good friends." She lowered her panini and turned to her mom. "And before you say, *Oh, but he's lonely,* believe me—he's not. He's a cute Brit in New York. He's not wanting for admirers."

"But does he buy them all gifts?" Sitting back, Maggie's eyes darted over Riley's head.

"Hey, don't wait for me!" Ben swooped down into his chair. "Get in, Riles."

Avoiding her mom's gaze, she bit into her sandwich.

THIRTY-NINE

One month later

"Rye, got any rum?" Erika's request battled to be heard over a loud playlist stuck in the eighties and the rowdy laughter of Ben's buddies from the diner.

Riley squeezed through the tight crush and past Casey, sitting tall on Piper's tower of suitcases. "Not unless Scott brought some." She lowered the music's volume slightly on her phone, hoping Ben's twenty-fourth birthday party wouldn't get shut down by her ever-vigilant super. He usually had circus class Saturday nights, so hopefully he was swinging on a trapeze somewhere for another hour.

Overdressed in Prada, Erika tapped a carrot stick against her empty cup of prosecco. "I'm craving daiquiris." Her eyes traced the twinkly strings of fairy lights stretching the short distance from the top of Riley's ladder to her photo wall, a glittery arch of stars hung for Ben's celebration.

"I can hit the liquor store downstairs. Riley, need anything else?" Erika's fiancé loosened his tie and unbuttoned his collar.

"You serious?" Riley inched past Piper heating up spring rolls in the toaster oven and laughed, pointing at the wine and beer bottles congregating around Ben's birthday cake. Baked by Maggie, its icing was beginning to melt in the June humidity. "I didn't realize BYOB meant 'bring your own *bar*' to you two. Scott, you shouldn't have to buy more."

"Hey, it's the least we could do. One day when you're a bigshot casting director in Hollywood and I'm a has-been hockey player, you can repay the favor." Scott kissed Erika's temple, weaved past Ben's co-workers, and slipped through the door.

"This is nice." Erika surveyed the room.

Riley wiped perspiration from her brow and adjusted the falling strap of her pink sundress, a steal from the bargain bin three summers ago. "It feels like a party in an airless elevator. My fan can only do so much—"

"No, I mean, nobody here likes hockey—well, except *you*. No one's hassling Scott about their playoff collapse. It's a relief."

"My relief was when Leia and Tyler declined my invite."

"It was nice you asked her. Did you invite Ben's roomie, the stripper guy?"

"Hunter? He's working—bachelorette party."

Pouting, Erika bit her carrot stick. "Aww, no Eggplant then..."

"*Eggplant*?" Piper butted in, leaning her chin on Riley's shoulder. "Overrated. I never find it satisfying."

"I know you don't!" Riley giggled, her eyes catching Cicely, Piper's date, talking to Ben by the window. He looked through the crowd and, spotting Riley, raised a smile and his bag of mini pretzels.

Piper's glittery lip raised into a snarl.

"What's the matter?" Riley grinned at Ben.

"Those dudes, munching chips and slopping beers on my bed."

Riley's loveseat creaked, swamped with Ben's bike courier friends wiping Cheeto dust on their jeans and vaping, filling the room with a fruity chemical stench. "Shit, I told them *twice!*" With a scowl, Riley squeezed past Casey to confront the smokers.

He slipped into the space she vacated. "Bet you're missing dorm life now, Pip."

"I am! Rye's great, letting me move in for four months, but she talks in her sleep, and it's like a 1960s commune here—no stove, no A/C." She pulled her asthma inhaler from her halter dress's pocket.

"People fuck in the shared shower! It's like biohazard central in there."

Shoving up his sleeves, Casey gulped. "Ugh, the horror."

"You could've rented a room somewhere else, you know." Erika's face pinched. "You're not the only one inconvenienced—Riley didn't have room to breathe *before* you moved in."

Erika's jealousy over Piper's friendship with Riley was flaring again. Casey ducked the firing line and faked interest in Riley's photo wall (now Josh-free) and Piper's tray of appetizers balancing on the chest of drawers, PEZ-less for the party.

"Hey! I *am* helping with rent, you know." Piper shook her inhaler forcefully. "I'm not a freeloader bugging her for beauty products, unlike *some* people—"

"Hi ya!" Ben, with Cicely in tow, interrupted the brewing argument. "You...all right? Who needs a drink?"

Erika's face softened. "Shouldn't we be asking you, birthday boy?"

"I've got a nice buzz on, cheers!" He raised his bottle of Stella to Erika. "Thanks to you and Scott helping with the booze."

"Anytime." Erika smiled sweetly.

Piper rolled her eyes and puffed her inhaler.

"Pip"—Ben bumped her shoulder—"lovin' the appetizers. Thanks, babe."

Piper inhaled deeply with a smile as Casey returned, eating a samosa. "My pleasure! So, how was the planetarium?"

Ben's eyes lit up. "It was brilliant! We went to Grand Central Station after to see the constellations on the ceiling. Stunning. I miss seeing stars—it's almost impossible with the skyscrapers lit all night." He smiled up at the twinkly lights. "Riley was determined I'd see some, even if they were strung across this room."

"If you want stars, try Broadway, baby!" Casey joked. "Speaking of, gone on any auditions?"

"Ah…no." Ben scratched the stubble shadowing his chin. "The diner's been insane and on days off, I'm doing the courier thing." He sipped his beer. "I keep getting lost. I punctured two tires and almost got punched by a cabbie, but apart from that, I'm a natural!" He smiled.

"How can you be a bike courier?" asked Casey. "Doesn't your visa—"

"I get paid cash," Ben mumbled quickly behind his bottle. He swung the conversation in a different direction. "So, hey, did you lot see Maggie's cake? It's a triple-decker!"

"The icing's sliding off." Erika fanned her face.

"I hope she's okay." Ben's forehead creased. "Riley said treatment left her exhausted this week."

"How many more to go?" asked Cicely.

"One or two more, not sure." Piper shuffled aside to allow Scott, arms full with a box of bottles, to access the counter.

"Ah, boozy reinforcements." Riley rejoined her friends, the vapers banished to the fire escape.

Ben looped an arm around her bare shoulder, his damp dress shirt—the same one he'd worn to the Salute the month before—cooling her hot skin. His hand slipped forward and for a brief moment, his fingers caressed her arm. *This is a first.* A jolt of heat sizzled up her spine. "Come on, your cake's turning into a chocolate puddle." She grinned. "Want to blow out your candles?"

"Sure!" He squeezed her shoulder and let go.

They eased past their friends to the counter where Riley lit two candles and led the room in an exuberant "Happy Birthday" followed by hollers of "Speech, speech!"

Ben beamed. "I never thought I'd celebrate my first New York birthday with all you lot…" He raised his beer. "Cheers, guys. Thanks to Maggie for this *awesome* homemade cake"—he locked eyes with Riley and took a deep breath—"and Riles, the girl who took me under her wing when God knows she had every reason not to. To quote those magnificent old biddies from *The Golden Girls*, thank you for being a friend. I don't know what I'd have done without you."

"Aw!" Cicely clapped.

"Make a wish!" Piper and Casey shouted.

"Or two!" said Erika. "Why stop at one?"

Riley bit her lip. *Two wishes, that's easy...wait, you idiot—you can't wish on someone else's birthday candles!*

Ben closed his eyes and, with a quick puff, blew out the small flicker of flame. The partygoers cheered and fell back into conversation. Riley set a handful of forks and a knife on top of a stack of dollar-store paper plates.

"I meant what I said," Ben whispered in her ear.

She smiled up at him like no one else was in the room. *I don't know what I'd do without you, either.*

The crowd at the shabby eighties club was wasted and sweaty, and one by one, Ben's birthday posse peeled away into the early hours of Sunday morning, spare the last holdouts: Riley, Piper, Cicely, and Casey. Taking a break, Casey went to the men's room while Piper and Cicely finished their drinks.

"Aw, look at them." Cicely clutched a weaving Piper, keeping her upright as they watched Ben and Riley twirling and laughing to "You Spin Me Round (Like a Record)". "They can't be drunk—all that spinning makes me barfy just watching them."

"I wish she'd stick her tongue in his mouth or grab his ass or SOMETHING." Feeling no pain, Piper gulped the rest of her cocktail. "This SONG, it's—*hic*—Riley. She's a freaking record, repeating on a—*hic*—loop: 'We're friends, we're friends.' FUCK FRIENDS. She should FUCK BEN!"

"Shh!" Cicely giggled. "They might hear you! But yeah, I agree. I think he's into her big time. She's all he talked about. Why haven't they hooked up?"

"Pfffft!" Piper blew out her lips. "I'm tired of being a spectacle, a spect—hater…spectator." She weaved forward. "You watch—I'm gonna make magic happen. It's time to—"

Casey's head leaned in. "To what?"

"FUCK!" Piper jumped. "You scared me!"

"To go home," said Cicely.

"Er—*hic*—ya." Piper's sticky hand playfully smacked Casey's face. "Bwit Twit! You look *sssssoooo* sleeeepy."

He swatted her away. "I had a Red Bull when you lot downed shots." He fist-pumped the air. "I'm buzzed. I could throw shapes for at least another hour—"

"Caseyyyyyyy." Piper's eyes widened like she was trying to force him into a mind meld. Her sparkly eyeshadow had migrated, creating silver splotches on her cheeks. "Cice and I need you. It's…"

"Nearly 2:45," Cicely filled in helpfully. "Pip's staying at mine, so how 'bout riding the subway with us?"

"NOW!" Piper stomped her flats.

"What? To the Bronx?"

"Ten points to Gryffindor! Duh!" Piper stumbled out of Cicely's grip, blocking Casey's view of Riley and Ben. "You staying at your parents', right? Makes sense to go togetha—pleeeeease?"

"Coffee's on me next time at Peet's." Cicely batted her enviable eyelashes. Unlike Piper, the dance graduate looked as neat as she had when she arrived at Riley's apartment.

"Fine! I'll go, but…" Casey peered over Piper's slouched shoulder. "Let's walk Rye home first."

"No!" Piper foisted her empty glass into the hands of a passing guy. He stared at it like she had handed him a dirty diaper. "She's got Ben. She's ffffine."

"Is she?" He narrowed his eyes. "That bloke—I'm not sure about him."

Piper smirked. "Yeah, he's a shapeshifter, all right—aren't ALL actors? The Tischie ones are…"

"If he wants to act so badly, why isn't he doing anything about it?" Casey scrolled on his phone. "I was on Facebook. He has like, ten friends—including you, Riley, and Maggie—but no Mark Keegan." Flipping the phone around, he shoved it in Piper's sweaty face. "His Instagram is nothing but food."

Piper chuckled, pulling the phone closer to her bloodshot eyes. "Ooh, noooo! Ben might suffocate Rye with a roti!"

"I'm being serious! I think he's lying about Mark. We know more about Keegs than he does. Something's off."

"Oh, stop acting like an overprotective brother." Piper shoved Casey's phone into his chest. "He's a nice guy, okay?"

Cicely nodded. "He's lovely! We talked about my move to London to try the West End."

"See?" Casey pursed his lips. "He never talks about *himself.*"

Piper's eyes leapt to the ceiling and fell back to Casey, a jolt of clarity making her stand up straight. "Lay off, Mr. Conspiracy Theory! Cice and Ben just met, for fuck's sake! He's not going to download his life story, is he?"

Cicely nodded in agreement.

"So, say goodbye now—or not. Do what you want, but I'm not dragging Riley out of here if they're having fun together. She needs that right now. Got it?"

"Fine," he muttered.

Casey followed Cicely and Piper through the crush, not waiting for the song to end.

"Dancing queens! *Hic.* We're goin'." Piper threw daggers at the gyrating elbows jabbing her back. "Have fun, catcha laters."

"Oh, okay." Lightheaded from twirling around, Riley breath-lessly giggled at Ben, wobbly-kneed and reeling. "We won't stay much longer. He has to open his present."

"A present?!" Unsteady, Ben bumped into Riley, his hand skid-ding down her back. "Hell yeah!" He flicked his hair from his eyes. "Goes without saying, I'll walk Riles home."

I'd like to do more than walk... Dizzy, Riley leaned into his chest as Ben's fingers pressed into her lower back, his warmth set-ting off goose bumps all over her skin. *Does Ben...? Or is he hold-ing on for balance?* Looking up, she caught Ben smiling at her.

Casey squinted, his eyes darting between the pair. "Rye, can I talk to you a sec?"

"Sure." She left Ben saying goodbye to Piper and Cicely.

"I can stay."

"Case, you can go, really."

He frowned. "Look, you don't need any more guy drama, okay? I don't want you to get hurt."

Overprotective, much? "I appreciate your concern, Case, but I'm a big girl, and Ben and me...it's not like that. I'll be fine, real-ly..." She looped her arm through Casey's, pulling him back to their friends. "Thanks for coming, guys. Get home safe, okay?"

Piper teetered into Riley, planting a sloppy smooch on her cheek. "All yours, Ben!" Her hazy eyes tried a wink but failed. She resorted instead to her old standby, a high five, but her aim was off and she swatted Ben's cheek mid-sway.

Cicely cringed and pulled her away. "Okay, night everyone!"

"Bye." Casey followed behind, glancing over his shoulder.

Ben didn't move until they were gone. "Casey doesn't like me."

"Don't be silly! C'mon!" Riley grabbed Ben's arms, encourag-ing him to jump back into the fast-paced song, but DJ Bob chopped it off mid-chorus with a new tune, slower in tempo with a steady drumbeat and sparse keyboards.

"Oh!" *YES! A slower song.* Riley giggled as people scattered and a brave few coupled up. *This reminds me of junior high. Ew, boys! Run for it.*

Ben leaned in, the music urgent and yearning. "You thirsty?"

Not for booze. Damn! Her shoulders slumped. *Ben wants to run for it. He was holding on for balance—stupid girl.* "Not...really." Her eyes darted, following the mass exodus they were about to join.

"Um, do you..." Ben rubbed his jaw like it would help loosen the words from his tongue. "Wanna dance?"

Want? Yes! Yes! YES! Her eyes widened, but she gave a non-committal nod. "If *you* do..." She suppressed her smile with a quick question. "What's this song?" Slipping her arms around Ben's neck, he reciprocated, embracing her lower back.

"Uh, it's by The Cure." His Adam's apple bobbed as he moved closer, his cheek resting softly against her temple.

Gentle and hesitant, they swayed together, each movement inviting Ben's stubble to press and tickle. His fingers shifted, searching her lower back for a safe place to land.

Is he uncomfortable? Being this close? Riley pulled back, meeting his eyes with a smile. *It's okay, Ben. I won't break.* She leaned in again, tightening her grip behind his neck, her confident embrace working its magic, helping him relax.

While I'm here... She nuzzled his neck and inhaled deeply. *It's so subtle...citrusy aftershave mixed with...Ben! And sweat. Holy. Hell!* A pang in her chest drew her closer, pressing against him as his words from the party teased. *"I don't know what I'd have done without you."*

She sniffed again and her eyes rolled closed, surrendering...to his scent, his words, and the music, its gentle beat competing with the pounding beneath Ben's shirt. *His pulse is racing.* Lyrics about home and love—*flying to the moon*—joined Ben's declaration swirling in her mind, hugging her heart and taking her somewhere she had never been.

Ben's fingers tensed, digging into her lower back. She pressed a soft smile into his shoulder, the firmness lurking underneath his damp shirt making her catch her breath. He tilted his head into hers, his weight comforting and welcome as they disappeared into the music...and each other, as if the song had been written just for them...their breaths rapid, their hearts whirling, everyone else on the dance floor vanishing as the singer crooned, *"I will always love—"*

Mid-chorus, the room plunged into stunned silence.

"Hey!" "What the fuck, Bob?" Sharp voices erupted around them. "Not a-fucking-gain!"

Riley slowly pried her eyes opened. *Fuck!* Her pupils recoiled, assaulted by the brightness of the venue's fluorescents flickering to full strength. Her flinch prompted Ben to lift his head and pull away, but his half-lidded gaze was soft and dreamy, not quite in the room despite the jeers from dissatisfied dancers infiltrating their ears.

"Party's over, folks." DJ Bob's gravelly voice, a souvenir of his two-packs-a-day habit, snarled over the complaints. Dust particles mocked the crowd, dancing alone in the beams of the colored spotlights.

Riley squinted, finding Ben's eyes waiting for her. "What was that song? It's gorgeous."

"Lovesong." He sighed, and then his lips curved into a sweet smile. "Let's get you home."

FORTY

Ben fidgeted on Riley's loveseat, his eyes drifting up to the strings of fairy lights crisscrossing overhead. *I feel like I'm taking advantage.* "But you already gave me a card…" A second slice of birthday cake waited on the milk crate beside his knees.

"Don't you know the nonnegotiable birthday rules?" Riley reached past his legs and pulled two gifts wrapped in racing Pac-Mans and ghosts from underneath the loveseat. "There must be cake, and there must be presents."

Ben shifted back into the cushions, the bag of mini pretzels from the party crinkling between his hip and the armrest. "Two gifts? Riles…you can't affor—"

"If I told you I used a gift card for one, would you shut up?"

"But—"

"Ben, please."

She handed him the two presents and sat down, the old loveseat's springs groaning under duress. "Open them!" A summery nighttime breeze blew a Funyuns bag off the windowsill, scattering yellow rings on the floor.

"Love the paper!" Ben picked up the smaller of the two gifts. *This one's soft and squishy.* His thumb popped the sticky tape…*pretzel-print socks!* His smile did the impossible and grew wider. "My favorite New York snack captured in hosiery!"

"You *do* have a thing for funny socks…"

"You been copping a sly look at my ankles?" Ben looked down. *Santa and Rudolph today.* "I hate to disappoint, but the daft socks weren't really a fashion choice. More like a beggars-can't-be-choosers thing…"

Riley tilted her head. "What do you mean?"

My mouth—fuck. Can't change course now. Just...say it quick! "The fucking hairless rat-cat my flatmate adopted got into my room, chewed all my socks. It was the middle of winter, my feet were freezing, and I was completely skint"—he winced, barely pausing for breath—"so I nicked some on Boxing Day from a pound shop." His expression tightened the faster his words flew. "I mean, it's not like the shop lost a huge profit because of me, and they're ugly and Christmas was over, so they needed a loving home—"

"Ben, I *get* it." Riley balled up the discarded paper and lobbed it into her bin.

Oh. She's not...shocked...

"Being broke and desperate..." She grimaced. "I've done things I'm not proud of, too."

"Like what?"

"You're going to think I'm awful." Riley stared at the unopened present in Ben's lap.

I doubt that. "Try me."

She swallowed. "I only said yes to Josh because..." Her eyes closed. "He said he'd help cover Mom's medical costs. She still doesn't know that's why I said yes."

Woah. So...you weren't heartbroken about Josh but...what the split would mean for your mom. Ben swept his hair from his eyes. "Well, nothing to be ashamed of there. You were being selfless, not selfish, and I get it—I'd do anything to help my mum." He glanced at the socks, a grin rising. "Thanks, Hope. I love 'em. Now I can bench Santa and the gang, mix it up for a while!"

The smile returned to Riley's face. She pointed at his second gift, a large flat square. "I hope you...ah, I'll just shut up."

Ben chuckled and ripped away the paper with one tug. *Oh...woah.* He froze, his jaw falling open. *She bought me a-ha.* His finger traced over the album's cover.

"Do you like it? The guy said it's their first album." She deflated slightly when Ben didn't respond. "I-I checked. That 'Take On Me' song from your phone is there, see?"

Flipping it over, he swallowed with a heavy nod. He blinked quickly. *Don't be a wuss.* "It's…"

"Secondhand, I know. I wish I could've afforded a new one—if they exist—"

"No. It's perfect." Ben pulled out the inner sleeve. A dusty scent accompanied the vinyl. "It's the real deal—from the eighties."

"That's good…right?"

"God, this brings back so many memories. When Mum got sick, I—" *Shit.* He tucked the sleeve back in the cover. *Go on. Tell her. She trusted you, now it's your turn.* He inhaled heavily. "I was put in a group home for a while."

"A group home? Why?"

"I had nowhere to go. Mum's adoptive parents and brother died in a car accident when she was eighteen."

Riley's mouth fell open. "Oh God!"

"So she couldn't look after me on her own. Doctors said her recovery would be long and painful after surgery. There'd be chemo appointments and homecare visits—too much to deal with. I was twelve and had never spent a night away from her. Mum packed up my bag, put a name tag on it. I kinda felt like Paddington Bear, being dropped off with instructions—*Please look after this Ben*—but with peanut butter sarnies instead of marmalade." A hint of a smile graced his mouth. "This record, though…Mum and I danced around to it while she cooked our tea. She gave it to me the day before she went in for surgery. I guess she thought it would help me feel close to her even when I wasn't."

"Aww, I bet it did."

"Yeah, for a while. There was an old record player in the home and I'd play it all the time, but one day after school, I heard yelling and banging upstairs. I shared a room with two other boys and one of them—not sure who—had smashed it to pieces. I burst into tears and they laughed their arses off, called me a 'sucky crybaby', which made me cry even more...about the record, about missing Mum—everything." He rubbed his nose. "The one thing she gave me to look after..."

"But it wasn't your fault."

A tear trickled down his cheek and his fist rose quickly, smothering it. "Sorry. This really took me back for a minute." *DAMMIT, get your shit together, mate.*

Riley wrapped her arm around his shoulder. "Hey, it's okay. I can't imagine. Twelve years old, being taken away from my mom—sharing a bedroom with bullies...I would've been bawling. I probably would've thrown up."

"Yeah. I did that, too." He cleared his throat. "I hated disappointing Mum then—I still do! You know how it is." Admiring the record, a soft grin rose on his face. "If we could talk to our younger selves now, eh? Dust yourself off, don't let the bastards grind you down, and always make your mum proud."

"Did you speak to her today?" Riley pulled her arm away, slowly.

"Yeah, this morning. She prefers chatting when I'm *not* pissed."

"You're pretty sober now, birthday boy." She stuck her big toe inside a Funyun on the floor.

He set his presents on the milk crate and playfully leaned into her shoulder. Riley didn't shift away. "Yeah, I paced myself. I wanted to remember my first birthday in New York."

"First of many."

"I hope so." Catching her eye, butterflies swirled in his stomach. *Should I? God, I want to kiss her so badly and...I think she does, too?* He tilted his head, staring at her lips. *A first kiss changes*

261

everything...

Riley stopped blinking and swallowed. Full lips parting slightly, she sucked in a breath, waiting.

I'm in over my head...what do I do? What if I fall in love with her and she doesn't love me back? Ben let out a jagged exhale, cursing his past. *And if she does fall in love with me...if I break her heart, I'll never forgive myself. I...I can't risk it.* He pressed his lips tenderly to her cheek and pulled away, retreating into the cushions.

FORTY-ONE

"Blew. It!" Piper's frown fought to reach her jaw. "I was hoping for a romantic sleepover with Cicely but instead of kissing *her*, I was hugging porcelain." Lying on the loveseat cocooned in an un-Piper-like tank and sweatpants combo, she scratched her messy nest of hair. "Oh..." She tugged her phone from her waistband and hit the voice memo app. "Buy toothbrush to keep at Cice's." She stopped recording and let out a groan.

Riley rustled a large trash bag, tossing plastic cups into it.

"Urghhh! Room, puh-lease stop torturing me?! I think the subway ride gave me vertigo."

You don't have vertigo! "You should've stayed at Cicely's. I was going to—"

"Invite Ben over for round two?"

I'm not in the mood for this. Pretending not to hear, Riley crawled across the floor, tossing Funyuns and popcorn into the bag trailing behind her.

"So, did Ben like his present?"

"He loved the record. He says they tour sometimes and we should go—"

"No, no, NO. That's not what I meant!" She propped herself up and froze, her smirk slipping. "Oh, fuck. You didn't...on my bed, did you?"

"No!"

Piper leaned forward, desperate for information. "*So...?*"

"He kissed me on the cheek and left. It was..." Riley yawned, scratching her jaw. "Almost 4 a.m." She resumed picking up junk food from the floor.

"Annnnd you didn't give him a hand-job? Or let him put his hand up your dress? What *is* this, *Downton Abbey*? I'd raise my eyebrows but they hurt!" Piper winced. "I swore you guys were gonna fuck last night. His little speech? My God—he has it bad! And he wouldn't leave you alone at the club. When you weren't spinning around like lunatics, you couldn't fit a piece of paper between the two of you—"

"Yeah, it was packed." Riley scooped up a Funyun. "Barely room to breathe."

"Seriously. I stay at Cice's to give you privacy and you waste it."

"Pip—"

"Don't say it!" Squinting, Piper rubbed her forehead. "You're 'friends'!"

"We are! I don't know why you have such a problem with that!"

Piper blew out her cheeks. "I don't, but I don't dance with friends like *that*."

"It doesn't matter anyway." Riley kneeled, dusting crumbs off her hands. "Even if we weren't friends, I'm not the type of girl Ben dates—if you can call what he does dating."

"Hey, *I* went on a date with him."

"You know what I mean." Walking on her knees, Riley dragged the trash bag to the milk crate. "Hey, have you looked at Mom's crowdfunding page? Erika shared it with Scott's teammates and it's up to two thousand dollars—"

"Don't change the subject! I think you're *exactly* Ben's type! Cicely said he wouldn't shut up about you."

"Yeah, I threw him a party—"

"Nope, it's more than that. He's crazy about you. We all see it—even Erika, and you know how badly she wants you and Josh back together."

"Ben's a flirt." Riley eyed his half-eaten bag of mini pretzels. "He's like that with everyone."

"But you're not. C'mon, I've known you long enough that—"

"Yeah, so you should know when you're crossing the line, Pip."

"If I can't cross it, who can? Rye, be *honest*—how would you feel if he started seeing someone, like seriously…as a girlfriend?"

"He's not into relationships—"

"But if he *was*…how would you feel?"

A heaviness squeezed Riley's chest. A familiar echo—*How would you feel?* She had banished that question to the cobwebs of her mind, dreading the day it demanded an answer. It was inevitable, wasn't it? Ben would tire of pick-up lines in bars and one-night stands. He wouldn't be on the market long; he'd meet a smart, pretty girl who loved books, new adventures, and eighties music, and she would do what everyone else had failed to—make Benjamin Fagan her own. He was too gorgeous, too fun, too beautiful *inside* to walk through life unattached. It was inevitable. One day, Ben would start seeing someone who wasn't just a friend, someone who wasn't…her, a sometimes-depressed girl with a sick mother and mounting debts. *Definitely* not Ben's type.

"C'mon—how would you feel?"

A sour taste rose in Riley's throat. *So jealous I would scream.*

"So?!" Piper stared, her annoyance at being kept waiting making her eyelid twitch.

So…now I feel even more stupid for thinking he liked me that way. Riley stared back. "I'd be happy for him, just like I am for you. That's what friends do." She grabbed the bag of pretzels and chucked it in the trash.

FORTY-TWO

Two weeks later

Laughter, heavy footfalls, and thumping bass from the Friday night rager upstairs drowned out the bathroom sink's faucet. Alone on the sofa, Riley explored Hunter's living room, AKA Ben's bedroom, for the first time. His possessions were scattered across the room: his mom's pink wheelie case flipped open opposite the sofa, a lone candy cane sock lying across his dress shoes, and a messy pile of concert tees tumbling from the gaping mouth of his backpack. The cherished a-ha record leaned against the black wall, safe from foot traffic beside two birthday cards: hers and one with a tartan heart announcing *Happy Birthday, Son.* A small, half-eaten cake sat on the crowded kitchen counter flanked by unwashed dishes, but the rest of the place was alpha-male central with Hunter's bicycle para-phernalia, protein powder tubs, and muscle-shredding free weights dominating the space.

Riley tugged the sleeves of her sweater over her wrists and smoothed her skirt, a jumbled knit blanket separating her from a messenger bag lying upside down. She looked up. *Red ceiling—not exactly calming. How does Ben sleep here?* Eyes returning to the coffee table, she spotted his phone. *Should I...? I want to know about Mark.* Curiosity gnawed her stomach. Ben was still busy in the bathroom...

She snatched his phone and woke it up. *Still no security code.* Entering his contacts, she guiltily scrolled the brief list...*a few guys' names, Hunter, several girls*—Riley paused, then kept going. *Piper, his mom, but no 'Mark', no 'Keegan', no 'Keegs. Hmm. Did they lose touch then...or were they never friends?*

She returned to the home screen and it buzzed in her palm. *Shit!* She dropped it on the table as if it had tasered her hand. A text from Hunter appeared: *Dude, hurry up! My night off means I need my wingman!*

Scooting backward into the cushions, the messenger bag shifted and something slipped out, falling to the floor. *Jeez! Such a klutz.* She bent over to scoop up the mess. *Oh! Unopened condoms—Hunter's prepared.* She chucked the handful back into the bag, returning it to an upright position against the armrest. A name tag flipped over on the handle—Benjamin Fagan. Her stomach pinched as the faucet drew silent in the bathroom. *Condoms, wingman—wise up, Riley. He's off to meet women—probably sexually adventurous women, women used to different things than you, things Ben probably enjoys.* Riley's heart ached. *What ARE you doing? This crush needs to stop now—*

"O-kay, all ready!" Ben swept into the room, the scent of soap and toothpaste following him. His face was smiley and his fluffy hair begged for attention, as did his ass, exquisitely displayed in dark jeans.

Ben's hookup ready. He won't be crawling into bed alone tonight.

"I'll let Hunter know I'm on my way and we can make a move." He glanced up at Riley. "This weather, eh? Last weekend in June and we're both wearing sweaters." His fingers slipped along his hem. "Thanks for dropping this off. Maggie fixed it perfectly—it's like new! You'd never know there was a hole."

"There were *five* holes!" Riley snickered. "I think it's time to buy another sweater. You can't live in New York with just one—"

Her phone lit up. *PARTY UPDATE—Josh brought a date! Leia stormed out, says his date is one of Tyler's puck bunnies. PLS COME SOON. Can't have bachelorette/bachelor party w/o ANY bridesmaids!*

Her shoulders fell.

"Is it Maggie?"

"No, Erika's freaking out." Riley looked up. "Josh brought a date, Leia left in a huff…"

"Shit! Are you okay—with Josh being…?"

"With someone? It's fine. I *want* him to move on, I just… It's going to be awkward, and I wish I didn't have to go."

Ben walked away, yanking his sweater over his head.

Riley's eyebrows pinched. "Too hot?"

"I'm changing. I can't let you walk in there solo, not when he's bringing someone."

What? He's coming…with me? "Ben, I'll be fine. You, on the other hand, are gonna face Hunter's wrath if you don't show in Soho soon." Her eyes traced his back, his muscles flexing as he whipped open the small closet by the door. *You're staring again! Stop!* She dove back into her phone.

"This party's *posh*, right? At some exclusive sky-high bar?"

Her phone buzzed with a text.

RYE HELLO! Did you get my msg?

"Yeah, but I dressed for the rooftop deck…warmth and comfort over style." She giggled, beginning her reply to Erika. "All Erika's fashionista friends will probably stare—"

Zzzzzzzip.

Riley glanced up. Ben was stepping out of his jeans, his navy underwear with several FCUKs on the waistband showing, along with so much more. *Oh—hello, tight butt!* He turned and she caught a glimpse of body hair before her eyes drifted…down…followed by her jaw. *Woah, Ben…!* She averted her gaze, her mind stuttering.

Ben pulled a dark gray suit from the closet. "C'mon, Riles, get your skates on!" A laugh left his lips. "Tonight's another first— we're partying under the stars!"

Thirty stories above the squawking taxis and Friday night madness of Midtown, Ben and Riley strolled down a moodily lit hallway that opened into The Skylark's main lounge, all floor-to-ceiling windows, leather couches, and Instagram-worthy views.

"See anyone you—wow!" Ben sputtered. "Look!" He pointed to their right where the Empire State Building glittered its breathtaking welcome.

Riley sighed. "Oh!" Smitten by the jewel in the dark sky, she stepped toward the glass. "She's stunning."

"Yeah, she is." Ben smiled softly, his eyes sweeping up Riley's back to the honey waves pooling over her shoulders.

"Rye, thank God!" Erika rushed through a cluster of Hugo Boss and Calvin Klein, her champagne-hued cocktail dress a successful score after schmoozing with designers at last month's Met Gala. "You're here…with *Ben*?" She side-eyed his secondhand suit.

I saw that Erika! Riley squeezed Ben's arm. "Yes, and don't we look amazing?"

His hand crept up his black tie. "I hope I'm not gatecrashing…"

"No, it's just—" Erika's flittering glance searched her guests.

"Josh is here—yeah, Riles told me."

Erika smiled tightly. "I can't deal with more drama."

"You won't get it from me, scout's honor." Ben scratched his whiskers. "Where's the bar?"

"Turn the corner, can't miss it." Erika pointed over her shoulder.

"Is it…"

"Free? Yes, Ben."

"Great! The usual, Riles?"

"Please."

With a nod and several 'pardon mes', he was swallowed up by

the well-heeled crowd.

"Is Stanley Pup here somewhere?"

Erika ignored Riley's question. "It's not serious, Josh and that girl—it's just sex." She couldn't get the words out fast enough.

Riley stuck out her chin. "It's none of my business." A gust of cool wind blew through the open patio door. "He's a free agent so…" She shivered. "Look Eri, I know you've known us both for ages and you're taking our split hard, but I'm happy with my decision, and obviously Josh is, too."

"I thought he would've begged to get back together."

Riley fell silent for a moment, peering at the lit skyscrapers puncturing the evening sky. "He doesn't need an unhappy fiancée trailing after him to Minnesota. He's got a bright future and should take advantage—even if that means hooking up with Tyler's cast-offs."

"Rye!"

"Josh never cheated on me. He could've, but he didn't. So, let him have some fun."

"As long as it's him having fun and not my Scott."

"Scott would never! He's infatuated, the most faithful hockey player ever."

"Speaking of unfaithful…" Erika's eyes followed a confident blond in a black suit back-slapping his way through the party. "That asshole didn't move a muscle when Leia ran out."

Riley scrunched up her nose. "I feel sorry for her."

"That was easier than I thought." Ben appeared at Erika's elbow with a tray of drinks. "Bride-to-be, champers for you."

"Ah, thanks." Erika claimed her flute.

He handed Riley an orange cocktail. "A sidecar for you—"

A vigilant server appeared at his side. "I can take that, sir."

"Ta!" Ben relinquished the tray and sipped his pint. "Erika, I saw Scott. He said someone from *Housewives* is asking for you—"

270

"What!" A hand flew to her mouth. *"The REAL Housewives?"* Riley waved her on. "Go!" She laughed as her friend tore through her guests. "It's Eri's dream to be on that show."

"I guess that's her TV happily ever after, eh?" Ben winked.

"The sun always shines on TV, right?"

Ben chuckled over the rim of his glass. "So, want to nose around?"

Riley led Ben through the throng, past cushy blue sofas and button-studded leather pouffes accessorized with all-star NHL players and their partners. The divide between flings, girlfriends, and wives was difficult to decipher when free booze was flowing and everyone looked like models. Riley gave Ben the play-by-play, whispering who the players were and how they were connected to Erika and Scott.

The bride-to-be appeared over Riley's shoulder, arms linked with a striking brunette.

"Riley, Ben! Have you met Olivia Chadwick-Smythe? Ben, she's from London!"

"Hi." Riley and Ben spoke at the same time. No one attempted to shake hands as Olivia's were occupied with a bulging white envelope and a roll of raffle tickets.

"Erika thinks all Londoners know each other." Olivia's posh British accent made Riley stand up straighter. "In lieu of Erika's no-engagement-gifts policy, we're doing a fifty-fifty draw. It's thirty tickets for fifty dollars or a hundred for a hundred. End of night, half the money raised goes to the winner, the other half to my theater charity for at-risk youth in the Bronx." Her long eyelashes blinked expectantly.

"Um..." Riley grimaced at Erika. *You know I would if I could...*

Ben squinted at her discomfort. "Oh, bugger..." His accent was distinctively more plummy sounding. He dug dramatically in his suit jacket pocket, smiling at Olivia. "I was running quite late and

271

managed to forget my wallet." His hand produced a crumpled five-dollar bill. "Best I can do, unfortunately, love."

Accepting the ratty bill, Olivia fought a frown. "Every *little* bit helps." She exhaled heavily, tore off a single ticket and slapped it in Ben's hand, turning on her heel with barely a "Cheers."

"Good luck!" Erika blew a kiss and followed Olivia to the next table.

"Thanks for bailing me out." Riley laughed. "But what the fuck was that voice?"

"Shut up! I can do posh!" Ben stuffed the ticket in his pocket. "I don't remember Her Majesty from the bachelorette."

"No, she wasn't there. I think Eri added her to her social circle recently."

Another drink later, Riley pointed out on-air TV personalities and several socialites, their enviable fashion show making her question her choice of outfit. *At least Ben looks lovely in his suit.* She stared down at her boots and tights, feeling like her lack of wealth and trendiness made her stand out. *It's so surreal. This party, the booze...how much of Mom's treatments and bills could be covered by all this?*

"I feel...guilty." Riley squeezed her glass. "Drinking expensive cocktails when I can't pay my loans, can't help out Mom."

Ben tossed back the dregs of his second pint. "That's why you *should* enjoy all this. You don't take it for granted, not like some of these spoilt brats." He eyed a parade of servers snaking through the party with trays of bite-sized indulgences. "I didn't eat today, did you?"

She shook her head. "I have ten bucks 'til pay day. I'm rationing cereal."

His warm hand wrapped around hers. "Not anymore, my lady." He flagged down passing waiters, making sure Riley sampled every option.

"Pigs 'n' blankets, pretzel bites—mac 'n' cheese cupcakes?" Ben's eyes lit up. "How does *that* work?"

He didn't stop hijacking appetizers until Riley groaned with satisfaction. She gave high praise to the Buffalo chicken lollipops while Ben broke away from his pretzel obsession to proclaim the BLT lobster rolls his favorite. "I've never had lobster before. It's lush!" A spot of bacon and tomato jam rode the corner of his boyish grin.

He doesn't try to be adorable—he just is. "You're got a little..." Riley motioned with her finger, and Ben's tongue licked his lip with a soft flick.

Lucky lip. Riley's gaze stuck, her memory rewinding to Ben's earlier surprise strip in Hunter's apartment, his tight backside, the impressive bulge stretching the thin layer of cotton... Heat spread up her neck to her cheeks. *Ben's obviously a show-er, not a gr—*

His eyebrows creased. "Is it still there? You're staring."

"Oh, no, you're good." Looking away, she hid behind her hair and scrunched her eyes. *SO good! Jeez, stop torturing yourself!* She inhaled a deep breath and exhaled into a smile, her glance skating across a silver table topped with flickering candles, half-drunk cocktails, and a guy leaning on the far edge, staring. *Josh.* A shiver crept up her spine. *Act natural.* She turned back to Ben. "Let's head to the roof deck."

"Sure." He laid his hand on her lower back, staying close and guiding her through the noisy crush.

"I don't think we've met."

The loud voice turned Ben's head.

Riley's jaw stiffened. *Great.* She painted on a breezy smile and glanced back. "Josh, hi."

His wall of a body weaved. "You act fast." Boozy breath lingered between them.

And he's drunk. Riley's eyes flirted with the ceiling. "Josh, it's not like that."

"Seriously, mate, we're friends." Ben shifted closer to Riley. "Calm down."

"Great." Josh snorted. "He's Australian?"

"Josh, Ben. Ben, Josh." Riley shook her head. "I'm here to support Erika and Scott, not to rub your nose in a new relationship. Speaking of which…where's *your* date?"

"She fucked off already." Josh swayed and whiskey slopped over the lip of his glass.

"Well, why don't you mingle? Introduce yourself around. It's the perfect opportunity to meet more NHLers, right?" Riley looked over her shoulder, hoping he'd take the hint.

"Yeah…*mingle*. I should meet teammates and…" Josh opened his mouth but forgot his point before the words came. "Get another drink." He staggered away, spilling a trail of whiskey.

"Nice save there, Riles," Ben whispered. "I wasn't relishing another broken nose."

"Let's head to the roof. I don't want Josh bothering us again."

Arriving on the thirty-second floor's east terrace, Ben was mesmerized by the sparkly lights of the city. "It would be peaceful up here if there wasn't a party going on."

A crisp breeze tousled Riley's hair.

"You warm enough? Want my jacket?"

Josh would never offer. Too bad I'm not cold… "That would be great!"

Ben swiftly wrapped it around her shoulders, and Riley fought the urge to bury her nose in it for a deep sniff.

They walked along the north side, marveling at the lights from Times Square as they passed clusters of beige couches filled with Erika and Scott's guests. Searching for seats, they shuffled through the crowd, passing the women's restroom where raised voices slurred and sparred. Riley snickered at Ben's wide-eyed headshake, the pair turning a corner where a tiny nook's gray L-shaped sofa sat vacant.

"Finally!" Ben fell into the cushions. "Work did a number on my back today."

"You're such an old man!" Riley dropped down beside him.

The yelling inside the restroom grew louder, closer, two angry female voices competing with Justin Timberlake crooning through the terrace speakers.

"That's why this couch was free." Ben chuckled.

"For fuck's *sake!*" a woman howled. "I can't go anywhere, not even to my best friend's party without one showing up!"

Shit! That's Leia. Riley bit her lip.

"Well, I didn't invite her!"

Holy crap—Tyler!

"Ooh, drama! Where's the *Real Housewives* people when you need them?" Ben laughed.

"Maybe we should give them privacy?" Riley stood up, grasping Ben's jacket at her shoulders so it didn't fall off. "I don't want to be in the middle of a domestic situation that ends up on Page Six."

"You fucking liar!"

Okay, that wasn't Leia. "Ben, let's go."

The warring couple careened out of the restroom, closely followed by a disheveled brunette, her dress half-unzipped, teetered on sky-high heels. The intoxicated trio blocked Riley and Ben's escape.

"Shit!" Ben frowned and looked over his shoulder. "Can we head back the other…?"

Is THAT the girl who came with Josh? Riley's jaw dropped.

"Leia, *calm down!*" Spying the slack jaws of Erika, Olivia, Riley, and his riveted teammates, Tyler buttoned his shirt and lowered his voice. "I think we've both had too much to drink. Lemme take you home—"

"Oh, listen to husband of the fucking *year*!" Leia looked angry but broken, mascara streaking down her cheeks. Riley felt pity for her.

"Leia, baby, c'mon. Don't do this. Let's get out of here."

"You *bastard*! You promised me—never again. You *enjoy* it, don't you, you sick fuck—hurting me?" Leia's wobbled precariously, steadying herself with the help of a table. As she gained her balance, her eyes widened, spotting Riley and Ben. "TWO can play that game." She pointed a wobbly finger at Ben. "See that guy? I fucked him *hard* in our bed."

FORTY-THREE

"RILEY! WAIT!"

A taxi screamed its disapproval as Ben stumbled into its path.

"Oh, fuck it!" The Brit went for it, darting north across West 39th Street, his sudden sprint unleashing a shrill chorus from the barrage of cars grinding to a halt.

Riley didn't dare look back. *Keep going, get to the subway— oww!* Her boots pinched as she rushed toward the colorful pandemonium of Times Square.

"WAIT!" Skirting bumpers and rude hand gestures from passing car windows, Ben swerved around the curb, turning right and crossing Seventh Avenue before a red traffic signal had a chance to end his chase. Legs pumping, he fought with his jacket, stuffing his arms through the sleeves. "RILEY!"

The glow of her phone caught her eye. *Mom? No, Erika.* In a texting frenzy.

Everyone's gossiping—I said no drama!

Srsly? Ben and Leia? WTF???

You OK?

Riley shook her head. *NO!* Turning it off, she began to run, jamming the phone in her purse. She frantically dug around inside, her fingers searching, the subway entrance half a block away. *Shit!* She flicked past her BBC security pass, Sephora name tag, and wallet. *Stupid MetroCard! Where is it?!* Boot heels scuffing the pavement, she looked over her shoulder. Ben was stomping to a halt, something on the ground grasped his attention.

He stooped, picking up her MetroCard.

FUCK! She turned away. With twenty dollars loaded on it, she couldn't afford to leave it behind.

"Riley! We need…" Heavy breaths fought through his words as he ran, meeting her on the corner of Seventh and West 40th. "To talk…please." His shaky hand grasped her elbow.

"Talk?" She whipped her arm away. "Why? We've talked for hours and it turns out I don't know you at all."

"Please, let me explain."

"No, let *me* explain." She leaned in, not backing down. "Your little secret with Leia embarrassed me in front of my friends, in front of my ex, and God knows who else! There were TV people there, Ben!"

"I'm sorry. I'd never hurt you on purpose, especially like this." An ambulance stuck on Seventh raised its shrill siren, urging traffic to move and prompting Ben and Riley to cover their ears.

"You slept with *Leia*!" she shouted and spun around, racing quickly past the crowd crossing West 40th Street, the chaotic flashing billboards around them no match for the electrical storm inside her head.

Ben darted after her. "I didn't even know her name was Leia until you told me. She said her name was Lisa!"

"Oh, spare me." She crossed her arms and kept walking, her boots barely touching the Fashion Walk of Fame disks embedded in the sidewalk.

"It's true! Look, I know you're pissed—you have every right to be—but give me a minute and I'll tell you everything."

"A minute?" She huffed.

"There's not much to tell. Please?"

She yanked her MetroCard from his hand. "One minute!"

"I met her my first night at the strip club, in the bar watching the guys. She introduced herself as *Lisa* and said she was checking out venues for a bachelorette."

"And?" The pedestrian crossing blinked 05, 04, 03—Riley

didn't wait. She ran across West 41st with Ben's long strides over-taking her. They reached the other side without a second to spare.

"She kept buying me drinks and flirted—a lot. I was flattered. A club full of fit blokes and she was giving *me* the eye."

"You weren't flattered, you were horny."

He exhaled heavily and looked up. Airbrushed actors and models, all Hollywood smiles and picture-perfect lives, passed judgment from gigantic ads. "Hunter came over and asked if I could stay out for the night. He was bringing some girl home. I had told Lisa—*Leia*—I was sleeping on his couch. That's when she offered."

"Sex..." Riley grimaced, weaving through the non-stop onslaught of people.

"Not upfront—no. She just said I could stay at her place for the night."

She shook her head. "She wanted to fuck you. You wanted to fuck her."

His face fell as he tried to catch her eye. "I needed a place to kip! And Leia never mentioned hockey or you. She told me she was a student, working on her master's at some fashion school."

"The Fashion Institute of Technology." A bus wheezed by with a *Lairds and Liars* season three advertisement stretched along its side, but everything beyond Ben was just a noisy blur.

"I swear, I didn't know she was married."

Yeah, right. Riley stared ahead, the dazzling billboards advertising everything the heart desires—cars, clothing, jewelry—but nothing she craved most: honesty, loyalty...love. "So that huge rock on her left hand didn't mean anything, huh?"

"No ring—her fingers were bare. I noticed at the bar."

"So, you *were* interested. Don't pretend you weren't."

"Riley, what hot-blooded single guy chatting to an attractive woman *doesn't* check for a ring? I checked your hand the minute I met you. And don't deny it—women do it, too."

Damn. Yeah, he's got me there. "Well, you would've seen wedding photos in her apartment. She has tons."

"I saw paint cans, a ladder, furniture covered with drop sheets." He scratched his head. "And to be honest, after five minutes, I wasn't exactly hunting around for evidence she was married..."

"Don't paint me a picture." Riley stopped abruptly, the dancing lights above the door to the West 42nd subway entrance inviting her in. *Your minute's up.*

"It was a mistake." He swallowed heavily. "I left in the morning. We didn't exchange numbers."

"No, just bodily fluids." She crossed her arms again and swayed back and forth, as agitated as she was chilly.

Ben dipped his head. "Two weeks later, she's at the club, *you're* at the club—I was fucking gobsmacked. Riley, I really liked you!"

And I liked you! You were lovely and respectful, dancing with me, and then... "You were a dick at the bar."

"I figured Leia told you about us sleeping together...but when it never came up, it was like...I dunno, a second chance."

"What? A second chance to fuck me? Yeah, 'cause that's what you do." Her palm tightened around her MetroCard. "You're just a fuckboy. You're all attentive and sweet until you get what you want."

"I know you think I'm a dog, but I've only slept with two women here, that's it, both one-night stands, and neither meant anything." He moved closer. "Riley, please, don't be cross—"

"I can't believe you slept with *her*. Of all people..."

"Yeah, she's not my type. You'd never catch Leia eating a chicken dinosaur."

Wha—? Oh. Riley's angry glare softened into a defiant pout.

"You said she wasn't a close friend, Riley, so I thought, great, lucky escape—it'll never come up. I was stupid thinking you would never hear about it. I should've mentioned it..."

"Yeah, you should've. I guess I was a real *disappointment* to you, offering a place to stay that night, *without* benefits..."

"Please don't think I stayed at yours expecting sex, Riley. You're...different..."

Here we go again. He thinks I'm some fragile born-again virgin. "I'm not a prude!" Her chest rose and fell as she spit out her response, earning a "You tell 'im, girl!" from a passing clique of women out on the town.

Ben edged closer, ducking his head to keep their conversation private. "I know you're not."

Riley lowered her volume. "What you or any of my friends do behind closed doors is none of my business."

"So then why does any of this *matter*?"

Chasing breaths, her mind raced. *Why? WHY? Because of Christmas socks and candy heart hellos, peanut butter breakfasts and bedhead hair. Because you make me laugh even when my heart is breaking. Because you ask and really listen to my answers. You see me like no one else has...you were my escape.* Her mouth gaped. *You were my island.*

"Riles, why do you care who I was with?"

Because... Riley swallowed, her heart pounding, leaping into her throat. "Because I—" She flung her arms around his neck and pulled him in, capturing Ben's mouth with her own. Soft and warm, his lips responded immediately, parting with a surprised moan as his hands claimed her waist, fingers digging in, tugging her close.

His lips...oh, wow...I'm not imaging this—this is happening! A pleasurable tingling sensation swept from Riley's chest through her body. She tilted her head and slipped her tongue in his mouth, kissing him harder, deeper, tasting him as her hands weaved into his hair, so fluffy and thick. She clutched fistfuls, refusing to let go, holding on so her knees—trembling with relief, excitement, lust—

didn't give way and end their impromptu clinch.

A heavy warmth grew in her cotton panties and she pressed her hips against his, prompting Ben's fingers to grip her sweater. *The sounds he's making...little moans in my mouth, and his kiss—so eager, so...confident, it's all unraveling me deep inside and it feels...amazing! HE feels amazing.* She reluctantly left his mouth, catching her breath.

Ben gasped with a smile and returned to her mouth, his tongue flirting along her lips. Riley let him in, desperate to taste him again, desperate to prove how much she cared. His hands roamed up her back, pressing her into his chest as if he was afraid he would lose her to the neon circus beyond their embrace.

More! Oh, God, I want more! Riley melted into him; all her pretending, all her denial surrendered to her desire and their kiss. The roar of impatient taxis and the glare of glittering billboards faded away as two lost souls found their escape in one another.

FORTY-FOUR

"The best and most beautiful things in the world
cannot be seen nor even touched, but just felt in the heart."
– Helen Keller

We're here...finally. A flutter danced in Riley's chest as the fairy lights, left behind from Ben's party, doused the darkness and twinkled overhead like a sky full of stars. "Ben...tonight, I've thought about this for ages."

He closed her apartment door, his gaze heavy and never wavering. "I have, too."

She reunited with his mouth, impatient to recapture the heat of his body, of his lips, and make up for lost time. She pressed him against the door and widened her stance, taking his thigh between her legs.

Ben didn't need any coaxing. Closing his eyes, he ran his fingers through her hair and kissed her deeply, sinking into the coat-covered door as Riley's hands slipped underneath his jacket and above his belt. One palm took a detour through the gap between his shirt's buttons. *Abs! Firm, mmmm! And hair—happy trail hair! Grown back!* Her cheeks flushed, but curiosity overruled shyness as the confident strokes of his tongue and the sounds coming from him urged her fingers to explore. *I love that he's not quiet! It's so HOT.* She chased the trail higher, her persistence sacrificing one button, then another, her fingers skimming the shallow dip of his belly button to drift and ride each subtle ridge of toned muscle. *Oh God, he feels SO good.*

Heat pulsed through her core, the wait to feel skin against skin dizzying, but Ben wasn't in a hurry. He moaned his approval against her lips as he took his time, caressing her back through her sweater, memorizing every inch. His hands roamed down to her skirt and lingered over the curve of her ass, his mouth kissing her with reverence, like she was a hard-earned prize. Such care and patience felt new to Riley. *Is he for real? Not that I'm complaining!* She couldn't remember a kiss with Josh that didn't feel like a hurried necessity, a means to an end-ing—always *his* happy ending. She had forgotten what real intimacy felt like, but as Ben savored their embrace and the sweetness of her mouth, it all came flooding back, how it felt to be appreciated, respected...adored. A smile graced her lips when Ben broke away with a soft groan.

"Riles, is Piper—"

She shook her head, her hand exiting his shirt to join the other, sweeping up the path of buttons to his collar. "Cicely's on Fridays." Her fingers swooped, teasing the soft hair at the nape of his neck as she sighed into another long, deep kiss.

Squeezing her ass, Ben's lips moved to her neck, each gentle lick and suck intensifying the ache in her panties. *I want to feel his mouth everywhere...but what I did with Josh...will that be good enough for Ben?* She gasped and Ben pulled back as if he sensed her uncertainty.

"We don't have to...*you know*..." His tone was breathy and playful with a vulnerable sincerity that made Riley's heart bolt into an even faster sprint. "We could just kiss...you're an *amazing* kisser, Riles."

Respect is such an aphrodisiac. "So are you. I could kiss you all night." She claimed his mouth again and pressed into his hips, feeling him hard, thick, and eager. *Ben wants ME!* A giddy euphoria bubbled in her chest, enticing her not to hold back. "I—" A shuddering breath parted her lips as she played with this hair. "I want

ALL of you, Benjamin Fagan."

He burst into a smile. "You sure now?"

The words barely touched her lips. "More than anything."

"Riley." Eyes drunk with desire, he licked his lip. "You took the words out of my mouth."

"Good, 'cause I want to leave you speechless." Her hands fell to his belt, threading it open.

He laughed, his hands leaving her ass to skim underneath her sweater, the first time his fingertips had ventured beyond her clothes. Confident yet gentle, they left a path of heat in their wake as they traced upward, lifting her sweater higher over her bra and her shoulders.

Raising her arms toward the crisscrossed strings of lights, Riley smiled under the passing wool. *I've wanted him so badly and it's actually happening!*

Her sweater's departure left her hair wild and falling into her eyes, but Ben's fingers tenderly swept it aside. "Beautiful Hope…I catch my breath every time I see you." He pressed his lips against her jaw, leaving sweet, barely there kisses in a path towards her ear, his warm breath on her skin teasing the heavy ache throbbing between her thighs.

"Come with me." Riley moaned and clasped his hand, leading him to the cozy rug keeping her loveseat company. Ben lowered himself to the floor, eyes not leaving her for a second as she pulled the throw onto the rug and reached into her toiletries box, turning around with a smile and a condom.

Entwined together under the soft glow of the glistening lights, they kissed and held each other, each sweep of a hand or tug of fingers removing his shirt, her skirt, his trousers, her tights…an intoxicating dance of rushed breaths and deep sighs, skin against skin pressing hot and tight.

Removing Riley's bra, Ben filled his hands with her breasts, his touch not rough or grabby. Ben was tender. Taking her in his mouth, his tongue flirted, peaking her nipple. *He's goooood.* Waves of pleasure rippled through her chest, pushing a sharp groan from her throat.

Worry clouded Ben's eyes. "Did I hurt you?"

"Nooo, I like it!" She pressed smiling kisses along his chest, shifting lower and hooking her fingers into the band of his boxer briefs. Tugging them down his thighs, she paused, stunned. *Ben...naked. My God, naked Ben. For real. ALL of him. All mine.* She wrapped her fingers around him, his skin smooth and hard and warm, desperate for her touch. She feathered kisses over his abs and stroked him to the tip...and back...tentative at first until she found a rhythm and felt Ben's hands dig into her hair.

Gasps escaped his lips. "Oh...!" Eyes fluttering closed, he pressed his head into the rug and groaned. "Ah, fuck..." His breath hitched again, tripping his words into gentle pleading. "Oh, keep doing...*that...please...*?" He moaned, moving against her hand. "Oh, fuck...Riley—no...wait—"

She released him and Ben pulled his underwear off, his hooded gaze holding a new purpose. Sitting up, he held Riley close, kissing her deeply before pulling back. "Will you show me what you like?"

A question? Not a demand. I'm not used to this... "I've fantasized about your mouth, your kisses...everywhere." Riley peeled off her panties.

Ben followed their progress then met her eyes. "You're not the only one."

He lay down between her legs and kissed her thighs, his stubble tickling her tender skin as he moved slowly upward, his mouth open and hungry. "You're perfect," he whispered, his soft licks and gentle sucks teasing Riley toward the brink.

Oh God, he's...! "Ben," she panted. "I'd like..." *To feel your weight over me, to grind against you...* She motioned upward, fighting ragged breaths. "You inside me when I come."

Ben answered without words, kissing up her stomach to her breasts then into her hair. Holding Riley in his arms, he moaned with bliss as her lips dragged along his neck to his collarbone and stars tattoo. They kissed and touched until their skin was damp with desperation and their racing hearts could take no more.

"Riley...?"

She smiled against his skin. "I want you so much."

Ben leaned back and tore open the condom. Riley couldn't pull her eyes away. *Ben Fagan, you are otherworldly...* Goose bumps prickled her chest. Whether it was the chill in the room, the absence of Ben's warmth, or her growing excitement, Riley wasn't sure. *I want to know everything: the sounds you make, how long you last...will you hold me after?*

Curling into him, Riley owned his neck with sucks and kisses, reveling in his warmth, the softness of his skin. *I don't have to pretend—not anymore.* She broke out into a joyful giggle and Ben claimed her open mouth with his own, a smile lurking behind his kiss, both of them discovering how it felt to be wanted for all the right reasons. With a shift of his hips, he guided himself slowly inside her, gasps escaping both their lips.

Riley wrapped her legs around his waist and Ben moaned, his eyes fluttering closed as he sank in deep. He slowly began to move above her. "Riley, you feel...*fucking amazing.*"

She clawed at his back and arched into him, meeting each exquisite roll of his hips, urging with her body for him to go faster, harder. Ben complied, leaning down to brush his lips across her cheek, leaving a kiss, then another. The heat of his breath, the pleasurable groans accompanying each thrust, deep in and out...she grabbed his ass, his thighs—the need to tug him closer, to touch all of him, all-consuming. Riley had never felt so greedy, but she couldn't rein herself in; there was something about Ben. Not only did he know how to please her, he was also attentive, considerate, giving—gasping through halting breaths that she could come first and he'd hold off until she did. Ben wasn't in a race to the finish line.

Riley couldn't get enough—or stay silent, crying out as Ben moved faster, deeper.

He opened his eyes, his heavy gaze landing on her mouth. "Riley, all right?" His words flew tight and quick.

She clutched his hips, frantic for more of him. A strangled "yeah" slipped through jagged breaths, the simplest of words evading her.

"Good."

Chatty Ben is at a loss for words.

Groaning, his head fell back. His mouth tilted into a smile and his eyes, drowsy with want, curved into the happy-go-lucky crescents Riley adored. Her heart felt heavy with desire, watching him moving over her, feeling his weight, their connection, body and soul.

Riley had never asked him how many women he had been with, but did it matter? All she needed to know was in the way he held her, kissed her, *saw* her. Being with Ben felt...almost predestined, meant to be...written in the stars. *You beautiful Brit boy—I adore you.*

Their eyes locked, but Ben wasn't smiling anymore, his tight breaths heating her cheek. *Is he close?* "Ben—?" The question sat on her tongue, the rest of her words an unintelligible moan. Her legs began to quiver and surging waves of pleasure, tingling hot and cold, grew stronger and stronger until they were too much. Pulled under, breaths shallow and halting...swept away. The stars overhead blurred into a hazy glow. She dug her nails into his hips. All she could do was hold on while letting go...

"Rye!" Ben groaned into a hitched breath and fisted the blanket, his body shuddering. He let out a final gasp and collapsed on top of her, hot and spent, both of them slick with perspiration. "Oh, wow," he whispered into her neck. "Mind...blown."

Unable to form a coherent response, Riley smiled and hugged him tight.

"Are you okay?" Ben shifted up onto his elbow, catching his breath. A grin spread across his face as he bent down, kissing her on the nose. "Was *that* okay?"

He's still inside me, warm...throbbing. This couldn't be more real. "Yes. *Yes!*" She smiled and cupped his face, brushing the hair from his eyes, so blue, so content.

"Gorgeous, Riley...you're amazing." Ben kissed her and reached down, holding the condom as he pulled out. He dropped it in the bin and grabbed the throw, draping it over Riley before diving under it with her. "I don't think we'll get much sleep tonight." He wrapped himself around her, laying a kiss on her forehead.

"You promise?" Riley cuddled into his neck and thanked the lucky stars dangling overhead for making one wish come true.

FORTY-FIVE

I can still feel his hands everywhere...hear the sounds he made...

Lying on her side, tangled with Ben in her twin bed, Riley watched him capture breaths and then gently set them free, each exhale from his lips faintly scented like mint toothpaste. *He looks innocent, so peaceful.* She had lost track of time, mesmerized by the occasional flutter of his dark eyelashes and the sleepy smiles that curved his mouth. His hair rebelled against the pillow, soft and messy. *Bae-watch: my new favorite show.*

The bright glow creeping around the edges of her curtain and the hush on the street below suggested that *maybe* it was six-thirty, seven o'clock at the latest, but Ben showed no hints of waking, holding her close even in slumber. *We're a human pretzel!* Riley's gaze happily strayed from his slightly parted lips to the sweep of dark hair on his chest, grown back from his short-lived stint as a stripper.

He was so lost on stage, fumbling and falling...nervous. Riley nuzzled into his chest and stifled her giggles, aware that the slightest shake could wake him up. *He didn't have performance anxiety last night...or this morning.* Her eyes drifted down to his abs, where her hand lingered, entwined with his long fingers. *Ben's still holding my hand. He never let go.*

Her attention shifted to the sheet and duvet bunched up near the bed's edge then back to her right leg flung lazily over his thigh where he dug into her leg. *Not all of Ben is asleep.*

"Riley...?" A raspy whisper rustled her hair. "You awake?"

She tilted her head, meeting his eyes. "Yeah. I couldn't sleep."

"Aww." A small yawn escaped his lips and he blinked like he

had been lost to the world for days, not a few hours. "You should've woken me."

And miss out on watching you sleep? Never. "You were down for the count."

"Is it any wonder? You were insatiable…" Pulling her tight, his smile pressed a lingering kiss to her forehead. "And perfect." He ducked below her jaw, leaving wet, openmouthed kisses along her neck. "*So…*" The little word hung in the air, cheeky yet heated. To underline its meaning, Ben released her hand and cupped her breast, his thumb lovingly circling her nipple, coaxing it to harden. "Riley?"

"Ben?" She inhaled sharply, goose bumps rising on her skin.

"Wanna go again?" His tongue slipped into the sensitive spot above her collarbone and Riley gasped, his lips sucking, teeth gently biting as he pressed into her.

I'm insatiable? He could drill a hole in the wall, he's so hard. "Yeah!" She quivered, an ache waking between her thighs. Her mind scrambled to form words before they floated away like a soapy bubble on a sunny day. "B-But…we need to talk…"

The kisses stopped and he lifted his head, the twin bed offering nowhere to hide. "Yeah." He sighed. "We do." He rubbed his eyes and sat up, pulling the sheet and duvet over them. Lying down again, he propped himself up on an elbow, ready to listen.

"I've been thinking and…I can't be mad at you for…" She swallowed. "You were single, I was engaged. I had no claim on you. I barely knew you."

Ben nodded, in no rush to jump in.

"But once we became friends and you found out I knew Leia, you should've told me. Last night was a shock. It was so…public."

"I know, and I'm so sorry. I hate that I embarrassed you like that." He scrunched his eyes. "And TV people were there…"

"They don't know me, they won't remember me. But Erika and

her friends…I hate being gossiped about." She twisted her mouth. "It hurt, Ben, finding out like that. We talked about Leia at the diner, the night of the bachelorette, and you didn't say anything."

"I thought about it, but you said that you weren't close friends and…we were getting along so well, making pinky promises, talking dyslexia—stealing spoons…" A grin flirted with his lips and then disappeared. "I was afraid if I said something, you wouldn't want anything to do with me. I didn't want you to think I was some…" He exhaled heavily. "Fuckboy wanker." Glancing down, his eyelashes beat slowly. "You called me a fuckboy in Times Square, but…I get it. I haven't really done anything to make you think otherwise, but after last night, after the last few weeks"—he met her eyes—"I hope you'll revise your opinion of me. Last night wasn't just sex, Riley. Not for me."

"It wasn't for me either." She rolled closer, tracing her finger along his bottom lip. He covered her hand in his and kissed her fingers softly. "I have a confession."

"Yeah?" He kissed her hand again and lowered it to his chest, holding it tight. "That I'm the best lover you've ever had, right?"

You are! "Maybe." Nose to nose, she blushed. "I've liked you since that night you stayed over."

"Ooh, well, it was my dedication to oral hygiene that hooked ya, wasn't it? Or…my exemplary toast-making skills?"

Riley played with a tuft of hair sticking up at his temple. "Any guy who wears Santa socks, loves peanut butter like I do, and well, *listens*."

Ben began a flurry of tiny kisses around her lips. She shifted closer, her mouth demanding something deeper. Cupping her face, Ben willfully gave in and melted into her. He pulled back slowly, a cheeky smile still close enough to kiss.

"You like me, eh?" He raised an eyebrow. "Birthday wishes DO come true."

"What was the other wish? You had two."

"Actually, it hasn't come true yet, so..." He mimicked zipping his lips and burst into a grin. "Riles, I've never met anyone like you."

"In a *good* way, right?"

"Yeah, in a good way. I fancied you from the minute I saw you, but getting to know you, watching you help people, help *me*?" He kissed her nose and hovered over her lips. "That did me in. I was a goner. You're beautiful inside and out."

"So, why the big friend speech at the diner?"

"I felt like I had to draw a line because you loved Josh—or I thought you did. I would've eaten my words if I'd known about your breakup. Why didn't you stop me and tell me you were single?"

"You kinda sold the whole friends thing like a done deal. I thought if I said something, I'd just embarrass myself. I know what it's like when someone likes you and you don't feel the same way. It happened to me in high school and ruined the friendship. I didn't want to ruin *our* friendship." Her fingers stroked his hip.

He exhaled a heavy breath. "You know, the minute you told me about dumping him, I had to fight the urge to grab you for a kiss right there! But—and now this feels stupid—I didn't know if you were into *me*. Then once we were up on that rock and I found out about your mom, it didn't seem right to crack on to you. I reckoned you needed a friend more than...well, this"—he waved his hand back and forth—"especially with everything you had going on. I almost kissed you on my birthday, but..." He shrugged. "I panicked. Then, I kicked myself for letting the moment go. I hoped if you *did* like me, you'd find a way to tell me, and lucky for me, you did!"

How 'bout a reminder? Riley's hand slid off his hip to where he waited, hard and ready.

"Oh, yes...*please.*" He growled as she kissed his neck. "Keep telling me, again and again." His eyes fluttered closed and his mouth covered Riley's, kissing her deeply.

CLICK! The door flung open.

They broke apart and Ben yanked the covers up to their necks.

"Rye, your phone's off, so I got breakfast burritos—" Piper spotted Ben's green and red candy cane socks on the floor and her eyes shot to the bed. "Holy FUCK!" She burst out in a bellyaching laugh, spitting out her gum. "Christmas came and...so did you!"

"Pip!" Riley hid her reddening face in Ben's neck. "Why are you back so early?"

"Hiya, Pip." Ben raised a sheepish hand.

"Cicely's grandma took her for brunch—she's trying to see Cice as much as she can before she leaves for London. Her grandmother's vegan so—yuck. Besides, I didn't think *this*"—her eyes scanned the discarded mess of clothes, the condom wrappers, and the balled-up throw on the floor—"would be going down!"

"I hope you bought enough for three." Ben smirked.

"Jeez, it's about fucking *time*, you guys!" Piper dumped the takeout bag on the floor and climbed the ladder, ducking around the strings of fairy lights to raise her hand for two embarrassed high fives.

FORTY-SIX

Two weeks later

Summer had taken New York City by the throat, and the second Friday in July was a t-shirt-soaking scorcher. Heat radiated off the pavement, everyone moved slower, and overworked air conditioners groaned across the city, their fight against the relentless humidity a losing battle.

LaGuardia Place in Greenwich Village sizzled in the early afternoon sun, but Ben and Riley had found one of the few shaded spots—a bench underneath the bubblegum pink awning of DŌ. They sat thigh to thigh, devouring their treats—a loaded brownie bar for Ben and a single scoop of Nuts for Nuts cookie dough jammed with Reese's Cups and Pieces for Riley.

Riley and sweets—I've never seen someone so happy. Ben watched behind his sunglasses, her spoon about to dig in again. *Two weeks in and she's still here. I'm still here, haven't bolted or ghosted—that's a first. Riles, what have you done to me?* Leaning in, Ben kissed her forehead. "Who'd have thought, eh? A fortnight of dirty sex and getting sozzled."

A wistfulness tainted her grin. "I wish! I've missed you, Ben."

Taking in her sundress and her long hair tied in a loose ponytail, his smile wilted. "Work's a bugger for keeping us apart, and so are our flatmates for being home. Two quickies in two weeks?"

"I know." She sighed. "I'm frustrated, too."

"If only one of us had a bedroom...or a car, somewhere private."

Riley kissed him and laid her head on his shoulder, his Duran

295

Duran t-shirt slightly damp. "There's always public restrooms..."

Wha—really? "Riles...?"

The rise in Ben's voice made Riley lift her head. "Well, needs must, right?" She sucked on her spoon. "And it checks *dirty sex* off that list—"

"I'm always up for that!"

"I bet you are!" Riley laughed, catching his naughty grin. "Oh! You're not joking? You've had restroom sex?"

"Ohhh yeah—*several* times." His eyes curved into cheeky crescents. "Haven't you?"

"No, but I've done it on a boat."

"Really?! Blimey, the Staten Island Ferry?"

"No!" She giggled. "At Josh's family cottage, upstate. We did it in the water, too."

"Ahh, mermaid sex? Yeah, that's hot." He leaned in and growled in her ear. "God, what I wouldn't do right now to slip you out of your wet bikini bottoms and take you in the sand."

Her eyes widened. "You're really not helping."

"The beach...California, yeah? One day." Leaving a kiss in her hair, he sat back, picking up the napkin-wrapped brownie from his thigh. He crossed his legs, hiding the growing ridge in his jeans. *Aw, mate, don't start what you can't finish.*

"One day, yeah." She smiled coquettishly, her gaze sweeping his crotch before returning to her spoon. "That's it for me, though. No other exotic locales to speak of, just a bedroom at a house party, in a closet—once. Oh, a pool table, but that was in my first boyfriend's basement. How 'bout you? Ever gone beyond the restroom?" She laughed.

"Oh, a few places."

"Like?" She licked chocolate off her thumb.

Ahh, Riles, what you're doing to me! "You don't want to know."

"Yeah, I do." She leaned in. "You started it!"

"Er, ooo-kay. Well...on the train from Windsor to London, in a TopMan changing room, an alley behind a pub—or two." He caught her arched eyebrows. "All right, *more* than two." *Okay, time to shut this down.* He nibbled his brownie and watched sweaty New Yorkers wilting in the shop's long line. "You know, just horny teenage stuff."

Riley bit her lip. "I lost my virginity in a backyard shed. There was a weird garden gnome staring at us the whole time."

"Ugh. I lost mine on a playground slide."

"Seriously? With your clumsy balance?" She laughed. "Where else have you done it?"

I like how she's not judgy or embarrassed. He set down his brownie. "A stairwell at uni, in a tent at a music festival, backstage at a theater—in my *Tempest* costume—"

"Ooh, did you finish with a standing O?"

He chuckled. "*Nearly* went all the way on the top deck of a London bus. Oh, yeah, at the Imperial War Museum—"

"A war museum? Not sexy!"

"When the urge arises..." Ben sighed and shifted again on the bench. "Ahh, Hope, too bad there's no restroom here."

Riley dug her spoon into her cup of peanut butter joy and left it there. Her shoulders deflated, disappointment in her eyes. "I wish you didn't have to work tonight. It's been six nights in a row."

"I know, it sucks." Ben put his arm around her and left a kiss on her temple. *I know she wants me to call her my girlfriend, and I want to, but I can't...not yet. Being emotionally attached, relied upon for more than shits and giggles—it's so new. I need to get used to it. I want to get used to it.* He kissed her again. "At least we have thirty minutes together before I have to head in, eh? And I'll call you on my break."

"I still feel bad about Thursday."

"*I* feel bad about you getting told off." Ben picked up his brownie again. "I shouldn't have dropped in on you. You can't blame your boss."

"No, but I can blame the new girl in skincare and her loitering boyfriend. Now, none of us can have visitors."

"Well, if you stopped in the diner mid-shift, I'd have to ignore you, too. It's tourist bloody central. Fuck, it's *nuts*, and I reckon it'll get more bonkers as summer rolls on." He gnawed the brownie's edge. "But they'll have to make do without me on July 27th..."

Riley's eyes brightened. "You...?!"

"Yep, got it off."

"YES!" Riley dove in for a kiss, sending her spoon falling to the sidewalk.

Ben held her close before pulling back slightly, his lips brushing hers. "Happy early birthday," he whispered and kissed her again.

"When did you find out?"

"Last night." Smiling, he tilted forward, pulling an extra plastic spoon from his back pocket, handing it to her. "So, I've got two weeks to work my magic! Come on, then, what would Ms. Hope like most for her birthday?"

She sucked in her bottom lip, her face reddening.

She's gonna cry. Oh, Fagan, what are you like! Ben's heart ached. He dropped his brownie on the napkin surfing his lap. "Aw, Riley." He pulled her in. "I'm sorry! Stupid question."

"No, it's not—"

"It is—what you want most, I can't give you..."

Her shuddering breath warmed his neck. "It's just...Mom hasn't been feeling great, and birthdays always make me think..."

"Think...?" He gently stroked her hair.

"What will they be like if...?" A sob stuck in her throat. "M-My mind keeps going *there*."

"Yeah, I did that when Mum was in hospital"—Ben kissed the top of her head—"I would play this awful game of 'what if': What if she got sicker? What if Mum didn't make it to my birthday?"

Riley nodded, understanding in her tearful eyes.

"I'd get so angry and upset—sometimes, so upset, I'd throw up, and then I'd feel even worse—guilty like, for not being positive and hopeful...almost like I was letting her down."

"Exactly." Riley wiped her cheek.

"One time, I was crying by the elevators and a male nurse came over." Ben rubbed his nose. "God, nurses are so underrated. He sat me down, bought chocolate buttons and milk, and let me ramble. He said, 'That's completely normal, son. It's *anticipatory* grief.' That was a bit of a mouthful for a twelve-year-old, so he broke it down, said I was grieving for the potential loss of my mum and my life as I knew it, but those thoughts didn't mean I was giving up on her and he said I shouldn't feel guilty about them. Amazing, eh? He saw this wee kid in bits and took a half-hour to sit down with me. I felt understood. I still had moments of 'what if', but I wasn't so hard on myself for having them anymore." Ben lifted his sunglasses to the top of his head, the plastic frames sweeping his hair back from his face. "Riles, you're grieving, fearing for your mom and the life you share." He brushed a loose wisp of hair from her eyes. "You *are* allowed to feel this way, and when you do, remember you're not alone, okay? I'm here for you, and so are Piper and Casey—and Maggie. From what you've told me, if anyone can beat this thing, it's her."

A tear slipped down her cheek as she shifted, finding the sweet spot in the nook of Ben's neck. "Thank you." She sniffed. "You just being here, holding me, makes me feel less sad."

Ben gave her a squeeze. "I'm guessing Maggie really celebrates your birthday big?"

She nodded. "Yeah, but not this year. Her last chemo treatment is that morning."

"Oh, really? That's a huge deal, yeah?"

"Yeah. I'd like to mark the occasion for her, but from past experience, I know she won't want a fuss." Riley sat back and looked at her spoon. "She'll be tired after being prodded and poked, so drinks and lots of people around are out, but that's the thing—she'll still want to throw some over-the-top birthday thing *for me*. I don't want her to overdo it, staying up late, but there's no telling her. When her mind's set..."

This is what you can give her—give them both. A soft grin tweaked his cheeks. "Well, I could organize something for you and Maggie that afternoon if you'd like?"

"Oh, Ben! That's really sweet, but you don't have to—"

"I know, but I *want* to. I mean, if Maggie's okay having me 'round after her treatment?"

"Of course! But you'd have to come out to Staten Island, take the ferry..."

"Ooh, Riles—you inviting me for a sexy boat ride?!" He raised an eyebrow. "You filthy minx."

Riley laughed. "That's me!"

He grinned. "So, who should I invite to your party?"

"Keep it small, Piper and Casey. I wanna cheer Pip up—she's been bummed ever since Cicely moved to London. You can skip Erika. She's in full-on wedding mode—oh! I *knew* there was something I meant to tell you: she invited you, right after I told her about us."

"Aw! Was she happy?" Ben's eyebrows rose gleefully.

Riley scratched her nose. "Um, yeah..."

She's fibbing. "Erika doesn't think I'm good enough for you."

"What?" She squinted. "Nooo!"

"You saw the look she gave me when we arrived at her party."

"No, I didn't—"

"Riley! C'mon, Erika's face gives *everything* away. She'd be shite at poker." He frowned at his sneakers. "Is it because I'm a waiter? Because of Leia? My clothes?" He looked at Riley quizzically. "I've always been nice to her—"

"It's because you're not Josh." Riley huffed.

"Oh. Well, thank Christ for that." His chuckle gave way to a concerned squint. "But why is that a bad thing? Doesn't she want you to be happy?"

"No, she does, it's just...Erika didn't want anything to change. If I married Josh and became a hockey wife like her, all the things she and I had in common the past three years would still be there. Josh and me breaking up meant I've broken that bond with *her*. I'm moving on and I think she's having a hard time with it."

"But you went to high school together. You've got other things in common, right?"

"I don't know if we do, to be honest..." Riley shrugged. "Not anymore."

"Aw, that's a shame." He pressed a lingering kiss to her forehead. "Well, see how things are after the wedding and take it from there? Maybe it's wedding stress making her weird?"

"God, I'm dreading going."

"Why? Because of Leia?"

Riley nodded slowly. "Not only her, but yeah."

"Hope, you have to talk to her sometime—you're both bridesmaids."

"Not by choice. Leia and I have never been close, so why start now? *Especially* now." Staring at her cookie dough, Riley retreated into silence.

This is my fault. If she doesn't want to talk about it, change the subject. Ben kissed her forehead again. "Sooo...birthday plans. Do you want me to order in or play Jamie Oliver? Jamie's not a stretch—he's dyslexic."

Riley's expression perked up. "Really? But *he* can cook!" She snickered. "Could we order in? Is that okay? It would feel like a treat."

"Fine by me. I'll get whatever you want: pizza, wings, burritos...?"

"Burritos...and cake?"

"Hell yeah! Can't break the Hope family's nonnegotiable birthday rules." He bit into his brownie and squeezed her closer.

FORTY-SEVEN

Two weeks later

A cutting from a Gerbera daisy stalk pinged across Maggie's kitchen. "Well, that's a work of art—not!" Piper snickered and wielded the pair of scissors again, poised to attack another stem.

Bollocks, it's lopsided. Ben slapped another spoonful of cream cheese frosting on top of his two-layer birthday cake. "What are you saying? Blokes can't bake?"

"No, just you." *SNIP!* Another slice of stem shot across the counter, landing somewhere in Ben's perilous stack of dirty dishes. "In the past month, I've seen you make toast, cereal, and peanut butter sandwiches—you *cook* like a twelve-year-old boy."

"Says the lass who lives on Chef Boyardee." Taking his time, he smoothed the frosting across the cake. "Granted, it's not the prettiest cake, but it'll be a nice surprise."

"Oh, it'll surprise her all right! It looks nothing like Maggie's cakes."

"It's Maggie's red velvet recipe."

She scrunched up her nose. "It is?"

"Careful, Pip, your face might stay that way." He leaned across the counter, checking his phone. "What time did Maggie say they'd be back?"

"Around four."

"We better get our asses in gear, otherwise Maggie will catch us in the act and try to help. When you're done with the flowers, can you hang the sign and then fill the chip bowls?"

"Yup." Piper adjusted the burst of blooms in a tall vase.

"Thanks for suggesting Gerberas. I had no idea smelly flowers might make Maggie queasy."

"Yeah, Gerberas tick all the boxes—no scent and they're gorgeous. I hope Maggie's all right. The last treatment is always a strange one. My mum was glad it was over, but felt too tired and sick to celebrate."

"Riley said your mom had a tough time, years back?"

Ben leaned away to admire his handiwork. "Yeah, but find a cancer patient who doesn't."

Piper frowned and transferred the vase of flowers for Maggie to the small table in the living/dining room where they joined a stack of board games and Ben's pot of forget-me-nots, Riley's favorite. She picked up the large HAPPY BIRTHDAY RILEY cutout, lovingly crafted from yellow construction paper. "How cute is this?! It must've taken Maggie forever to cut out the letters. Rye's shown me photos of her kiddie birthday parties. Friends come and go, but this thing was always there!"

"Tada!" Ben lurked behind her shoulder, a plate with his gooey cake proudly in his hands. "Icing hides a multitude of baking sins."

"Hey, I'll never tell," said Piper with a wink. "I know I've been teasing you the whole time, but if a dude baked a cake for me, I'd be blowing more than just his candles." She stepped onto a small stool, the birthday sign and its ties dangling from her hands. "I'd say you're getting lucky tonight. Good thing I'm staying at Casey's."

"Yeah, thanks for that!" He did a double take, catching a flicker of sadness cross Piper's face. "I'm sorry you and Cicely split."

"I really liked her, but doing long-distance…" She shook her head. "That's what sucks about graduating and finding jobs. Everyone scatters."

"It's your turn next."

Piper tacked one end of the sign above the entrance to the

kitchen. "Yeah." Her shoulders slumped slightly. "That's what I'm most sad about. I miss Cicely, but it's not like how I'm gonna miss Rye. Four years together, almost every day…she's my heart."

"Riley will miss you, too." Ben set the cake on the table. "Pip, you know her best. Can I ask you something?"

"Sure."

"I've been online, trying to read everything I can about depression but…what can I do to *help* her? I just want her to feel safe, you know? Understood and supported."

"Well, just keep doing what you're doing—be there for her, and don't try to solve it with a quick fix."

"But that's it—I just want to fix it so badly."

"But you can't, Ben." She pushed a tack into the string on the right side of the sign. "I don't mean to sound like a textbook, but we learned about this in class. Depression ebbs and flows. Every day is different. Every person is different. Be patient and take your cues from her. If she seems distant or lost, ask what she needs and go from there. Depression can be really isolating. No one should have to struggle alone." She hopped off the stool and popped her gum. "Just the fact that you're asking makes you a superstar in my book. So many people think the depressed person just needs to snap out of it, you know? Cheer up and smile more, go exercise, and stop eating crap, like that will solve everything, but that's bullshit! That's why people like Riley end up with smiling depression in the first place— the stigma doesn't allow them to be themselves."

"I want to do everything I can for her. Riley's the first girl I've—" He caught himself. "Really been into."

"Yeah, I know." Piper patted his arm. "I hate to say it, Ben, but you're not *that* great an actor!"

It's the cutest thing ever! Sitting on the floor, Riley leaned into Ben as he closed the clasp on her bracelet. On her wrist, a small silver puffin charm dangled from a delicate chain. "Cake AND puffins!" *Ben is just...* Her heart pounded, refusing to slow down. *It's happening—I'm falling for him.* Her eyes left the bracelet, finding Ben gazing at her. *And maybe...he might be falling, too?* She smiled warmly and kissed him then turned to her mom, who was curled up beside Piper on the sofa. "Isn't this gorgeous?"

"It's adorable, sweetheart," said Maggie, cutting into her slice of birthday cake. "So perfect—you did good, Ben!"

Still grinning, he glanced back at Riley.

"I've always meant to ask." Piper swallowed the last bite of her butter chicken burrito. "Why puffins, Rye?"

"Well, like me, they love cliffs, rocks, swimming, and islands. And they look like clown birds—"

"You hate clowns," said late-arrival Casey, sitting down with his plateful of cake.

Riley laughed. "I know, but puffins are cute, and they look happy all the time."

"I always thought that old stuffed thing with no eyes lying on your bed was a mangled parrot." Piper set her empty plate on the coffee table and scooped up a handful of pretzels. "His neck's all floppy."

"No, he's brilliant." Ben smiled at Riley. "Just because he's been around the block doesn't mean he's not lovable."

"Exactly." Riley noticed Maggie yawning between bites. "Mom, do you want to lie down or have some more water?"

"No, I'm good, sweetie. Just a bit tired, but that's not stopping me from enjoying this cake!" She met Ben's eyes. "It's really good, Ben. Have you baked before?"

Cheeks full, Casey froze and looked up. "You made this?"

"Uh, yeah." Ben scratched his clean-shaven chin. "Mum taught me to bake, but I never mastered icing or decorating..."

"Who cares what it looks like?" Riley licked her fork. "It tastes just like Mom's."

Casey nodded begrudgingly. "It does."

"Well, that's Ben's compliment, not mine." Maggie smiled at him. "I can teach you icing."

Ben glanced at Riley.

"Means more ferry rides out here for you, Ben." Riley snickered into her plate. "Say yes."

"That would be great, always willing to learn!" His face lit up. "Cheers, Maggie."

"And you know what else is great?" Riley smiled at Ben. "Come on, tell them."

Casey stopped chewing.

Ben scratched his neck. "I've...got an audition."

"No! You kept that quiet!" Piper threw a pretzel at him while Casey looked underwhelmed and dove back into his slice.

"Ben! Congratulations!" Maggie smiled. "What's it for?"

"It's a scripted comedy TV series." He popped Piper's projectile in his mouth and chewed slowly. "A small part, the boyfriend of one of the main characters. It's non-union so pay won't be great, but it's something to slap on my CV."

"I think it's amazing." Riley beamed.

"You say that now. Wait until he has an on-screen kiss," said Piper, cutting herself a large slice of cake. "Or a nude sex scene!"

"Oh, he'll be *great* at that," Riley blurted out uncensored, forgetting Maggie's presence for a moment. She bit her lip and leaned into Ben, stifling a giggle.

His complexion began to turn pink.

Maggie smiled kindly. "I hope you get it, Ben." Her eyes hopped to her daughter. "Riley, should we get out the Monopoly board or Jenga? I've got Operation around here somewhere..."

Mom's tired. We should do something relaxing. She might want

307

to doze. "Let's have a *Lairds and Liars* marathon. Is that okay?"

"YES! I'm soooo in." Balancing her cake plate, Piper slipped her feet under her butt, making herself comfy.

Casey nodded. "Season three just got added to Netflix."

"Okay, let's go to Scotland!" Maggie smiled through a yawn as Riley set down her plate and stepped around Ben.

"Lean forward a bit, Mom..." She plumped up Maggie's pillows and scooped up the throw from the sofa's armrest, unfurling it over her lap. "Pip, cue up the first episode and we'll get more snacks." She signaled for Ben to follow into the kitchen.

"You gonna make me watch Keegs in a kilt?" He chuckled, grabbing several sodas from the fridge. "You owe me, Hope."

"And I'll gladly pay up." She filled her arms with bags of Funyuns and Doritos then shot him a teasing glint. "Guess what Piper gave me this morning—Twister bedsheets."

"Wahey!" Ben slapped Riley's butt and followed her back to the living room.

FORTY-EIGHT

Three weeks later

Riley's eyes hopped from a fog-embraced castle to miles of emerald green hillside overlooking a serene blue sea. The breathtaking images housed in rustic wood frames felt more travel agency than cancer center, but it made a refreshing change from the usual prim watercolor paintings found in most hospital settings.

"I'm guessing Ireland?" Riley turned to Maggie, sitting beside her in the doctor's office, its cheery robin's egg blue chairs further underlining the 'We're not a medical center' décor.

"Hmm, it looks like something out of *Lairds*, so I'm going with Scotland. Wherever it is, we should add it to our dream tour itinerary." Maggie scratched at the soft fuzz growing underneath her head scarf. "I bet Ben would know where it is. Have you heard from him?"

"Just a text saying to message when we're done. If he doesn't answer right away, he's in his audition."

"I hope he gets the part," said Maggie. "It's a good sign he's been called back twic—"

"Maggie, sorry to keep you waiting." A familiar face above a pristine lab coat slipped into the office and closed the door. Carrying a file folder thick with papers, Maggie's oncologist, Dr. McLoughlin, sat down at her small desk. "It's great to see you and Riley." She logged into her computer and opened the folder, her chin dipping toward the top page. "How's your summer been?"

"Good, too muggy for my liking, but that's New York." Maggie shrugged while Riley nodded in agreement, her knee jittering under the tote bag lying on her lap.

"Yeah, coming from Arizona, I never get used to the humidity here." Dr. McLoughlin looked up from her paperwork, poker face in full effect. "Well, the results came back for your scans and blood work. The cancer in your liver hasn't spread, but I'm afraid it *has* grown slightly—"

"Grown...?" Riley's eyebrows furrowed with confusion. "But—" *Third time lucky...*

"So, what does that mean?" Maggie reached over the armrest, her warm hand enveloping Riley's.

"Well, we have options." Dr. McLoughlin nodded. "We can try a clinical trial for a new drug, but...I'll be honest, its success hasn't been proven with your type of cancer. If you decide to try it, we'll weigh the benefits against risks and side effects—"

"Sorry, wait." Avoiding Riley's stare, Maggie jumped in. "In April, the cancer was advanced. I could *live* with it...but now, what does a slight change in size *really* mean? Is it...?"

Is it...what? Riley's eyes darted from her mom to the oncologist.

"Maggie..." The oncologist shifted in her chair. "The cancer has grown, but it hasn't spread beyond your liver. *If* it does, we'll make you comfortable for as long as possible. We'll relieve your symptoms, control your pain..."

"You're..." Maggie's voice cracked. "You're...talking about palliative care?"

Palliative—what?! No! A vice clenched Riley's stomach, its suffocating squeeze traveling higher and higher. Her mouth fell slack as words—jagged, horrific, life-changing words—burned the back of her throat, unable to escape. *Symptom relief...pain control? Palliative care? Isn't that just a fancy way of saying, 'Sorry, there's nothing we can do'?*

Dr. McLoughlin didn't nod, didn't shake her head. Her lips

pressed together, like they were unwilling to surrender the inevitable.

Say it. Riley swallowed, but the thickness wouldn't budge. *It's easy. Just say NO, it's not palliative!*

"Yes, but there are..."

Yes?! Riley clenched her Mom's hand. "No...*no*," she choked out, her lungs desperately fighting for air, but it felt thin and nonexistent, like all the oxygen had been sucked from the room, like she was going under.

She swore her heart stopped.

For how long, she had no clue.

Valuable seconds with her mom...

...one...

...by...

...one...

...slipping away, vanishing...gone—lost forever. Memories flashed and then twisted, fading into a dizzying spiral of thoughts, drowning her...

How long until...? A year, six months...one month?

I don't know how to make your red velvet cake.

What will birthdays be like? Mother's Day?

Who will watch cheesy Christmas movies with me?

Share donuts, walk shelter dogs?

I'll miss the smile in your voice

when you realize it's me on the phone.

Will I forget your scent?

How you can wear a sweatshirt and still look chic?

What happens to your stories, the ones I don't know?

Will they be lost—forever?

Who will walk me down the aisle on my wedding day?

If I have kids, they'll never meet you, learn from you, love you.

How will I make you proud?

When time runs out…
How do I do this?
Alone…
…without you.

Female voices floated in and out, but they were garbled like an underwater conversation as the thrashing of Riley's heartbeat pounded through her ears. Words formed on her tongue but weren't spoken.

Or were they?

Did I say something?

She felt pressure…her hand…a squeeze? Maggie's touch reawakened her senses. Riley turned to her mom, her pretty face and head scarf blurry in a wash of pink, blue, and green. *When did I start crying?* The drone in her ears began to shift, and a few fragments spoken by the doctor ricocheted around her mind.

…"unresectable bile duct cancer"…

…"liver transplant"…

…"national wait list"…

A warm chuckle invaded the words, pulling Riley back to the surface. *Mom?*

"Yes, do it." Maggie's voice was firm, assertive—the quiver from earlier gone. "Add me to the list. I'll wait for as long as it takes."

"A liver transplant?" Riley wiped her eyes, streaking her hand with teary mascara smudges.

Offering a box of tissues to Riley, Dr. McLoughlin's gaze hopped to Maggie. "Well, you'll have to be evaluated by a transplant hospital to see if you're *healthy* enough for surgery. They'd run a series of tests, both physical and psychological, and then a committee discusses the findings and makes a decision. If it's a yes, you'd be added to the wait list, but I have to tell you, Maggie, there's no guarantee you'll receive a liver. The list is…extremely long." She typed something into her computer and scrolled the screen. "Right now, there are over thirteen thousand people waiting around the country. Most of them…" The oncologist took a deep breath. "Won't live long enough to receive a transplant."

"I'm not most patients." Maggie held Riley's hand, refusing to let go.

"We have to try." Riley sniffed behind a tissue.

"I don't want to dissuade you, but you should know the reality," said the oncologist. "Every person on the list is ranked based on how urgent their need is within the next three months. This protocol places the sickest patients at the top of the list."

Maggie nodded. "You said my type of cancer can grow quickly—would that make me an urgent case?"

"Not necessarily. Bile duct cancer cases aren't always accepted by transplant centers, and livers from deceased donors often go to people with more curable diseases."

Maggie looked confused. "So, a transplant wouldn't cure my disease?"

"No, there's a good chance it could since your cancer is localized to your liver, but we're dealing with a numbers game—the need for donated livers exceeds the supply and living in New York state makes it even harder to receive an organ."

"Why?" Riley's stare bounced between both women. "I thought the wait list was national?"

"It is, but organs are shared regionally, not nationally, so areas with higher populations, like New York or California, have a greater need and a longer wait."

"So, if I lived in…" Maggie shrugged. "Idaho, my chances of receiving a liver would be better?"

"Yes."

Seriously? Death by geography? Mom will lose out on a liver and die because she lives in the wrong state? Tears trickled down

Riley's cheeks.

"There is one other option." The oncologist sat back. "A living donor."

Living donor? I could save her—ME. Riley sat up like she had been given a shot of adrenaline. She rubbed her swollen nose, her eyes wide. "I'll do it. I'll give Mom my liver—"

"Honey, just...wait." Maggie patted her hand. "You're not giving anything—"

"Why not?!" Riley leaned forward, swiping tears away as quickly as the words rushed out.

Dr. McLoughlin half-smiled at Maggie then back to her daughter. "Riley, there's *a lot* to consider—it's major surgery and recovery can be painful."

Riley refused to be dissuaded. "How does it work?"

The oncologist shifted in her chair. "Well, the liver is comprised of two lobes—the left and the right. The donor gives their right lobe, about sixty-percent of their liver, to the recipient."

Maggie grimaced. "More than half?"

The oncologist nodded. "But the amazing thing is the liver will regenerate itself."

"Really?" Riley listened intently.

"Within six to twelve weeks of surgery, the donor and recipient's livers will have grown back to about eighty percent their original size."

"That's amazing." Riley gripped Maggie's hand tighter.

Dr. McLoughlin softly smiled. "The body can do some incredible things to repair itself."

"Well..." Riley swallowed, trying to mute the quiver brewing in her throat. "Sign me up." Her puffy nose made her voice come out nasal.

Maggie shook her head. "Riley, you're not doing this."

"I AM." Eyes flashing, Riley pleaded with Maggie. "I'm an

adult, Mom. You can't stop me—"

"Riley—"

"There's nothing you can say that will change my mind."

Even when things are at their worst, I refuse to believe all is lost.

I will never go down without a fight.

Riley wiped her eyes a final time, straightened her posture, and turned to the doctor. "What do I need to do?"

Ben squinted into the afternoon sun, his shades left behind at his audition in Chelsea. *She's jumping in so fast.* "Are you sure about this?" He threaded his fingers through Riley's, giving her hand a squeeze as they walked to the convenience store near Maggie's apartment. "It sounds… risky."

"All operations involve risk, even simple ones." She swerved, pulling Ben off the sidewalk, so two boisterous kids on scooters could fly past, their golden retriever loping behind. "So, whatcha hungry for? I'm gonna make Mom quesadillas. I might have pasta—no! A burger."

Now's not the time to talk burgers! "This isn't wisdom tooth surgery. It's removing half a vital organ—an actual *organ*, Riles! And how do you know you're a match?"

"I'll find out after an evaluation." Her eyes, still puffy from crying earlier, lingered over her shoulder, following the dog.

"You mean tests, right?"

She smiled, watching the pet disappear.

She's stalling. His posture stiffened. "Riley, what tests?!"

"Oh, nothing scary." Her voice was cheery as she flashed a 'Don't worry!' grin. "It's stuff like a chest x-ray, abdominal ultrasound, CT scan. There's also a psych assessment, which…" She lifted her chin. "I'm thinking of starting therapy again."

315

"Really?" Ben's tight expression eased slightly. "Riley, that's great." He raised her hand to his lips and kissed it. "I'm proud of you, going back."

She grinned and resumed swinging his hand in hers. "Mom mentioned it a few months ago, but I wasn't ready. I am now. I'm going to do this properly, all of it—therapy, the donation, blood tests, *liver biopsy...*" Glancing away, she quickly mumbled the last two words, taking in a jagged breath.

What? Did...? Ben's eyes widened. "Did you just say *liver biopsy*? Jeez, Hope! That's—"

"The biopsy isn't for sure. It's a...maybe." She tugged him to the right, turning onto a side road.

"Did you sign something already?" Tinged with worry, his voice rose an octave.

"No, not yet. Mom's appointment with the transplant hospital is Monday. They'll decide if she's a good candidate and put her on the list."

"You going to that?"

She shook her head. "She wants to go on her own in case it's bad news. I said that's why she *shouldn't* go on her own, but she won't budge. I have to pick my battles. I've won the 'I'm donating' fight, so I'm not pushing it."

"So, she still goes on the waiting list even though her liver is coming from you?"

"Yep, and once she's on the list, her insurance company is notified, and *then* I go for my evaluation."

"So, you're on hold for bit."

"Kinda, but I can find out my blood type on Monday. It only takes a few minutes. I'd go tomorrow but..."

"Oh, yeah, Erika's wedding."

Riley frowned. "My heart's not really into bouquet tosses right now."

"But you're a maid of honor—you can't blow it off."

She sighed. "I know, but…Erika and I, we're not as close as we were, and with everything with Mom—"

"Riley, I've already said I'll hang with Maggie." He adjusted his backpack on his shoulder. "Tomorrow is booked off, and it's not like Erika will miss *me*."

"But *I* will. I'd have fun if you were there, *taking the piss* out of everything." Riley smiled. "But I'm glad you'll be with Mom. Today was hard and I know you'll cheer her up."

"Yeah, she said she can't wait to tell me her embarrassing teenage Riley stories!"

"Hey!" She stepped in front of him, blocking his progress. "Be nice to me, Brit boy. I've got blood tests on Monday, remember? Big scary needles…"

"You'll be fine! It will hurt for, like, a second. Just think of the lollipop they'll give you afterward." He kissed the top of her head and they started walking again. "Do you want me to come with?"

"No, you can't afford to take time off."

"Will Maggie's insurance pick up the cost?"

"Retroactively, yeah. They'll pay for all my tests and hers, but we'll be out of luck on living expenses, rent, my lost wages…"

"Bollocks, yeah…you'll be off work for a bit. Well, what about that crowdfunding thing? Could you pull money from there?"

She shook her head. "I hoped it might pay for the bills Mom already has, but it won't even do that. We've only raised two thousand of the fifteen-thousand-dollar goal."

"That's better than nothing."

"Yeah, but it barely makes a dent, especially now that she needs a transplant. I kinda wish we hadn't done it; I haven't told Mom about it yet…"

"She still doesn't know?"

"No. It's depressing, seeing such little interest." She smiled tightly. "So, I have to take all the Sephora shifts I can get and keep saving like Scrooge. It's not like I have a choice."

"Isn't there anyone else in your family who could do this? I worry about you. Call me selfish, but I don't want anything to happen to my girlfriend—"

"Girlfriend?" She stopped, jerking Ben to a halt.

Well, that just slipped out. "Um..." Still holding her hand, he moved closer. *There's no sense denying it—not anymore. I'm ready for a commitment. I can't lose her—to anyone or anything.* "I know we haven't talked about being exclusive, but...I think you know I have been, and I want to...with you. So, yeah...I want to be your boyfriend." *Agh!* Ben held his breath. *Did I do that right? I feel like I'm fourteen! First time for everything...*

Her smile grew. "You like me, huh?"

"Yeah." His gaze fell to her lips. "Quite a lot, actually."

Grin widening, Riley cupped his face and kissed him softly as Ben slipped his arms around her waist. He settled in, the need to go deeper reserved for another day when hospitals and organ donations weren't at the forefront of their minds.

A passing car laid on its horn...several times.

Gotta love New York. Ben laughed against her lips and broke away, reclaiming Riley's hand as they moved forward.

"So, *boyfriend*"—she giggled, ducking under a low-hanging tree branch—"don't worry, I'll be fine, and so will Mom. I can feel it."

"There's no talking you out of this?" Ben gripped a dangling leaf, pulling it with him.

"Nope."

He let go and the leaf snapped back. "You're amazing. You're also scaring the bejesus out of me, but I get it."

"Good." She swung his hand, walking in silence for a few steps. "So, how did the audition go?"

"Eh...all right."

"Just all right?"

"I don't think I'm what they're looking for."

"Really? But you read for them three times."

"Yeah, but all the callbacks today were blond, captain-of-the-football-team types. I felt like the brown-haired runt of the high school litter."

"But runts are more interesting. They're stupid if they don't pick you."

"Riles, if only you were the casting director." Ben wrapped his arm around her.

"Well, never say never. I was looking at BBC job postings yesterday when I was supposed to be doing data entry and I found a casting position in LA. Not that I'm qualified, but a girl can dream..."

"Maybe one day, eh? See anything else that looked good?" *She deserves a break. She works so hard.*

"A few entry-level jobs in production, a part-time assistant and a full-time one—right here in the New York office."

"You should apply." Ben squeezed her shoulder.

"I already did! I know it's not LA, but I need to keep my options open." She shook her head. "I don't want to be scared about the future anymore. I need to focus on *now*, on Mom—you—" Her smile grew. "Mom's appointment today was scary, but when the doctor said there was an option to donate...Ben, I felt so *empowered*! From now on, it's like I'm scaling rocks again—I'm using everything I've got to hang on and keep climbing to help Mom beat this, once and for all."

"You'll like this, then." Ben reached into his backpack. "I got you something the other day." He pulled out a re-sealable plastic pouch.

Riley's eyes immediately lit up. "Climbing chalk!"

319

"For a better grip on your climb, brave girl." He kissed her cheek.

"Thanks, Ben, really…"

"Boyfriend did good?"

"Yeah, you did good, but it's more than that." She squeezed the pouch in her hands. "Thank you…for believing in me."

You're so much braver thank you think you are.

FORTY-NINE

Children darted around topiary and happy in-laws oohed and aahed as Erika and Scott—the new Mr. and Mrs. Perrault—kissed for the photographer, their loving embrace mirrored in the sunken garden's reflecting ponds. Their historic venue, built in 1919 on Long Island's wealthy Gold Coast, looked like a fairytale castle and was famous for celebrity weddings, movie shoots, and music videos. When Erika discovered Taylor Swift had filmed her "Blank Space" video there, she chose the gorgeous mansion for her and Scott's special day.

Dodging the couple's two hundred-plus guests, Riley led bow-tie-wearing Stanley Pup on his leash around the vast property, careful to avoid grass stains on the hem of her lilac bridesmaid dress. Her sojourn also allowed her to elude Josh and his date as well as Leia, who had only traded stilted small talk throughout the festivities. *So far, so good.*

Stanley paused to gnaw on some grass, so Riley checked her phone, finding a text waiting from Ben.

Hey pretty mer-maid of honor, don't cop off with any hockey-playin ushers!!! He also added to his '4 Riles!!!' playlist with "I'm Your Man" by Wham!.

She giggled and glanced up, her breath catching. *Shit!* Leia, wearing an identical lilac dress, was striding toward her. Dread fluttered in Riley's stomach. *Great. Can I slip behind this tall bush?* She checked in with Stanley. He was lifting his leg for a pee, scuttling her escape. *Argh, right now, Pup?!*

"Hey." Leia raised her hand in a static wave, a blush of sunburn on the tip of her nose. "Beautiful day, huh?"

"Yeah." Riley glanced skyward, trying to smile like she meant it. "Erika always gets what she wants."

"I know. It's sickening, isn't it?"

Riley swallowed, trying to soothe the ache in the back of her throat. Stanley strained at his leash, sniffing Leia's dress. *What does she want?*

"Um, I just wanted to have a private moment to...uh..." Leia sighed and clutched the diamond pendant resting on her décolletage. "Listen, what happened with me and Ben..."

Taking a deep breath, Riley stared Leia in the eye. *Yikes, where is this going?*

"Can I share my side of what happened?"

Riley responded with a wary nod.

Leia toyed with her pendant. "I was checking out strip clubs for Erika when I got a text, another rumor about Tyler—more cheating, a different girl. It felt like fucking *Groundhog Day*. I wanted to lash out and forget. I wasn't sure what to do." She shrugged. "I watched the dancers, had a few drinks, but they didn't dull my anger. I could feel the need for revenge burning through me, so I thought, *Fuck it.* I took my rings off, hid 'em in my wallet, and then Ben sat at the bar...all friendly, blue eyes you could get lost in, and that British accent..."

For fuck's...I don't need to hear this! Riley broke eye contact and glared over Leia's shoulder.

"He didn't say he was a dancer. We got to talking and drinking, and that purple thong guy showed up. He pretty much begged Ben not to come home that night. He had nowhere to sleep, so..."

So, you fucked him—yeah, got it. Riley crossed her arms, met Leia's gaze again, and saw...regret? Pain? *Wait, she's...not bragging. She's...ashamed?*

Leia squeezed her necklace tighter. "I slept with Ben to get back at Ty. I shouldn't have bothered. I thought it would make me feel better…it didn't." She cleared her throat, the sparkly brilliance of her necklace, cushion-cut engagement ring, and diamond-encrusted wedding band firing glinty flares. "I used Ben to cheat on my husband. I broke my vows, something I thought I'd never do."

And I never thought I'd use Josh, even if I thought it was for a noble reason. I've made mistakes, too, in the name of love. Guilt rose in Riley's throat and her expression softened. *What good is this doing, being mad at Leia? For what? Sleeping with a single guy? One you barely knew at the time. It could've been any guy sitting there that night, but it just happened to be Ben. You've forgiven him. Forgive her, too.*

Riley nodded. "We've all been there, we've all done things we regret—I know I have." A slight grin raised her cheeks. "Relation-ships, huh? They're never easy."

Leia's brows relaxed and she let out a relieved breath. "Erika says, you and Ben…?"

"Yeah."

"He seems like a *nice* guy." Leia nodded.

"He is."

"You'll have to tell me what that's like sometime. I'm happy for you." Leia let go of her necklace and pointed over her shoulder. "Well, I should get back to Ty…"

Riley smiled kindly. "I hope things work out for you, Leia—really."

"Yeah, me, too." Leia gave a pained smile, a tinge of sadness muting her blue eyes. "Good luck with Ben." She tucked a curl behind her ear and walked away toward the glamourous party, return-ing to the life Riley had left behind.

Two round, single-layer cakes sat on Maggie's counter, both coated perfectly with a smooth layer of white buttercream icing. One was

Ben's work-in-progress canvas; pink dots and green swirls speckled the cake's top, each colorful decoration a little neater than the one that came before.

Ben mopped his brow with the back of his hand and lifted the piping bag full of frosting away from his latest squiggle. *Bugger, that was rubbish.* His mouth twisted. "Maggie, you've got the patience of a saint."

"Nonsense. You're learning faster than I did." She shifted off her tall stool, moving a cake smoother and several piping tips to the side to make more room for Ben to work. "If you apply a little more pressure to the piping bag and hover the tip just above the cake, you'll get much better control, see?"

Okay, try again. Deep in concentration, Ben's tongue slid along his bottom lip as the star-shaped tip of the piping bag inched above the cake, depositing a thick ruffle of pink and white buttercream goodness. *NOW we're talking!* Ben's face lit up at his fancy finishing touch. "Look at THAT. It works!" He pulled back, full grin on display.

His attention shifted past the cake to his phone, a new text waking up the dark screen. Riley's latest add to the '4 Benjamin' playlist had landed: "Throw Your Arms Around Me" by Hunters and Collectors. *Oooh, girl! How'd you find that steamy eighties gem?* A fan of the song's sensual lyrics, Ben smiled wider. *Wait 'til I see YOU tonight, lady!*

Maggie leaned in to check his work and Ben quickly nudged the phone aside. "I'm having a great Saturday!"

Maggie laughed. "You don't regret staying behind?"

"No. Riley had her maid-of-honor duties, and I dunno, I think she needed to socialize solo with her friends. I don't want her to drift away from people she's known forever just because there's a new boyfriend on the scene. Friendships are important, especially ones from way back."

"But you could get to know them, too?"

A text Riley received from Erika two days ago popped into his head.

Aw, not being funny, please remind Ben—no vintage Ts, ok? ;)

Erika seemed to think he was incapable of dressing appropriately for her wedding. *Like I'd choose a concert tee over a dress shirt. Gimme some credit.* "Yeah, I'm starting to, but I'd rather do it when Josh isn't around. It's just a bit awkward. He and Scott are pretty tight." He hunched over the cake with the piping bag, practicing another design.

Maggie nodded, smiling at Ben's progress. "Oh, angle the bag a *little* less…"

He lowered the bag so it was practically perpendicular to the cake's edge.

"Looking great, Ben. Did you bake a lot with your mom when you were a kid?"

"Hell yeah." He paused and licked icing off his finger. "Ingredients cost a bomb and she worked all hours, but when she had a few quid and time going spare, she made brownies, chocolate chip cookies, and heart-shaped gingerbread. She called them 'little bites of home-baked love'". His smile grew. "I found baking relaxing—and fun. And I got to play DJ with her old vinyl when we did it."

"And an eighties music fan was born!" Maggie glanced down at Ben's Police t-shirt and reached across the counter, switching on the radio. Smooth, poppy vocals filled the kitchen. "Ah, Boy George!"

"I know this! 'Time' by Culture Club. You a fan, Maggie?"

"Yep—my first concert. November 1984, the Brendan Byrne Arena in Rutherford, New Jersey. I was fourteen. My poor dad didn't know what hit him. God, the things we put our parents through."

"Why didn't your mom go?" Ben leaned over and lowered the icing bag again.

"She died when I was five."

He straightened up, a sad look on his face. "Oh, I'm sorry! I didn't think..."

"It's okay. It was a long time ago." Maggie patted his forearm. "Dad stepped in, did all the things Mom would've done. He even bought me makeup. I went to the concert as Boy George!"

"Really? You had the braids and everything?"

Maggie nodded. "Red eyeshadow, crimped hair, neon clothing..."

Ben chuckled. "Mum dressed up in pirate gear with a white stripe across her nose."

"Like Adam Ant!"

"Yeah, when she wasn't being Bananarama, wearing crop tops and rags in her hair."

"I bet she looked amazing!" Maggie bobbed her head to the music. "We had *fun*! Dad even bought me a fedora so I could copy Duran Duran."

"It's kinda like cosplay today, innit? But instead of dressing up for comic cons, you lot did it for gigs." Ben aimed the piping bag at the cake again. "Were your brothers and sisters into it, too?"

"I'm an only child. My dad died before Riley was born, so it's just us."

"No wonder you're so close." Ben grinned, but Maggie's words twisted his stomach. *'It's just us.'*

It's true, then. There wasn't anyone else—Riley really was Maggie's last hope. Ben swallowed heavily and returned to decorating the cake.

FIFTY

The crook of Riley's elbow pinched each time she straightened her arm. Waiting outside Hunter's apartment, she picked at the small cotton ball, as fluffy and white as the clouds floating free in the blue sky. But this little cloud wasn't free; it was trapped, pressed into her skin underneath a cheap plastic bandage.

"Tear it off quickly, you'll barely feel a thing," the nurse had said after taking a sample of Riley's blood less than an hour earlier.

Her fingernail couldn't leave it alone, pushing under the sticky plastic to torment the cotton, pulling wisps from the ball as hot tears streamed down her flushed cheeks. Some slipped under her chin, others fell, soaking the scoop neck of her yellow tank top. *How? HOW?!*

Cheery music blaring from an ice cream truck parked a few doors down on Canal Street did nothing to soothe her anguish or blot out the joy-filled giggles of several little girls, nose deep in soft serve cones. Their mothers stood watch—chatting, happily sipping their to-go iced coffees. *Moms and daughters...* Envy left an uncomfortable lump in Riley's throat as sobs broke through her lips. *Why me? Why us? What did we do to deserve this?* She wiped her snotty nose on her forearm, her shoulders slumping toward her denim skirt.

"Riles!" Ben's brakes squealed as his bike shuddered to a stop. "Oh, love, I got here as soon as I could."

Everything was blurry. Riley wasn't sure how Ben got off his bike, where he locked it, or how he helped her upstairs to Hunter's apartment. She wasn't sure of anything except that Ben was by her side, hugging her, rubbing her back, kissing her hair, which was damp with tears. "It's okay, it's okay," fell from his lips repeatedly.

"I can't...I..." Tissue pressed to her nose, Riley sat down on the sofa and began to slowly rock back and forth.

Worry creased Ben's forehead as he dug a hand through the front of his hair, a chaos of tangles left behind by his bike helmet. "I'll get you some water, okay? Just...I'll be a sec."

He crossed the room and filled a glass, watching Riley over his shoulder the entire time.

"I'm sorry...I didn't mean for you to ditch work."

"Don't worry about that." Ben set the water down on the table and wrapped his arm around her shoulders. "Your text...I panicked. Thank God I was only a few blocks away." His attention darted from her bloodshot eyes to the bandage, one end lifting from her skin. "I'm so sorry, love. I should've been there to hold your hand. Tell me what happened."

She shook between sobs, gulping for breaths. "They pricked my finger to figure out my blood type. The nurse said results would take two minutes, and she began to take blood from my arm while we waited. It stung when the needle went in, but I was fine after that."

His fingers traced circles on her bare shoulder as he listened.

"While the blood filled the vial, the nurse looked at the finger test and said I was type A positive. I was like, *Okay...and?* It didn't mean anything to me. She looked in my file and..." Anger sizzled in Riley's belly as her face grew red and sobs broke through her lips. "She..."

"It's okay, Riles. Take your time."

She gasped. "She said my blood type isn't compatible."

Ben shook his head, confusion clouding his gaze. "But how's that possible? Don't mothers and daughters share the same blood type? I thought it was a given."

"So did I, but apparently, that's not how it works. She said some people with different blood types *can* share organs, but Mom has high levels of antibodies in her bloodstream. That means there's a greater chance her body could reject my liver." Her chest shuddered. "She said I probably have my dad's blood type. So, I can't help Mom who means *everything* to me"—she gritted her teeth— "but I could help *him*. I couldn't believe it. I asked the nurse to check again, but it...it wasn't a mistake."

"This isn't fair." Ben closed his eyes, fighting back his own tears.

"So, then everything stopped. She pulled out the needle, slapped on a Band-Aid—in five minutes, everything had fallen apart." Riley continued to rock, desperate to ease the pain crushing her heart. "I didn't know where to go. You and Piper were working, Casey's on vacation...I couldn't speak to Mom—not yet."

"You can always call me, 'kay? I'll drop everything." Ben pulled her into his chest and cradled the back of her head. "I'm so sorry."

"I can't believe it's over...it hasn't even begun." She hiccupped into more tears and buried her nose in the softness of Ben's t-shirt. "It's not fair. She even has the most common blood type..."

"Which is what?"

Riley cried through her reply. "O positive, but who cares! Mine's not compatible...I can't *save* her, Ben!"

Swallowing thickly, he rocked with her in his arms, his hand gently rubbing her back. Their embrace was silent except for Riley's sobs and Ben sniffing his nose. After holding her closely for a few minutes, he whispered into her hair. "Riles?"

"Hmm?" Nose congested, she sucked in breaths through her mouth.

"Maybe...I can?"

Riley lifted her head from Ben's tear-soaked shirt.

"Maybe I can help Maggie."

"You...? How?"

"She's O positive?"

"Yeah?"

"Well...so am I."

Wide-eyed, Maggie sat down at her table as her daughter, Ben, and Piper—who had faked a stomach bug to flee work—served up mac 'n' cheese and salad. "I...I don't know what to say."

Riley grinned, her eyes still puffy from crying hours earlier. *I don't either. How do I even begin to thank my new boyfriend for offering to donate his liver?* She set a plate down in front of Maggie. "Mom's speechless—well, that's a miracle!"

Maggie gave Riley one of those looks only a mother can give and then turned to Ben, warmly covering his hand with hers. "Ben, that's incredibly kind of you, but I can't let you donate."

Ben sipped his water and smiled. "But I want to. Look, I know we haven't known each other long, but you and Riley mean a lot to me and"—Maggie opened her mouth to interject, but he cut her off, blurting the words out as fast as he could—"I can't sit back and do nothing, not if I can make a difference. I'd never be able to live with myself."

Riley's mom shook her head. "Ben, you can't rush into this."

"Believe me, I'm not." He grinned. "Riley and I talked—for hours."

"Yeah, we talked and cried and talked some more." She smiled back at Ben. *He's seen me at my worst and didn't walk away.*

"Riley only agreed on two conditions: one, I wasn't offering because I felt like I had to, and two, I wouldn't try to win future arguments with 'but I gave your mom my liver!'"

Riley leaned into Piper. "I mean, talk about fighting unfair."

Ben picked up his fork. "So, we called the coordinator. One of the transplant surgeons was free, so we had a wee chat. He asked me some questions, made sure I understood booze is a no-go if I want to donate, and gave me the thumbs-up—I meet the initial criteria to be your donor."

Tears brightening her eyes, Maggie squeezed his hand. "Ben, this is too much to ask."

"I mean, it's early days. I've passed the blood type test and nothing else, but"—he let go of Maggie's hand so she could wipe away a few tears—"it's worth a shot, right?"

Riley leaned in and kissed him on the cheek.

"Well, Benjamuffin, I'll say it if no one else will—dude, you're my frickin' *hero!*" Piper winked and sprinkled pepper on her dinner. "This is the most romantic thing ever, saving the life of your girlfriend's m—" Riley kicked Piper under the table. "Ahhh—well, it is!"

Ben blushed over a forkful of salad. "They emailed me an info packet, so we started to make a list of questions for Thursday."

"So soon?" Maggie glanced at her daughter.

"His blood work, physical, and liver CT scan are Thursday, which means, no eating after 10 p.m. Wednesday."

Ben made a face and chewed quickly, swallowing before talking. "And I'm seeing a liver doctor, a psychologist, and an ethics specialist." He looked at his girlfriend. "Did I forget anyone?"

"A living donor advocate and a surgeon." Riley dug her fork into her salad and exhaled, feeling the weight of the day. "It's gonna be a busy one."

Ben nodded. "And then Friday is a chat with an anesthesiologist. What else...oh yeah, a heart test and a MR-something."

"MRCP, another test that looks at the liver," said Riley, reading notes on her phone. "They said Ben should know if he's donor material by late next week."

Piper gulped her Fanta. "Before Labor Day weekend? They

don't waste any time."

"Nope," said Ben. "So, surgery could happen early September. You ready, Maggie?"

"Everything's moving so fast. I wish you'd think about this a bit longer." Maggie scratched her head, the patchy regrowth of her hair—once brown and wavy—coming in auburn and straight.

"I've done my thinking. Now it's time to get rolling." Ben smiled, sampling the cheesy macaroni.

"Mom, don't bother trying to change his mind." Riley smirked at him. "You think *I'm* stubborn…"

"But what about missing work?" Maggie leaned in.

"I'm pretty fit from cycling, and the doc said that works in my favor. The healthier I am, the easier the recovery, the earlier I can go back. Hunter will be cool about time off, and Stavros, my diner boss, will understand. He just marked five years with his sister's kidney!"

Maggie shook her head. "But you'll lose thousands in lost wages. My insurance will cover some of your medical bills, but not all, and it won't take care of your food, travel costs, rent…"

"The doc told me about a few organizations that offer short-term financial assistance."

"But you have to apply…oh, Ben, I don't want you taking out loans for this."

"I'll be fine, Maggie—really."

Mom's not backing down. Riley's chest tightened. *Should I…?*

"Ben, I can't let you donate AND get yourself into debt, it's too—"

Riley cut her off. "The crowdfunding page will help."

"The what?" Confusion clouded Maggie's gaze.

"Uh…" Riley winced. "In April, we started a fundraising page for your medical expenses."

"Fundraising?"

"Yeah."

"It was *my* idea, Maggie." Piper came to Riley's aid, opening the page on her phone and handing it to Maggie. "Sorry. I shoulda asked first." She gulped.

"Strangers…" Maggie squinted at the screen, reading. *"Two thousand dollars*?!" Her mouth fell open. "People donated this…for me?"

Riley nodded.

"It'll pay for some medications, taxis to the doctor, a few bills even," said Ben.

"I *was* going to tell you…" Riley leaned toward her mom.

"You kids…" Maggie shook her head as she blinked back sudden tears. "I don't know what to say. *Thank you.*"

"You're not mad?" asked Riley.

Maggie shook her head. "You did this out of love, wanting to help…" She fanned her face, unsuccessfully trying to curb her tears. "Come here, *all* of you." Riley, Ben, and Piper left their seats to gather around her for a group hug.

Ben tried his best to keep it together while the girls found Maggie's tears too contagious.

"Okay, let's stop this crying." Maggie laughed, wiping her eyes. "Ben, I've got one condition: if you have the operation, I want you to move in with me while you recover."

"Uh, really?" Ben raised his eyebrows. "Why?"

Maggie touched his forearm. "That crowdfunding money could help both of us and stretch a lot further if you stayed here. You wouldn't have to pay rent or buy your own groceries, and we could schedule follow-up appointments together, take one cab to the hospital instead of two."

"Yeah! I'm not letting either of you take public transport while you're recovering." Riley tossed back her water with an emphatic glug. "And selfishly, both of you living here would be a huge help.

You could keep tabs on each other. I'd worry a lot less when I head back to work."

"And Riley would only have to visit one place to see both of you—saves time." Piper popped a cucumber slice in her mouth, proud of herself.

"I know my foldout couch isn't the Four Seasons, but—"

"Believe me, Mom, your foldout is better than that sad sofa Ben sleeps on at Hunter's." She pointed her fork. "Don't deny it. You're always complaining about how lumpy it is."

"I don't know..." Ben winced, shaking his head. "I'd feel like I was imposing."

"You won't be—I want you here," said Maggie. "I can't let you do this without a little mothering."

Riley nodded at Ben. "She's right."

"I'm not gonna win this argument, am I?" Ben smiled and reached for Maggie's hand. "Deal."

FIFTY-ONE

Nine days later

Ben wouldn't stop playing with the plastic anatomical model of a liver he'd found on the doctor's desk. "I *know*, right? Hunter is such a legend! He didn't even let on he was doing a fundraiser, crafty bastard!"

"Twelve hundred dollars? How many lap dances is that? I have to thank him. Can you give me his—" Looking up from her chair, Riley did a double take. "Ben, put that back! The surgeon will be here any minute. You might brea—"

The plastic gallbladder pinged off. "Ahh, shit!" He ducked out of his chair, retrieving the errant organ from across the desk.

"Ben!"

Just my luck! He couldn't get the gallbladder to snap back into place. "What's the crowdfunding page at now, then?" he asked, examining the two organs closely, trying to see how they might reconnect.

"Just over four thousand—Ben, *hurry*—"

"Sorry to keep you waiting." Dr. Ricer, one of the surgeons on the transplant team, strode through the door, shutting it behind him. "Please, have a seat."

Ben smiled, hid the broken organs behind his back, and sat down.

"Beautiful day today." Riley smiled, trying to distract the doctor.

"Summer's last gasp—must enjoy it while we can." Dr. Ricer opened Ben's file on the desk. "So, I'm not sure congratulations is

336

the right word, but Benjamin…you're in!" The surgeon grinned behind his neatly trimmed beard. "The donation team agreed you'd be a suitable donor for Maggie."

"Brilliant! Drinks are on me!" Catching the doctor's smile slip, Ben corrected course. "Just joking!"

Dr. Ricer flipped a page of Ben's medical notes. "Kidding aside, giving the gift of an organ is a generous gesture, and a serious decision. I know you've thought long and hard about this, but as we've already discussed, you *can* change your mind at any time, Benjamin, right up to the day of surgery—"

"*Ben*, please, and I won't change my mind." He squeezed Riley's hand and let go.

"Your gift has a high likelihood of curing Maggie's cancer, but there's always a chance it will come back and your sacrifice won't have its intended result. Some donors decide they can't go through with it because there's no guarantee of a positive outcome."

"I realize that, but what in life *is* guaranteed? I could get run over by a bus leaving here today." Ben shook his head. "Nope, we have to try."

The surgeon smiled and scratched his shoulder through his scrubs. "I know it sounds like I'm giving you the doomsday take on living organ donation, but we just have to make *certain* you're aware of all the facts and risks before we move forward."

"Gotcha. Yeah, it's a huge decision and I'm not taking it lightly." Ben reached over and swept a piece of hair from Riley's eyes. "I've become close to Maggie, and I know how much she means to Riley. Look, if this was happening to my mum, I'd hope someone would do the same for her. So…I'm all in."

Riley let out a shaky breath and blinked back a tear, a smile flirting with her mouth.

"Well, it's good you have the support of Riley and Maggie." Dr. Ricer turned over a page in Ben's file. "Now, I see for family, it's just you and your mother? And she's aware of your decision?"

He nodded. "Yeah, just me and Mum. She's concerned, obviously, but she respects my decision."

"Good." The surgeon wrote something quickly in the file. "Now, I'll run through the risks a final time, and if either of you have questions, don't hesitate to jump in."

Both Ben and Riley nodded.

"Donor surgery involves general anesthesia, and like any medical procedure where the patient is unconscious, there can be complications including blood clots, heart problems, and bleeding that might require a blood transfusion. These complications don't happen too often."

"That's good." Riley exhaled nervously.

"Now, when we look at post-operative risks directly connected to liver donation, it's important to note that a small number of donors have had *some* sort of complication. They can be mild, like post-surgery nausea, constipation, small bile leaks from your liver, or minor wound infections. These problems usually resolve—" The surgeon's phone rang. Dr. Ricer glanced at it then flipped it over, face down. "Within a few weeks."

Wait, wait, back up. "A leak?" Ben chewed his lip. "How would you know...?"

"Well, you'll have one or two small drainage tubes in your abdomen to drain any blood or bile that may leak from your liver. Those tubes are usually removed after two or three days. If there's a lot of bile in the drainage and it's accompanied by chills, nausea, or swelling, we'll intervene and operate right away."

Christ, that sounds bad. Ben screwed up his face.

"And that's a *minor* complication?" Riley fiddled with the puffin charm on her bracelet. "What are the major ones?"

The surgeon folded his hands on the desk. "Serious complications can include failure of the remaining left lobe to function or death, but the chances of either happening are very low."

Riley shifted in her seat and wrapped her arms around her middle. "Low...but not impossible." She swallowed and stared at her boyfriend.

She's fretting. Lighten the mood. Ben looked ahead, serious and reserved. "And when can I drink again? I'll need a pint when all this is done."

Riley's expression softened.

"One of the great ironies," said the doctor. "Unfortunately, Ben, you'll have to hold off on having a hard-earned drink for six months after surgery—"

Shit-bollocks-fuck it! "Really? That long?"

"And even then, just small amounts for a while. Your liver will be recovering and growing. Metabolizing alcohol won't be at the top of its to-do list."

"Slacker organ." Ben leaned forward, his gaze unwavering. "What about sex?"

Riley did a double take.

"Oh, Riles, I gotta ask." He laughed.

"Sex will have to wait, too. During the post-operative period, specifically the first three months, you might feel weak or have some discomfort in your abdomen. Some donors have reported lower sexual functioning—that's issues with erections, having orgasms—during this time, but those problems *do* improve and return to normal as recovery progresses."

No booze, no sex...I didn't even think... "So what you're saying is, I'll basically be livin' like a monk for a bit?"

The surgeon nodded slowly. "Your body won't return to normal overnight. It's major surgery, Ben."

Toying with her bracelet again, Riley shifted in her chair. "I read something about the gallbladder being removed, too. Is that true?"

Yeah, it's behind me! Ben stifled a chuckle, pretending it was an awkward sneeze. Riley shot him some side-eye.

"Yes. I'll show you why…" Dr. Ricer's eyes searched his desk.

Shit. He's looking for the model. Ben stared into space.

"Hmm, one of the interns must have it. Well…" The surgeon pointed at his own abdomen. "It sits in front of the right lobe of the liver here, so it has to be removed to enable access. The gallbladder aids in digestion, but Ben shouldn't have any major issues without it. Sometimes digesting fatty or spicy foods can cause discomfort. Our nutritionist will go over a meal plan with you, post-op. It's usually recommended that you avoid certain foods for a while, things like French fries, ice cream, potato chips."

"No crisps, no booze, no sex…got it." Ben cleared his throat. "And how long will I be off work exactly?"

"Every donor is different, but we find most are off for three to six weeks post-surgery, longer if the job is physically demanding." Dr. Ricer referred to his papers again. "You're…a bike courier and a waiter—you'll have to play it by ear, Ben. Cycling around Manhattan and bussing tables is about as far as you can get from a desk job."

Jeez. It all feels so real now. Ben's face fell.

Pulling her jean jacket sleeves over her hands, Riley looked down, her green eyes glassy.

"Look." The surgeon took a deep breath and leaned forward. "Being a living organ donor is not easy. It's no surprise people change their minds. It's an enormous ask."

Ben chewed his lip. *But Maggie never asked—not for cancer, not for recurrences—and she'd never ask me or Riley—or anyone— to save her life.* He inhaled deeply and let the breath slowly exit his lungs, watching Riley quiet and still, staring at her lap like she was determined not to sway him one way or the other. *It won't be easy, but…I can skip all the fun stuff for a few months. My 'suffering' doesn't compare with anything Maggie's gone through—or the ag-ony she'll go through if I don't do this...* He blinked and sat up, put-ting his hand on Riley's knee. "It's a big ask, but I still want to do it."

Riley's lips parted. "You sure?" she whispered.

"Yep." Ben ran his hand through his hair. "Can we set the sur-gery date now?"

"We can. We had a cancelation for next week."

"Someone dropped out?" asked Ben.

Dr. Ricer didn't answer and kept scrolling on his computer. "We'd like to schedule Maggie's transplant as soon as we can. It's always tricky to book these things as we need two operating rooms, two surgeons, two teams of nurses and anesthesiologists...okay, right. Here it is. What are you doing a week from now—Tuesday, September 4th?"

Ben turned to Riley and smiled. "Saving your mom."

FIFTY-TWO

Three days later

Riley's phone lit up with a photo of Ben basking in April sunlight atop Rat Rock.

"Hey!" She cradled it in the nook of her neck, her hands busy typing an email on her laptop. "I was just gonna call you. I got an interview! A week from today for the full-time BBC assistant job!"

"Seriously? Aw, Riles, that's just grand! I knew they'd consider you."

"Oh, and you left without your lunch."

"Ahh, well, that's all down to you, that is," Ben whispered through the phone. "After sex that good, my brain shuts down and I basically become a vegetable."

"*Yeah...*" Riley's mind drifted: Ben's fingers gripping her hips from behind...his eager mouth biting her shoulder, owning her wet skin...their gasps and moans muted behind the plastic curtain... "Just don't tell Piper. She'll never shower in there again."

He chuckled. "What she doesn't know won't hurt her." Muffled voices and laughter rose in the background. "Hey, listen, if you're free, can I meet you and grab those sandwiches?"

"Uh, yeah, if we meet halfway somewhere." Riley glanced at the plastic container holding Ben's lunch hostage. "I have to be at Sephora at two."

"Oh, I thought you were scheduled off today?"

"I got called in. Someone's sick."

"Ahh, okay...well, meet me at Wagamama?"

"What? A few blocks away?

"Yep. My last delivery was nearby."

"Why do you need sandwiches if you're eating noodles?"

"I'll save them for dinner. Please? Come meet me now!"

"'Kay, be there in five."

Pulling open the door to Wagamama, Ben's favorite restaurant chain from London, Riley walked into a wall of noise: laughter, clinking cutlery, and John Legend crooning somewhere through the speakers. A cluster of hungry diners waited ahead of her, perusing menus and checking their phones. She glanced past them, spotting Ben wearing his Duran Duran t-shirt, waving her toward a teak booth beside the window. *Who's he with?* Someone in a ball cap and a woman with a long blonde ponytail sat across from him.

"Riles!" Ben climbed out of the booth. "I want you to meet some friends."

She turned—and her heart froze. *Whaaaa...is it...?*

The chaotic lunchtime noise, the dim light, yummy smells—everything except the male sitting in front of her, got sucked up into a massive black hole of unimportance.

IT IS! OhmyGodohmyGodohmyGod!

Riley's stomach dropped in the most spectacular, giddy freefall. She stared, mouth agape, her lungs paralyzed, all ability to form words gone.

Ben chuckled, removing the tub of sandwiches from her arms. "Riley, meet Mark and Alex!"

Mark Keegan. Keegs. Your fave actor...he's real. He's HERE!

Grinning from ear to ear, Mark Keegan was almost unrecognizable, his pitch-black hair, long and shaggy, barely contained under his ball cap. Sunburn tinged the tip of his pale Irish nose and he was wearing navy knee-length shorts with a baggy New York Yankees t-shirt that hid his toned chest.

"Hey, Riley."

That Irish accent!

Mark stood up and kissed her on each cheek. "It's such a pleasure to meet you." He gave her a soft bear hug, her nose buried in his neck.

He smells ah-may-zing! What is it about Irish and British guys and their...oh! Crap! My hair's in his face! ARGH! The ONE day I don't shampoo...

Mark pulled back, gifting Riley the full impact of his brown puppy dog eyes. *Holy crap! He's even more gorgeous in person! And...shorter? Shorter than Ben.* "Hi...it's nice to meet *you*."

Mark motioned to the pretty blonde in a blue sleeveless shirtdress. "This is my girlfriend, Alex. She's from Florida..."

"I know!" *Shit. Great—now I sound like a total stalker. Alex will know you read online gossip. Speaking of which, they're here...together—they're back together! Oh God, wait 'til I tell Pip!* "Hey, Alex. It's *so* great to meet you."

Mark sat down and Alex waved from the end of the booth. "Hi! This is amazing. I *finally* get to meet Ben, and now you, too. I'm so happy to have friends in this crazy city."

Ben held the sandwich box and shifted along the seat, nudging his bike helmet and messenger bag with his hip, making room for Riley to scoot in.

Alex Sinclair wants to be friends! "Oh, you're moving here?" Riley's eyes lit up and roamed the table—no food, just drinks. Ben was following donor pre-surgery protocol and was sipping ice water, not alcohol.

Mark nudged up the peak of his cap. "New York's great, but no, London's home, eh, Mouse?"

Mouse? Mark calls her Mouse. Okay, I'm dying.

"My play is transferring from London, so I've been here working with the producers." Alex toyed with the straw in her soda.

"We're flying home tomorrow, but I'll be back for casting in April."

"And opening night in May." Mark sipped his beer. "Can't wait for that! *Thirteen* is a great production. I'm proud of my girl."

Alex's eyes lit up. "You guys should come!"

"Wouldn't miss it." Ben wrapped his arm around Riley and whispered in her ear. "I ordered you a ginger ale."

Riley smiled breathlessly at her boyfriend. *How is this happening? We're sitting with MARK AND ALEX!*

"I was just apologizing to your man, here." Mark smiled, his eyes crinkling in the corners. "It's my fault we lost touch, mate. I'm glad you reached out to Freddie." He looked at Riley. "Freds is my best mate back in London."

"Freddie's a top bloke." Ben swept his hair from his eyes. "I'll never forget when you guys came to my play at the Old Red Lion Theatre. Tough gig. You were the only people in the audience, if you don't count the bar staff."

"I wanted to tag along that night. I was trying to get *this one* to notice me." Alex looked lovingly at Mark. "We were all at the Castle pub earlier in the evening…"

Mark nodded. "That's where Alex and I met."

"Well, met *properly*," Alex said with a smile.

"May 30th, 2015, a night I'll never forget—but not for Benny's acting." Mark dodged back as Ben swatted at him across the table.

Benny?! Riley stifled a laugh.

"Ahh, The Castle. I love Islington. I love that pub," said Ben. "Riles, when we're in London, I'll take you there."

When we're in London…? Riley's heart fluttered into a frenzy.

"We'll get the whole gang out: Lucy, Harry, Simon, Tom, and Naomi!" Alex nodded enthusiastically.

"Well, if the rest of them are as great as Freddie…" Ben smiled. "He gave me Keegs' new number yesterday. I rang Mark to catch up, and voila—the bastard's right HERE."

The server stopped at the table with the ginger ale, and Riley noticed how Mark pulled down his cap and ducked his head. Once she dashed off, his chin lifted and he rejoined the conversation.

"Yeah, I've barely been home this year. I don't know if I'm coming or going. I lost my phone and had to change my number because some fans got hold of it. And I lost most of my contacts. I'm not great with technology."

"You've always been shite at replying to texts." Ben stroked Riley's shoulder.

"But I'll have you know, Fagan, I rang Spencer months back, trying to get in touch."

"Oh…" Ben shifted in his seat. "Erm, she's…"

She? A girl named Spencer?

Mark laughed. "What did you *do*? She refused to give me your number."

"I just owed her some rent…" He winced, turning to Riley. "Spencer's my old flatmate—we met at uni."

"Oh." She sipped her drink. *Ben's never mentioned her.*

"And the owner of an *awful* hairless cat." Mark scrunched up his face.

"Cat?" Ben sneered. "More like a rat. He used to nip my feet."

"Yeah, not cute, not like Pizza Rat." Mark picked at the label on his beer. "We actually saw him last week—for real!"

"I love Pizza Rat. He's so cute—in a grubby New York way!" Riley turned to Ben, who looked both confused and creeped out. "There's this video of a rat dragging a dirty slice of pizza along the subway tracks." She laughed. "I'll show you later."

"My first celebrity spotting in New York." Mark chuckled. "Yeah, I like it here. We did Central Park on my first day, went up the Empire State Building, walked the High Line, and visited Coney Island—I almost got Lex on a roller coaster, but she chickened out."

Alex frowned. "Ugh, I hate them."

"I don't blame you," said Riley.

"What?" Ben leaned in to his girlfriend. "You'll scale boulders and rock walls, but a rollercoaster gives you the willies?"

"It's not the height. It's the lack of control I don't like."

"Ahh, now, *that* makes sense." Ben kissed her on the forehead and turned back to Mark with a smile. "So, when does filming start? It's *Full Throttle 3*, isn't it? Lots of car chases…"

The inside scoop on a movie shoot! Riley couldn't mute her huge grin if she tried.

"No, I dropped out weeks ago." Mark met Alex's gaze and they shared a soft smile. "The script was total bollocks—a ton of plot holes and CGI explosions, zero character development or heart…it just wasn't for me."

"Phew, that's a relief, mate. Now I don't have to tell porkies." Ben scratched his stubble. "Those *Throttle* films are shite!"

"Yeah, I'm sticking with stuff I love: season four of *Lairds* shoots in October, and then I've got *A Doll's House* at the Old Vic. Previews begin in February."

"Old Vic? Blimey, Keegs, well played. That theater is life goals." Ben nudged Riley. "It's like two hundred years old and stunning inside—another for our London to-do list."

"Can't wait." Riley beamed like she could burst.

"How's it been for you, finding work out here?" Mark took a swig of beer.

"Oh, you know. I'm auditioning…no luck yet. I'm doing jobs on the side."

"I'm guessin' courier by the helmet—good, keeps you fit. Bartending, too?"

"Close! I'm a singing waiter in a diner for tourists!" With a smile, he sarcastically raised his glass to Mark.

"And a *lifesaver*." Mark clinked his beer bottle with Ben's glass and grinned warmly at Riley. "This fella here…he may be clumsy as fuck and a bit of a klepto, but he's got a heart of gold. He's a good 'un. I don't mind tellin' ya, if I was donating my liver in four days' time, I'd be absolutely shitting it."

"Well, what can I say? Some of us are made of stronger stuff, Keegs." Ben pulled up his sleeves to show off his modest guns.

Riley rolled her eyes, slapping Ben's arm playfully as the two old friends laughed.

Alex smiled sympathetically. "Ben told us about your mom, Riley. I hope surgery goes well and she feels better soon."

"Yeah." Mark nodded. "We'll be sending positive thoughts and lots of love."

"Thanks, guys. Mom'll love to hear that..." *Should I ask? For her?* "Mark, would it be possible to get an autograph for her?" *I hope that isn't weird!*

"Oh, absolutely!"

Riley pulled out a spiral notebook and a pen from her tote, handing them over.

"Maggie, yeah?"

Riley nodded, and Mark took his time, writing a message while she chatted with Alex and Ben. Alex asked about Riley's time at NYU and her BBC internship, and they exchanged contact details. She added Riley on Instagram and Facebook and insisted they stay in touch so they could meet up when she returned to New York in April.

"Here you go, love." Mark handed Riley her notebook. "Maybe next time we can meet Maggie, too."

"That would be great!" Riley tucked Mark's note in her bag. She didn't read it, saving it as a surprise for both herself and her mom.

"I wish we could actually have a meal and stay a bit, but Lex has a final meeting in Midtown."

"Oh!" Riley checked her phone. *Noooo!* "I gotta go to work, too."

Ben fished a few dollars out of his pocket and left them on the table beside money left by Mark.

"Let's not leave it so long next time, eh?" Mark stuffed his wallet back in his shorts. "Text me when you're in London?"

"Definitely, mate." Ben nodded, tossing his messenger bag over his shoulder. "But before you go, let's get a pic like old times."

Riley beamed. *Ben, I frickin' LOVE you! I so wanted to ask for a photo.*

"Christ, remember the photos we took during drama school? The London Dungeon costumes…?" Mark slipped out of the booth and offered Alex his hand so she could exit easily with her purse and shopping bag from Duane Reade.

"That tourist attraction? You acted *there*?" asked Riley.

"Yeah, we played historical Londoners." Ben nodded at Mark. "Jack the Ripper here begged me to join him."

Mark rolled his eyes. "Tough crowd, long days—bloody hot, too! At least we had a laugh together, scaring tourists."

"I didn't know you played Jack the Ripper, Mark!" Alex giggled.

"With Keegs' charisma? He KILLED it, geddit?"

"Ben!" "Oh, God!" His friends groaned.

He nudged his hair from his eyes. "I was hoping to play Guy Fawkes, Henry VIII—someone awesome—but nope. I was a jester and the plague doctor."

Mark snickered. "Ben spent most of his first term at Guildhall washing off fake blood and puss."

"Eww!" Riley and Alex cringed with laughter. "That's just gross!"

"I'd keep those photos under lock and key, Keegs. They'll be worth a mint one day." Ben winked. "Riles, use your phone? Mine's cracked to fuck."

The four of them gathered around the edge of the table and Ben took several selfies. Mark adjusted his hat back down over his eyes and hugged Riley. "Be sure to text me those, 'kay?"

"Stay in touch." Alex embraced Riley, too. "We have to hang out when I'm back in the spring."

This is surreal. "For sure." Riley picked up Ben's sandwich box and caught a glimpse inside Alex's small plastic bag. *Packages of Twizzlers?!*

The two couples headed outside into the bright sunlight on Third Avenue. Mark promptly put on his shades and nodded at a discreetly idling SUV. "All the best for Tuesday, yeah? Riley, make sure this one behaves." Mark snickered, smacking Ben's hand and pulling him in for a one-armed hug. "Ben Fagan, liver donor— never in my wildest." Mark gave Ben a squeeze and let him go. "I'm proud of you, mate."

Ben responded with a tight-lipped smile.

The famous actor and his playwright girlfriend climbed into the SUV's back seat and waved from the window, driving north through the Friday afternoon traffic.

Riley stood slack-jawed. "You forgot your lunch on purpose, right?"

Ben hugged his helmet and twisted slightly back and forth. "Got you here, though, didn't it?"

"Did *that*…really just happen?"

"The look on your face…bloody priceless!" Ben leaned in to kiss her, but Riley's phone went off in her hand.

She reluctantly pulled away and handed Ben his sandwiches. "Sorry, could be Mom…oh, Casey. Just let me…hel—"

"OH. MY. GOD." Casey's shouting made her wince. "RILEY! HE WASN'T LYING!"

"Case?"

"I was SO wrong about Ben. I'm texting you. Take a look—call me RIGHT BACK!"

Riley lowered her phone. A screenshot appeared by text, then another. The first was a shot from Mark Keegan's Instagram, a photo of Maggie's crowdfunding page with a caption saying: *Please spread the word and help my friend if you can. Much love, Mark xo*

The second image was Mark's Instagram bio with a link so his fans could donate directly to Maggie's campaign.

"Oh my God. Mark's sharing Mom's..." Riley jabbed at her phone, opening up the crowdfunding page. Scrolling, scrolling...

A slow smile crept across Ben's face.

"Mark donated five thousand dollars and brought us up to just over nine thousand five hundred! And his *fans*! They're giving ten, twenty...a hundred dollars! You *told* him about this?!"

"It might have come up."

Riley shook her head in awe. "I can't...I just can't believe you did all this. Thank you so much...*Benny!*" She smiled and leaned into him for a long, deep kiss.

FIFTY-THREE

Ten hours...almost half a day...six hundred minutes—the only thing separating Ben from his life-changing decision. Before and after...what would *the after* be like? How does someone feel after saving someone else? Happy? Empowered? Scared? For the past three days, Ben could think of little else, and the whispers in his head were getting louder, more demanding, feeding the seeds of anxiety in his belly. Normally, he'd turn to alcohol to block out unease or sweat away his troubled thoughts in a crowded club, but that morning as a fiery sliver of sun broke through Riley's curtain, exposing the disarray in the darkness, his girlfriend helped him silence the noise. He wouldn't have had it any other way.

A sock dangled from the counter, discarded jeans covered the milk crate, and a fuzzy pair of handcuffs lay open on the loveseat. Ben's dress shirt, stained with soy sauce from dinner, lay crumpled beside a heap of Twister bedsheets. Several PEZ dispensers, taken out by Riley's bra flung in a moment of passion, mingled on the floor with a tipped over bottle of lube and condom wrappers, both torn and unopened, just beyond Ben's splayed fingers gripping the rug.

Remember every second. Ben panted above Riley as his hips shifted, thrusting in and out. *It might be weeks—months—before I can feel her like this again.*

He buried his face in her hair, losing himself in the subtle orange blossom, jasmine, and musk of Riley's summery perfume. He couldn't get enough of its sensual tease, unlocking frequently visited daydreams of her skimpy swimwear and sex in the warm sand, the sun-kissed holiday they joked about but couldn't afford to take.

Her fingernails dug into his ass. "Ben?"

Riley's breathy gasp lifted his head. "Yeah?"

"Switch...me on top."

"You read my mind." Ben rolled onto his back, pulling her on top, her thighs fitting perfectly around his, pinning him to the floor. His hands squeezed her hips, digging in as she rocked against him. *Beautiful Hope. Fuck yes. Let me watch you...take me deeper. Oh, sweet lord...* His head pushed into the soft pool of Riley's discarded dress, his heavy gaze flirting between her breasts and the soft smile curving her mouth.

Few words were spoken. Every kiss and lick, every moan and name whispered across skin, through the night and into that morning, had said all they needed to say, yet somehow...it still wasn't enough.

Before going under tomorrow, I want to remember... Ben sighed and traced his thumb down her hip and in between her legs, circling her, coaxing her to the edge.

A gasp escaped Riley's parted lips. "Oh, God, I'm close." Moving faster, her breaths drew short and quick, and for the first time, Ben noticed a blush of pink around her mouth and chin. *Stubble burn.*

"You feel so *good.*" His hand left her hip and slid around, squeezing her ass and holding her tighter, trying to slow his excitement down. *Let Riley come first. Let her remember...how good we are together...* With a satisfied groan, his eyes fought to stay open, desperate to watch as he felt her begin to tighten around him.

"Oh—!" Her fingers spread out on his chest. She cried out, her body shaking until the spasms subsided.

Fucking hell, Riles...I can't hold on much longer.

His own rampant desire took over as he leaned forward to kiss her breasts, focusing on what he needed. Thrusting deeply and fighting sharp breaths, his tongue swirled around her nipple with a

353

feverish urgency until his head fell back, releasing a deep groan. He clutched her hips as his thighs began to twitch and his body followed, jerking upward with a final thrust. "Fuck!"

Riley clasped onto his hands, steadying herself as he sank back to the floor, breathing heavily.

"That was..." Eyelashes flickering, his eyes rolled back, and the grip he had on her hips relaxed. "Bloody hell."

"We're gonna be sore." Riley nudged her messy hair off her forehead.

"And every time we feel a twinge, we'll remember..." Ben leaned up on his elbows and reached between them, anchoring the condom as Riley moved off him. He peeled it away, dropping it in the bin with the others.

Lying down, covering Ben's nakedness with her own, Riley left tender, loving kisses along his chest, a glint of sweat dampening the fine hair on his pecs. Her hands roamed up his body, following her mouth to his neck.

Caressed in her sighs, Ben caught his breath and held her tight, marveling in her warmth, her exquisite softness, and her lips pressing smiles into his skin. *I never want this to end. I want to stay right here, like this.*

She looked up, his silence raising a glimmer in her eye. Her lips teased his with brief kisses that softened into longer, deeper ones.

But if I don't wake up tomorrow... His tongue danced with hers until he couldn't stay silent any longer. *You need to tell her. Take a leap of faith.* His heart began to hammer in his chest. "Riley?" Her name lingered between their lips. "You and I are now...we."

Riley caught the intense look in his eyes. "We? Yeah, 'course we are. We're exclusive."

No, that's not it. Say the actual words...c'mon, say them! His finger traced her cheek, brushing hair out of her eyes. "Yeah, but Riley, what I mean is...I love you—I absolutely love you! I think

I've loved you all along, but I didn't know what that meant or how to say it. I know now, though. I *know*, Riley! I love you so *fucking* much that I think my heart could burst out of my chest..." He stopped talking, gazing into Riley's eyes. "Please say something."

"Oh, *Ben*. Oh my God." A smile flickered on her lips before parting them for good. "I love you, too!"

"You *do*? Really?" His eyes pleaded, searching hers for clarity. "You're not just sayin' that 'cause of tomorrow? I mean, if that's why, that's okay—I'll take whatever I can get—"

"Ben." Riley held his face in her hands. "I *do* love you for helping Mom, but that's not *why* I love you. There are so many reasons...and they all clicked in Central Park up on the rock. It's not every day you meet someone who sees inside your heart and *completely* gets you, but you did."

Ben kissed her nose and pulled her tight against him, leaving a kiss on her forehead. "You know, when I landed here, my goal was to have maximum fun—nothing serious, no commitments, just some good times while I figured things out. It was never in my plan to meet a beautiful girl and fall for her, and it definitely wasn't in my plan to give away a liver to anyone!" He smiled. "But then you showed up out of the blue with your pink suitcase... Everything changed. I feel happy...content."

"That makes two of us." Riley cuddled into him, lying silent for a moment. "Hey, will you call your mom before surgery?"

The nervous knots he'd felt in his stomach earlier began to twist and pull again.

"I know the five-hour time difference makes it tricky, but you could call her now?"

Ben let out a heavy exhale. "Riley, there's something I have to tell you." He closed his eyes, afraid to see her reaction. "Mum doesn't know I'm doing this."

Riley's jaw dropped. "What?! Why?"

He bit his bottom lip and looked at her. "We haven't been speaking for quite some time now and...that's my fault. She was all for me coming out here, but I haven't picked up any acting work...she spent so much on drama school, and for what? For me to wait tables and have my bum pinched by grannies from Florida? I want to make her *proud*, Riles. I hate disappointing her, but that's all I ever seem to do."

"But if she knew about tomorrow...helping Mom—"

"Maybe." He nodded, flipping over his phone on the floor. *6:32 a.m. Monday, September 3. In less than ten hours I'll be gowned and on a hospital gurney, spending the night.* "But just let me get through it, okay? Let's make sure Maggie's all right, I'm back at work, and things are back to normal. Then, I'll tell her about it, and all about us, okay?"

"O-kay..." Her brow remained creased. "But I don't agree with it. She's your mom, Ben. She'd want to know. You're risking your life—"

"I know, but please, Riley, I don't want to argue right now. Remember what the doc said—rest and *relax*."

She nodded. "Right...sorry." She caressed his bottom lip with her finger. "I'm dreading leaving you and Mom at the hospital."

He kissed her fingers and laced his hand in hers, holding it against his heart. "I'll see you tomorrow morning, right? Before they whisk me away?"

"Yeah." She rested her face against his chest. "Ben, are you scared?"

"A little bit, but I want your mom to be okay...more than anything." He caressed her cheek lovingly. "I'm a so-so actor with dyslexia who can't get work, a pretty shit waiter, a really shit stripper— I've never been good at *anything*! But this one time I might really make a difference. I might save Maggie's life! And knowing how close you two are, if I can do that...well, in a way, I can save you, too."

"Aw, Ben." Getting teary, Riley stared into his eyes. "You're the sweetest, kindest guy I've ever known. I love you so much." She placed a long, lingering kiss on his lips.

"I love you, too." Ben smiled, playing with the puffin on her bracelet. "I'm so glad you like this."

"Well, that's a given, Fagan—it's from you." Riley sighed as her fingers ran across his stubble. "I wish they'd let me stay with you tonight at the hospital."

"Well, you say that now, but I don't think you want to be there for bowel prep. From what I've been reading, it ain't gonna be pretty, girl! Funnily enough, Mark was bang on—I will be shitting it!"

She laughed and slapped him playfully on his chest. "Oh, way to go and break the *mood*, Benjamin."

You can never say "I love you" enough, and the people you love can never hear it too much. Say it warmly, say it often.

FIFTY-FOUR

In the hospital's pre-op area, Riley stood by her mother's bedside, trying to stay out of the way of the nurses and the IV line inserted into a vein in Maggie's hand.

"It's quicker to fly to *Dubai*, you know. I looked that up on my phone last night." Maggie stifled a laugh, mindful of the other patients beyond her hospital curtain. "I'm glad you dressed comfy."

Riley tugged at her baggy NYU sweatshirt that stretched past her leggings-covered butt. "The transplant coordinator said *up to* twelve hours. Could be less."

"You could grab breakfast, go see a movie or three, then come back..."

"I'm not going anywhere." Riley held her mom's hand and inhaled deeply, the sharp lemony scent of disinfectant from the damp, recently mopped floor waking her up. "I brought a book, and Piper and Casey will keep me company." Her eyes strayed to the squiggly lines and blinking lights on the monitor beside the bed, tracking Maggie's cardiac rhythm, blood pressure, and oxygen levels. "The nurse said the surgeries are happening in reverse order. The living donor usually goes in first, but they're taking you before Ben. She said it's something to do with your cancer?"

"Yeah, they have to do an exploratory lapa-*something-or-other* first to make sure it hasn't spread. If it has, they'll call off the transplant and Ben's liver stays put."

"My ears are burning..." Ben peeked around the privacy curtain, a cheeky smile on his tired face. Wearing a hospital gown, a bathrobe draped over his shoulders, and slippers, he clutched his phone in one hand and his IV pole in the other. A bag of saline swung from a hook on the pole, its rubber tubing tethered to the back of his left hand.

Maggie smiled up at him. "Ben! Come in."

"Hiya, Maggie." He flung his non-IV arm around Riley's waist and nuzzled into her ear. "Morning, gorgeous. I missed you last night."

Riley leaned into him, his warmth, his familiarity feeling like home. *My head fits perfectly on his shoulder.* "Did you sleep okay?" The dark circles under his eyes answered her question.

"Like a log, but I had stripper flashbacks this morning." He rubbed his tummy and frowned. "They shaved my abs!"

Maggie laughed. "If it makes you feel any better, they shaved my stomach, too! Oh, before I forget, now that you're both here— thank you for that lovely note from Mark. He's a doll."

With a smile, Ben looked over his shoulder and pulled the curtain closed. "How you feeling, Maggie? Ready to play Operation?"

"Yeah! Hopefully, a buzzer won't go off and my nose won't light up if they touch something they shouldn't!"

"They better leave your 'spare ribs' and 'bread basket' alone." Ben's eyes kept darting to the bottom of the curtain, his strange behavior punctuated by a nervous giggle. "They can take my 'butterfly', though."

Why is he acting weird? Curiosity halted Riley's exhale. "Ben, does your nurse know you're here?"

"Does he heck! I made a break for it, said I needed the loo." Scratching his messy hair, the hospital ID bracelet slipped down his wrist. "I wanted to see Maggie—"

"Maggie?" A young nurse with a Welsh accent pulled the curtain aside. A female aide lingered behind her. "We're ready to take you to the OR now."

So soon? "Can we just…" Riley glanced at her mom.

The nurse nodded, hearing the tremor in Riley's voice. "Of

course. I'll be back in a sec." She turned away and checked on another patient.

Ben stepped back and toyed with his phone, giving mom and daughter privacy.

"Riley, please...don't worry. Ben and I are in good hands. It's going to be fine."

How do I say everything I want to say in a minute? Riley's lip trembled. *Do NOT cry! You don't want her upset before she goes in.* Holding back tears, she squeezed Maggie's hand. *But what if it doesn't go well...* "I love you, Mom."

"Sweetie, I love you, too. You're my life."

Now I'm really gonna cry. Riley leaned over the bed's rail, kissing Maggie on the cheek. "Third time lucky, right?"

"Yep! And this time, it's personal!" Maggie chuckled, patting her daughter's hand as the nurse and aide returned, ready to go. "Oh, wait! Where's Ben?"

"I'm here." His IV stand squeaked as he shuffled to her bedside.

Maggie's eyes glowed with tearful gratitude. "I can't thank you enough. I think an angel sent you to us. You've given me hope where there wasn't any."

Ben looked awkward, his eyes flicking down to stare at his slippered feet. "You'll be fine, Maggie. Can't wait to have this stupid ol' liver whipped out of me and put to good use."

"Gimme a hug!" She lifted her arms to pull him in, whispering in his ear. "If anything happens, please give Riley the letter in my nightstand at home? And look after each other, okay?"

"Maggie—"

"Liver or no liver, you'll always be part of our family, Ben."

"Thanks." Pulling away, he ducked his quivering chin.

The nurse squeezed past with a warm smile and unplugged the monitor from the wall, its battery pack beeping. She attached it to a pole at the head of the bed as the aide unlocked the bed's brakes. Riley and Ben shifted out the way so she could steer Maggie clear and toward the doors leading to the hallway.

This is going to be the longest day of my life. Riley's stomach lurched with nausea.

"Love you. I'll see you when I see you." Maggie squeezed Riley's hand one last time and let go, her eyes locked on her daughter until she was out of sight. Riley followed the bed, only breaking her gaze when it vanished behind the closing OR doors.

"Code yellow: missing patient. Surgical floor. Code yellow."

Riley's eyes widened. "That's not *you*, is it?"

Ben grinned sheepishly. "Shit, I think I've been rumbled."

"Mr. Fagan, you shouldn't be strolling the halls." Annoyance prickled the male nurse's words as he snapped the rubber tourniquet around Ben's upper arm.

"Oww!" Ben scowled. "Flo Nightingale you ain't, mate!"

"It was time for your blood work and you weren't here. Your walkabout could've delayed surgery."

Riley smirked, holding Ben's free hand. "You're a transplant troublemaker. They're not going to invite YOU back again."

"Ahh, story of my life. Always the bridesmaid, never the bride."

The nurse stuck a needle into the crook of Ben's right arm, just above his Pac-Man blue ghost tattoo. Riley flinched and looked away.

"Thhhhhh!" Ben sucked in a breath. "Fuckity bollocks!" He glared wide-eyed at the nurse. "You're doing that on purpose now, aren't you?"

His question fell away, ignored as a full vial of blood was removed and an empty one was clicked into its place.

"Well, one thing's for sure: with the big abdominal scar I'm going to have, my stripping days are well and truly over!"

"In public, maybe." Riley stared at the wall. *Is it over yet?*

Ben swallowed several times. "I'd kill for some water, and my stomach is growling like an alien's about to burst out."

The nurse untied the tourniquet and pulled out the needle, quickly covering the skin puncture with a cotton ball and a Band-Aid. He nodded at an aide standing in the doorway. "Right, Mr. Fagan, we're moving you downstairs to pre-op—"

No. Riley's stomach rolled. "Already?" Eyes flitting between the aide propping open the door and the nurse undoing the monitors from the wall, she loosened her grip on Ben's hand. "But...my mom has only been in the operating room for thirty minutes—if that."

"We need Mr. Fagan close to the operating room so we can finish his pre-op prep. The anesthesiologist needs to meet with him again, too."

Ben fiddled with his phone, lying on the blanket. "Riles can come, yeah?"

The nurse shook his head, untying the patient call button from the bed rail. "We'll be inserting an epidural catheter in your back to help with pain relief. We don't allow family there when that's done. I'm sorry."

Ben squeezed Riley's hand as her phone buzzed in her tote. Eyebrows peaked, she whispered, "So..."

"So..." Ben squirmed in the bed. "Riles, please hang on to my stuff? The bag on that chair..." He motioned toward it, lifting his chin.

The nurse handed the bag to Riley and she looped its long strap over her shoulder, next to her tote.

"Oh, phone, too." Ben placed it in her hand. The bed shook and squealed as the aide unlocked its brakes.

It's happening too fast... Riley looked up, fighting the urge to cry. "Come back to me, Benjamin Fagan."

"Hey, that's a first. I never get asked back!" His wide grin sank into a scared gulp. "Riley, if I—"

"Ben..." She leaned over the rail and ignored the impatient stare of the aide standing behind the head of the bed. "You'll be all drowsy the next time I see you..." Riley bit her lip, but tears spilled through her lashes and wouldn't stop. "I love you."

"I love you, too, and I want you to know..." With a peaceful smile, he swept the tears from her face and caressed her damp cheek. "I've never loved any one 'til you," he whispered. "You were so worth the wait, Hope. You're my first, my always."

You're my last, my always. Riley gasped and met his lips, sharing a lingering kiss flavored with salty tears. She hoped Ben's final memory before going under would be of kisses and plans for their future together, not tears and worry over what could go wrong. She smiled softly and squeezed his hand. "As soon as you're feeling better, we'll tackle that to-do list: dinner at that pub in London, go see a-ha in concert somewhere, see a play at the Old Vic Theatre..."

"It's a *date*, gorgeous." Ben punctuated his promise with a wink that released a tear.

Riley let go of his hand to dry his cheek, but the bed moved forward and Ben was no longer within reach.

FIFTY-FIVE

Curled up on a couch, a copy of *Emma* on her lap, Riley didn't realize a worried frown had taken up residence on her face. She twirled her ring round her finger. *At this rate, I'm going to be completely gray by the time they're both out of surgery.*

"Rye...it must be going well." Sitting beside Riley, Piper licked her finger and flicked a glossy page of a waiting room magazine. "Seven hours, no word. No news is good, right?" She glanced at Casey sitting across from them, a venti quad, no-whip, extra hot mocha with coconut milk, caramel drizzle, and extra butterscotch topping hovering by his lips.

"Pip! Don't lick your finger in here. God knows where that magazine has been!"

"Case, if this place is such a nightmare, go outside, hit up Walgreen's, and bring back Swedish Fish, Funyuns, and Fanta."

"Hello? What's my number one rule?" Scrolling his phone, Casey grimaced. "I never buy food where sick people shop."

Piper loudly flicked another page.

"Hey, have you seen the crowdfunding page?" Casey raised an eyebrow. "It's over twenty thousand dollars now. Mark's fans are a bloody army!"

"Keeganites rock," said Riley.

"I still can't believe you got to meet him." Piper tossed her head back against the sofa, bored. "Anything interesting in Ben's bag of junk?"

"I haven't looked." Riley had felt so guilty looking through his phone contacts, she didn't even think about snooping through his belongings.

"Heard from the princess?" Piper enquired as she yawned, referring to Erika.

"She's still honeymooning, and kinda out of the loop." Riley's phone buzzed in her tote. "She doesn't know about the transplant."

"How?!"

"You know better than to ask *that*, Pip." Casey sneered like he smelled something rotten. "Erika's all about Erika. Bridezilla-itis only made it worse."

"To be fair, I didn't tell her." Riley dug into her tote, rifling past Ben's phone to find her own.

Casey shook his head. "Yeah, because what's the point?"

Riley looked at a long text running off the screen. *Speak of the devil.* It wasn't like Erika to reach out during a self-indulgent vacation.

Hey. Life as we know it is over! Chillin on beach and Scott's agent texted. Scotty's been traded! To WINNIPEG. I HATE the cold, what am I going to—

Woah! Traded? Riley stopped reading. *But...jeez, the sky's not falling. Trades are part of hockey—she knows that! I'll answer later.* She spied two other texts. *Ben? That buzz in my bag before they took him away...was him?*

Ben's first text: *Riles!!! Look inside my bag—for a bag!!!!*

She giggled. *You've got to be kidding me.*

Piper stared over Riley's arm. "That boy uses too many exclamation marks."

Riley reached inside, past his bracelet and clothes. She pulled out a white paper bag with thick Sharpie writing on the side: WAITING ROOM BOREDOM KIT. *Ben made me a care package!* Contents included: an apple, two packages of Reese's, a bottle of grape Fanta, a Keroppi PEZ, a small bag of Funyuns, and three packets of Fun Dip. Her hand searched inside again, touching something plastic. She peeked—the gallbladder from the surgeon's office! *BEN!*

She left it in the bag and grabbed a roll of candy. *Smarties? No, it's bigger.* She pulled it out, and Ben's accent swirled in her head. *"Once you go Brit, you just can't quit."*

"LOVE HEARTS? British ones!" Piper's hand dove toward the bag.

Opening an end of the roll, Riley pulled out pale-colored candies exclaiming, 'Ever Yours', 'Be Happy', and one that featured a winking emoji. She put the wink in her mouth, catching the next message waiting inside the roll—'Don't Cry'.

"Aw, lucky ducky." Piper held out her hand. "Can I see?"

Savoring the sweet lemon candy melting on her tongue, Riley handed over the roll and shared the peanut butter cups with Casey. She checked Ben's second text, three new songs joining his growing '4 Riles!!!' text playlist:

"Doctor, Doctor" by The Thompson Twins

"I Just Can't Stop Loving You" by Michael Jackson

"Absolute Beginners" by David Bowie

She rooted in her tote for her earbuds.

"Riley?"

She jolted, almost dropping her tote and Ben's plastic bag. Dr. Ricer walked toward her, his light green surgical mask untied and hanging down on the chest of his scrubs.

"Yes!" She sat up. Piper nervously stuffed several Love Hearts in her mouth, and Casey chewed the brim of his empty cup.

"Ben's surgery went well. He lost some blood so we gave him a transfusion, but he's now resting in recovery and will be taken to the surgical intensive care unit."

Thank God! Happy tears stung Riley's eyes.

"That's a relief," said Casey as Piper blew out her cheeks.

"Can I see him?" asked Riley.

"Soon. Once he's awake, a nurse will take you to him."

Riley accepted a tissue from Casey. "Any news on my mom?"

367

"It's going as planned. Her surgeon will be able to tell you more once she's in recovery, but she'll still be a few hours. Do you have any questions?"

She shook her head. "Thank you for taking care of Ben."

"He's young and strong. He'll be sore for a bit, but he's over the worst part." He nodded and left the room.

Piper waited to speak until he was out of sight. "Rye, did you buy a naughty nurse costume?"

Casey rolled his eyes as Riley threw Piper a tired smile. "No, Pip, it *completely* slipped my mind."

"It's okay, babe—I'll lend you mine," said Piper, winking theatrically as she moved in to hug her best friend.

Monitors beeped and flashed their lights as Ben groggily blinked, his eyes hazy and unable to focus. "Heyyyyy..." His hand lazily swatted at the tube in his nose. A second tube, thinner and more flexible with prongs for each nostril, was out of place and blowing oxygen below his lips.

"Hey you." Riley leaned over the bedside railing, a smile brightening her whisper as she brushed his hair from his eyes. "Thanks for the Love Hearts and the...uh...gallbladder."

His hand pawed his nose again.

"Benjamin, you've got to keep your hands away from your face." The surgical intensive care nurse, an older Filipino woman with a shock of bright blue in her gray hair, placed the oxygen prongs back in each of Ben's nostrils. "If you do it again, I'll have to put you in wrist restraints, you understand?"

His lips curved up, feeling no pain as his watery gaze landed on Riley. "Ooooooooo...yassss, tie...tie meee UP..." His scratchy voice dissolved into a dopey giggle.

Riley tried to stifle a laugh unsuccessfully.

"We've got a live one here." The nurse winked at Riley. "He might settle down a bit if you hold his hand, keep talking to him."

"Oh, good. I wanted to."

"The oxygen is just a precaution, but the nasogastric tube in his nose shouldn't be pulled." The nurse adjusted Ben's pillows, propping him up higher. "It goes down into his stomach and helps keep it empty. We don't want him throwing up. Ants in his pants aside, he's a good kid."

Riley nodded and held his hand, careful not to touch the tape and tubing from his IV. She smiled. "Ben, you did *good*."

"Yaaaaaay." He tried a shaky fist pump, but his rubbery arm flopped down on the blanket. "Soooo, I neva donut an orgun bfoe..." Woozy but determined, he swallowed a few times and wouldn't shut up. "I 'ave more *neva-duns* than yooo. Game ova. I-I wwwin, Wiles."

"Yeah, you win, Ben." *And so do I, because you came back to me—you kind, unselfish boy.* She kissed his stubbly cheek, and a crooked smile slowly crept across his face.

A few hours later, a nurse retrieved Riley from Ben's bedside and took her to the intensive care unit. The ICU was similar to where Ben was resting, but the care was reserved for the hospital's most fragile patients. Visiting hours and patient monitoring were more controlled, and the row of small, private rooms were eerily quiet apart from the soft beeps of medical devices.

Relief and hope swirled in Riley's chest. *I can't wait to see her! A few days here and then she moves to the transplant recovery floor. Then, she'll start to feel better—hopefully, cancer-free.*

Holding her breath, Riley peeked into Maggie's small, dimly lit ICU room.

Mom...?

All the questions in Riley's head, the hunger in her belly—everything hit pause.

Her mother looked so tiny and pale.

The jolt drew tears to Riley's eyes.

Tethered to several glowing monitors, Maggie slept in the middle of a web of cords, tubes, and cables that crisscrossed the bed. The trail of wiry, tangled spaghetti leading from her hands, arms, and chest constantly fed information back to the nurses' station. A plastic tube similar to Ben's was inserted in one nostril, whisking away fluids from her stomach. More cords—a catheter and three drainage tubes in her abdomen—snaked away from the blankets, but it was the ventilator that had Riley reeling. Despite being warned by the nurse, the image of her strong-willed, vibrant mom with lips parted by a large breathing tube, and her chest inflating and falling like clockwork—was a shock. *"It's normal, only for a few days,"* the nurse had said, but the reality of seeing her mom breathing with the help of a machine was frightening, no matter the nurse's explanation.

The windowless space gave no hint at the time or weather outside. Life elsewhere didn't exist. Riley's uneasy fingers played with her puffin charm. She didn't know what else to do.

"Your mom will be asleep for a while," said the ICU nurse, jotting down new readings on Maggie's chart. "But she's doing well. You can stay as long as you like."

"Thank you." Riley grinned softly as the nurse left them alone.

She pulled a well-worn chair to the bedside and covered Maggie's cold hand with her own. "Mom, I'm here." Seeing her mother lying motionless brought goose bumps to her skin. Maggie didn't *do* still—ever.

"Ben's okay and they said you're doing great…no complications," Riley whispered, laying her head on the blanket. "Third time lucky, Mom…you did it."

FIFTY-SIX

The next six weeks were a rollercoaster of pain, appointments, and boredom for Ben and Maggie, and a blur of worry, long commutes, and skipped meals for Riley. Life in the post-transplant bubble was hard and tiring with plenty of tears and a few short (pain-induced) fuses. Still, Riley wouldn't have traded the rocky path for anything. Each day was a gift, and every night before she curled up beside Ben in Maggie's foldout couch, she said a silent thank you for her mom's third chance at life and the extraordinary British boy who'd given it to her.

Putting away groceries while Maggie finished her shower, Riley giggled. Ben's favorites shared shelf space with hers: Frosties and Reese's Puffs, smooth and crunchy peanut butter, grapes and apples, all side-by-side. In a way, it felt like they were playing house, especially before Maggie's discharge from hospital, when it was just the two of them.

Released six days after his operation, Ben had moved into her mom's Staten Island apartment. Maggie wouldn't be discharged for another eight days due to a wound infection and a reaction to her anti-rejection drugs. Riley suspected that without supervision, Ben would get in all sorts of trouble. He had already been caught twice trying to lift his backpack at the hospital (lifting anything heavy could open his incision and jeopardize healing), and he regularly forgot to use the handheld incentive spirometer, a plastic gadget for breathing exercises. Abdominal surgery patients found coughing, sneezing, and deep breathing painful post-op, and this toy-like 'game' helped clear lungs of mucus and hopefully kept pneumonia away. To keep Ben in check, Riley left Piper and St. Mark's Place, temporarily moving back in. When she wasn't at her BBC internship or working shifts at Sephora, she cooked healthy meals, took Ben for slow walks around the neighborhood, and challenged him to board game tournaments. It almost felt idyllic apart from the pain meds, the ban on sex, and the absence of greasy foods from their diet—chicken dinosaurs and smiley face potatoes had been temporarily axed, doctor's orders. But, this latest grocery shop was the last of its kind. Maggie was doing well enough to be on her own, and Ben was itching for more privacy. He'd be moving back to Hunter's, and Riley would be returning to her East Village shoebox by the end of the week.

A text landed on her phone from Ben. *Back soon x*

Daily walks were part of both Ben and Maggie's recovery regime, but today, Ben's stroll was productive, picking up goodbye tiger lilies for Piper.

Riley's heart sank. *I can't believe the day's come. Piper's really leaving.*

It seemed like yesterday, Piper bursting into their narrative television production workshop squealing, "They want my puppets on their show! October in LA, baby!" Back in April, it felt like a distant promise, something at the far end of summer, but tonight, her best friend was flying home to Chicago for a quick pit stop before heading west to follow her TV dream. Riley had no doubts—Piper would eventually rule children's television production, one adorable puppet at a time.

She watered the orchid Erika and Scott had sent over before they rushed north to Winnipeg, replaced the water in the weekly Gerbera delivery from Alex and Mark, and opened up the 'Good Luck' card waiting to be signed on the counter. *I'm so proud of Pip, but that won't fill the hole in my heart from missing her.*

She cleared her throat and picked up a pen. Once Maggie was ready and Ben was back with the bouquet, they would be meeting her for lunch one last time.

A key clicked the lock. *Ben's back.* Riley kept writing.

"Riles?" He sounded distressed.

She dropped the pen and turned around. "What's wrong?"

"Gimme a hand?" Ben's face was hidden by an enormous vase of pink lilies, Gerberas, and roses.

"Uh, you went a little overboard!" She took the vase from his arms. "And it weighs a ton! Ben, you still can't lift heavy stuff."

"It's not from me. I met a delivery bloke outside." Wincing, Ben reached over his shoulder and rubbed his aching upper back, a lingering side effect of slouched posture. For the first three weeks post-surgery, Ben's abs had hurt when he stood or sat up straight, the nerves and muscles unhappy to be stretched. To avoid that pain, he'd hunch over, but now he was paying the price. "They're for you, I think?" A small wrapped bundle of tiger lilies for Piper dangled in a shopping bag from Ben's forearm.

"Me? From who?" Riley set the monster bouquet on the table and pulled out a thank you note-sized envelope that was nestled in the blooms. "Someone has a lot to say…" She opened the letter and started reading the unfamiliar handwriting.

Riley, my apologies for not sending my wishes sooner. The flowers are for your mom, but please keep reading—this note is for you.

"Who sent them?" Ben looked over her shoulder.

Erika's been busy settling in Winnipeg, so I only heard about your mom's transplant yesterday. Please accept these flowers along with my sincerest hopes for a swift and complete recovery. I know how close you two are and can only imagine how stressful and scary it must've been the last few weeks.

Riley turned the notepaper over. Ben squinted at the bottom of the page. "Seriously?"

I'm taking time away to figure things out. I've started divorce proceedings against Tyler. Maybe when I'm back in NYC, you and I could go for lunch (my treat). I've always admired your strength, Riley, and I'm so sorry we got off on the wrong foot. You were RIGHT about Ty, of course. I should've had more self-respect than to let him treat me so badly. I doubled (tripled!) down, going cold on anyone who called him out for what he was, because I was still clinging to the hope that I'd be the one who changed him. It's a rotten excuse, and so unforgivable on many levels, but I hope it's not too late for us to be friends.

"That's big of her." Ben scratched his chin.

Anyway, before I moved out, I cleared out our joint accounts. I've donated today (properly) to your mom's crowdfunding page. If I'm going to make Tyler pay for all the pain he's caused, what better way than to share the money with someone who would benefit most. I hope it helps make life a little easier for her. Moms are precious, and you know that better than anyone.

Take care, Riley.

Much love, Leia xo

"Wow!" Riley lowered the paper, dumbfounded. "I know we made our peace at the wedding, but I never expected this."

"Bloody hell. How much did she give?" Ben whipped out his phone, opening up the bookmarked site. "Blimey O'Riley!" He showed her the screen, holding his stomach as he laughed in disbelief. "She donated ten thousand dollars! She's pushed the total past forty-two thousand! You've more than doubled your goal."

Riley, Ben, Maggie, Casey, and Piper filled several oversized armchairs in Beans & Leaves, a Staten Island café famous for its Belgian waffles. They toasted Casey on beginning his master's, laughed at Ben's retelling of his numerous hospital gown malfunctions, and congratulated Riley on her job news from the day before—after three rounds of interviews, she had accepted the assistant job supporting the VP of TV sales and co-productions in the BBC's New York office. Despite feeling fatigued, Maggie grinned the entire time. Nothing was going to mute her joy. She had her daughter and her health was returning—life had never tasted as good.

Taking a break from the oversized waffle she was sharing with Ben, piled high with Reese's Pieces, gooey fudge drizzle, and marshmallow fluff, Riley raised her fork to get everyone's attention. "I want to say a few words about my girl, Pip."

"Don't you dare make me cry," said Piper, taking a bite of her Cap'n Crunch waffle.

"I'll never forget how we met. Four years ago, first day at Tisch—"

"Waiting in line in the NYU bookstore," Piper interrupted, elbowing her best friend.

"Ahh, not quite! You were *leaving* the bookstore, yapping on your phone. Your face! It was bright red—"

"I was mid-argument," explained Piper.

"You were stomping around in four-inch wedges and tripped over your own feet!" Riley laughed. "It was epic! NYU magnets, Swedish fish, and a bottle opener all went flying."

"I remember that opener!" Casey, sitting across the table, wiped his mouth with a napkin. "That's how Pip and I met in the dorms. I had the wine and a massive hangover, she had the opener—and a cast on her foot."

"And I thought I was clumsy." Ben laughed.

"It wasn't *funny*, Ben." Piper leaned across Riley to playfully slap his arm. "It really hurt! I thought I had broken my ribs and wrist, too."

Maggie winced.

"Pip was crying. She never cries," said Riley. "She had scraped her hands up pretty good, too, and her phone got flattened by an open-top tour bus."

Piper bumped Riley with her shoulder. "This one ended up late for class because she waited with me for the ambulance. I spotted the Benedict Cumberbatch *Sherlock* pin on her backpack and that was it—friends for life."

"I love how you met," Maggie smiled.

"Fandoms rock!" Riley nodded.

"I only survived my first weeks at NYU with my cast and crutches because of Riley," said Piper. "She carried my books and got me from class to class. Rain or shine, she was there for me, and when my cast came off, she still was—every day, for four years."

Ben kissed Riley on the shoulder.

"She even waited outside Rockefeller Center in a blizzard to get me Cumberbatch's autograph. Who does that, huh? Riley does! Actor crushes, boyfriends, and girlfriends may come and go, but Rye never failed me." Tears glistened behind Piper's false eyelashes. "I honestly don't know what I'm going to do without you. I miss you already." She sniffed. "Dammit! I wasn't going to *cry...*"

"Oh, Pip." Riley's nose prickled with impending tears as she sank into Piper's outstretched arms. "I'm so proud and excited for you! And this isn't goodbye. A best friend like you is for life. I'm going to text and FaceTime you so much, you'll be begging for a restraining order."

"You better come visit." Piper wiped her nose. "And when you're ready to move to LA, I'll be there, playing tour guide."

Casey chuckled, cutting his churro waffle. "Are you going to do this all over again at the airport tonight?"

The girls laughed through their tearful hug. "Probably!"

FIFTY-SEVEN

Two days later

"Hey, man! Welcome back!" Ben's diner buddy slapped him on the back. "Oh, shit...did I hurt you?"

Fuck, yeah. Ben bit his lip. "No, I'm good. It's been just over six weeks...goin' a bit stir crazy, to be honest."

"I'll bet." The server flicked through his notepad and looked over his shoulder at a table of seniors wearing *Hamilton* sweatshirts. "We've missed you...and we weren't the only ones. All those school girls stopped coming when they realized you weren't here."

Yeah, that's me, Mr. Popularity! Ben chuckled. "Well, I'm itching to come back. Is Stavros about?"

"Stavvy? Nah, he hit the road."

"Ah, bollocks." Ben sighed, stuffing his hands in his hoodie's pockets. "I'll try him tomorrow, then—"

"No, he's gone, dude, like, no-longer-here gone. Family stuff."

Concern darkened Ben's eyes. "Oh, shit. Is he okay?"

"He's fine. They moved upstate...beginning of October." His co-worker pointed to a stocky guy with muscles for days flipping through paperwork at a far table. "Talk to Ethan. He's taken Stavvy's place."

Ben broke into a smile. "Oh, cheers, mate."

His friend nodded at a customer waving for his attention. "Great seein' ya, Ben! Let's grab a beer when you're back."

"Definitely!" Ben weaved past diners and servers, pausing several times to say hi to his co-workers. A few new faces slipped past with meals aloft, but such was working life in a restaurant. The revolving door of employees was always spinning.

With a big friendly smile, Ben caught Ethan's eye. "Hello!"

"Hi. What can I do for you?" A confident grin brightened Ethan's face.

"Ethan, I'm Ben Fagan." He offered his hand to shake and the diner boss accepted. "I worked as a server for Stavros."

"Okay." Ethan released Ben's hand and cocked his head, his eyes straying and coming back, keeping tabs on the restaurant.

"I've been on medical leave for six weeks and I'm ready to come back. I realize my day shifts have been given to someone else, no worries—"

"Day shifts?" Ethan blew out his cheeks. "Sorry, but I don't know who you are and we don't have any jobs open."

Who is this joker? Ben smirked and leaned in. "Stavros was holding my job for me. He was renewing my visa and—"

"Nope, no, sorry." Ethan shook his head, his eyes escaping down to his invoices. "I don't know anything about your visa."

You've got to be fucking kidding me... Ben narrowed his eyes. "What?" His heart began to hammer in his chest. "Stavros had all the paperwork..."

Ethan chewed his lip. "Visa renewals went in for the kitchen staff, but Stavros didn't leave immigration forms for any *servers*. Things have been slow since summer, and we're in the middle of a hiring freeze. I had to let two staff go last week."

This is a mistake. Surely he can fix it? "Okay, but look—Ethan—I'm a *total* grafter. I can work double shifts with no notice, and I'm popular with customers. You can ask—"

Ethan held up his palms. "Listen, Ben, I get it. Stavros made you a promise, but it's not my fault he didn't tell *me*. He left in quite a hurry and I guess some things got lost in the transition. My hands are tied. I wish I could help, but...I'm sorry. Look, I'm sure you'll find something. If you need a letter of recommendation, gimme a call." He grinned tightly and returned to his invoices.

With no visa, I'm fucked. Ben gulped, a sick taste burning his throat. *What am I gonna do?*

Hunter scratched his bare chest. Even in his cramped courier office, he worked half-naked. "Ben-dude, you okay? You look like you ate some bad shrimp."

I'm sweating like I'm in a sauna. "I'm in trouble, mate." Ben sagged into a chair. "The diner didn't hold my job—they didn't re-new my visa. The three weeks left on it are tied to *that* job in *that* restaurant. I can't legally work here anymore."

"Jesus, yeah. Lose the job, lose the visa—and hey, good luck finding another restaurant to hire you and file paperwork in time."

"Cheers." Ben exhaled, worry gnawing at his gut. "That *really* makes me feel better."

"Sorry." Hunter grimaced as he shifted a bike made from spare parts.

"What the hell am I going to tell Riley?"

"Hey, maybe she'll marry ya!"

"Fuck, *I* wouldn't marry me." Ben frowned and picked the peeling paint on the wall. "Don't get me wrong, I'm crazy about her, but I'm nowhere near ready to be a husband."

Hunter tapped his fingers against his lips. "Hmm, there *is* a guy I know who might need bar staff. Would be legit, too. He got that same visa for some guys a few months back. I saw on Facebook he's chillin' in Miami, but I'll call him this weekend when he's back."

Hunter's impressive contact list saves the day again. "Ah, that would save me. Thanks, mate!" Ben's smile gave way to a yawn, his stamina still not back to normal. "And I'd really like to get back on my bike, do some deliveries—is that cool? Some tax-free cash would be really helpful."

"Job's yours, you know that, but you sure you're ready to ride?"

"Yeah, no problem!"

"But they cut your stomach muscles, man." Hunter picked up a spare tire. "I'm no doctor, but I know a bit about abs. You need your core to cycle. If your muscles aren't completely healed, you should probably wait—"

"No, I'm good. Never felt better! I can start tomorrow…if that works."

"I could definitely use you, but I dunno…"

"Hunter, dude, I'm *ready*!" Ben looked around the small room. "Where's my bike?"

"The new guy has it." Hunter's phone began to ring. He motioned to three bikes near the door. "Grab any of those tomorrow."

"Brilliant!" Ben's grin faded as Hunter answered his call. *But what if the bar job doesn't come through…?*

Ben set plates down on Riley's tiny counter. *I'm not hungry, not after the day I've had.* "How was therapy?"

"Good." Riley filled a tortilla with romaine lettuce, chicken, and Caesar dressing. "We talked about Pip leaving and me living alone again, and we did another CBT exercise together."

"Coping strategies…that cognitive behavior stuff works, eh?"

"Yeah, it takes practice. It's not easy replacing negative thoughts with positive ones, but I'm really trying. I feel like I'm rewiring my brain—in a good way!"

"Well, I think you're amazing—and brave. Asking for help is a huge step. I'm proud of you, Riles." Ben leaned over, kissing her temple.

"Thanks." Riley glanced over her shoulder. "Last night was so quiet without the chaos of Pip." She pouted. "I miss her."

"Have you spoken yet?"

"Yeah, she landed two hours ago. Her first stop was Kermit the Frog's star on the Hollywood Walk of Fame."

"She really does live and breathe puppets, doesn't she?"

"Yup." Riley rolled up the tortilla while Ben filled glasses with tap water.

"What about Erika? Still off the radar?"

"Seems so. I texted again, but I guess out of sight, out of mind. What's that phrase? *Fair-weather friend*? We were great as teenagers when everything was gossip and crushes on boys, but things got real two years ago with Mom and that's not her scene. The Josh stuff didn't help either..." Riley sighed. "It's still sad, losing a friend."

Ben rubbed her back and left a kiss in her hair.

She changed the subject. "How's Hunter? I bet he's happy you're back."

In more ways than one. "Yep. I'm a dream roomie compared to the bloke who stayed while I was at your mom's. Get this—the dude was a naked sleepwalker! Freaked Hunter right out, which is ironic considering..."

Riley laughed. "Is he okay holding your job a little longer?" She sliced through the homemade wrap and placed half on Ben's plate.

Shit. I knew she wouldn't forget what the doctor said Monday: start back slowly, no heavy lifting, try riding a bike in the gym first.

"Yep." Ben picked up a bottle of malt vinegar and doused the opening of his wrap. "But starting tomorrow, he's paying me to organize his paperwork, answer the phone for a bit." He slipped her a quick smile. "So, don't worry, I won't lift anything heavy."

FIFTY-EIGHT

Jeez, this is tougher than I thought. I'm exhausted. Thighs burning and gasping for breath, Ben pumped the pedals on his bike, just making it across the intersection of West 54th Street and Seventh Avenue before the traffic light switched to red. He stuck to the relative safety of the bike lane, avoiding cars parked by the curb on his left and the mid-Friday gridlock of honking taxis on his right, heading east toward Sixth Avenue.

Three deliveries down, two to go, then lunch!

Passing a car rental place, an SUV pulled out behind him a little too close for comfort, almost clipping his back wheel. Ben kept pedaling, increasing speed and creating distance, but his body was no longer used to that type of exertion. His butt ached and his back cracked. A side stitch had been pinching for the past fifteen blocks, reminding him that it had only been a short six weeks since his surgery.

Get to Sixth then take a rest at the fountains. Just a few minutes with some water should do it.

He stood up on his pedals and dug in, puffs of his warm breath hitting the cool October air as he pushed himself, but the strain he felt in his core, back, and hips forced him back in the saddle.

Then it came out of nowhere.

Ben didn't see it.

A passenger-side car door flew open from the curb into the bike lane.

He didn't stand a chance.

Smashing into the car, Ben was thrown into his handlebars and over the vehicle's door, his momentum sending his messenger bag soaring from his shoulder. It landed under the wheels of a passing truck. Ben followed, tumbling into a crumpled heap on the asphalt, the air in his lungs knocked free. His bike didn't fare much better, bending into a crude right angle.

A screechy "OH MY GOD!" from the car's open door echoed across the street.

"FUCK!" Ben's abs and hands felt like they were on fire. "You fucking twat!" He glanced down. Blood and dirt streaked his hands and patches of skin had been shorn off his palms, but worst of all, his right wrist was bent funny. *Oh Jesus, I'm gonna be sick.*

"Oh, I'm soooo sorry!" A nasal accent sailed over the still-open passenger door, but the man and his wife, departing guests from the hotel overlooking the scene, kept their distance.

"You all right?" A doorman crouched by Ben's side. His hotel co-worker was on his phone, calling 911. Several pedestrians lingered, cars slowed to rubberneck, and two cyclists swerved to pass the bicycle lane roadkill.

"Yeah, I..." Ben shifted to sit up. His back ached and the burn in his stomach flared, stealing his breath.

"Don't move, buddy." The doorman raised his hand, afraid to touch him but also wanting Ben to stay put. "You might have a concussion or something. Can you feel everything? Your legs, hands?"

That's just the problem—I'm feeling everything way too much. He lifted his throbbing right arm, slowly. "Yeah, but something's wrong with—"

"Your wrist looks broken," said the doorman with a distasteful gulp. "Stay right there. Ambulance will be here soon."

A siren screamed from the direction of Seventh Avenue. Competing from somewhere... the sidewalk, underneath a parked car... was the intro to "Take On Me".

Shit, my phone...where is it? With one hand, Ben tugged off his helmet and dropped it on the ground. *I need to call Riley.* His eyes lingered over his clothes: torn jeans, ripped hoodie…his bracelet, missing. His heart stuttered and began to race. *I have to get out of here.*

"The police are here." The concierge from the hotel appeared with a bottle of water and a towel just as Ben crawled to the curb.

Two NYPD officers strolled over. "Second case of dooring to-day." The female police officer shook her head at her male partner. She flipped open her notebook and turned to Ben. "Can I have your name, please?"

Do we really have to? My life is scattered across the road and my wrist—fuck! Hugging his stomach, Ben rocked back and forth on the curb, his gaze frantically searching the pavement for his bracelet and now-silent phone. *I feel dizzy…*"Benjamin Fagan." Sweat began to soak his t-shirt.

"Can you tell me what happened, Benjamin?"

Ben recounted what he remembered along with the doorman and a few tourists who saw the incident unfold. The reckless car door opener, hyperventilating and fretting over what he thought was an impending heart attack, sat in his car talking to his lawyer on the phone, and was the last to give his side of the accident.

After a twenty-minute wait, paramedics arrived and took Ben's medical history, his liver donation sparking tons of new questions. They inspected his chest, ribs, and abdomen for injuries, his L-shaped surgical scar still pink. They cleaned cuts on his face, hands, and knees, and placed his broken wrist in a sling that would have to do until he could be transported to a hospital. When they were done, the female officer returned to his side, asking questions about his background and employment.

Ben pawed at his hair. *Say as little as possible.*

"You're from England? How long have you been in the States?"

"Since February."

"So, over ninety days. Do you have a visa?"

Shit. Not a visa that allows me to work as a bike courier. I can't lie my way out of this one. "It's an H-2B…I was acting in an indie film but found work in a restaurant and they renewed it."

"So, you're an actor and also a waiter?"

Ben nodded, his eyes spotting his broken leather bracelet lying in the bike lane. *I need to get that!*

The cop eyed a large envelope of legal documents and a flattened box poking out of Ben's messenger bag in the road. "And a bike courier…?"

Pain seared through Ben's stomach causing him to reply through gritted teeth. "No, just today. I'm helping a friend." A sour taste rose in his throat. *Ugh. I might throw up.*

"Hey, Viv." The cop's partner called over from Ben's broken bike. "Come 'ere."

She stood up and left Ben's side.

Can I reach it? Bracing himself on his good hand, Ben stretched his left leg, trying to use his shoe to pull the bracelet closer, but his stomach muscles weren't happy. He grimaced through the pain and dizziness but kept trying. *Fuck it, I gotta crawl over.*

"You want that?" The female officer stooped down and picked up the bracelet, handing it to Ben.

"Thanks." He tucked it safely in his hoodie pocket and glanced away. The sidewalk gawkers had moved on, and the doorman was welcoming high-tipping hotel guests again.

"So." The male officer returned. "Your bike's missing its registration decal. I ran its serial number in the system and it's been reported stolen."

"Stolen? No, my bike was—" *Fuck. Loaned out to another bloke.* Ben's face fell. *This isn't my bike. It's that random one Hunter built from spare parts…*

"I'm sorry, Mr. Fagan, but you're in possession of stolen property. We're gonna have to arrest you and take you to the station."

"But I...I didn't steal anything! And my wrist—"

"We'll take you to the hospital first, get that looked at." He opened up his handcuffs.

That's gonna hurt like a... Ben's eyes grew wide.

"Chuck, he's already in a sling." The female officer shook her head. "He won't be trouble."

Be trouble? No. IN trouble? Definitely. Ben groaned as the cops helped him up to his feet.

Holding Ben's police-issued 'personal belongings' plastic bag, Hunter followed his friend out of the police station. Sunlight was long gone, replaced by empty office buildings alight in the dark sky. "I feel like I'm in a movie, being your 'one phone call' guy." Hunter's warm breath trailed away, riding the chilly October breeze.

His gait slow and stiff, Ben winced, threading his plaster cast through the right arm of his torn hoodie. "I couldn't call Riley and get her upset. It was her last day at Sephora." Hand free, he wriggled his fingers and sucked in a sharp breath. "Owwwff!" *Docs said to move my fingers, keep the blood flowing, but the pain is sharp as fuck.* "She's going to be so pissed. I told her I was working in your office."

"She'll get over it."

"I lied to her, Hunter."

"Yeah, well...I'm sure she'll calm down when she hears what happened. You're lucky, man. The charge was dropped, and more importantly, you're alive! Could've been much worse, bro."

Wrong. It can't get much worse. Ben wearily looked at his left hand, dirty with ink from being fingerprinted.

Hunter peeked at Ben's stuff, his helmet, messenger bag—all the broken remnants of the crash. "I nearly shit myself waiting to see if the cops believed me. I mean, how was I supposed to know the frame came from a stolen bike? We're both innocent. Thank fuck they didn't press charges. I tell ya, that's the last time I go to the dump for parts."

"Thanks for telling the police today was a one-off."

"Well, it wasn't a lie." Hunter nodded at Ben's cast. "You won't be riding for a good month with that thing. If you want, I can still put a call in to my buddy this weekend, but you're not gonna look great in the interview, if you know what I mean…"

Shoulders stooped and eyes glued to the ground, Ben gnawed his bottom lip. Worry creased his brow, making him look even more tired and racked with pain.

Hunter frowned. "Cheer up, though, dude. You escaped jail— that's a *good* thing."

Ben looked up and stared into the darkness. "Could you text Riley for me? My phone's dead."

"Uh, sure." Hunter wrestled his phone out of the front pocket of his jeans, the time 11:16 p.m. "Don't be mad, bro, but she texted earlier and I didn't reply. I didn't know what to say."

Fuck, Hunter! You could've just said I was busy. She's going to be out of her mind with worry.

Hunter grimaced, taking in Ben's frown. "What should I say now?"

"Just…say my phone died and we're out—*not* having drinks! I still can't drink. Just say we're grabbing a bite, discussing work shit, and I'll be there soon." Ben gasped in discomfort and held his stomach, dreading what was to come.

FIFTY-NINE

Leaning against her windowsill, Riley's fingers absentmindedly rolled and unrolled the hem of her sweatshirt. "I left three voicemails. I thought, *He's just busy, he'll call back later*, but you never did—not even when I finished work. You *always* call me when I'm walking home. Always! So, I texted Hunter, and he didn't answer either. Ben, I was freaking out."

Broken wrist throbbing with each heavy beat of his heart, Ben bowed his head and shifted on the loveseat, searching for a comfortable position to rest his bruised and broken body. "I'm *so* sorry. I would've called, but they took away my phone on the street."

"I even went looking for you. I went to Hunter's, the Red Lion. I didn't want to upset Mom, so I called Casey. He said he'd keep looking while I called hospitals. I thought something happened with your liver."

I've really fucked up. "You have every right to be angry. I would be."

"Then Hunter texted me—finally! I could breathe again." She shook her head, a soft smile fighting through her frown. "Oh, Ben…" She sat down, wrapping her arm loosely around his shoulders, careful not to bump his cast or squeeze him tightly. "I'm still annoyed, but I'm *so* relieved you're okay." Her body relaxed, holding him close.

Ben released a tight breath. *I don't deserve her sympathy.*

Her fingers skimmed his cast. "This must hurt like hell." A pained expression pinched her face.

"It's uncomfortable…the cast feels tight. I think my wrist is swelling."

She sighed. "What *was* the rush? The surgeon said you could start cycling *in the gym*. He didn't give you the green light to go full-on super courier!"

Ben chewed his thumbnail. "But he also said to listen to my body. If I felt strong enough...it was worth a shot—"

"Yeah, a shot that almost got you killed."

"But it didn't."

"Thank God!"

Ben dropped his hand from his mouth. "To be fair, Riles, what happened had nothing to do with rushing back. It was just wrong place at the wrong time..." His voice trailed off, regret immediately tying a knot in his belly. *Jeez, did you break your brain when you flew off that bike, too?*

"You think?" A sardonic tone tainted Riley's retort.

No, not really. Damn, I wish I could take that back. Ben's eyes fell to his jeans, the knees torn and dirty, a large Band-Aid visible through one of the rips. *Today's mess has everything to do with rushing back. If I hadn't been in such a tizz over being bored at home, I wouldn't have touched that bike. I wouldn't have been rushing, trying to deliver those packages. I wouldn't have been at the hospital or the cop shop. This conversation wouldn't be happening.*

Frowning, he raked a hand through his hair. "Actually...no, I don't. I'm a fucking *idiot*. I should've waited. I've been so restless and down about things, and it was starting to get to me, you know? It sucks not earning any money. I hate that Maggie's crowdfunding cash has been paying for me. I'm not a sponger."

"Of course you're not! Ben, you know the surgery and recovery costs are always paid by the recipient."

"I know, but I feel useless."

"You're hardly useless. Your liver saved my mom's life! Still, I get it. Being broke and stuck at home would bother me, too."

"It's been almost seven weeks...I thought I'd be back to normal by now." A lump grew in his throat. "I've become a burden."

"You are not a burden. Come here." Riley pressed a kiss to his lips and pulled him in. "I can't imagine how hard it's been. Sitting still isn't your thing, is it? And missing out on the foods you love, drinking pints, sex—God, I miss sex with you!"

The softness of Riley's sweatshirt, the scent of her shampoo...Ben's chest began to ache, but it had nothing to do with the accident.

"Maybe now that you're in the city again, you'll start to feel more like yourself? Independent, back in Hunter's man-maze of bicycle parts." She giggled and curled her fingers in his hair. "I love you so much. It scares me half to death, though, thinking I could've lost you today."

Oh, Riley. Deep in their hug, looking over her shoulder, the window began to blur. He blinked quickly, suppressing his tears. "Hope—"

"But I didn't, and you're here, and we'll get through this together. Maybe Hunter can *really* give you some paid work in the office. And then in a few weeks, you'll go back to the diner, start auditioning again. We'll have Christmas together—everything will be okay, you'll see."

"But it won't be," Ben mumbled in her hair.

Riley pulled back. "Won't be—what?" Her wide eyes glanced down at his t-shirt. "Did something else happen? Ben, you hurt your liver?"

My heart... "Riles..." His voice cracked and he shook his head slowly. *If I could do it over again, I wouldn't have touched that stupid bike.* "The police ran an immigration check on me."

"Yeah, so? That's normal, right? If you're not a citizen, they'd totally do that." She caught the slight quiver of Ben's chin and froze. "But..."

"I have to go home." He gulped, fighting the urge to cry. "The diner isn't renewing my visa."

"They're...?" She jerked forward, eyes wide. "But they promised!"

"Stavros left. I found out yesterday. So, I told Hunter and he said—"

"Wait? You told Hunter...before me?"

"I told him because I needed help. He *knows* people, Riley. He was trying to hook me up with a job in this bloke's bar. The guy's gotten visas for staff before and..." He stared up at the ceiling and the twinkly lights overhead. So many beautiful memories made, so many secrets shared under those dollar-store stars. "Then, today happened, and when I finally got to the police station after the hospital, an immigration officer was waiting for me. Apparently, the diner was obligated to notify immigration if my employment ended before my visa expired. So, I was flagged in their system. They just had to find me, and they did—with a broken wrist on West 54th."

"But you've got three weeks left on your visa."

"It doesn't matter. If I don't have that diner job, the current visa is void. I'm here illegally now."

Her breath began to quicken. "You have to go?" She held his left hand and Ben reciprocated, squeezing it tight. "When?"

"The lawyer at the station recommended voluntary departure."

"What does that mean?" Tears gathering in her eyes, she blinked quickly.

"I agree to leave the country quickly and voluntarily so I won't be kept in custody or have a removal order on my file. I'll also avoid a period of inadmissibility."

"Meaning...what? You wouldn't be banned from *returning* to the U.S.?"

Ben nodded.

Her face relaxed. "Oh. Okay! So, you leave and then come right back." She wiped away a tear with her free hand.

"I could, but only as a visitor—not staying for longer than ninety days, and I wouldn't be able to work. I was lucky getting that visa the first time, even luckier getting it renewed, but the chances of it happening a third time are slim to none. There's no 'third time lucky' for me, Riley. I have to be realistic."

"Well, stay illegally, then!" Riley nodded, like she was trying to convince herself it was a great idea. "Lots of people do. You could work for Hunter. You know he'd keep you on."

"Yeah, but what kind of life would that be? Always looking over my shoulder, making next to nothing as a courier. You can't afford to pay my way, and I'd never expect you to. I want to make something of myself. I want to make *you* proud of me." Tears trickled down his cheeks.

"I *am* proud of you, Ben." She held his face in her hands, his damp stubble scratching her palms.

"And if I stayed here illegally, I'd never be able to go home. The minute I flew to London and then tried to come back here, U.S. immigration would be all over my ass. They'd scan my passport, see how long I had been in the States, and I'd be refused entry. The immigration guy said illegals who do this get banned for *ten years*. A decade, Riles!"

Bowing her head, tears raced down to her chin and lingered before dropping to her sweatshirt.

Ben bent his neck to look into her eyes. "Riley love, it's not worth risking, not if it stops me coming back to see you."

She looked up, all mascara smudges and determination, fighting through her tears. "Well…marry me, then."

He chuckled and slipped into a soft smile. "Hope…"

Riley didn't laugh. "I'll marry you. I'm serious."

"Gorgeous girl, I know you are." Ben swept her hair, damp from tears, off her cheeks. "But I'm on immigration's watch list now. They wouldn't believe we were in love. They'd say we did it for the green card and then we'd *both* be in trouble." He kissed her forehead. "And think about it, love—be honest—do you really want a husband right now? When you're starting your career? When opportunities are coming your way? You begin your job on Monday, Riles. After everything with Josh, I think we both know the answer—"

"But I'm in love with *you*! That's the difference."

"And I love you, but that's why we shouldn't rush to beat some stupid deadline."

She tilted her head and fresh tears raced down her cheeks. Ben put a finger under her chin, lifting her face up to meet his.

"Hey, I would marry you *so* hard!" He chuckled wistfully. "But I want to do it right. I want to give you a romantic proposal one day that will make you snog my face off. I want you to say yes—but at the right time and for the right reasons. I want us to last. Riley, it would kill me to lose you for good..." He kissed her softly, her salty tears on his lips. "I'll go home to London, get a job, save enough money, and come back."

Riley shuddered, trying to catch her breath. "When do you have to leave?"

"Well, they said I shouldn't delay. The sooner I leave, the faster I can come back—"

"Ben..." She pleaded, looking into his eyes. "When?"

"Wednesday."

"Wednes...that's only—" She struggled to swallow. "In five days, you'll be gone."

"But I'm here now." He took her face in his hands, tenderly kissing her lips.

Recycling trucks were doing their noisy best to rouse St. Mark's Place at 3 a.m., but Riley was wide awake. Lying in bed with Ben's head resting on her chest, she stroked his hair while her mind worked overtime. *When all the bad stuff piles on, I tell myself 'this too shall pass' and I try my best to believe it, but…that means I have to accept that the good things in my life—moments like this with Ben—will pass, too, and that breaks my heart. Sometimes I don't feel like I'm savoring the sweet moments as much as I should, and by the time I clue in, they're gone and it's all too late.*

"Ahhh, that feels nice," Ben purred.

"You're awake?" Riley whispered. "Do you need another pain killer?"

"Not yet." Raising his head, Ben groaned and shifted back onto the pillow, his abdomen bruised from hitting the bike's handlebars. "Have you slept?"

"No. I can't stop thinking…" Riley pulled up the duvet so it covered both of them. "What are we going to do?"

"What we talked about earlier—the long-distance thing. You've done it before, so you're a pro!"

Hardly. "It's not easy. You have no idea what you're in for."

"Well, yeah—I reckon juggling time zones will be a total pain in the arse, but you're worth it!" He blinked sleepily, his puffy eyes mirroring Riley's. "You know me—I like a challenge."

"This isn't fun like our Never Dunnit game."

"I know…"

"It's no joke, Ben. Being apart can eat away at you. There's all the missed FaceTime calls, delayed texts, silences that make your mind leap to the worst thing, and the worry you'll fall out of love without physical contact…"

"But you and me, we're not like that."

"I used to think Josh and I weren't either."

Ben inhaled a deep, painful breath.

"I just don't want you *unprepared*, that's all." She swept his hair from his eyes.

"Coach me, then. Tell me what to expect."

"Ben, it's late. Don't you want to sleep?"

"I want *you* to sleep, and I don't think you'll be able to until we discuss this." He kissed her nose.

"Okay." She exhaled heavily. "Well, birthdays and most holidays will be spent apart."

"Not if I can help it."

"Unless we win the lottery, we'll be lucky to see each other once a year…"

"Guess I'll start buying lottery tickets, then!" He smiled. "Carry on."

"You'll see friends coupled up in the pub, and you'll feel so lonely your bones will ache. You'll have to come home early on nights out if you want to catch up with me over FaceTime. All your money will go into calling, texting, saving for flights, and when we *are* together for a rare visit, we won't just pick up where we left off—we'll have to get used to each other again, and it will feel a bit awkward until we do. You'll find your memory plays tricks. Annoyances you never thought of before will pop up, like 'I don't remember her hogging the duvet,' 'She smacks when she eats—'"

Ben laughed. "You don't smack! Did Josh say that?"

She shook her head. "Plus, long distance means months without hugs, kissing, sex—"

"Physical contact sex, yeah, but not *FaceTime* sex! Riles, I've done many things in bed, but I haven't made love through a screen before…I'm a FaceTime sex virgin!" He raised his eyebrows. "You'll have to teach me, but please, be gentle!" He chuckled. "Look, I know it'll be hard, but I promise, I'll do whatever it takes. I want you, Riley. I *love* you."

I know he loves me, but if he's had problems committing to relationships before in person, how will he handle one separated by an ocean? "I love you so much. I just want this to work."

"And it will. I know it'll be a test, but we'll smash it, Riles. Seriously, it'll take more than some daft ocean to separate us, okay?" He kissed her nose. "Now get some kip, sleepyhead. Maggie won't be happy if we doze off in her frittata."

SIXTY

The news of Ben's accident and pending departure left an air of resignation hanging over Saturday lunch at Maggie's, the usual laughter and eighties tunes sadly absent.

A wet paper towel traveled across the counter underneath Maggie's hand, mopping up melted butter and eggshells. "I feel completely useless," she said quietly.

You and me both. Riley stuffed her hands in oven mitts and squatted down, keeping an eye on the skillet underneath the oven's broiler, their spinach, cheese, and red pepper frittata gifting the kitchen a delicious aroma—not that anyone was hungry. *How am I gonna eat this? I feel sick.*

"I wish I could make them change their minds." Maggie dropped the garbage in the bin and washed her hands, her face still wide-eyed with shock. "You'd think they'd make an exception on compassionate grounds..."

"I don't think immigration knows what compassionate means." Leaning against the kitchen doorjamb, Ben pulled up a pair of ill-fitting purple sweatpants. That morning, Riley had helped him shower (with a plastic bag covering his cast), but afterward, Ben realized he couldn't do up the buttons on his jeans by himself. Riley raced over to the NYU bookstore, returning with the deeply discounted—and ugly—sportswear. If there ever was a reason to learn how to fasten buttons one-handed, those sweats were it.

"It's just wrong, making you leave now," said Maggie. "You're not fully healed from surgery, and you've got doctors here who know your case inside out."

"I told them that, but they didn't care." Ben shrugged. "One of the immigration guys laughed and said, 'Nice try, buddy,' like I was moaning about a cold or something." He caught Riley's gaze and smiled softly. "It might take a while, but I'll find a transplant specialist on the NHS to keep an eye on me."

"You won't have to pay for checkups, right? England has national healthcare?" Maggie set down three plates and dug around in her cutlery drawer.

"Yeah, thank God. They'll take care of me."

"Where will you live?" asked Maggie.

The lump grew in Riley's throat. *Far, far away from here...might as well be another planet.* For Ben's sake, she was trying to be upbeat, but it felt like her heart was being crushed.

"Walthamstow, northeast London. I sweet-talked Spencer, my old flatmate, this morning. My old room's full of her wakeboarding stuff, but I can have it as long as I pay the back rent I owe. Hunter's spotted me some money, so that's taken care of. I'll give Mark a bell, too. See if he knows of any work going."

"Thank goodness you've got people there who care about you...but I still think you should be staying here."

"Well, Maggie, at least *part* of me is staying here."

Maggie laughed and stepped over to Ben, hugging him softly so the embrace didn't hurt him. "Saying 'thank you' will *never* be enough. After everything you've done for us..." She sighed. "It all seems so unfair."

You belong here with me. Riley could feel Ben's eyes on her. She glanced over her shoulder and Ben was already there, waiting for her.

"I'm going to miss you both something rotten." He sniffed, a lost look in his eyes as he mouthed, "Love you," to Riley.

"We'll miss you, but just think how happy your mom will be to see you. You are such a credit to her." Maggie's voice broke. She cleared her throat and loosened her hug.

Thanks, guys. Now I'm gonna cry again. Riley pulled a loose thread on Maggie's oven mitts, busying herself so she could blink away tears unnoticed.

Maggie returned to the drawer, gathering forks and knives. "Before you two head back on the ferry tonight, I'll give you a note for your mom, Ben. Don't let me forget."

A quivering smile betrayed Ben's usually easygoing façade.

"We'll just have to come visit," said Maggie with a confident nod. "Take that trip we've planned forever, right, Riley?"

The smell of burning egg and cheese urged Riley to remove their lunch from the broiler, giving her an excuse to answer without meeting Ben's gaze. "Yep!" The empty promise pinched her heart. *Mom's trying to keep things positive, but she knows we can't afford a UK trip—not now or anytime soon.* She pulled out the frittata, and its eggy smell stoked another wave of nausea in her belly. *I have to face the facts: Ben will go back to London, and we might never see each other again.*

SIXTY-ONE

It's funny how time can drag when you're waiting for something good—Christmas, a much-anticipated vacation, cookies in the oven—but when something you're dreading is placed in your path, days can feel like hours, minutes like seconds, kisses—gone in the blink of a teary eye.

For Riley and Ben, his last days in New York City—Sunday, Monday, and Tuesday—careened toward Wednesday without mercy. The life they had known for the past seven months had hit its expiration date. That evening, Ben would be on a flight to London, and Riley would be riding the subway back to Manhattan, alone.

Her new job had kicked off two days before, but Wednesday morning Riley couldn't face it and called in sick. The thought of spending another day training alongside her pushy predecessor with his stinky ass-breath while Ben was packing his suitcase alone had left her hyperventilating in the shower at 6 a.m. When she didn't return a half-hour later, Ben went looking for her.

They didn't get very far. Closing the door to her room, Riley met his mouth and fisted his t-shirt, pulling him gently to the shaggy rug on the floor. They had kissed so often, so desperately over the past five days, their lips were red and slightly puffy, and Riley had become a fast learner at covering hickeys (or 'love bites', as Ben called them) with makeup.

She wasn't about to let Ben leave with only deep kisses to think about on the plane. Since his surgery, Riley had freed Ben from his boxers several times, teasing him with her mouth, and his tongue had reciprocated, inciting wave after wave of orgasmic fireworks, but that morning their seven-weeks abstinence of hip-to-hip, toe-curling sex ended. Ben was ready, and Riley wasn't about to let her new job make it a measly quickie.

They moved to her loveseat then had a session in her cramped bed, showing each other how much they were cherished, how much they were loved.

Riley, mindful of Ben's bruised, broken body, caressed him and kissed him and told him how much he had changed her life for the better. With the hours counting down ruthlessly, she moved above him, thinking only of their present, not that evening or the next day when, instead of Ben, loneliness would wrap itself around her.

My beautiful Brit boy, pretend this is the beginning, not the end.

Ben held her each time like it was their first, losing himself in her, committing her sighs, her soft skin, her taste to memory, all of his senses firing...over and over. Exploring with his hands and mouth, along her stomach, between her thighs—if he couldn't stay, he would take her with him the only way he could: in his heart.

My darling Riley, I could die happy right now.

Wrapped in each other, sighs, pleasurable moans, and laughter filled the small room until the darkness outside the window began to swallow up the daylight, and one by one the twinkly lights—the stars on strings that had lovingly kept watch above their heads—began to flicker out.

Ben's bubblegum pink case, with its white polka dots and *B. Something* name tag flapping farewell, scooted along the conveyor belt and tipped, disappearing into the abyss of the airport's bag drop. Riley's heart did a belly flop. *What brought us together is now gone.*

"Let's get out of here." Ben's hand grasped Riley's and led her away from the discount airline's check-in desk.

A twisted sense of déjà vu unsettled her. They were in a different airport—Newark, not LaGuardia where they had met—but Ben was wearing almost the exact same layers: the slim jacket (*so ill-suited for winter!*), his favorite purple hoodie, a flannel shirt, baggy jeans almost abandoning his butt. Even his right hand was injured, albeit wrapped in a cast instead of a bloody bandage. In seven months, Ben's outward appearance and taste in clothes hadn't really changed, but the way Riley saw him now couldn't be more different. *What you see on the outside, never tells the true story of someone's heart.*

"What did you get? Aisle or window?" Riley bit her lip. *Be brave. Be CHEERY. Don't be that red-faced girl bawling at departures.*

Ben yawned. "Middle."

"Nooo! The worst!"

Ben paused a few feet away from the entrance to security. Tired and sore, his abdomen ached from their passionate morning and afternoon. He looked up at the clock above the departures board. "Oh, before I forget..." He let go of her hand and slipped Riley's going-away present, her much-loved Strand Bookstore tote, off his shoulder, rooting past his carefully packed a-ha record and two black-and-white cookies to pull out a plastic bag. "For you. A 'see you soon' prezzie."

It's too firm to be Fun Dip. "You just put a four hundred-dollar airline ticket on your maxed-out card. You can't afford gifts!" She smiled and reached into the bag, pulling out a thin book: *The Duchess of Bloomsbury Street* by Helene Hanff.

"Oh, babe, you shouldn—" She stopped herself. "Wait...did you steal this?"

"No! I didn't—honest!" Ben laughed and adjusted the backpack on his shoulder. "I saw it on an outdoor cart at the Strand. I bought it back in August and was saving it for Christmas but..."

Riley admired the book's worn cover. "That makes it even

more special—thank you."

"Your good habits have rubbed off on me. No more stealing, even if I'm hungry…or sockless." He kissed her on the head and lowered both the tote and his backpack to the floor. "You've already read *84 Charing Cross Road*—this is the sequel. It's when she finally gets to London, something I hope you'll do soon, too." His eyes flitted up to the departure board again.

Ben's worried glance felt like a kick to Riley's gut. "It's time?"

His smile dimmed. "Bugger, yeah. I still have to get through security." He picked at the end of his cast like a nervous little boy. "Riley…"

"I'm not ready." She hugged Ben's gift, halting breaths and suppressed sobs tightening her chest.

"I don't know how to do this…" He reached for her hand, his voice shaky. "Leaving you…"

"I don't want you to go." Riley lunged, throwing her arms around him. She hid her face in his neck, choking back tears. "How will I get up each morning knowing it will be a day without you in it?"

He squeezed her tighter and rocked back and forth. "You will. You did before and you will again…for a little while, anyway. You're stronger than you think, Hope." Despite his best efforts, hot tears slipped underneath his eyelashes and down his cheeks.

She clutched him so tight, her knuckles paled. "I-I…can't."

"Beautiful Riley," he whispered, his hand smoothing her hair as he kissed her temple. "I'm still yours. It'll just be different until we sort things. I'll text and call, you'll see—I'll be a right bloody nuisance."

Just when I've found you…you go. She cried into his chest. Who would listen now? Who would understand her? Her mom was amazing, but some things you don't tell your mother. Piper was several time zones away. Casey, while a dear friend, wasn't the best

403

listener…not like Ben. "It's not the same as you *being* here."

"I know." Ben blinked quickly, but the tears wouldn't stop. "But, I'll be with you"—he pulled back slightly, placing his hand gently over her heart—"here, cheering you on, loving you with every breath."

My Brit boy. "I love you…so…much." Shaking, she could barely get the words out.

"Copycat. I said it first." His tear-soaked grin looked like it pained him. "You are my first, my always." Ben caressed her cheek and claimed her mouth for a kiss that melted into something more…a promise, perhaps, that this embrace wasn't the end.

Riley's fingers laced through his hair, digging in, keeping him close. *Remember this, remember everything. Memories might be all we have left.*

They kissed and held each other until a shrill announcement for Ben's final boarding call broke them apart.

I'm not ready! Oh, God. Her hands slipped from his hair down his arms, her right hand grasping his left, refusing to let go. "Ben…"

He leaned his forehead against Riley's and whispered, "When you feel sad, just close your eyes and remember, 'kay? And we'll be together again." Ben squeezed her hand and released it, picking up his backpack and tote. "I'll text you when I land." He wiped his cheeks and backed away, ducking behind the security wall with a hand raised in farewell.

Riley stood there for several minutes, drowning in tears, hoping Ben might pop back for another kiss or hug, but he didn't.

You are my last, my always…

Out of breath and sweaty from the last-minute sprint to his gate, Ben wiped his nose with the back of his hand and dropped into his middle seat in the last row of economy. He rifled through his backpack, reorganizing his belongings post-security check before the flight attendants forced him to stow it under the seat. *The t-shirt Riley sleeps in, a bag of grapes—half smushed, bugger! My birthday cards, Maggie's note addressed to Mum.* He plunged it back inside, his hand meeting something smooth and pear-shaped. *What? I didn't pack anything like that...* Confused, he pulled it out for a better look. *The plastic gallbladder!* Ben burst into a laugh, holding the organ aloft, drawing stares from his bemused seatmates. *Oh, you get me, Riles. You really get me.*

Sleepy eyes staring at the ceiling, Riley paused Ben's '4 Riles' playlist and checked the time. *4:45 a.m. He should've landed by now.* Mid-yawn, a-ha was cut off by Sia's vocals, making her jump. Her fingers scrambled to accept the call. "Hi!"

"Hey." His voice was low and sleepy. "Landed—with a thud."

"Oh, no. Bad landing?"

"No. Plane was fine. I meant my heart," he mumbled quietly. "I miss you."

"I miss y—" Her whisper broke. She gathered her breath, halting a surge of new tears. *How do I have any left?* She rolled onto her side, over a bunch of damp, balled-up tissues, souvenirs of her tear-soaked night. "It must feel good to be home, though."

"Ahhh, this isn't home, not anymore. Home is you."

Riley clutched her stomach, the ache of missing his warmth almost breaking her in two. "I love you."

"Uhh, I'm getting daggers from the customs bloke. Better go. Love ya, Riley."

He hung up and Riley hid under her duvet, dreading day one without Ben.

Sixty-Two

A week later

Waging war against a stubborn head cold, Riley blew on a steaming spoonful of her dinner—chicken noodle soup. Heavy-lidded, she blinked at her iPad, propped up against Ben's green Bruins cap. The tablet's live FaceTime feed showed the California sun beating down on Piper, turning her bleached blondness into a retina-burning glow.

Riley breathed through her mouth and answered Pip's question with a nasal twang. "Not an hour goes by that I don't think of him."

"Aw, Benjamuffin. I'm sorry you're missing him so much." Piper frowned underneath her huge white sunglasses. "Does he FaceTime a lot?"

"No, but he wasn't a big FaceTimer or Skyper when he lived here, either. He calls and texts, though, all the time: photos of his breakfast, his walk to the library, doing laundry. It's kinda funny how detailed he is."

"Maybe he thinks if he's not a constant presence in your phone, you'll forget him?"

An ache squeezed Riley's throat. "I could never forget him." Eyes getting misty, she bowed her head and set down her soup. *Here come the waterworks again.*

"Rye...?" Piper lifted her sunglasses, concern narrowing her eyes.

Change the subject. "So, how's life, Cali girl? Anything new from two days ago?" Riley smiled and wrapped a tissue around her streaming nose.

"Nope. Still pinching myself. Give me ALL the felt, googly

406

eyes, and feathers! It's puppet-making heaven! But I could do without the lame team-building t-shirts they make us wear. Check it..." Piper shifted the phone, showing off the banana yellow tee hanging shapelessly above her silver tutu, 'I'M A PUPPET PAL!' scrawled across her chest in a swirly red font.

Riley grimaced. "It looks like you rolled in mustard and someone squirted ketchup on your boobs."

"I know, right?" Piper snapped her gum. "I love puppets, but I don't need to declare it while walking along Santa Monica Boulevard. No wonder I haven't made any friends."

"You will." Riley dragged her spoon through her soup. "*Oh!* Tonight's Halloween! You should go to that party you told me about Monday. You'll meet fun people there, and hot ones, too—LA's full of 'em, right?"

"*Meh.* Women here think I'm weird, and the only men who give me the time of day are limp and made of felt."

Riley giggled. *Thank God I didn't have soup in my mouth.*

"I was listening to this girl at work bragging about her weekend hookup. She said he was a girthy seven inches. Can you imagine? I swear, I was a mess with the hot glue gun that afternoon. Come quitting time, I rushed home and pounced on Sherlock." All of Piper's sex toys were named after characters portrayed by Benedict Cumberbatch.

Picking up another tissue, Riley squealed with laughter. "Oh, Pip, never change!"

Piper snickered. "How's work going? Has Ass-Breath left?"

"Yep. I like it up on that floor, but my desk isn't near anyone else, so it's a bit lonely. I'd wander and say hi to my co-workers, but it would look bad if my boss needed me and I wasn't around."

"The joys of being an assistant." Piper sighed. "If I worked there, I'd make a point of becoming best friends with you."

"I know you would, Pip." Riley blew her nose. "I really miss you guys." *It feels like that's all I ever say.*

"Aw, I know, I feel the same—" Riley's phone rang and Piper squinted through the screen. "Oh, is that Maggie?"

"No…Nick, my boss. I'll let him go to voicemail. He probably wants to quarantine me. He's flying to London on Friday."

"So, how *is* Maggie doing?"

"Good!" Riley's face brightened. "She's tolerating her anti-rejection meds much better now."

"That's great news. Give her a hug from me?"

"I will, once I'm over this stupid cold." Riley sniffed. "Those meds weaken her immune system, so I can't see her until I'm better."

Piper scowled at the screen, noticing the time. "Shit, I should head back. I have to finish an elephant puppet."

"Pip, I really think you should go to that Halloween party—"

"Maybe. Look, Rye, what you said about missing everyone—you seem really down."

"Oh, I'm just sick and…being dramatic. I'll be fine." *I will. I just have to keep telling myself that.* "You should go—"

"No, you're not being dramatic. Look, gimme five? I'll call my boss, say I have a period emergency and need tampons. I'll FaceTime you right back."

"That excuse always works with male bosses." Riley grinned. "Pip, really, I'm okay. It's just so new…"

"But just because I'm not *there*, it doesn't mean I'm not *here* for you, okay? You're not alone."

"I know, but there's really no need to '*buy tampons*'." Riley still felt lonely but laughing with Piper had boosted her mood considerably.

"When's your next therapy session?"

"Tomorrow, and they're helping—a lot. I just…slip backward sometimes. My therapist says that's completely normal."

"Well, okay, but if you want to talk—"

"I'll call you." Riley nodded.

Piper snapped her gum. "You better mean that!"

"I do!" A genuine smile graced Riley's face. "Pip, just seeing you makes me feel better."

"Me, too." Piper blew her a kiss.

"Now, go! My soup's getting cold—bye!" Riley waved and hit disconnect.

Riley tapped Ben's name in her FaceTime app. *It's worth a try. 7:30 p.m. here is...thirty minutes past midnight there. He's probably still up reading.*

The annoying dial tone gave way to a half-assed Harry Potter.

"Riiiiiilles!" Ben's blue eyes creased with happiness behind round plastic eyeglasses. The Band-Aid on his forehead from his accident was gone, replaced by a smudged lightning bolt between his dark eyebrows. A loose red-and-yellow striped tie curled around his neck, outside the collar of a half-buttoned white dress shirt, and his hair was standing up like he had stuck his finger in an electrical socket. He laughed and stumbled over something, which only made him laugh harder. "Aw, baaaaaaabe, I've missed yooooo."

He's drunk?! "Ben, where are you?"

"Home..."

"Where *were* you?"

"Out!" His face disappeared from the screen, replaced with a swinging glimpse of clothes on the floor, the crotch of his jeans, and a small lamp. When the phone stopped its travels, it looked like Ben was flopped down on an unmade bed.

"At a Halloween party?" She sniffed her stuffy nose.

"Yeppers." He waved his cast at his face. "I'm Hazza Potter!"

"Y-Yeah, I see that." Riley's forehead creased. "Ben, how

much beer did you have?"

"Not much…maybe two halfs."

"One pint?"

"Yup."

"Ben, it's been only eight weeks. You're not supposed to have *any* alcohol."

"I've been a bad boy, Riles." He laughed and fumbled his phone. "Whoops! Spank me, dirty girl!"

"Ben! It's not funny!" The congestion in her sinuses started to throb. "The doctor told you no booze for three months. Your liver can't process it. That's why you're pissed on one pint."

"I only had a lickle bit." He exhaled heavily like he was annoyed. "Stop yellin' at me."

"I'm not—"

"Can't do *this*, can't do *that*…Spencer says I should have fun, says I deserve it." He gave a woozy frown.

Spencer—yeah, she's an expert on liver donation. Great.

"She dressed me like dis and we went to…Hallween party. I wasn't having anyting, but…go onnn, have a half." He closed his eyes, his words slow to materialize. "Then, someone gave…more…"

Riley scowled. "Was Mark with you? Or that Freddie guy? *BEN*?!"

He startled, fighting the urge to sleep. "Blimey O'Ri…" His face scrunched like he was in pain. "Do you think of me…?"

What…? Just play along. "Do you think of *me*?"

"Ohhhhh, Riles! All the fuckin' time. I think of you at the library, I think of you while eating toast, I think of you when I have a wank." He groaned and closed his eyes. "Ohh…"

"Ben?"

"Riles!" Breathless, he sprung up to a sitting position, the Potter spectacles hanging off one ear. "Let's phone fuck!" he growled.

"Uh…sure." She blotted her runny nose with a tissue.

"Hey! Guess what?! I was celebratin'!"

"O-kay? Why?"

"Just back from Aberdeen—that's Scotland."

"Yeah, I know it's Scotland, but the photos you sent me yesterday were in London—"

"Fooled ya! SURPRISE! Keegs, bless 'im, got me walk-on part in *Lairds*."

"Really?" A warm, happy feeling filled her chest. "Oh, Ben! That's incredible!"

"Yup. I was a messenger! From another clan. Said two lines"— he flung his hand away, his cast a white blur—"then fucked off."

"I'm so proud of you! That must've been fun."

"Yup…but Riles, ma' wee lassie, I had nothin' on under ma' kilt. I wuz bollock nekked…"

Nice! "Well, I would've liked to have seen that…"

"I…show ya now!" He yawned and lay back, trying to stuff his phone down his jeans. Riley got an eyeful of his belt. "Let's 'ave…" He closed his eyes. "Sssssssex…" His voice trailed off into gentle snores.

Next morning 6:05 a.m. in NYC / 11:05 a.m. in the UK

Riley slept through the arrival of Ben's text.

Riley!!! Last nite, SO sorry. I was happy cuz Lairds *but missing you + frustrated AF. I'm an idiot. Please 4give me? Luv u. xoxoxoxoxoxoxox*

A second text landed. '4 Riles!!!'—a new addition to his eighties playlist: "Tenderness" by General Public.

SIXTY-THREE

Three weeks later

"Hey, kids! Could one of you toss that bag of marshmallows to Frank?" Can of cranberry sauce aloft, Casey's mom, Tina, squeezed past Maggie, who was busy stirring a mixture of pork, cumin, garlic, and chili powder in a sizzling skillet atop the crowded stove. The delicious smell, along with the aroma of roasting turkey, was too much for Riley's growling stomach to ignore.

"I've got it." Hugging her parka, cheeks still pink from watching the Macy's Thanksgiving Day parade with Casey and his three sisters, Riley handed his dad the final ingredient destined for his sweet potato casserole.

"Thanks, Riley." He smiled. "Case, can ya grab that bowl with the corn husks over there?"

"I haven't had a chance to wash the parade off my hands yet." Casey huffed, removing his coat.

Frank nodded to a card table in the corner of the kitchen, a staging area for his Thanksgiving feast. "Careful! Don't spill the water."

"I wish we were having Yorkshire pudding." Rolling his eyes, Casey picked up the soaking husks and turned, stopping just short of chinning his youngest sister, Carrie, with the bowl.

"Aww! I thought *I* was stuffing the tamales!" the ten-year-old pouted.

"Carrie, I'm getting them ready for you." Maggie grinned over her shoulder. "Come dry the husks, and then you can spread the dough and add the pork."

"'Kay!" Carrie beamed. "Just gonna dump my coat."

"Oh, Care Bear, take mine?" Riley pulled her phone from her parka's pocket and stuffed her coat in Carrie's waiting arms. "How can I help?"

Frank wiped his brow with the back of his hand. "Well, Maggie's got the tamales taken care of, I'm finishing the casserole…Tina's opening the occasional can—"

His wife swatted his butt with a dish towel.

"Peel some potatoes?" Frank shrugged.

"I'm on it!"

Casey's twin eighteen-year-old sisters, Cherie and Chastity, opened the fridge, gawking at the homemade desserts Maggie had brought as a thank you for the kind invite.

Frank shook his head. "What's wrong with this picture, huh? My guests are workin', and my kids—"

Riley's phone awoke with a request from Ben. *Yay, he's FaceTiming! Fourth time this week!* Happiness warmed her from head to toe.

"I'll start the spuds," said Casey. "You go."

"Thanks! I'll be just a sec." She ducked out of the kitchen and hit accept.

Ben appeared with an equally wide smile, his right hand—cast marked up with colorful doodles—running through his hair. "Riles! I just got in." He was clean-shaven and wearing a blue sweater Riley hadn't seen before.

Ben now owns TWO sweaters! She giggled. "Did you see my photos? Sorry I sent so many…"

"I loved them! Balloon-a-palooza! Fuck me, now that's what you call a parade. I wish I could've been there." Ben sipped a steaming mug of tea. In London, it was around 8 p.m.

"You would've loved it! They had star balloons and a turtle!" She stepped over the sweeping tail of the family's chubby cat. "We're at Casey's now."

413

"Nice! Who's there, then?"

"A few aunts, uncles, and cousins are coming. I swear, they're making enough food to feed all of the Bronx. Mom's on cloud nine, cooking up a storm." She swerved around Carrie in a rush to stuff tamales and sat down at the dining table just as the doorbell rang. Casey's adopted Pomeranian went into full-on guard dog mode, barking its fuzzy face off.

Ben sat up straight. "Oh. Do you need to go?"

"Uh..." Riley looked over her phone.

Chastity shooed the dog away and opened the door. She hugged a man who looked like Frank's twin and then another middle-aged guy, a woman, and three teenage boys. "No, I can talk for a few minutes. If Case's dad needs me, he'll holler. When he heard Mom and I were doing Thanksgiving on our own, he insisted we come."

"That's really nice. Can I can say hi to Maggie?"

"Yeah, sure!" Riley craned her neck. "Oh...she's...still busy with Casey's sister right now, making tamales. His dad's recipe is to die for, sooo good."

"I'm glad Maggie's feeling well."

"Yeah, she looks so much healthier. She's even started to put feelers out for marketing jobs. It's twelve weeks next Tuesday, Ben—three months since surgery." Laughter rose in the kitchen and Riley glanced up, catching Casey mid-eye roll walking to the bathroom with a 'Families, huh?' grimace.

Ben dunked a cookie into his tea. "I'm looking forward to my last checkup—well, last one for a few months anyway."

Riley smiled at him, biting into his shortbread. "And you can have a pint next week to celebrate."

"No. I learned my lesson on Halloween."

Every time we talk, he apologizes. "Ben, I know you're dying for a pint. It's okay to have one or two." An irritating laugh pulled her attention away. *What?* "Shit!" Riley lowered her voice. "He's in the kitchen."

Ben tilted his head. "Uh, who…?"

"Casey's uncle with the hyena laugh. His dad wants to set Mom up with him."

"Yeah? Is Maggie keen?"

"No! Mom hasn't dated for…I dunno, five years? And this guy, he's all octopus hands and cheesy lines, from what Casey's told me. She might need rescuing."

Ben leaned in. "Oh, but before you go, I've got news—and a surprise!"

"What, another role?" Riley leaned over to pet the dog. "I can't wait for *Lairds*! Piper freaked when I told her! She was like, 'Holy shit, Ben's in a kilt?!'"

"No, no kilts this time. I have to wear undercrackers at this gig." His grin grew, twinkling his eyes. "Riles, I got hired by Waterstones, the huge one on Piccadilly!"

"The bookstore? That's terrific!"

"I know! Finally, full-time hours, a regular pay packet. I'll be on the third floor where the theater and film books are. I think my drama degree helped me land this one. I'm really chuffed!"

"You should be! You'll be amazing there."

"Yeah, and Spencer's only a floor down in the young adult section, so I'll have a friend from day one."

He lives with her, works with her—when isn't he with Spencer?
"Oh, did she put in a good word for you?"

"Yep. I needed all the help I could get."

"No, you didn't. You're a dream hire, you're friendly and amazing with customers, and you love books."

He smiled, unable to sit still. "Now, surprise time. Remember I was hanging with Mark and Alex in their new flat a few weeks ago?"

"Yeah…"

"It was like a potluck. We all brought food and stuff, so I made cookies and brownies from Mum's and Maggie's recipes—and everyone *raved*."

"No way! Mom will love to hear that!"

"And Mark dared me—"

"Oh God." Riley cringed.

"No, it's nothing bad. He dared me to get a legit table at a weekend market, see if I could make a few quick quid. Most places won't let newbies have a go, but I found one and I did a one-off last weekend…"

"What, like a food audition?"

"Yeah." He chuckled. "A food audition. So, I went and…" He did a fist pump. "I sold out! I made ONE HUNDRED AND FIFTY FUCKING POUNDS! For just two hours' work—in the rain. Imagine if it was sunny."

He's so cute—and happy! "Mom's cookies *are* really good! I'd stand in the rain eating them."

Ben bounced in his chair. "And today they called, asking me back!"

"For another Saturday?"

"No, for the next *six* weekends. It's a proper tryout, starting this Saturday. Isn't that hilarious? Mark will have to pay up massively, the plonker!"

"That's funny! Is it close to you?"

"Nope. It's in Bermondsey—southeast London, the Maltby Street Market. It's about a ten-minute walk from Tower Bridge—you know, the one you keep calling London Bridge?" He giggled. "When you visit, I'm taking you to both bridges so you'll see the difference—and believe me, there's a HUGE difference."

'When you visit.' With what money? "Ben, have you given any more thought to when you might visit *here*?"

He took a breath. "Oh, love, that's all I think about. With these

416

two jobs, I reckon I can save up, maybe be there for our anniversary."

Oh? The end of June...eight whole months away.

Her frown made Ben laugh. "Hope! You're thinking June, aren't ya?"

"Well, that's our anniversary."

"No, don't be daft! I mean St. Paddy's Day—our *airport* anniversary! The day we met!'"

"Ohh! GOOD! I can't wait eight months to kiss you..." Riley did a double take—Casey was hovering with a bowl of half-peeled potatoes.

Ben's eyes drifted like he was trying to see what Riley was looking at.

"Rye, sorry." Casey leaned in and waved through her phone. "Hey, Ben. Sorry, mate."

"Hiya, Case, all right?"

"I will be when today's over. Relatives—who needs 'em." He squinted at Riley. "You might want to come. My uncle is cracking on to your mom." Casey shivered with revulsion and walked back to the kitchen.

Gross. Riley curled her lip.

Ben grimaced. "Go save Maggie. Call when you get home?"

"It won't be until late, like 3 a.m. your time."

"No worries. I'll keep my phone near. I love you, Riley. Happy Thanksgiving."

I have so much to be thankful for. "I love you, too, Ben."

Sixty-Four

Sunday, November 25, 1:24 p.m. in NYC / 6:24 p.m. in the UK

A photo and text message popped up on Riley's phone: Ben beaming with pride, holding a small chalkboard with BEN'S LOVE BITES scrawled across it.

Sold EVERYTHING this wkend! xo

Riley giggled and typed a message.

How cute are YOU? Ben's Love Bites? Mmmm, my fave! LOL! Are you sure you didn't eat more than you sold, Cookie Monster?

Three minutes later.

And eat my profits? No! I'm all about £! £ = me w/u in NYC. Froze my bollocks off but getting all toasty thinkin of u.

You want sexy FaceTime?

Within seconds of Riley sending her text, she received a FaceTime call from Ben.

Christmas Day, 8:46 a.m. in NYC / 1:46 p.m. in the UK

Sitting by Maggie's tiny Christmas tree, Riley smiled at the tartan change purse given to her by Piper and hit send on her latest text.

Merry Christmas Benjamin Fagan, love of my life! x

Twenty-five minutes passed—no text. Riley gave up waiting and had begun mixing waffle batter when Ben's reply arrived.

Happy Chrimbo, gorgeous!! Soz for late reply. On train. Give Maggie kiss! xo

Riley happily abandoned breakfast prep and picked up her

phone, replying. *FaceTime?*

Can't. Really low battery. 4got my charger!! Shite reception. On way to see Mum.

Her lips let out a satisfied sigh as she texted back. *You two made up?*

Yep. Open my prezzie?

Riley glanced under the tree. Inside an opened box was a photo book of their New York memories and a cute ring featuring a real Love Heart candy preserved inside a glittery red resin heart. The candy's message: Catch Me. Ben had also included a handwritten card: *It's not that you need catching, but if you ever did fall, I've got you. xo*

Her fingers flew with her answer. *I loved it. That ring will look perfect with my red Christmas dress.*

Aw, Hope...sounds hot—send photos later?!!

She giggled, hitting send. *Will do! Did you like mine? Did you like Mom's sweater?*

She didn't receive an answer. No further texts arrived that day.

New Year's Eve, 6:52 p.m. in NYC / 11:52 p.m. in the UK

Phone buzzing, Riley slowed her walk through the frozen slush. *Finally!* She pulled off her mitten and read Ben's text.

I miss your lips!! I need a snog at midnight!!! xoxoxoxoxoxox

A chilly breath caught in her throat. *Who WILL Ben kiss at midnight?* That question had been burning a hole through her heart the past several days, ever since Ben had reunited with his phone charger post-Christmas and told her about Mark and Alex's New Year's party. The news had tripped a switch inside her, allowing depression to push its way in, wrapping itself around her palpable loneliness, and no amount of cute dog GIFs from Casey or ugly

Christmas sweater photos from Piper could pull her free. Riley hadn't felt this low since saying goodbye to Ben at the airport. *Someone will kiss Ben during Auld Lang Syne—and it won't be me.* She texted back.

I love you, Ben. x

Ben's FaceTime invite invaded her screen. She accepted it without pause.

"Riley!" In a crush of people, Ben was wearing sparkly 'Happy New Year' head-boppers and the purple dress shirt she had bought him for Christmas. "Where are you? It's dark. You outside?"

He looks so good. Watching him so far away, surrounded by friends felt like a bittersweet punch to the stomach. Riley's nose began to prickle. *Don't cry in the street.* "I'm walking to Mom's."

Mark leaned over Ben's shoulder. "Riley! Happy New Year, darlin'! This one's *really* missing you."

Hearing that made Riley stand a little taller. "Hi Mark. I'm missing him, too."

Mark slapped Ben on the back and left him to it.

"Ahh, I feel better for seeing you!" Ben only had eyes for Riley. "Things all right, gorgeous?"

They are now. "Yeah. Gonna have a quiet night, watch Times Square on TV."

"Good! I don't want you off kissing blokes at midnight in Times Square!" He laughed. "Riles, I've got news! They've offered me a permanent spot at the market."

"That's fantastic!"

"I get a proper sign and everything." He beamed. "And that's not all—I'm definitely coming to New York in March for our airport anniversary!"

YES! YES, YES! Oh my God...I'm gonna cry. "Ben!" she squealed. "I really needed to hear that today!"

"Aw, love!" He laid his hand over his heart. "You can meet me at terminal D and we can have a do-over with kisses and Funyuns and street pretzels instead of stolen luggage! Whatcha say, gorgeous—"

"BEN!" A brunette with mischievous brown eyes and a swingy bob lurched into frame, cuddling into him. She was wearing a stunning blue dress; Riley was pretty sure she had coveted the same one in the window of Ted Baker in Soho. A colorful tattoo on her shoulder—a Rubik's Cube—stole Riley's attention.

"I need you—now!" The woman demanded. "Love pest by the sausage rolls. Idiot won't take a bloody hint. Save me!"

Ben looked off screen and turned back to the interloper. "What? Again? Jeez. This is the *last* time I pretend for you." He wrapped his arm around her shoulder possessively. "Happy now?"

Riley frowned. *Who's she? Is that Lucy, the girl Alex mentioned at Wagamama?*

Ben tipped his head toward the woman. "Riley, meet Spencer. She's a right pain in the arse."

That's Spencer? Spencer's...pretty...and there—with Ben's arm around her.

"RILEY?!" Spencer waved. "Ben doesn't shut up about you!"

Good. Back off. Riley mustered a smile. "Hi."

Ben held the phone closer, cutting Spencer from view. "Riles, I have to play Good Samaritan otherwise I won't hear the end of it when we get home..."

'When WE get home...' Riley's jaw clenched. *Ben's roommate is pretty. She's probably seen him in his FCUK pants. Maybe she's seen him WITHOUT his FCUK pants...* "Okay, I'll...let you go?"

His eyes pleaded. "But I'll call tomorrow, okay, first thing? I want to start the new year off with you, not a hangover."

Big Ben's iconic four-note chimes rang through her phone. Someone must've cranked up the London festivities on TV.

"Okay. Love you!" Riley's words were lost in the tune.

"The countdown's starting!" Spencer shrieked off camera, her jumping up and down jostling Ben.

"Ten...nine..."

"Riley? You okay?" He leaned in, his expression pinching like the party and Spencer were too much. "It's too noisy! I love you!"

"...five..."

Riley's heart felt heavy as she raised her voice. "Happy New Year—LOVE YOU."

Ben pointed to his ears in frustration and lowered his phone, but FaceTime wasn't disconnected, and Riley could still see and hear.

Spencer yelled, "Ben, that perv's coming over..."

"...three..."

"I'm not kissing you, you daft cow." Ben shook his head and shifted the phone, cutting off Riley's view.

"...one..."

His phone jerked and Big Ben bonged. "HAPPY NEW YEAR!" burst though Riley's speaker.

"Ew! Freddie!" Spencer wailed. "You kiss like a fucking fish!"

Hitting disconnect, a relieved smile warmed Riley's face.

Valentine's Day 2019, 4:55 p.m. in NYC / 9:55 p.m. in the UK

Red roses and lilies graced her co-workers' desks, but Riley wasn't envious one bit. She admired the blue forget-me-nots beside her computer. "My flowers, Ben! They're perfect, and I've eaten half the candy already." She peeled the plastic off her microwaved lasagna, letting a curl of hot steam escape.

"Good, glad you like 'em, love!" Ben's image bounced and the background behind him—books, shelves—flew past as he quickened his pace. "The florist over there tried to talk me into roses. I reckon they thought I was a cheap bastard."

Riley giggled, digging a fork into her hot dinner. "Did my present arrive?"

"Yeah! *Equinox Ten*—'Star-drive to maximum power!'" He mimicked the cult TV show's iconic salute and laughed. "I've wanted that box set forever! Cheers, Riles."

"Did you get my latest addition to the '4 Benjamin' playlist?"

"No, don't think so. Send it again?" He stared into his phone. "Uh, you're just eating lunch now?"

"No, I'm staying late—this is early dinner." She fiddled with her phone, sending him the missing playlist text—"When I Think of You" by Janet Jackson. "I'm going all out on a report for my boss. There are rumors of amazing job postings soon, so...I want to stand out, you know?"

"Right." He spotted her text and smiled but seemed preoccupied, jogging up some stairs.

"Is everything okay?"

"Uh, fine. I'm...finding a quiet corner. Fourth floor should do it—no one will look for me in Economics."

"You're working a late one, too..."

"Yeah, 'til closing." He ducked into an abandoned alcove of tall bookshelves. "Riles, they told me this afternoon—they're sending me on a course." He didn't look happy.

"Is that...good or bad?"

"Both, I guess. I'll get paid a bit more afterwards, but I have to make a decision."

"Oh?"

He lowered his voice. "If I want to get promoted here, I think I'll have to pack acting in. There's no way I can do both."

"Oh! So...how do you feel about that?"

"I love the books and chatting to people—and the steady pay packet." He shrugged. "Acting-wise, I've done nothing since that *Lairds* one-off...I haven't even been on an audition."

"Yeah, but being an actor is like that, right? I guess you have to ask yourself if you'd miss it."

"Well, I'd miss my acting buddies and how fun it is to be someone else, but the rest—the shit money, zero job security, being told I'm too tall, too skinny, too pale—*hell no*! My heart's not in it. I think my talents might lie elsewhere…"

"Like the kitchen? Alex texted me saying she visited the market and you had fawning customers. Ben, you've got fans!"

"Wouldn't say 'fans'…regulars, maybe."

"Same thing! I'm so proud of you." She smiled. "To think you were practicing icing with Mom only seven months ago."

He tugged the red Waterstones lanyard around his neck and looked away. "Yeah…"

He still looks unsure. "Ben, you know, you don't *have* to quit acting, not if you still want to do it. I'm sure you can find a balance—"

"No, it's not the acting that's bugging me…" Ben closed his eyes and grimaced, opening them again. "I can't visit you next month."

He's not coming. Ben's not coming to New York. The hunger gnawing her belly twisted into ice-cold nausea. She abandoned the fork in her lasagna.

"The course is that week, and then I have to be in the store over the St. Paddy's weekend—I'll even miss the market."

Her face fell as she swallowed hard. *We've missed Christmas together, New Year's, Valentine's, and now our airport anniversary. Will four months apart grow to six…ten…a year?*

"I'm so sorry." Ben lowered his head. "I saved enough for my flights and everything—"

He's heartbroken, too. It's not his fault. She lightly pressed her lips together, glancing at her 'Catch Me' ring sparkling on her finger. "Ben, it's okay. Really."

He looked up through his hair. "Riley—"

"The trip wasn't definite anyway, and…you can't let this opportunity pass. It wouldn't look good." She offered a smile.

"After the course, I'll get a new job title, few more quid, but I can't have any proper holiday time, not for the first three months. So, I'll come over in June—for our real anniversary, yeah??"

Four more months, but what choice do I have? She nodded. "Yeah."

SIXTY-FIVE

Two and a half weeks later

Fresh from a celebratory afternoon wandering around the MoMA with Riley, Maggie beamed as she dug into her small strawberry cheesecake 'Blizzard' in the Staten Island Ferry Terminal's Dairy Queen. "Six months post-transplant and I *finally* feel like life's returning to normal."

"A year ago, things were so different." Riley chewed a peanut butter cup from her frozen treat.

"Like night and day. My energy and appetite are back, my new job stars next week—I can't wait to earn a paycheck again." Maggie placed her hand over her daughter's. "And that crowdfunding money—it's taken away so much worry. I couldn't be more thankful."

Riley smiled at her phone, Ben's most recent '4 Riles' playlist addition front and center: "I Melt With You" by Modern English. *Well, job done, Benjamin—I actually like eighties music now.*

"Want to try Ben?"

"Yeah. He should be home." Riley tapped his contact info. "I know he wants to congratulate you!" She propped her phone against a napkin dispenser and scooted over to her mom's side of the booth. The live FaceTime feed opened to Ben in his bedroom.

"Hey! Working girl!" He laughed. "Staten Island's loss is New Jersey's gain! Congrats on the new marketing gig, Maggie. That's brilliant!"

"Thanks! I'm dreading the switch from jeans and sneakers to nylons and heels, but I'm also grateful for the chance to complain about it!"

"Damn straight! I'm glad my liver's behaving itself." He chuckled. "Here's to our six-month anniversary—I might have a proper celebratory drink tomorrow."

"You've earned it, sweetie," said Maggie.

"*And...*" Riley bounced in her seat. "Mom's cancer-free."

Ben leaned forward, his smile out of control. "You got the all clear?!"

"Not in so many words, but there's no sign of any cancer, so they're calling it a remission. I'll still have regular checkups, but they seem optimistic I'm not going anywhere anytime soon." Maggie smiled.

"Amazing!" Ben sat back, elated. "I'm two for two—that was my second birthday wish, you being well again."

"Really?" Riley couldn't stop grinning.

"Well, it worked, and I'm enjoying each day as it comes." Laughing, Maggie waved her ice cream teasingly at the phone's camera.

"Blimey." Ben licked his lips. "What I wouldn't give to be tucking into that! What did you get, Riles? Peanut butter something? When you visit, I'll take you to one of those 'freakshake' places."

"Those loaded milkshakes on your Instagram?"

"Yep, with the brownies, Oreos, pretzels—all stuffed in. Don't show Piper—she'll get cavities just looking at them."

"Oh, we are SO going there on my first day!"

"Yeah?" He chuckled.

"I'm serious."

"I pity the fool that comes between you and your desserts!"

"Well, step aside, Fagan." Riley couldn't hold back, the words racing from her lips. "Work might be sending me over there!"

His eyes widened. "Work? Oh my God, for real? How?"

"You know Elstree Studios, the huge production place outside

427

London?"

"Yeah?"

"Well, the BBC is taking someone from here for a six-month placement. It's an assistant's position, like I have here, but the idea is that we'd learn more about the company, cultivate new relationships, and then bring that knowledge back home."

Ben blew out his cheeks. "Jeez, that's just...if you got it..."

"I know! So, I've been working stupid hours, trying to get noticed. I didn't say anything earlier because everyone's applying for it and my chances are slim—I didn't want to get your hopes up."

Maggie nodded.

"But I'm doing everything I can to be with you. I even got my passport! It arrived last week, so I'm ready to jet out—*if* I get it!"

"Oh, Riles!" Ben cleared his throat. "That's...great. Wow!" He sat back and fidgeted with the strings on his hoodie.

Why is his smile stiff? Isn't he happy?

"When would you be over?"

"Soon—spring, if it happens. I'll know this week."

"That soon, eh? That's grand! Erm, will they put you up somewhere or...?"

Or? Riley squinted, waiting for him to continue, but he didn't. *This is when you offer for me to stay with YOU, Ben.* "I don't know all the details yet—"

"I'd love for you to stay here, but Spencer's flat...it's so cramped, you know?" Ben looked away, his eyes skimming his room. "I don't even have a closet. My clothes are crammed in my suitcase..." He shook his head. "You can't swing a rat-cat in here." He chuckled nervously. "Uh, I could ask Alex. Maybe you can stay in their spare room? You'd have privacy and a lot more space..."

He wants to pawn me off on his friends...what the fuck? Why doesn't he want me there with him? Is he not telling me because Mom's here? "I don't need tons of space, Ben. You've seen where I live—"

"Sweetheart…" Maggie's eyes darted from Ben fidgeting on his bed to Riley's confused frown. "Why don't we wait and see if you get it, and *then* you can figure out all the details?"

Ben's nod dissolved into a yawn.

Maggie patted her daughter's arm. "There's no point asking Alex or doing anything until we know."

Ben yawned widely again. "Sorry! I'm just…knackered. Two jobs…" He rubbed his eyes. "Riley, I really hope you get it, love."

You're not acting like it. Riley stared into her dessert and closed her eyes, hoping her mom—but most of all, Ben—wouldn't spot the tears of disappointment threatening to dampen her lashes. His loving words from the airport swirled in her head, mocking her.

"When you feel sad, just close your eyes and remember…"

Right now, though, Riley wondered—was Ben forgetting?

Seeking comfort in pajamas and a fuzzy blanket, Riley curled up on Maggie's foldout couch and settled in for the night. Eyes puffy, she typed out a text to Ben but then deleted it. *I'm still too upset.* She opened her laptop and dove into work emails. *How does one day off trigger an avalanche of messages?* She scrolled through, accepting requests for meetings and confirming her boss's travel itinerary for a TV festival in Banff. As she flagged some emails, a three-word subject line sent her pulse into a sprint.

Elstree Studios Placement

Riley bit her cheek and opened her boss's message.

From: Nick Balfour
To: Riley Hope
Sent: Monday, March 4 at 3:25 p.m.
Subject: Elstree Studios Placement

Riley,

Human Resources delivered their decision this afternoon regarding the Elstree Studios placement. I wanted to tell you in person, but since you weren't in today and all applicants are being notified ASAP, email will have to suffice. As you're well aware, the timeline for this placement is tight, and Elstree wants the successful applicant settled in London no later than Wednesday, March 20.

Forget butterflies, Riley had the cast of *The Birds* flapping inside her belly. *I'm afraid to look.* She took a deep breath and read on.

In the three years you've been with us (internship and fulltime), your hard work, enthusiasm, and dedication to the group has been duly noted, and it's with great pleasure I say, 'Pack your bags! London's calling!'—the six-month Elstree placement is yours. Please take this evening to think it over and let me know your answer in the morning. We'll be meeting with HR tomorrow at ten to discuss details and answer any questions you may have.

You've been such a great addition to the New York team and I'll be lost while you're gone, but you've earned this chance, Riley. Congratulations and well done!

Best, Nick

Oh. My. God. She read it again, in case the emotional exhaustion of the day was making her hallucinate. *No, it's real—the job's mine. London's mine!* Her hand trembled as it met her mouth. *I wish Mom were awake. I wish Ben wasn't being weird. Shit! I really need to tell someone...Pip! I'll Skype her...*

She answered right away, a wet towel twisted into a beehive atop her head. "Hey! Sorry I didn't answer your text earlier—I was elbow-deep in glue and feathers most of the day! Great news about your mom, huh? Remission! Thank God!"

"Yeah. Couldn't have come at a better time."

Pulling her bathrobe closed, Piper pressed her lips together. "You okay?" She angled closer to her computer screen. "Your face is weird...what's up?"

"I just found out...I got the London placement."

"WHAAAAT?!" Piper bounced up and down in her chair, her wet towel wobbling. "Holy shit, Rye! You'll get to see Ben!"

Riley's grin slipped. "Well, I'm glad you're excited...he sure as hell isn't."

"He's not?" Grimacing, Piper halted her Tigger impression. "This is Benjamuffin Fagan, right? Didn't his brain explode with happiness?"

"Nope. We were FaceTiming this afternoon, before I knew the Elstree thing was mine...I said I *might* be moving over, and he rattled off these weird excuses why I couldn't live with him—"

"Oh, Rye!" Wincing, Piper rubbed her forehead. "Did you *ask* to move in?"

"No, but why didn't he...you know...offer? If he's missing me as much as he says—"

"Rye, stop! All this long-distance shit has warped your brain."

"No, it hasn't!"

"It has! Look, don't hate me, but I agree with Ben. I know you shacked up post-op, but it's *wayyy* too soon to live together properly. You've only been dating for like, eight months or something— and half that time, you've been on opposite sides of an ocean." Piper popped open a box of Pocky; the chocolate-coated sticks were her favorite Japanese snack.

"I know, but—"

"And doesn't he live in a dump with some girl and her cat?"

Riley pouted. "Yeah, *Spencer.*"

Piper snapped a cookie stick in half, chewing through her response. "I remember him saying her flat was barely big enough for one person. Rye, it's cramped as fuck."

"I can do cramped! I've done it for the past four years."

"But it's a different story when there's three of you. Ugh, it's the worst! Trust me—I'm living that nightmare right now."

"I thought you liked your roommate and her boyfriend?"

"I do, but we're constantly stumbling over each other, lining up for the stove when we cook." Piper swallowed and shook her head. "*He* eats all my Chef Boyardee, *she* hogs all the shelf space in the bathroom, and don't even get me started on sex. It's a good thing I'm having none because the walls have ears. I feel like I'm in the middle of a three-way every time they do it."

Hmm, she has a point. "Ben suggested moving in with Alex and Mark because they have a bigger place with a spare room."

"Ooh, do that! God, imagine bumping into Mark frickin' Keegan in the hallway after he's had a shower! *Whoopsie*…his damp towel slips from his waist—"

"Pip! Stop drooling!" Riley giggled. "But seriously…it's like Ben wants to keep me at arm's length."

"No, it's like he wants to take his time, not rush into anything. That's what you should want, too…especially after Josh."

Ah…shit. She's scored another one. Riley sighed. "Yeah…"

"I know being long distance has been hard and you miss him, but please don't read into every little thing he says. To me, it sounds like he's being honest. There's no room at the inn—period!" She crunched another Pocky. "Seriously, do you really want to move into *that* clusterfuck?"

"That's what Mom said—sorta."

"You should be glad Ben's with it enough to realize you wouldn't be happy there."

"Yeah, that's true." Riley checked her phone, wishing there was a message from Ben…just something to back up Piper's advice.

"So, when are you gonna tell him? I'm surprised you didn't call and wake him up."

"I would've, but I was still mad at him…"

"Imagine his face when you tell him! Oh, wait! You know what's even better?! SURPRISE him—in person!"

"What, just show up on his doorstep? Don't tell him I got the job?"

"YES! I've always wanted someone to do that for me." Piper swooned. "It would be sooo romantic."

"Not if Spencer answers."

"Well, surprise him at the market."

Now THAT would be amazing. Riley sat back, the tension from earlier in the day melting away as a big grin lit up her face.

Sixty-Six

Riley had no time to spill the beans. For the next two weeks, her hours were filled with packing her apartment, training her replacement at the BBC, and spending time with Maggie. Casey helped her move back to Staten Island and, along with Piper, continued a social media guise supporting Riley's '*Can't wait for spring in NYC*' charade. To seal the deal, she had told Ben the morning after their awkward Dairy Queen FaceTime call that the Elstree placement had sadly gone to someone else. He commiserated with her and promised to book his June NYC flights the next month. Operation Fool Fagan was moving along without a hitch.

On the morning of St. Patrick's Day, their one-year 'airport' anniversary, Riley planned to call Ben early before he became ensconced in Irish shenanigans. Maggie was out at a Sunday market, so Riley had plenty of privacy for a FaceTime chat.

"Ben!"

"Happy Paddy's, love." Weaving and slurring, Ben held his phone in one hand and a pint of Guinness in the other. It was 6 p.m. UK time and he was already sloppily pissed.

Riley laughed. "Benjamin Fagan, have you been pre-gaming?"

Ben's arm swayed, so Riley's view of him did, too. "Yup. Got buzz on at home…" The purple dress shirt he was wearing was crispy ironed, but it had a large wet stain on the front and was unbuttoned mid-chest, showing off a few wisps of dark hair—not Ben's go-to style at all.

He's a bit of a mess, but he's allowed to have some fun. "Who's out with you?"

Ben wobbled and tripped into someone, spilling most of his

pint. "Oh! Sorry, mate, soz." He leaned to hug his victim, but the guy pushed Ben away and he stumbled backward, fighting to keep his balance. "Oh, well, bollocks to you, ya wanker!"

Yikes. "Ben...?"

He jerked his phone close to his face, blinking wildly like he was trying to clear the fog and focus. "So—*hic*—ahhh, Riles, where...where are...?" He bumped into another guy and slumped against a wall, staring into the phone. "Whatcha wearin'?"

"Uh, a tank and sweats." *He's so drunk, he can't tell. I should've lied.* "I'm at home. I wish I could be with you, today of all days. Happy Airport Anniversary, Brit boy."

"Aww. Sweet, sexy Riley. My Ri..." His words spilled out in a slow, thick mumble as he slid down the wall to the floor, landing with a thud on his ass. "I miss kissing you...it hurts, not holding you." He abandoned his glass on the floor, his chin trembling.

He looks like he might cry. "Ben, are you okay?"

"Everything's SHITE, Riles." He pulled his knees to his chest. "The course was shite, the—"

"The course? But yesterday you said it went well."

"Nope. Was pissin' awful. My dyslex-ya fucked me..."

Oh, shit. Her brow wrinkled. "I'm sure it wasn't that bad. What did they say?"

Eyes glazed over, he silently drummed his fingers on his knee, the phone's camera shaking.

Is he alone? "Ben, who's there with you? Is Mark there?"

"Somewhere..." He waved the hand holding his phone, giving Riley a woozy view of the wall behind him. "With Alex. I'm sick of lovey-dovey couples, sick of being on my own. It's BOLLOCKS. Work's bollocks, Spence's fuckin' rat-cat bit me...I don't blame him..." He winced.

"The cat *bit* you?"

"It was a bad idea, moving back there...*hic*...everything's fuckered. I'm so lonely..."

I've never seen him like this. Damn. Should I tell him? It'll still be a surprise... "Babe, look, everything's going to be okay. We'll see each other soon! I'm—"

"I'm a fuckin' stupid arse who doesn't deserve anythin' good, 'specially you..."

Where's that coming from? She narrowed her eyes. "That's not true—"

"No, nooo, it is. Riles, I..." His hand pawed through his hair, pulling it off his forehead. "I didn't mean...it just *happened*. I didn't think..." His face crumpled. "Maggie's gonna hate me."

Why would Mom hate you? "Ben—?"

"Forgive me?" His hand released and his hair fell forward, messy. "Please...? Riley, I'm sorry. I am..."

Forgive?! Riley's heart tripped. "Forgive...what?" *What did you do, Ben Fagan?*

His bloodshot eyes opened wide as he spotted someone in the crowd.

"Ben? You don't look so hot..." A familiar American accent cut through the pub's ambience. Alex squatted down and squinted into his phone's screen. "Riley! Hey!" She lifted Ben's hand, raising his phone higher so Riley could see them both.

Thank God he's not alone. "Hi Alex. I'm happy to see you!"

Alex nodded and side-eyed Ben, concern creeping into her sunny smile. "I'm gonna get Mark."

Ben flinched. "I don't need Keegs..."

"Well, I do. We're going home, and you're coming with us, mister." Alex looked at her buzzing phone. "Shit. Spencer..."

"Spence?! Where?" Ben's hand shakily swept his hair from his eyes again as he looked beyond his phone.

"She wants me in the toilets *now*." Alex bit her lip. "But I'll get Mark first. Wait here." Rubbing Ben's arm, she turned to Riley.

"Don't worry, honey. We'll look after him." She ruffled Ben's hair sympathetically and stood up, disappearing from view.

Alex is friends with Spencer. Mark is friends with Ben. Alex and Mark, Spencer and Ben—great. Sounds real cozy.

"Riles, you gonna hate me...I haven't..." He picked at the tear in the knee of his jeans. "I should've been honest..."

"About what?" Unease grabbed her by the throat. *Ben, what the fuck is going on?*

"I'm ssssoo sorry, darlin'." He disappeared from view as he tried to get up, but his phone slipped out of his grip, clattering across the pub floor.

Shit! Riley felt sick. "BEN?!"

A passing boot kicked his phone, spinning it several times until it smacked against the gum-scarred leg of a metal table. The impact killed the picture and sound, pushing Riley into a panic.

I need to know what's going on! Tears of worry and frustration stung her eyes.

She texted Alex and waited.

Hours later, slouched on Alex and Mark's sofa with an empty coffee cup on the table in front of him, Ben hid beneath his hands, his head still spinning. *I've been so stupid...*

Alex gave Mark a worried look. "Riley sent me three texts. I told her Ben was here and had been sick a few times but was resting now. Should I say anything else?"

"It's not up to us, Lex." Mark shook his head. "Christ, he looks *rough*." He set down a glass of water for his friend. "Mate, you gotta be honest with her."

Sixty-Seven

Sitting in Casey's dorm room in front of his laptop, Riley recounted the previous night's St. Patrick's drunken debacle to her best friends. It was 4 p.m. on the west coast, so Piper had slipped out of Monday afternoon puppet production to grab some gum and join the chat. She leaned against a palm tree in the glorious Los Angeles sunshine. "London, Rye—LONDON! You'll be there in TWO DAYS! I'm so freakin' jealous!"

"Don't even start on the London envy," said Casey, sipping from a Starbucks cup that held an unusually simple venti white mocha with almond milk. "At least I'll live vicariously through *this* one." He playfully elbowed Riley, who sat to his left with an untouched Insomnia peanut butter cookie in front of her.

"How's Maggie holding up?" asked Piper. "I bet she'd stow away in your luggage if she could."

"She's way more excited than I am," said Riley. "I wish she could come, but it'll be a while before we can afford any travel."

"Flight paid for, a shared flat arranged for you near the studio...your rent is gonna be in POUNDS, Rye!" Casey dreamily looked into space and tsked. "I should've gone into production instead of documentaries."

Riley gave him a bittersweet grin.

"You should be doing cartwheels over all this!" Piper snapped her Juicy Fruit. "I wish I could jump through the internet and give Ben's head a good shake."

"Yeah, what's he playing at? He should know he can't drink like he used to." Casey broke apart his Snickerdoodle cookie, the three friends maintaining their Monday afternoon ritual one last

438

time, even if it meant Piper was forced to drool from afar. A second box of cookies sat in reserve on Casey's bed. "Thank God Alex texted last night. At least you know his phone was broken and he's not lying in a dumpster somewhere."

"I'm glad he barfed his brains out," said Piper. "That'll teach him, hopefully. It's also karma for making you so upset."

Riley winced. "I stayed awake last night, waiting for him to call. Ben doesn't do silent, especially when he's drunk." Appetite AWOL, she nudged the peanut butter cookie away. "He was a total wreck. He looked depressed—then he said something about Mom never forgiving him."

"Fuck…" Swallowing hard, Piper's shoulders tensed as she glared at a motorcycle thundering past. "He mentioned *Maggie*? That makes me think he…"

Is Pip thinking what I've been thinking? "Mom would only be furious if…" The lump growing in Riley's throat made her voice raspy. "If he did something that would hurt me."

"Bastard better not have!" Casey curled his lip.

"I just wish I knew what that *something* was before I get on the plane tomorrow night." Riley sniffed. "If we're breaking up—"

"Rye, don't even *think* of not going."

"Casey's right," added Piper. "You can't bail on that job."

"No, I want to go, it's just…the timing's the *worst*. What if I end up alone and brokenhearted in London—"

"What broken heart? You're jumping the gun," said Casey. "And as for timing—fuck timing. If we waited to do stuff until everything was perfect, we'd never budge. *You* told me that!"

"I know, but it's easier to give advice than take it."

"True enough." His phone buzzed and he glanced down, a smile warming his face.

Piper swatted away a wasp. "Rye, you've spent these last few years living your life for your mom." Riley opened her mouth to interject, but Piper doubled down. "I *know*—it was the right thing to do, and you did it out of love—but she's well now and it's time for you to 'fly, my pretty'. I know it's not Cali, but it's the next best thing, trust me. England's *awesome*."

"The swimming's not," Casey mused. "Pebbly beaches."

"Really?" Riley scrunched her nose.

"But that's no reason not to go! You *love* him, right?" asked Casey.

"Yeah."

"Then you should be with him." Casey sighed. "Look, I have no idea what his drunken speech was about—probably *nothing*, and if it's *something*, you'll sort it out."

Piper giggled. "Since when are *you* offering love advice, Oprah?"

"Uh, since Ben proved he wasn't a liar—" Casey caught himself. "I mean, since he proved he knew Mark Keegan and he stepped up to save Maggie." He turned to Riley. "Ben's crazy about you. You just have to talk to him and be honest with one another."

"I'm trying to! I can only leave Alex so many messages asking for him to call me."

"You should talk face to face. Tech is great, but there's nothing like an in-person conversation." Casey waved a cookie at his laptop's camera. "*Amiright*, Pip Pip Hooray?"

"Argh! Our Monday cookie ritual sucks as a spectator."

Casey's phone buzzed a second time and Riley caught a name on the screen.

"Uh, Case…who's Sophie?"

"Sophie?" asked Piper. "We don't know a Sophie."

"Ah, *we* don't, but I do." Casey's cheeks began to flush.

"Ohmygawd!" Piper screeched. "You had SEX!"

"No, I didn't!"

"But you want to!" said Piper.

"It's not like that! Well...maybe." His cheeks tinged bright pink. "I don't know!"

"Wait a minu—is that extra box of cookies for her?" Riley sat up. "Do you have a date *tonight*?"

He scratched his nose. "Yeah...our second."

"Aw, Case." Riley gave him a hug.

"When did *this* start?" asked Piper.

Casey let go of Riley. "I met her in Duane Reade...buying hand sanitizer."

"Really?" Riley squeezed his arm. "She's a germophobe, too?"

"Hardly. Sophie's doing an infectious disease fellowship at the Langone Medical Center."

"Noooooo!" Piper doubled over with laughter, swallowing her gum in the process.

"She hates Harry Styles, too..."

Piper fought through a coughing fit. "Oh, fuck! Stop! I c-can't—ahh, you're really taking a risk with this one, Case."

"I think she might be worth it. I think it's time, you know? Watching you guys move away and try new things...I've realized I should, too. Being hurt in the past isn't a good enough reason not to try again."

"Well, I'm not going to monopolize you if Sophie's waiting," said Riley. "I'll pop to the washroom and then head to Mom's. I've still got packing to do. Back in a sec, Pip!" She stood and left the room.

"Case..." Piper leaned in. "Is she gone?"

"Yeah."

"So, Sophie—she's real?"

"Yep, she's real." He chuckled.

"And does this mean...?"

"It does." Casey exhaled heavily. "It's been four years—three with Josh, nearly a year with Ben. Riley's never going to see me in that way. Seeing her so happy with a *nice* guy like Ben…it's helped me make peace with it. I'm over the whole unrequited love thing, but please, Pip, keep your promise and don't say anything."

Piper winked. "You're good, sweetie. I swore on Kermit's life, remember?"

"Yeah. I think you'd like Sophie. She's fun, loves British TV, and dogs."

"Case, this is great. You'll make an awesome boyfriend—I just know it."

"Thanks." He smiled. "I really want things to work out for Ben and Riley. I'm gonna miss her a lot…but I want to see my friend happy."

Riley returned to the room, catching his last few words. "What friend's that, then?"

"You, you silly moo." Casey laughed and playfully punched her arm.

Riley sat back on her heels, her large suitcase stuffed to the brim with clothes, favorite novels, and two photo books of memories: the one Ben gave her at Christmas, and a going-away present from Maggie. Her smaller pink case, the one Ben had taken by mistake a year ago, was flipped open with just enough room remaining for Puffin. *I'll have to sit on both these beasts to get them zipped up.*

Maggie hovered nearby, too restless to sit. "Is there anything else you need, sweetheart? I can make you sandwiches in the morning? Airplane food is always hit or miss, right?"

Riley unzipped her backpack, checking its contents again. "Hmm, not sure, Mom. My stomach keeps flipping. I'm so nervous."

"That's just butterflies! You know what, I'll make you some anyway. You don't have to eat them." Maggie ran a hand through her auburn pixie cut. The short style suited her so beautifully, she had decided not to grow her hair back to shoulder length. "When you get to London—" She stopped herself. "Listen to me, *'When you get to London'*...oh, Riley! Your first transatlantic flight—to a job in England—at the BBC! Proud mom alert!"

I couldn't be more homesick, and I haven't even left yet. "Thanks, Mom." Riley took a deep breath. *We've never been apart. You've always been a ferry ride, a bus trip, a local phone call away.* "California always felt like a big leap, but this...being on my own..." Her eyes began to sting. *I knew I was gonna crack some-time.* "What if you get sick again? I'll be so far away."

"Oh, honey." Maggie swooped down, giving Riley a hug. "I haven't felt this good in seven years! And London won't feel so far with FaceTime and texting. I'll be with you every step of the way." She kissed her daughter's temple. "It's your time, Riley. It's time to put yourself first."

"But I'll miss you so much..."

"I'll miss you, too, but I'm more excited than sad. You'll see everything you've dreamed of and more. The world is finally get-ting to meet Riley Hope, and it's going to love her." She brushed her daughter's hair from her eyes. "You won't feel homesick for long—not in London, not with Ben! You're going to have the time of your life!"

Riley hadn't told her mom about Ben's St. Paddy's meltdown or his drunken claim that Maggie would 'never forgive him'. If she didn't know what Ben was talking about herself, there was no point worrying her mom about it.

"I hope so."

"I *know* so!" Maggie sniffed away her own tears and smiled, giving Riley a squeeze. "Now, c'mon—let's check you in online and find space for Puffin."

Sixty-Eight

London, five days later

The double-decker buses, the iconic red phone boxes...for Riley, London was like a postcard come to life. It was also rainy, extremely crowded, and lonely, but when in Rome... *Stiff upper lip, 'Keep Calm and Carry On', and all that bollocks, as Casey would say.* Tightening her scarf as the sun played hide and seek with the clouds, Riley tried to ignore the jitters in her stomach. *I'll make my time here count, regardless of what's to come.*

Walking with purpose along a southeast London street, she pulled her phone from a new Strand tote and double-checked her directions. Three days into her life abroad, her track record for getting around was laughable. Despite living only ten minutes away from Elstree Studios, she got lost on her first day and got turned around heading home on her second. *Thank God, it's Saturday and I can start fresh—in more ways than one.*

Laughter and music coaxed her around a corner. A bustling market tucked between a railway viaduct and a high wall sparked a surge of adrenaline through her veins. *Is this it?* Her already racing pulse beat faster underneath her parka. *But the sign hanging above the entrance says 'Ropewalk'...?* Strolling toward the lively hangout with its colorful flags and bunting waving over the heads of hungry shoppers, she spotted a chalkboard leaning against a table: MALTBY STREET MARKET: Saturday 10-5, Sunday 11-4. *Ben's here...somewhere.*

Piper had told Riley stories about London's outdoor markets but being immersed in one was a delight for the senses. *So many accents! And it smells SO GOOD!* Sizzling steaks, grilled cheese, freshly made waffles drizzled with maple syrup. People crammed the narrow alley and flocked around its tables, their vendors peddling artisan coffee, Scotch eggs, Japanese gyoza, tandoori breads, and so much more.

Standing here, it's so real now. Am I doing the right thing? Surprising him?

On Tuesday, the day of her departure, it'd still felt like a good idea. Ben had finally reached out via text. He brushed off St. Patrick's Day as "a bender gone off the rails" and apologized, swearing off drink for the foreseeable and saying how mortified he was for getting in such a state. He claimed he could "hardly remember a thing," so whatever might have required her (or Maggie's) forgiveness never came up—and Riley didn't push him, afraid if she found out, she'd be a tear-soaked mess on her long overnight flight. Since her arrival in London Wednesday morning, they had continued to text, but she'd declined his FaceTime requests, blaming long hours at work—a white lie that kept her location secret...until now.

Zigzagging through the throng, Riley searched for Ben's adorable bedhead hair, his easy smile, his 'Love Bites' table sign, but no luck. *Did I miss him somehow?* She dodged preoccupied eaters with messy burgers and got stuck behind a large group of slow-walking tourists devouring shrimp po' boys, their every...plodding...step stoking her agitation. *Jeez, can I get around them?* Squeezing past, a cheeky laugh stole her breath.

It's him... Her heart, beating out of control, catapulted into her throat.

She darted through a break in the crowd, following the sweet sound and...found him, half-hidden beneath a gray Tottenham Hotspur beanie with a cluster of customers swarming his table. *Oh, Ben! You look...so well. So happy. So gorgeous.* Afraid he'd spot her, Riley ducked behind two tall guys reading a London map, keeping her presence secret as she watched Ben smile and laugh and hand over baked goods in exchange for colorful British five- and ten-pound notes. *I'm so proud of you! Look, you've got customers— lots of 'em!* A heady rush of memories came flooding back: her hands lost in his messy hair, his kisses tenderly tracing a path down her neck, his promise in Central Park to always be there for her.

But then a tall blonde and her two friends were served next, and Ben dialed up his charisma to eleven, playing to his female audience with smiles, compliments, and offers of free samples. The women were all over him, touching his arm and complimenting him, their obvious interest in her boyfriend reminding her of St. Patrick's Day and those words that kept her up at night.

"It just happened...forgive me?"

But *what* happened? The question gnawed at her relentlessly.

Purchases in hand, the flirty women reluctantly moved on from his table, and Riley got a clear view. Ben, comfy in a puffer vest, hoodie, jeans, and an apron, used the lull in business to reorganize his dwindling stock: a few cookies and a lone slice of raspberry cake. Riley snickered. *Nice blue plastic gloves, Ben. Very fetching.* He turned away and popped open a container of something decadent, his back to the market's foot traffic and Riley.

You can't stand here forever. Talk to him. Stepping out from behind the human wall, she approached his table, clearing her throat.

"All right, love?" Back still turned, Ben spoke over his shoulder and sliced through a pan of cakey brownies. "What can I get ya?"

It's now or never. She swept her hair from her face and smiled nervously. "Do you have anything with *American* peanut butter? I hear it's the dog's bollocks."

Ben froze mid-slice. "Riley...?" he whispered, turning around.

Their eyes met.

Ben. Her breath caught in her chest.

Dropping the knife, a smile took off across his cheeks, his eyes disappearing into happy-go-lucky crescents. "It's YOU! Holy sh—" A plastic-gloved hand flew to his mouth as he gave her a lingering once-over. "Blimey O'Riley, you're *really* here!"

"Hi Ben." Her voice cracked as she spoke his name.

"What the hell—c'mere, gorgeous!" He clambered out from behind the table, removing the barrier between them. "My Hope!" Wrapping his arms around her waist, Ben lifted her up.

Riley clutched his shoulders, the feel of him flooding her heart with bittersweet joy.

"I can't believe I'm actually *holding* you. I just…oh, bollocks, just *kiss me*, Hope!" He held her tight and pressed his lips to hers. She reciprocated, but her body language signaled the kiss would go no further.

I can't…not until I know what's going on.

Ben set her down and Riley let go, his happy demeanor fading as he sensed something was wrong. "So, I'm completely gob-smacked…and confused, too." He chuckled nervously, his hands falling from her waist. They aimlessly flitted along the knotted belt of his apron. "Yesterday you were texting about delays on the Staten Island Ferry and now you're here! Did you just arrive?"

"No, Wednesday."

"Wednesday?" His forehead creased.

"I texted you from work, from the BBC."

"What?" His face wavered between a smile and a frown. "They changed their minds?"

"No, it was mine all along." Riley bit her cheek.

"So, why'd you…fib?"

She winced. "I wanted to surprise you…but after St. Patrick's Day, I didn't know if *this* was a good idea." She looked away. "I still don't…"

"Why?" Ben tilted his head, trying to meet her eyes. "Riles, what's happened?'"

He's asking ME? The fucking nerve. Her nose began to tickle. *Hold it together.* "Funny you say that…I was going to ask you the same thing."

A customer stopped at Ben's table and glanced around, searching for assistance.

Shit. I knew I shouldn't have come.

"Fuck," Ben uttered under his breath, rubbing his chin with his forearm. "Riley, *sorry*—just gimme…" He smiled tightly at the man and slipped back behind his table.

Fighting tears, Riley stared at her boots until, one raspberry cake slice and four brownie sales later, Ben's undivided attention was hers again.

He reached out to her. "Riley, let's—"

"No." *I can't wait any longer.* "What were you afraid to tell me on St. Patrick's Day?"

Avoiding her gaze, he hugged his stomach and ducked his head like he was bracing himself.

"That wasn't the *drink* talking, Ben! You were upset, and not about some cat biting you or the Waterstones course—it was like you needed a brewery's worth of liquid courage to speak to me." Her jaw and shoulders tensed.

He slowly nodded and chewed his bottom lip.

"You kept apologizing, saying you were lonely, that it was a mistake to move in with Spencer…and then you asked me to *forgive* you." She gulped for breath. "You said *Mom* wouldn't forgive you." Eyes damp with tears, she whispered, "So, what did you do, Ben? Did you sleep with Spencer?"

"*What?*" He looked up, meeting her eyes again, his dark lashes blinking rapidly. "*Riley.*" He raised his hands to cup her face but remembered his food-service gloves and peeled them off, his face softening into an uneasy grin. "Spencer's a university friend. She's like a sister to me." He dropped the gloves on his table. "I swear, we've never snogged or slept together. That would be…weird."

Never? "But…what about New Year's, you and her on FaceTime…"

"Ohhh, *that!*" He scrunched his nose. "That was me, acting up a storm. I was playing her boyfriend to save her from a handsy bloke for the millionth time. It's something we first did back in uni—she asked Mark and me to help her get rid of some loser in the students' union bar. Mark already had his arm around some girl. Me, on the other hand…" He scratched his chin. "I can't just stand there and do nothing, but you *knew* that, right…?"

The tension in her body eased slightly. "I feel like such an idiot."

"Don't." He smiled. "But is it wrong that I find it hot—you being jealous?"

Riley rolled her eyes.

"Look, I'd never cheat on you, Riles. Never. You've got my heart—you've gotta know that, okay? No matter…what happens…" He lifted her hands to his lips and kissed them gently, his eyes closed.

Confusion and concern swirled in Riley's head. *I believe you, Ben—completely—and my heart's yours, too, but you're keeping something from me…I can FEEL it.* She pulled her hands away and tugged on the straps of his apron in frustration. "So, what am I supposed to *forgive?*"

His face fell. "It's…Christ, I don't know how to tell you…"

Oh God, tell me WHAT, Ben?

He nodded solemnly. "I have to…"

Her stomach tightened.

"Will you come with me?"

"Where? *Now?* But you're working—"

"Mo will watch my table." Ben turned to an older guy working

449

the next stall. "Mate? I've gotta go. Something's come up."

Mo eyed Riley and flashed a toothy smile. "I bet it has…go on, get out of here!" He waved Ben off and dropped several falafels into a bubbling pot of hot oil. "I'll look after things. See you tomorrow."

"Cheers, mate. I owe you one." Ben removed his apron and stuffed it in his backpack. He tossed it over his shoulder and bundled half of his cookies into a paper bag. "For the journey." He clasped Riley's hand.

"Where are we going?"

"Paddington Station—to catch a train. I'll explain everything when we get there, I promise."

"At Paddington Station?"

"No, at our destination—Reading."

"But…wait—how far is that?"

"Uh, thirty, forty miles, maybe? Tube and train—won't be more than an hour. You'll have lots of time to catch me up." He kissed her cheek. "Tell me about where you're staying, this cool job you scored…I want to know everything, okay?"

So do I, Ben. So do I…

SIXTY-NINE

As the express train roared through the countryside, Riley filled every awkward silence with stories about her roommate and her first two days at the BBC. She told him about her mega-accomplished female boss and the welcome flowers waiting on her desk. Ben nodded and smiled and asked thoughtful questions, but his mind kept veering off track as they traveled towards his truth.

My hands are clammy and I'm sweating like mad under this puffer vest. Riley's been sweet and hasn't said anything—God, I couldn't love her more, but will she feel the same when she finds out? I thought I'd have more time...I'm not ready for this, and I don't know if she is either. She seems happy, chattering away, but she's talking way too fast and is stress-eating cookies.

"...Ben's all silent and closed off now."

Eh? Hearing Riley speak his name, Ben's attention swerved back to his girlfriend. He shook his head, clearing the cobwebs. "Sorry, who?" *Me?*

Riley brushed cookie crumbs from her lips. "Big Ben."

"Oh, *right*. Yeah, he's being restored." Ben looked out the window, the sensation of the train slowing down, teasing the butterflies in his belly. "You won't hear his bongs or see him without scaffolding, not for four years."

"That sucks." She half-laughed, nervously.

"Uh, this stop's ours..." He let go of her hand and fumbled in his pocket, pulling out their tickets.

Riley stashed the bag of half-eaten cookies in her tote.

"Here..." He handed her two tickets. "The top one you need to exit at street level. Feed it into the barrier and it'll open. The second one is your return trip."

"Okay, cool." She glanced at the orange and yellow tickets, spotting 'Reading Stations' in a smudged computerized font.

Leaving their overheated train carriage, the midafternoon sunshine was no match for the biting wind and plunging temperature outside. Riley shivered and fought with her parka's stubborn zipper as she copied Ben's long strides, hurrying across the station courtyard. She yanked sharply on the zipper's pull and lost her return ticket to the crisp March breeze.

"Shit!" She chased after it, leaving Ben alone at the station's taxi line.

"Riley, it's okay...I'll buy another." Ben pressed his lips tight and leaned into the open front window of a black cab, giving the driver their destination. He reached for the door's handle as Riley returned, shaking her head.

"Sorry, I'm such a klutz."

She's nervous. She's not the only one. He opened the door, letting her climb in first.

The driver joined the Saturday afternoon traffic and left central Reading. Neither Ben nor Riley spoke. Ben fidgeted with the knotted leather bracelet on his right wrist, the healed fracture aching from the damp. Riley watched town center businesses, narrow streets, and small terrace houses morph into suburban shopping plazas, tree-lined roads, and large semi-detached homes.

"Oh." Ben sat up suddenly, leaning toward the opening in the clear partition separating the cabbie from his passengers. "Mate, can we stop here?" He turned to Riley. "Won't be a minute."

The cab pulled into a gas station and Ben dashed out the door, picking up several skinny bouquets of daisies from a bucket outside the kiosk. While he paid, Riley reapplied her lipstick and pulled her hair into a neat ponytail, still unsure where they were headed.

Jeez, could they look any cheaper? Ben hopped back in the taxi,

452

handing Riley two modest bunches. "Just a little...something."

"They're pretty." A sweet happiness brightened her face, erasing her confused pout. "Thank you."

Shit petrol station flowers, no proper kisses—this is the most awkward reunion ever, and it's not her fault...it's all on me. Heart pounding through his chest, Ben shook his head, his hand clasping two identical bouquets. *I wish we could do this over—do it all over.* He pulled his phone from the pocket of his vest.

Riley's eyes fell to the cellophane-wrapped flowers crinkling in his hand. "Who are those for?"

2:45 p.m. We're good for time. He stuffed his phone back in his vest. "My mum."

"Your *mom*?!" Eyebrows raised, Riley's grin grew and nudged her voice up almost an octave. "Oh! I was *hoping* we might be going there!"

Ben slumped against the window, his eyes darting from one impressive detached home to another, their mature leafless trees guarding the upscale road. *I wish we were going anywhere but there.*

Watching the increasingly luxurious houses fly past, Riley took in her jeans, old parka, and worn sneakers. A self-deprecating chuckle slipped into a whisper. "I wish I'd dressed up—" She frowned and dove into her tote, her fingers finding something that reunited her cheeks with her smile. "Oh, I totally forgot..."

"Forgot?" Ben glanced over as Riley pulled out a plastic bag...with flats. She set the shoes down on the cab's floor.

"I usually leave these under my desk at work, but I'm so new there, it felt...oh, I dunno..." Nervously rambling, she bent down, tugging off her socks and sneakers. "I forgot they were in here. At least I'll look a little more presentable now."

"You look fine, Riley, really, you don't need to..." Ben pulled off his wool hat, dumped it in his half-zipped backpack, and patted

453

down his hair, but it stubbornly flicked up again. His hand skidded across his forehead as the taxi drove through a set of stone gates and down a long driveway. *Shit. I'm burning up.*

Leaning over, Riley's head hovered at her knees. "I *hope* I look fine!" She slipped her bare feet into the flats and rubbed away a scuff mark.

I need air. I can't...breathe... A thickness plagued Ben's throat, not helping his already queasy stomach. He stared at the familiar landscape of scattered brown leaves, bare trees swaying in the wind, and the winter-scarred grass, the hint of sunshine chased away by clouds. He tilted toward the cab's partition. "You can stop here, mate."

The taxi rolled to a stop and Riley stuffed her sneakers in the plastic bag before placing it into the tote. She lifted her head, her eyes drifting from Ben stuffing a ten-pound note through the hole in the cab's partition to the wilted flowers and weathered gravestones waiting outside.

SEVENTY

What? No...no! It can't be...

Stepping out of the cab, Riley trembled, the cellophane surrounding her flowers rustling against her parka in the brisk breeze. "Ben? It's not..." Words she never thought she'd say choked her throat. "Your *mom...?*"

He nodded, closing the car's door behind them. The slam unnerved several crows loitering in nearby trees, their abrasive *caw-caw-caw* filling the stilted silence between the couple as the cab headed back toward the main road. Ben swept his hair from his eyes and wrapped his arm around Riley's shoulder, guiding her off the cement path. A warm breath left his lips in a shudder.

The safe, familiar feel of Ben holding her close was of little comfort. Walking through row upon row of moss-covered gravestones, her eyes, dazed with disbelief, filled with tears. Her shoes sank into the spongy sod with each fraught step. *This is every child's nightmare.* The tingling in her nose intensified with the cemetery's earthy smell of damp, freshly turned dirt. *Poor Ben!* "When...when did it happen—?" Her voice broke.

Ben bowed his head, staring at his boots scuffing over the flattened grass. "Riley, I wanted to tell you so badly..."

Is this really happening? Her body felt stiff, uncooperative, like she had forgotten how to walk. *His mom...dead. That's why he canceled his St. Patrick's visit, why he seemed lost, got so drunk. Why didn't he say anything? I wish he'd told me!* Gathering tears stung her eyes. "Were you with her...when...was she sick?"

"She's here..." he whispered, stopping in front of a modest gray headstone, simple in design, without cherubs or crosses, and

455

dwarfed by its more expensive neighbors. A burnt tea-light candle in a small mason jar lay tipped over in front.

Shannon Catherine Weir

Oh...! The sight of his mother's name carved into stone felt like someone had reached into her chest and ripped out her heart. *It's true. Oh God, it's true.* Hot tears spilled down Riley's cheeks. *His dear mom.* She leaned into Ben, who remained stoic, but the slight quiver of his chin told Riley he was barely holding himself together. "Oh, Ben," she whispered into the wind. "I'm *so* sorry!"

He wiped his nose and let her go, sinking to his knees. He dropped his backpack on the grass and righted the little candle then removed his flowers from the cellophane.

Riley leaned forward, her eyes drifting past Ben's hair waving messily in the breeze. *He looks so alone. I should've been here for him.* She slowly read the engraving as he lovingly placed the daisies on his mom's grave.

Shannon Catherine Weir
April 18, 1975 – September 6, 2008
Beloved mother of Benjamin
"Love you until the last star fades"

So beautiful, so Ben. She traced upward again. *April 1975 to September 2008—wait. 2008? But...* Her breath caught in her throat. She looked at the grass under her flats—grass that hadn't been dug up for some time. *She didn't die recently?* A chill spread through her core, slowing the arrival of fresh tears. "Ben...your mom died...*eleven years* ago?"

His watery eyes darted over his shoulder. "*Riley...*" Ben stood up, his fingers curling under the bottom of his vest.

"You lied? I don't underst—you said—" Her stare narrowed as she stuttered. "You said she was *alive*! Why...why would you *lie* about that?"

Ben met her confused, pained glare, his chest chasing breaths. "I knew it was wrong, but..." A wince pulled his head back. "I was trying to...protect you."

"Protect me?!"

His hands fled to the zipper on his vest and up into his hair, where they roamed and tugged. "Look, everything I told you, about my dad, moving from Scotland, Mr. C—all of it's true, but me and Mum..." Closing his eyes, he exhaled into a whisper. "I couldn't..." His lashes flickered open slowly. "Look, I need to tell you now...tell you everything. *Please*, Riley. Hear me out?"

Anger and sadness whirled in her head. She couldn't look at him, her gaze dropping to Shannon's gravestone: 'Beloved mother of Benjamin'. Her heart ached, revisiting those words. *A twist of fate—that's all that separates me and Ben. If we never met... wouldn't I be in his shoes? Wouldn't I be heartbroken, laying flowers beneath 'Beloved mother of Riley'?* She slowly looked up, meeting Ben's pleading eyes. *He needs compassion, not a fight. He's listened to me...so many times. I owe him that.* Her tight-lipped "okay" gave him the go ahead.

"Thank you." He exhaled, rubbing his forehead in relief. "Me and Mum...we were *just* like you and Maggie. She was my world and I was hers. We only had each other, so we were inseparable. Even when I was, like, nine or ten, I'd hold her hand, give her a hug at the school gates. I got teased sometimes, other lads called me a mummy's boy, but sod it." He shrugged. "There are worse things than being uncool. She was my best friend. It was me and her versus the world, especially after my father made it clear he had no interest..."

I know that feeling well. Riley nodded.

"I loved reading with her. Every Friday lunchtime, she'd go to the library. She'd come home at night, books tucked under her arm, all for me: atlases, books about space, books about animals from faraway places. I think she spotted I had reading problems pretty early on. She took loads of time with me, going over each word. When I was diagnosed with dyslexia, she said it wasn't anything to be ashamed of, said it just meant I had to decipher each word one at a time. The specialist I saw told Mum that, like a lot of kids with dyslexia, I was a sensitive kid—*empathetic* was the word he used, but I didn't know what it meant. Mum said it was this amazing superpower—I could see *through people*. I listen well. I pick up little clues about people's feelings that someone else would miss. I get it now, but back then, I'd no idea what they were on about with their 'compassionate listener' bollocks."

"It's not bollocks—you *are* a great listener."

"Shame it didn't impress the school bullies..." He pressed his lips together. "Mum told me over and over, *'You're just different, Ben, and different is great!'*"

Pulling her coat tighter against the wind, Riley's expression softened. "She sounds wonderful."

"Yeah. She always loved me...even when I was naughty. She'd tell me off, I'd apologize for whatever I'd got up to, then she'd give me a cuddle. One time, she dragged me into the kitchen to help her bake. I thought it was punishment, but the more I mucked about, squeezing brown sugar and butter between my fingers, making a right old mess, I began to love it." His face lit up. "I'd look *forward* to it. I think it made her happy, us making brownies and biscuits together." His fingers crept up his right wrist and hooked his bracelet. "Mum always wanted her own bake shop..." Looking away, Ben blew out his cheeks, buying time.

His market stall? A lump grew in Riley's throat.

"When I was twelve..." He rubbed his eyes with the heel of his hand. "One day, I got in and she was already there, sat on the sofa, waiting. Mum *never* came home early. Her eyes were puffy, but her makeup was perfect, like she had just reapplied it. I-I wasn't fooled—I knew she'd been crying and wondered if my father had done something to hurt her again. The year before, Mum had sent him pictures of me in the school play, but he'd sent them back unopened. I shrugged it off, but Mum...I *hated* how he made her feel unimportant. I went over and gave her a big hug and..." Ben's breath hitched. "That's when she told me."

You never forget that moment. Tears stung Riley's eyes. *Mom waiting at home, after school...my arms full with my science project, an untouched coffee in front of her. Her words suffocating the room, extinguishing the light, shattering my heart...*

"We clung to each other." Tears glistened in Ben's eyes and his Adam's apple bobbed as he swallowed heavily. "I thought cancer was something old people got, not Mum. She said, *'We'll have to be apart, but only for a wee while, Benjamin. The group home will be like a sleepover with kids your age.'* But I didn't want to hang with some rando kids...I wanted Mum."

Riley stepped closer, clasping his hand. "You must've been so scared."

He choked back tears. "I couldn't stop shaking...I-I *begged* her to let me stay, promised I'd be good, promised I'd look after her, told her *'We don't need anyone else.'* She burst into tears and said, *'But Benjamin, love—this time, we do.'* I buried my face in her neck and sobbed my heart out. I've never felt more helpless."

"Ben, I'm so sorry." Riley squeezed his hand and sniffed back tears. "Did...did they begin treatments?"

"Yeah. I bawled the first time I saw her after surgery: part relief, part shock. She was totally out of it. Her cheeks were gray. There were tubes everywhere..."

Riley nodded. "It's so scary."

459

Ben pushed his hair off his forehead. "Mum opened her eyes and smiled when she saw me, though, so I held her hand until she fell back asleep. The next visit was better. She told me to hop onto the bed so we could snuggle while I read to her about planets and stars. That became our thing, me reading to her, even when she left hospital and started chemo treatments. It was *me* looking after *her*...for a few hours anyway. I was only allowed to visit twice a week.

"Before Halloween, they let me move back home with her. It was the happiest day of my life. Mum was mine again. We baked and played her old records—it was perfect...and then, it wasn't. She got sick again...ten months later. I went back to the group home. Mum went..." The words caught in his throat. "Into palliative care. I'd cry into my pillow, scared of *that* phone call in the middle of the night, I missed her so badly, but Mum never came home again, and neither did I." His voice trembled with tears.

What does that do to a little kid? "Ben..." Riley pulled him into a tight hug, her tears falling quickly.

"I wasn't with her when she died." He wept over her shoulder. "I was in fucking PE class and the headmaster pulled me out and marched me back to his office. I *knew*. I knew before the social worker said a word. I *felt* it. I felt like something sharp had ripped my heart open...and all the love and everything good spilled out."

Riley cradled his head with her hands. "Did you...say good-bye?"

"No. They wouldn't let me see her." He pulled back from their embrace and more tears slipped down his cheeks. "The social worker drove me home and said to grab what I needed because I couldn't live there anymore. She had brought Mum's suitcase from the hospice—the pink dotty one. I was in shock. I had no clue what to do. I flipped it open and found Mum's photo album, my stuffed turtle, some clothes. I buried my face in her cardigan and that's when I lost it. Her scent…brought her back to me." Letting Riley go, he dug in his pocket and found a tissue. "I couldn't stop crying. I scooped up the rest of her clothes on the floor and curled up in a ball with them. I don't know how long I was like that. The social worker came back and told me we had to go. All I could think of was packing as much of Mum's stuff as possible. I put the clothes in the case and opened her old trunk." He wiped his nose and took a shuddering breath, his tears slowing their descent. "She hid her 'wee treasures' in there. I found the eighties t-shirts, her notebook full of recipes, some jewelry." He lifted the cuff of his hoodie and his thin leather bracelet slid to his wrist.

"It was hers?" Riley touched it gently. "That's why you never take it off…"

He nodded, pulling his sleeve down. "There was one other thing that meant the world to her. She'd save it for best…that silver bracelet with a puffin charm…"

Riley's mouth fell open, her eyes darting to her own wrist. "This?"

"Yeah, Mum brought it back from a school trip in northern Scotland." Ben fidgeted, ripping apart the tissue in his hand. "You love puffins so much, I wanted you to have him…Mum would've, too."

"Oh, Ben…" Holding the little silver bird between her fingers, Riley felt the knots in her shoulders and chest release.

Trembling in the cold wind, Ben's sad smile faded. "I ran into my bedroom, grabbed some clothes, and found the last birthday card she gave me, but that's all I took. The social worker said we had to get going and she'd make sure my books and Mr. C's telescope were sent on to me…but I never saw them or the flat again. I found out later, social had called my father, hoping to place me there, but he didn't return their messages…I had no one."

He was just a kid…with nobody left to love him. A deep ache overwhelmed Riley's chest.

Ben nudged the grass with his boot. "It was raining...the day of her service. It was in the crematorium, over there. The vicar was kind; he asked me about her. Then he stood up and said some nice words, how she was a 'great mother to Benjamin Fagan,' how she was with the angels now." Ben stared off into the distance. "The thing was, I was the only one there, if you don't count my two social workers and a lovely nurse who treated Mum at the hospice."

That fear... Riley swallowed heavily. *Being entirely alone...I thought about it all the time while Mom was sick, but Ben has LIVED it.*

"I rattled around the foster care system until I turned eighteen. I lived with four different families—"

Riley's eyebrows lifted. "Four?"

"Four years, four homes." He sniffed and stuffed the shredded tissue in his pocket. "The first foster parents hit me with a belt. The next home was with a thirty-something woman who wasn't around much—she was just in it for the payments from social services, I think. So, I fended for myself, having cereal almost every night."

"You must've been so lonely, Ben."

"Yeah, and angry. I missed Mum so badly, I couldn't stand it. I ran away a few times, got hauled in by the cops for underage drinking. I smoked joints, had sex...didn't have many friends. When stuff went missing at school, I'd get blamed by the teachers. Back then, I *swear* I didn't steal, but I soon figured, 'Well, if they're blaming me anyway, might as well get something out of it.' I knew it was wrong, but..." He shrugged. "When I was sixteen, I joined foster family number three, in Windsor. They were an older couple, proper strict: no computer games, TV for only an hour a night after homework, household chores. They laid down rules, but it felt like they *cared*, you know? I liked them. We got along pretty well after a few months. I overheard them talking one night about *maybe* adopting me…"

"But they *didn't*?"

"Their next-door neighbor's daughter…" Ben glanced away. "We…had sex a few times. She got pregnant. I got blamed." He looked up, gauging Riley's reaction.

He's got a kid? She gripped her flowers, trying not to look alarmed.

"They told me having sex at sixteen made me a 'bad influence' on their *own* kids…" He shook his head. "I told them I'd been careful, it couldn't be mine, but they weren't having any of it. They called social services, sent me packing. Of course, the real father came forward when the baby was born, but by then I was already with foster family number four. I kept my head down, studied, went to my drama school audition, and counted the days 'til I turned eighteen. I hightailed it on my birthday.

"I know fostering helps lots of kids, but when no one wants you…you turn *inward*. All I had was my memories…and grief. I was told I'd 'get over it', but grief isn't something you get over, or move on from. Grief sticks. It finds its way into your bones and changes you. I felt like I'd lost myself. I wasn't Shannon's son anymore. If Mum could've seen me, she wouldn't have recognized me." He squinted into the sky, the sun sneaking out from behind a gray cloud. "That August I moved to London for uni, met Mark— the first real friend I had in a bloody long time. Through him I met Spencer and…*other* girls." Ben began raking the toe of his boot through a pile of windblown leaves. "I think I was looking for someone who might love me, but…I was pretty fucked up. I confused lust and sex with love. I thought if they fancied me, they *cared* for me. Took me a while, but I realized the girls most interested in drunk, no-strings sex weren't going to be there when I felt lost or couldn't afford bus fare." He tilted his head, meeting Riley's sympathetic stare. "It triggered those old feelings of not being loveable, you know? And if I felt anything resembling love, I didn't trust it. So, I'd have sex and move on, ditch them before they ditched me. Why stick around for rejection? I've had more than my fill." He ran a hand over his frown. "I'm a bit ashamed, looking back. I wasn't doing it to be an insensitive dick. I was desperate for companionship, even if I didn't know their names the next morning..."

I called him a fuckboy. Riley's stomach soured. "Ben, I'm sorry I called you a—"

"Fuckboy? If it quacks like a duck..." The corners of his lips turned up. "No, it's okay. I own it." He looked away. "I know it sounds weird, but I think I forgot how to care about anyone, or how it feels *to be* loved..." His eyes found her again. "And then, this pretty New Yorker stole my suitcase..."

"Uh, you *know* you've got that backward," said Riley, in on the joke.

He smiled lovingly. "You were like this rare, beautiful comet lighting up the dark sky. You helped me find my way again... helped me find *myself* again. You saved me."

Her eyes dropped to the ground and her grin broke free, his kind words and the feel of his unwavering gaze raising a warm blush to her cheeks.

"If you'd left me in the shitty strip club that night, God knows where I'd be...what I'd have done." He reached up, freeing a rogue leaf from her ponytail. "I owe you *so* much..."

Lifting her chin, she caught his eyes. "Well, I owe you more— Mom and I both do."

A wistful look washed over his face. "That day up on the rock in Central Park, you went to get ice creams and were laughing with the vendor. I remember looking down at you and thinking I could never get tired of that smile. I pulled out my phone and saw Maggie's crowdfunding page on Facebook. It floored me. I didn't know what to do or say. All that fear, the helplessness I had when I lost my mum, it all came flooding back..."

Riley gripped Ben's hand tightly as he continued.

"I know it was stupid, but I thought it was the right thing at the time, just a little white lie. I wanted you to know I'd been through something similar, but I couldn't bring myself to tell you the truth. I didn't want to be *that* person—the idiot who tells someone in the middle of the battle, 'Oh, yeah, my mum had cancer. She had surgery, chemo, but none of it worked and she died.'"

He refused to be a Grim Reaper—he was just trying to protect my heart.

"You didn't need to hear my unhappy ending, Riley. I wanted you to keep fighting for her, still have hope. So...I said Mum had *beaten* her cancer, because—God's honest truth—I wanted that for you and Maggie, more than anything in the world..."

A surge of warmth—gratitude—filled her chest. Riley pulled him into a tight embrace, fresh tears in her eyes. "Ben, I don't like lying, but..." *He didn't do it maliciously; he knows what it's like—losing hope when the odds are against you.* "I understand why you did it. You were sparing me more hurt. You were trying to be kind..."

Ben held her in his arms, his head on her shoulder. "I think...sometimes...it's easier to help someone else with their pain than to deal with your own, you know?" Pulling back, a gentle smile softened Ben's face again. "And I was already falling in love with you—so badly. That mad feeling...it knocked me sideways." He laughed, playfully. "I was giddy and dopey, wanting to be around you all the bloody time. I'd fight dragons—*NO!*—I'd pick up *spiders* for you and..." His grin faded, a hushed tone imbuing his voice. "Lie about the worst day of my life...if it would help lift you up." A sigh passed his lips as he let her go and slid his hand around hers, his thumb strumming her skin. "Riley, I love you *so* much, you know that, right? You're my everything."

And you're mine. A rush of goose bumps rose underneath her parka. All the tender moments they'd shared, cherished in memory, wrapped around her heart. She gave his hand a squeeze. "I love you, too."

Ben squeezed it back. "That day, when you told me Maggie's blood type? I know we'd only been going out for a little while, but...I can't really explain it. It's like I *knew* I could help her, and it was maybe, you know...a second chance. There was nothing I could do for my mum, but I felt like maybe I was meant to meet you and Maggie when I did. Sounds daft, I know..."

"No, it doesn't." Riley's offered an understanding smile.

Ben slowly shook his head in frustration. "I didn't mean to do any harm, but the longer it went on, the lie sorta took on a life of its own. I was afraid you'd dump me the second I told you the truth. When you called to celebrate six months post-op, I behaved terribly, and I'm so sorry. I was actually over the moon that you might be moving here for work, but I was afraid you'd ask to meet Mum if you came. It all started to eat away at me. So, I decided if you didn't get the job, I'd tell you and Maggie in June, face to face when I visited New York, and if you did come over, I swore I'd do the right thing and bring you...here." He glanced at his mother's gravestone, his face crinkling into a worried frown. "I can only imagine what Maggie will think when she finds out. If she doesn't want anything to do with me, I'll understand—"

"Ben, it's *okay*." Riley released his hand and stepped closer, her heart pounding, screaming in her chest—*just kiss him!*—but she didn't, taking his face in her hands instead. "We'll explain it to Mom. She'll understand...just like I do." As she stroked her fingers delicately over his cheeks, Ben's worried expression faded, replaced by a soft grin. "But, please, no more secrets, okay?"

He rested his hands on her waist. "Definitely, no more secrets.

It's a huge relief, actually, telling you..." A soft breath left his lips. "Riles, I miss her so much."

"Ben." Riley gathered him in, desperate to ease his pain. "I can only imagine..."

Safe within her embrace, he gave in to his grief. "You know, it's always there, under the surface. Some days—Mother's Day, her birthday—I brace myself, knowing it's gonna be bad, but it's weird—a regular day can feel worse. I'll be in a shop and hear a song she loved or see someone wearing a coat like hers and..." His voice cracked. "It breaks me so hard. It just comes at me and I can't stop it..." His hand swiped tears from his eyes. "I miss telling her my good news and hearing her laugh. I know it sounds daft, but I keep our old number in my phone. I like seeing it there."

Stroking Ben's back, Riley nodded. "My mom carries her dad's driver's license in her wallet. She can't part with it. She talks to him sometimes, too."

"Oh, I do that—all the time. I don't need a church or a grave, I just...wherever I am, I share how I'm doing, how much I love her, and...how much I love you." He pulled back, meeting her eyes.

An ache stirred inside Riley's chest. *Five months, three days and...too many hours! Just KISS HIM!* Slowly breathing him in, her lips joined his, the softness of his mouth feeling like home. Ben's hands shifted upward, pressing through her bulky parka like he couldn't hold her close enough. From the tenderness of his kiss, his eager embrace, Riley knew Ben was as devoted to her as she was to him. She leaned back, smiling as his hair danced in the wind across his forehead.

"I've never kissed in a cemetery before. Have you?"

"Um..." Ben bit his lip.

"I'll take that as a yes, then!' They shared a quiet laugh.

Ben gently swept a lost eyelash from Riley's cheek. "But I've never been in love in one...until now."

"Well, that makes two of us." She wrapped her arms around his neck, the touch of her fingers reveling in his hair, eliciting a groan of longing from his lips.

"You don't know how good it feels to hear that." Ben nuzzled her ear and a new burst of goose bumps tickled her skin, causing her to shiver against him. "That wind is picking up. Want to head back?"

"When you're ready."

Ben pulled back slightly. "We could go to mine. Spencer's away on a hen weekend—"

"YES!" Riley flinched at her own outburst. "I mean...yeah, that would be great." *More than great.*

He laughed, pressing a smiley kiss to her mouth, and let her go. "I'll call a cab."

Riley watched him on his phone, chatting with the dispatcher. He looked happy, relaxed—his old self again. *I owe Shannon so much.* She removed the plastic on her daisies and kneeled down. "Thank you...for sending him to me," she whispered, setting her flowers beside Ben's. "I promise Ben will never be alone again."

SEVENTY-ONE

Riley and Ben achieved a new record—within seconds of slamming the door of Spencer's tiny flat, they were naked and lip-locked and tangled in each other on his unmade single bed. While a tour of his London home would've been nice, Riley didn't care. All she wanted to see was Ben liberated from his boxer briefs. After their hour-long taxi/train/Underground journey (where their amorous acrobatics were limited to a full-on snog and under-the-parka, over-the-clothes touching), her self-control had been pushed to its limits on the Victoria line.

Ben didn't leave the Underground unruffled, either. Despite making it his mission to tease Riley into a pent-up frenzy, Ben's desire for his girlfriend got the better of him—he exited the Tube station carrying his backpack in front of his crotch.

Behind closed doors, the promise of a slow, sensuous reunion dissolved into a desperate quickie of open mouths, arching hips, and fisted bedsheets. In the heady aftermath, Ben's small room looked like it had been ransacked: a once-orderly stack of books lay in a pile of literary rubble, discarded clothes were scattered everywhere, and the bedframe's incessant banging knocked a framed photo of Riley off the wall to the threadbare carpet. Even his small floor lamp was upended.

Happy? Euphoric? Sex drunk?! Yes, THAT'S how I feel! I've missed him, how I feel with him. Lightheaded and breathless, Riley flopped backward onto the crumpled sheets and discovered why Ben always slept on the right side of the mattress. "Oww!"

He looked over his shoulder, the damp sheen of exertion glistening on his back. "Careful now, Riles. I told you, this mattress bites." He laughed as he dropped the used condom in his empty bedside bin.

Not even a painful spring could deflate Riley's orgasmic high. Taking delight in Ben's toned backside, she raised an eyebrow and hugged herself, the bliss of *finally* having skin-against-skin sex after five months apart still coursing through her body. "Benjamin," she purred. "Come back *here*."

Ben snickered, searching for his underwear. "If you want a nice home-cooked supper tonight and more of *this*"—he waved his hands over his body like it was a prize on a TV game show—"you gotta let me pop to the shops for groceries and more condoms."

"Didn't that restroom vending machine give you more than one?"

"Nope. Stingy fucker." Ben leaned over, setting the broken floor lamp back onto its feet.

Watching him at the end of the bed, Riley ached for the weight of him moving over her again. "Don't go yet. Kiss me—now." She eased up on her elbows, daring him to come back.

Ben's eyes swept over her pale skin, bathed in a sliver of street-light, creeping past his polyester curtains. "Bossy." He laughed. "And that's a compliment!" He climbed back onto the bed and lay between Riley's thighs, leaving gentle kisses first, then warm licks and sucks, each teasing flick of his tongue pushing Riley's hands farther into his hair.

Ben lifted his head, a cheeky glint in his eyes. "Argh—you're getting me all riled up again. Sorry, you'll have to wait for more, missy!" He shifted up, pressing brief kisses along her chest and her neck, finally reaching her mouth. He smiled into a long, deep kiss as Riley's hand slipped past the scar on his abdomen, curling around where he was eager and ready for another round.

With kisses and caresses, they spoke to each other in sighs, thankful their love was stronger than any ocean or secret conspiring to keep them apart.

Riley's lips brushed Ben's. "I think I'm going to like London—a lot!" They shared a chuckle as her finger traced the two hollow stars tattooed beneath the curve of his left collarbone. The beautiful sentiment from his mom's gravestone tugged at her heart. *Until the last star fades...* "I used to think this tattoo was a tribute to astronomy or that crazy *Equinox* TV series you geek out about, but...it's for your mom, isn't it?"

He nodded, a wistfulness in his eyes. "Yeah. It's me and her. This way, she's always with me. I don't get to the cemetery as much as I used to, only birthdays and Christmas, really." He propped himself up on his elbow. "I want to make her proud. It's why I've been working so hard with Love Bites—it feels like I'm doing it for her as much as me. I've even started taking orders for weddings."

"No way!"

"Yeah! First one was before Christmas. A customer took my details and hired me to make brownie wedding favors. Then, three of *her* guests, called me up for three different corporate parties in the City. I ended up baking all night and rolled into Waterstones half asleep, but it was so worth it! Those jobs turned into more bookings and they just keep coming, mostly word of mouth, referrals. Riles, if demand keeps growing like this, I might be able to do Love Bites full-time, maybe get a small shop, even..."

Her hand flew up to meet her smile. "That would be perfect!"

"I know! And I'm doing *everything* by the books. I've met with a bloke at the bank, I drew up a proper business plan over Skype with Hunter, and Mo has been giving me advice. He started with one market stall five years ago, and now he's got three stalls, two shops, and online sales, too! His son is a website wiz, so he's been working on my new site. It goes live next month!"

"Ben, this is amazing! Can you...imagine what your mom would say?"

"Hmm, she might be a *wee* bit proud...and hopefully you are, too?" He raised an expectant eyebrow.

"Like you have to ask!" She planted a kiss on his forehead. "I wish I could've met her."

"Oh, she would've *loved* you...and Maggie. I—oh!" Ben froze. "Just give me..." He rolled over and off the bed, his hand zeroing in on the envelope Maggie had sent over for his mom. It sat on a narrow shelf screwed to the wall. The a-ha record, two birthday cards, the *Equinox Ten* boxset, a much-loved stuffed turtle, and the swiped plastic gallbladder were the only other residents. "Maybe you can sorta meet her..." Envelope in hand, he sat back on the bed.

"But that's *my* mom's note—she wrote it to your mom." Riley looked confused.

He pulled away a second envelope, stuck to the back of Maggie's. "It sticks to everything. Mum sealed it with tape. She always went overboard—took me ten minutes to open a Christmas present once." He flipped it over, placing it in her hand. "Here."

For Benjamin. Riley stared at the swirly handwriting; its penmanship matched the *B. Something* tag on his pink suitcase. "What is it?"

"It's the letter Mum wrote me...before she died." He nodded. "You can read it...if you want to."

"I can't read it. It's private."

"Well, suit yourself, but she wouldn't mind." He leaned forward and kissed her temple then gathered his blankets into a cozy nest around her. "Now that you're snug as a bug in a rug, I'm running out to the shop. I'll get some basics: bread, eggs, bacon...oh, and prawn cocktail crisps—you'll like those! Be right back, 'kay?"

She nodded, her eyes falling back to the envelope.

Ben shimmied into his boxer briefs and inched along the small pathway between the bed and the wall until he located his jeans, t-shirt, and hoodie, all buried under his books. Blowing Riley a kiss, he left the room and the flat, the door locking behind him.

Heart heavy, her tentative fingers slipped inside the envelope and pulled out a folded piece of paper, its edge jagged from where it had been torn from a spiral notebook. Taking a deep breath, she began to read.

9 August 2008

My darling Benjamin,

I'm sitting in your room with a pen and notebook, writing you this letter. I'm happiest here. I love your room so much; it's the heart of our home. I can hear your cheeky laugh, feel the warmth of your hugs. Your cherished possessions—your astronomy books, Mr. C's telescope, the chessboard I gave you last year, stuffed turtle, even the half-eaten packet of prawn cocktail crisps (Oh, Benjamin, those stinky crisps!)—make me feel closer to you. I just want to take it all in, remember every precious moment with you until you return from the library, books under your arm and stories to tell, and then I'll hug you like there's no tomorrow...like I've done a million times before...and put this letter away for you, my beautiful boy, to read after I'm gone.

I've never wanted for anything except more time with you. Fourteen years isn't enough, but then neither would twenty, forty, or sixty. Sometimes the heart wants what it can't have.

I always thought I'd see you go on your first date, graduate from school, get married, but I'll miss all those milestones. That thought makes my heart ache, worse than any pain I've ever felt. There are so many things I wanted to do, wanted to say...but I'm running out of time. I hope this note will give you comfort and guidance when I can't, my love. It's a collection of little things to remember, and maybe when you do, you'll remember me, too.

Benjamin, always be polite. Say please and thank you, hold doors open for others, take your shoes off when entering someone's home. It's common courtesy (except I don't think it's very common anymore). Be the exception.

I want you to try new things whenever you can. If you feel nervous, that's good! It means what you're doing matters to you.

Always be open to new friendships. The person you chat with in line at the supermarket might become your best friend or even your soul mate.

Don't feel that you need to be fashionable, cool, or rich to matter. None of those things will make you happier, not really.

Don't compromise what you believe in your heart just to be popular. It's better to stand alone and be true to yourself than in a crowd, regretting your choices.

It's okay to have dessert for dinner—or eat more than one slice of cake! (Just not every day, okay?)

You already do this, but a gentle reminder can't hurt. Brush your teeth at least twice a day. See a dentist. Girls won't kiss you if your teeth are nasty (or missing—trust me on that one!).

Be wary of falling for someone who wants to change who you are, because that's not the person you're meant to be with.

Explore! See the world. Even a visit to a new town will open your eyes and introduce you to new people. A simple 'hello' could change your life.

Bake (and use ALL the chocolate chips!)

Dance, my darling. Dance like it's "1999"! (Prince rocks, and so did 1982).

Big dreams are never silly. They help soothe a bad day and give us something to reach for.

One day, you'll probably own a mobile phone. Please don't walk and text—you'll hurt yourself and others in your path. Plus, you'll miss out on the amazing things happening around you. Be present, Benjamin. Put the phone down and engage with life.

Failure isn't a bad thing. It can hurt, but it's how we learn, how we figure out what's right for us. I'd rather you try and fail than never try at all.

You can never say 'I love you' enough, and the people you love can never hear it too much. Say it warmly, say it often.

If you believe in nothing else, please believe in love. It can make miracles happen.

You're so much braver than you think you are.

Grief might make you turn inward for a while, but please, my love, try to look outward. Embrace your superpower; listen carefully. Look for people who might be hurting, who are silent in their pain and aren't asking for help. The best way to heal yourself is to help someone else.

Benjamin, please don't be sad for me or angry that your father left. The love I was supposed to find wasn't his; it was yours. Always yours. You've made my life so happy, so full—my funny, brave, thoughtful son. I'm so proud of the young man you've grown to become.

Please don't be scared. I'll be there by your side and I'll love you until the last star fades.

Love, Mum
xoxoxoxox

Gasping through tears, Riley folded Ben's cherished letter, her heart heavy with sorrow and loss for an extraordinary woman she loved but would never meet.

SEVENTY-TWO

One month later

"Mom, check it out. Isn't this *cool*?"

Riley held her phone high and did a slow sweep of the flags, shoppers, and food so Maggie, wrapped in her bathrobe post-shower, could feast her eyes on the Maltby Street Market through her tablet. A cloudless, sunny April sky, more typical of a spring day in New York City than London, had brought people out in droves, every stall surrounded by customers hungry for a lunchtime deal. Ben had mentioned to Riley an hour earlier that he'd be lucky if he had any Love Bites left by 2 p.m.

"*Mmmmm!*" Maggie squinted through the screen over her breakfast. "Are those the loaded waffles you keep Instagramming?"

"Yep! They smell even better than they look!" Riley swiveled, giving her mom a close-up of the batter being poured into the nooks of a sizzling griddle. "You can get them piled high with marshmallows and chocolate sauce or go healthy with fruit." Riley's phone returned to her face. "So, come on—spill, Mom. Did Casey bring Sophie last night?" Before Riley left for London, Casey had promised he'd visit Maggie regularly to check in and make sure all was well.

"He *did*. We had pizza and watched a movie. Sophie is lovely and absolutely adores Casey."

"Aw! He texted me some cute photos from her cousin's wedding last weekend. I'm so happy for him. I was worried he might retreat into his dark editing cave with me and Pip gone."

"Well, he has, but he's not alone." Maggie spread strawberry

477

jam on her toast. "Sophie's helping him with his new documentary."

"Couples that work together..." Riley glanced over her phone and spotted Ben a few stalls away, handing a box of Love Bites brownies to a customer. "I love it."

"So, how did it go yesterday afternoon?"

"Mom, it was AMAZING! I shadowed the series director! I swear, it felt like I learned six months of stuff in a day. On the studio floor, she introduced me to one of the BBC's casting directors, and *she* invited me to spend half a day with her, too. I told my boss and she said I can go. Can you believe it? The *two* things I want to do most!"

"Well, sounds like you're not missing the California dream at all!" Maggie took a bite of toast.

"I'm not!" Riley winced, squeezing through the crowd. "I mean, I'd be lying if I said I wouldn't prefer the weather—and having Pip around—but I adore London, really like my new therapist, and *love* my job—and my boss! She's been like a mentor to me, and get this: she's not supposed to say anything, but she gave me a heads-up about two coordinator jobs being added this fall. She told me I should apply but..." Riley looked away with a shrug.

"*Riley*." Maggie set down her toast. "We talked about this."

"I know, but I'm so far away, Mom. What if something...happens?"

"Sweetheart, please don't worry. I'm feeling great! I'm busy with work, friends, my book club, and I'll feel even *better* if you're living your life, enjoying yourself. If a job comes up while you're there and it's something you want to do, apply for it. I'm fine, fit as a fiddle—if I wasn't, I would tell you."

"I know," Riley said quietly. "But I miss you."

"Oh, honey. I miss you, too, but I'm always just a call away. We talk more *now* than when you lived here, silly!" Maggie laughed.

"But I can't *hug* you."

"But you will...soon! And I'll bring you Funyuns, and Ben some black-and-white cookies—a little taste of home." Maggie picked up her coffee and took a big sip.

Riley slipped behind Ben's table. "I can't wait!"

"Can't wait for what?" Ben waved a blue plastic glove at Riley's phone screen. "Oh, hiya, Mags!"

"Hey, Ben!" Maggie beamed over her mug. "Look at you, our young entrepreneur!"

"Mom and I were talking about her coming over with Piper in August. Thank God for seat sales!"

"I booked that week off," Ben half-shouted toward the phone, handing a sample of his pretzel-topped brownie bites to a teenager. "Riley's making a huge must-see list: the crown jewels, St. Paul's, Platform 9 ¾ at King's Cross—"

Riley interrupted, bumping his shoulder. "Ben will probably be dressed up as Harry Potter."

He smirked. "Jeez, you dress up *one time...*" He caught the eye of a thirty-something guy with his five-year-old daughter. "Sorry, just a sec, Maggie!" Ben stepped away and slipped back into work mode as two women and a cluster of seniors joined the swarm eyeballing his cookies and cakes. "All right? What can I get ya?" The dad asked for a large slice of red velvet cake, triggering Riley's smile to stretch into cheek-aching territory.

"See that, Mom?" She reversed the camera and aimed at the table. "They're buying *your* cake! Ben says your red velvet and Shannon's peanut butter brownies are his bestsellers."

She reversed the camera once more, her mom's face back on the screen.

"His mom would be so proud..." A hint of sadness dimmed the brightness in Maggie's eyes. "Riley, when I'm over, I'd like to visit

Shannon's grave. I'm sure somewhere, somehow, she knows what Ben means to us, but I want to tell her myself, mom to mom."

Riley smiled warmly. "Yeah, of course we can—"

"Oh, Mags, did Riles mention?!" Finger poking the air, Ben jumped back into frame and the conversation. "Mark's invited us to Aberdeen for a day or two while you're—"

"*BEN!*" Riley punched his arm.

"Oww!" His eyes scrunched with a hurt 'What was that for?' glance. "Oh...*bollocks.* Yeah, sorry...it's a *surprise*, right?" He loomed large into the lens towards Maggie, his face a sheepish half-smile. "Ermm...*surprise!*"

Maggie looked awestruck. "*Really?* We're going to see where they film *Lairds and Liars?!*"

Riley nudged her way back on screen, smiling. "Yeah. We'll fly up with Alex, hang out on set, and all go for dinner together. I thought if *anyone* was going to let something slip, it would've been Piper, not *you*, Fagan!" She laughed, pointing an accusing finger.

"Soz, love—my bad! Look, I'm retreating...back to my baked goods!" Ben chuckled and greeted newly arrived customers, his stock almost sold out.

Riley gave her mom a 'guys, huh' eye roll and moved a few steps out of the way. "Hey, I hope Piper's not too exhausting on the flight."

"*I* might be the exhausting one." Maggie licked jam from her thumb. "I'm so excited! My first transatlantic flight! Piper might need earplugs and a sleep mask if she's sitting with me; I don't think I'll sleep a wink!"

"I pity the person in the third seat." Riley chuckled. "Every time we talk, Pip's even more buzzed about coming to the kids' TV show taping at my work. I'm hoping she'll apply for a job while she's over. She's got dual citizenship, so..."

"Well, she loves it over there, so you never know." Tugging the neck of her bathrobe, Maggie noticed the time on her tablet. "Oh, seven-thirty already? Sweetheart, I've gotta run! I've got a date with an orphaned cocker spaniel at eight."

"Aww, give the shelter pups a cuddle from me." Riley smiled. "I love you, Mom. Talk Monday?"

"If not before." Maggie tucked a short piece of hair behind her ear. "Love you! And give Ben a big squeeze." She waved and the FaceTime session ended.

Ben appeared over her shoulder. "Bollocks. She's gone?"

"Yeah, she's off dog walking, but she was thrilled to see you in action." She kissed him on the cheek and pulled out a roll of Love Hearts from her denim jacket. She popped one in her mouth and smiled blissfully. "I *love* this, you know...spending weekends here with you."

"Yeah, me too..." Noticing a pause in business, Ben tugged off his food-service gloves and motioned to the back of his stall. "Love, c'mere for a sec."

"Sure. What's up?"

"Remember we said no more secrets? We'd be completely honest with each other?"

The urgency in his voice made Riley wary. "Yeah?"

"Well, I've got a confession..." His smile tightened as he scratched his messy bedhead. "I *hate* long-distance relationships."

That's his confession? "Um, tell me something I *don't* know." Riley giggled and wrapped her arms around his hips, her fingertips slipping underneath his apron and shirt into the waistband of his jeans. "But I don't remember any *distance* in our relationship this morning." Her lips brushed his ear. "Remember how hard you came when we...?" she whispered teasingly.

Ben closed his eyes and a naughty smile swept across his face.

Riley kissed his lips. "Next Saturday, I'll leave my flat earlier so we'll have more time at yours."

Jolted out of the memory, Ben's eyes popped open. "See? That's what I *mean*, Riles. We're *still* long-distance!" He frowned, hugging her close. "On a good day, our flats are an hour and a half away from each other, and it's not even a direct route. A train and two bum-numbing Underground rides—it takes forever, right?"

Riley nodded. "Yeah..."

"So..." Ben took a deep breath. "How 'bout moving in with me?"

Whaaat?! Holy crap! Riley's smile flickered then slipped away. "Uh, at Spencer's...?"

"Oh, Christ, no! We'll rent our own place—Elstree, maybe, near the Beeb? If we can find something small, affordable enough. It wouldn't be a palace, but..."

"I wouldn't even know what to do with a large place."

Ben pulled her closer. "Just think: no flatmates, no long commute...more time in bed every morning and night..."

Good God, that's definitely a bonus. Riley plucked a piece of lint off his shoulder. "But I might be jobless in five months."

"I doubt it. I think your boss is prepping you to stay. Companies don't invest time like that if they're planning to send you packing, and if she's already hinting about you applying for upcoming jobs, I'm betting you're quids in." He kissed her on the nose. "And that's the other thing, Riley—you've seen it yourself—Love Bites is *crushing* it. Seriously, I can't keep up with demand! It's not just *this*—it's the extra money from those corporate gigs and weddings. I know I've still got a ways to go before I have my own shop, and we'll have to scrimp and save for a while, but it's kinda romantic, right? You and me, taking on the world, living off peanut butter sandwiches...shagging until we can barely walk." His fingers traced along her back.

Riley laughed. "Yeah, we'd be limping around...but with stupid big smiles."

Ben grinned. "For the first time, I'm really excited about the future. For the first time, I don't want to *escape*. I want to make my own happily ever after…with you, the girl who gave me stars on my birthday and a reason to believe in myself again, a reason to love again. What do you say, gorgeous? Play house with me—for real?"

Oh, my dear sweet Ben, I'd give you the stars and more if I could. You stole my heart and saved it from being broken, and now it's yours, completely. Riley looked at Ben, his smile bright and selfless, his soul open to love and ready to let the hurt of his past fall away. He was too gorgeous, too fun, too beautiful *inside* to walk through life unattached. *And you want me by your side.*

The market's foot traffic was getting heavy again, but Ben wasn't in any hurry to get back to work; the only sweetness he wanted was from Riley, and she wanted him right back. *I want to kiss you so hard right now.* She captured his lips and hugged him tight, her kisses slowly melting away to reveal her answer, spoken in a confident whisper. "Yes, Benjamin. It's a yes!"

"Yeah?" Ben's smile could've lit up all of Bermondsey. "Well, snog me again, then—before more customers show up!" He tenderly cupped her face and leaned in, kissing her softly until she parted her lips, her quiet gasps promising she was his.

Benjamin Fagan, the Brit boy who stumbled into my life and changed everything.

It was inevitable, just as Riley had thought.

One day, Ben would meet a smart, pretty girl who loved books, new adventures, and eighties music.

But Riley had cast the girl all wrong.

Ben's girl…was her.

ACKNOWLEDGEMENTS

Thank you so much for reading *Until the Last Star Fades*!

A few years ago, I wouldn't have called myself a mental health warrior. I hid my anxiety and fought through panic attacks, but when I wrote Alex Sinclair's struggles with anxiety in my first two books, I saw my mental health challenges in a new light. I saw how they might help others. So, instead of leaving Alex to bravely face the mental health stigma on her own, I joined her. I haven't been silent about mental health awareness since.

With Riley Hope, I opened up about my own smiling depression. The diagnosis sounds funny, but it's no laughing matter. Ignorant notions about people with my type of depression abound, but I can tell you, none of us are weak. We're resilient and we feel everything so much—that's *our* superpower. It's time to tell the ugly stigma to, as Ben would say, "do one." I hope in some small way, I've done that with this book.

The mom storyline in *Until the Last Star Fades* was incredibly hard for me to write. I lost my mum a few years ago and it changed me like nothing else has. Even though she's not "here", I talk to her all the time, and she lives in these pages—just little things that mean everything—as well as the gut-punching challenges with cancer, summers spent in hospitals, the endless hope for good news, and the crushing despair when it's elusive. I've been there, and my heart breaks for anyone who's been there, too.

Until the Last Star Fades also gave me another chance to explore organ donation (I wrote about it for a magazine a few years ago). Back then, I interviewed living donors, organ recipients, and family members of deceased donors. For this book, I also received invaluable insight from the 'Living Donors Online' Facebook group. Three liver donors shared personal stories with me: Heather Badenoch, Megan Hornseth, and Meghan Hanley. It's one thing signing up to donate your organs after you die (if you haven't, please do!), but it's quite another to selflessly give the gift of life when you're living. These women are heroes.

I'd like to thank Heather, Bill, Tobey, and my family and friends for always supporting me. Love you so much.

Sending all the Pizza Express doughballs (plus hugs) to Vicki and Charlie. Cheers for the line that describes Ben perfectly (even though you thought of it for a different Ben!). Love ya!

Cristina, your talent inspires me, and I wish we could hang out more. Here's to seeing Whishy together soon.

To my wonderful beta readers, thank you for all your help!

Caitlin (Editing by C. Marie), sorry for being a crazy comma lady! Thank you for the polish and your kindness.

Thanks to Steve Scanlon for your beautiful back cover photo.

Crystal Patriarche, Taylor Brightwell and the BookSparks team—you are PR rock stars!

Author shout-out! Thanks to Renée Carlino, Andrea Dunlop, R.S. Grey, and Colleen Hoover for blurbs and Instagram photos. One day, I hope we meet so I can thank you personally. Kristin Contino & Nicole Trilivas, I *have* met you both and adore you!

Darren & Zoey—you're everything! I love you. You're my life and my heart. I couldn't do any of this without you.

To the Bookstagrammers, BookTubers, and bloggers who have read and supported my books: you're so creative and AWESOME! Thanks for taking a chance on this indie author. Big hugs.

And to the Keeganites in my FB group! You make bookmarks, candles, have tea parties—celebrating my books! Cool doesn't even begin to describe you guys and what you do! I love you to the moon and back. Thank YOU! xoxo

GLOSSARY

Some people, places, and things mentioned in *Until the Last Star Fades* might not be familiar to all readers. Here are a few helpful explanations:

Drafted: Between the ages of 18-20, male ice hockey players are 'drafted' by National Hockey League teams while they're playing college or junior hockey. Some players go pro and join their NHL teams the following season, while others like Josh finish their college education and then join the team that drafted them.

FOMO: Short form for 'fear of missing out'.

Smiling depression: Also called high-functioning depression. People with smiling depression appear happy on the outside but feel sad, emotionally numb, or shut off from the world inside. Friends and family often have no clue that their loved one is depressed because they hide it so well. Sufferers are often high achievers and/or perfectionists who seem to have everything going for them.

Chef Boyardee ABCs: Pasta ABCs in tomato sauce from the American makers of canned ravioli.

Page Six: Society and celebrity gossip column in the *New York Post* newspaper.

Playoff beards: Hockey players are very superstitious and many grow beards for good luck during tournaments and playoffs.

Upcycling: Upcycling is the process of taking something no longer used and turning it into a product that's more beautiful, interesting, and in some cases, valuable. Upcycling often gets mixed up with recycling, but they're not the same thing.

Chemo brain: Term used by cancer patients to describe a foggy-brained feeling after chemo.

Muppet: British insult meaning idiot (not a cute and fuzzy puppet!)

PEZ: Small, rectangular hard candies that are kept in plastic dispensers featuring the heads of pop culture characters (Snoopy, Santa, Chewbacca, etc).

Back of the net: British phrase using football/soccer analogy for scoring a point in conversation.

FCUK: Stands for 'French Connection UK' — used by British clothing company, French Connection.

Up herself: British phrase meaning a woman is conceited.

Tisch Salute: Tisch students have two graduation ceremonies. The first one is NYU's All-University Commencement, which in Riley's graduation year, was held at massive Yankee Stadium. Then a few days later Tisch holds its 'Salute', their own ceremony featuring student performances and speeches from department chairs.

Cognitive Behavioral Therapy (CBT): Therapy used to treat a variety of mental health issues including anxiety, panic attacks, and depression. With CBT exercises, a therapist helps the patient identify negative thoughts that can trigger anxiety, depression, etc., and works to replace them with positive or more realistic thoughts.

HEALTH RESOURCES

If you or someone you know suffers from depression, help is available.

United States
Anxiety and Depression Association of America
www.adaa.org

Canada
The Canadian Mental Health Association (CMHA)
www.cmha.ca

United Kingdom
Mind
www.mind.org.uk

Want to learn more about organ donation?
Find more info here:

United States: www.organdonor.gov
Canada: www.organtissuedonation.ca/en
United Kingdom: www.organdonation.nhs.uk

Want to read more about Mark Keegan & Alex Sinclair?

(and see how they met and their relationship developed in London, Manchester, Dublin and NYC),

Please read my first two books...

A contemporary coming-of-age story with a touch of romance.

And its sequel, a contemporary romance which can also be read as a standalone.

London, Can You Wait?

Available in paperback and ebook from all major retailers.

Until the last star fades

Enjoyed this novel? Please consider leaving a review on the retailer's website.

Stay in touch! Follow Jacquelyn:
Instagram: @JaxMiddleton_Author
Twitter: @JaxMiddleton
Facebook: JacquelynMiddletonAuthor
and join her private Facebook readers group.

Sign up to Jacquelyn's email list for exclusive giveaways at
www.JacquelynMiddleton.com
and visit for playlists, behind-the-scenes posts & news.